Darcy & Elizabeth

Hope of the Future

DARCY SAGA PREQUEL DUO BOOK 2

SHARON LATHAN

Edited by Gretchen Stelter www.gretchenstelter.com
Published by Sharon Lathan www.SharonLathanAuthor.com

 Created with Vellum

TABLE OF CONTENTS

ಔ

Hope For a Different Future 1

1~   Optimistic Expedition 11

2~   Unforeseen Complication 39

3~   Invigorating Interaction 55

4~   Illuminative Conversation 79

5~   Aristocratic Reception 93

6~   Capital Exploration 123

7~   Sensational Revelation 159

8~   Festive Commemoration 193

9~   Relative Transition 221

10~   Dramatic Interruption 251

11~   Significant Introspection 281

12~   Supreme Temptation 309

13~   Matrimony Finalization 325

A Hopeful Future Begins 347

BOOKS BY SHARON LATHAN

~

THE DARCY SAGA "PRIDE & PREJUDICE" SEQUEL SERIES

Mr. & Mrs. Fitzwilliam Darcy: Two Shall Become One

Loving Mr. Darcy: Journeys Beyond Pemberley

My Dearest Mr. Darcy

In the Arms of Mr. Darcy

A Darcy Christmas

The Trouble with Mr. Darcy

Miss Darcy Falls in Love

The Passions of Dr. Darcy

THE DARCY SAGA PREQUEL DUO

Darcy & Elizabeth: A Season of Courtship

Darcy & Elizabeth: Hope of the Future

DEDICATION

To my wonderful husband, Steve.
He is my Mr. Darcy,
and without him I would not have
survived my rough times.

❧

To Regina Jeffers, my dear friend,
and Austen Authors partner.
She stood by me when others did not.
Constant, faithful, and supportive;
she taught me what true friendship is.
I can never thank her enough,
and will cherish her friendship forever.

HOPE FOR A DIFFERENT FUTURE

~PROLOGUE~

Rosings Park, Kent
Early October in 1816

he candle's flame licked the tip of the stick, melting the gold wax into a shining rivulet whirling into a blob over the paper's seam. The engraved end of a brass seal flattened the hot wax, and a steady pressure was maintained to ensure Lady Catherine de Bourgh's insignia hardened into a defined shape. The Earl of Matlock would recognize his sister's seal, and the gold wax was chosen to emphasize the critical nature of the letter, guaranteeing he would open the correspondence forthwith.

While waiting for a servant to respond to her summons, Lady Catherine crossed to the window for a visual reappraisal of her only child's condition.

Anne de Bourgh lay on a cushioned swing secured to a branch of an ancient oak. One corner of the blanket draping Anne's thin legs fluttered as the bench gently swayed, the movement a result of the intermittent pushes by her companion Mrs. Jenkinson. The latter read aloud from a book in her lap.

Probably one of those novels Anne gravitates toward, Lady Catherine brooded.

Anne's eyes were closed, thick black lashes a stark contrast to her pale cheeks. If not for an occasional smile curving her bloodless lips in response to the recited story, Lady Catherine would have concluded her daughter asleep. Worse than the corruption of Anne's mind by the nonsense in a novel, the sun's position had shifted since Lady Catherine's previous inspection, and the swing was no longer fully in the shade. Rays of sunlight beamed between the leaves to touch Anne's chalky forehead and one translucent eyelid. Angrily pursing her lips, Lady Catherine clasped onto the window's latch, but, in mid-twist, a footman entered the room.

"You rang, my lady?"

"Obviously," she snapped. Delaying the order of Anne back into the house, she stepped away from the unopened window and extended the sealed envelope. "This is to be sent with due haste and delivered directly into the hands of the Earl of Matlock in London."

The footman promised to carry out the instructions—Lady Catherine ignored his pointless toadying—and then pivoted smartly. Halfway to the door, he stopped and turned back around. "The Countess of Starkley's carriage has entered the drive, your ladyship. Shall I escort her directly into the parlor?"

Expression bland yet somehow conveying her contempt—as per design—Lady Catherine peered at the servant in silence until a swift darting of his eyes to the side signaled her message of disapproval had been received. Speaking with a practiced blend of condescension and menace, she asked, "Is Lady Starkley not invited to Rosings Park as my guest today?"

"Yes, my lady."

"Would you deem it appropriate to have her wait in her overheated carriage on the drive? Or perhaps you considered relegating her to the library or butler's pantry? Or were you intending the upstairs loo?"

Stiffly he bowed, wisely not attempting a rebuttal. "I shall see to Lady Starkley's swift arrangement and every satisfaction, your ladyship."

"See that you do. Tea and refreshments as well. And mind that the other matter is not forgotten," she concluded, pointing at the letter he held before turning away dismissively. The footman would complete her orders or soon be seeking a new employer...without a reference.

Returning to the window, she reached for the latch but paused before twisting open. Anne had shifted position on the swing and tilted her face to bathe in the sunlight. A hint of pink colored Anne's cheeks and moisture sparkled prettily across her brow, but the brightness accentuated the sharp bones under her translucent skin. The picture was a tragic mixture of delicate loveliness and infirm fragility.

"Oh! My poor, darling girl! Who will care for you when I am gone?"

Trembling fingertips pressed against her lips, and for a moment— only a moment—she was nothing more than a mother filled with despondency for her child. As swiftly as it came, the despondency disappeared, replaced in a heartbeat with fury directed solely at her nephew Fitzwilliam Darcy.

How could he behave so heartlessly? How could he ignore his duty? How could he choose that woman over Anne?

"Catherine, leave the window latched!" a female voice bellowed. "The air today is a miasma determined to congest my chest and curdle my blood. I daresay the noxious vapors forced me to breathe through my handkerchief from the carriage to your door! I nearly succumbed and shall wheeze for hours. Why drivers cannot halt a carriage without stirring up the dust, I'll never understand."

"Your ladyship, Lady Starkley has arrived—"

"I am quite aware of Lady Starkley's presence."

A curt flick of her fingers sent the footman scurrying for the door, but his escape was not speedy enough to evade Lady Starkley's extensive order for refreshments. Delivered as vociferously as her dire health predictions a moment ago, she displayed no outward signs of diminished lung capacity. On the contrary, while well into her sixtieth year with graying hair and spidery wrinkles on her face, the countess appeared the picture of health. Lady Catherine usually tolerated her friend's obsessive preoccupation with illness, but today there were urgent matters to report. No time to spare discussing her aches and afflictions.

"Millicent, my friend, sit and be comfortable," Lady Catherine sweetly interjected, hoping to stay Lady Starkley's complaint-laden monologue, adding a second dismissive gesture toward the lingering footman. "I already ordered tea to be brewed, the restorative herbal concoction that heals your pains, and the sweets best for regaining your strength. You are quite pale, poor dear. Was the road from London especially treacherous?"

"Indeed! You know how they claim to maintain the roads, Catherine, increasing the toll fees and taxing us blind, yet the conditions remain appalling."

Emitting a strained grunt as she sat on the settee, Lady Starkley continued to grouse while drawing an enamel-painted vinaigrette from within the ruffles of her fichu. Flipping open the glazed, jeweled lid, she waved the perforated cover under her nose and inhaled. "Rosemary, mint, and hyssop," she explained, not that Lady Catherine had asked. "Another of Dr. Higgins' miracle concoctions."

Lady Catherine attempted to maintain a neutral expression, but an uncontrollable facial contortion of some sort must have snuck through.

"Disapprove if you must, Catherine," Lady Starkley chided. "One day you shall admit what I and many others have learned: Dr. Higgins has a gift for creating medicinals. His Tears of the Poppy elixir has eliminated all my tremors! And his blemish salve, *la Veloutine*, has erased years of careworn lines from my visage."

"Be that as it may, he is no more a doctor than I am. That is the source of my disapproval. People should not claim to be what they are not, especially in exalting themselves to a station above what is divinely accorded."

"Now, now, Catherine. Dr. Higgins boasting his credentials, if he is—and I'm not conceding the allegation—would be nothing more than clever marketing. What this Miss Bennet is attempting with your nephew Mr. Darcy is detestable. Wholly unacceptable! This is why I was eager to assist in preventing such a travesty. These disturbances in the natural, God-ordained social order must stop, or the world shall fall into chaos! It is our Christian duty, as those whom I spoke to agreed."

Unable to sustain her rigid pose of self-possession, Lady Catherine dropped into the sofa across from Lady Starkley and leaned forward. "Tell me!"

At that moment, the footman reappeared with the tea and treats. Setting gingerly onto the low table between the two ladies, he proceeded to serve them as if each piece of the tea service weighed a hundred pounds!

Why does such an ordinary, oft-repeated procedure take so long to complete? Lady Catherine wanted to scream. Then, augmenting her stress, Lady Starkley insisted upon drinking half of her tea and consuming three sweet cakes before uttering a single word. Finally satisfied, the countess launched into her tale, between delaying bites and sips.

"Alas, the ladies of substance abiding in Town this time of year are woefully lacking. Most are off to the country, resting in peace and celebrating Michaelmas."

Lady Starkley paused to sigh pitifully, Lady Catherine ignoring the melodrama. With no sympathy forthcoming, Lady Starkley resumed, after an extended sniff from her vinaigrette.

"I despaired of our solemn task bearing fruit. Those available were thrilled to meet with me, naturally. My august presence was a welcome intrusion into their boredom. In fact, one and all were effusive in their delight, so much so that I was guilt ridden to pass on such horrific news! As often as I repeated the scandal of Mr. Darcy's betrothal to this Miss Bennet, knowing the truth of it, my dear Catherine, as you do not possess the ability to tell a falsehood or hurt a living soul without just cause, the greater the shock of it sunk into my heart. I daresay, if not for my unwavering trust in you, I would not have entertained the notion of Mr. Darcy—a fine, upstanding gentleman of breeding—stooping so low as to ask the hand of such a creature! It was this conviction which enabled me to convince our esteemed coterie of the truth and of the necessity to do all in our power to prevent his marriage."

It was Lady Catherine's turn to sigh. She relaxed into the cushions, a tiny stream of tension leaving her body. The scheme to break Mr. Darcy's engagement to Elizabeth Bennet was well underway, but not yet accomplished unless something positive had transpired in the two days since the countess had quit London. Lady Catherine could not afford to relent in her quest, for Anne's sake.

"So they agreed to disseminate the details of this ghastly affair?"

"With passionate resolve! Upon my word, once informed of the situation, I could not have stopped any of our friends had I exerted my towering influence to do so. Rest assured, Catherine, though small in number, down to the last they are on your side, which is, needless to say, on the side of righteousness. You have, I presume, written to Lord Matlock?"

"Yes. Thrice. I am unclear as to my brother's precise schedule, but in his last letter from Bath, he alluded to returning to London by the middle of October. He and Lady Matlock were not in residence when you left?"

"Not unless we passed each other upon the bridge crossing the Thames. Be encouraged on that front, my friend. His lordship cannot possibly see the advantage of such a union. He shall support your cause, I am sure of it."

"I wish I could be as confident. Forever has my brother been contrary, and he was a great friend to James Darcy. I fear his fondness for our nephew may sway his opinion."

"Pray it isn't so!" Lady Starkley appeared severely stricken at the possibility. Withdrawing a fan from her reticule, she flipped it open and began waving it vigorously before her face. "What are we coming to as an advanced society? I can hardly bear it and wonder if I am not blessed to be in waning health to avoid long years of witnessing the further degradation of our core values. If a worthy man of the gentry like Mr. Darcy of Pemberley can fall to the seductions of an ill-bred country chit, who is safe? How can a man of his caliber be so heartless to Miss de Bourgh and shirk his sworn duty?"

Lady Starkley's query, the words nearly identical to the questions Lady Catherine had thought minutes before the countess's arrival, brought all her anger rushing to the surface.

"I wish I could comprehend his actions myself," she roared, launching up from her seat. Fists clenched, she stormed to the window. Relief to find that Anne and Mrs. Jenkinson were gone— hopefully indoors where it was cool and protected—had limited effect on her roiling emotions. "For years I have been the saint of patience, Millicent, and what has it gotten me? For two years after Darcy's father died I said nothing, waiting as he grieved and adjusted to his new role as Master of Pemberley. Then, when I gently reminded him of the earnest wish of his mother, my sister, bless her soul, to marry my Anne and of the arrangement agreed upon by all, he refused to acknowledge it."

"Unfathomable!"

"Believing his refusal to commit to Anne and fulfill his promise was merely a request for more time to sow his wild oats, as the saying goes, I politely dropped the subject. I understand that young men require a period of recklessness and freedom before settling down. Not that the matrimonial state inhibits most men from satisfying wandering lusts and selfish needs for entertainment elsewhere. We both know this truth from personal experience."

Lady Starkley nodded gravely, although without a trace of judgment or disapproval. Lady Catherine, preoccupied with her irritation, barely noticed.

"How long was Anne supposed to wait? A man can take his time, age not affecting him as profoundly. Women are not as fortunate. My poor Anne, forced to pretend she was not heartbroken to see her youth slip away, all while the man promised to protect her, to give her a future and a family, ignores his duty to family and our rank. Oh! The shame of it!"

"Did he show no remorse? No heart when you pleaded with him?"

Lady Catherine hesitated before turning away from the window. The countless exchanges with Darcy regarding Anne flashed through her mind, particularly the most recent one in the Darcy House billiard room after leaving her distasteful audience with Elizabeth Bennet in Hertfordshire. Lady Catherine shuddered at the memories, not quite sure which one caused her the most pain and outrage. Over the years each conversation with her nephew had grown increasingly hostile. Darcy rigidly maintained that he and Anne had no affection for each other and that any "arrangement" agreed upon had no hold upon him.

She could remember, however, early discussions when he spoke with tenderness, pleading softly with her to understand. Anne, too, had echoed her cousin's sentiments, begging for an end to the topic.

Lady Catherine had flatly rejected doing so. For a host of reasons, a union between Darcy and Anne was the sensible, only acceptable course. Now, with the latest repugnant development, Lady

Catherine's conviction of her superior wisdom was stronger than ever.

Setting her jaw, she fixed a stony glare on her guest and, in a voice of iron declared, "The past is irrelevant. Darcy *will* marry, and it will be to my Anne, not a worthless country girl lacking a drop of noble blood. Whatever it takes."

1

OPTIMISTIC EXPEDITION

October 27, 1816
Darcy House in London

Fitzwilliam Darcy dipped the tip of his sharpened quill into the silver ink jar, tapped it onto the edge to remove the excess fluid, and etched a precise X inside the square for the twenty-sixth of October.

Smoothing one hand over the calendar page while returning the quill to its stand, he gazed at the rows of squares, each with a bold X indicating the date had passed. It was tempting to mark today as complete, but doing so would be premature, considering his breakfast tray sat on the table, and the pot of coffee remained half full.

Best not to violate the rules, no matter the satisfaction in seeing precisely one month remaining until the day scheduled for his marriage to Elizabeth Bennet.

In one respect Darcy did not wish to rush the time. Each day within this season of courtship brought new delights and increased the hope of their future happiness together. The remaining month promised to be especially splendid. Managing to keep a tight grip on his passions, he determined, was the only obstacle to a blissful engagement period!

Coffee cup in hand, Darcy relaxed into the chair and lifted his eyes to the window where sunlight glistened on the drops of dew coating the panes. The small patio outside his bedchamber had transformed from the lush, green-shrouded privacy of summer with bright colors of wisteria, lilac, and potted flowers, to an open terrace of faded blooms and semi-bare branches with clinging leaves of oranges and yellows.

While perhaps not as gloriously beautiful, Darcy tended to prefer the rustic, earthy colors of autumn. For some, this season too vividly illustrated decay and death. To Darcy, autumn marked a gradual easing of life's busyness and ushered in a period of restful, solitude. For as long as memory served, he had embraced the tranquility of winter at Pemberley. This upcoming winter, with Elizabeth in his life, anticipation for the season was multiplied tenfold.

Nay, after yesterday's miraculous revelations, make that a hundredfold.

Before arriving in London two days ago, the rapport forged with Elizabeth in the month since their engagement had exceeded Darcy's wildest imaginings. He had lost count of the times when their easy conversation, similar humor, and reciprocated insights had amazed him. Gradually his guilt over past missteps had faded, as Darcy accepted that by some miracle Elizabeth loved him—almost as deeply as he loved her.

On this fine autumn morning, Darcy freely admitted to his error on two points.

One, Elizabeth *already* loved him as deeply as he loved her, this being the first miracle revelation from yesterday's fiery encounter in his mother's bedchamber.

The second miracle revelation was how thoroughly Elizabeth understood his heart and mind. Clearer than he did, as it turned out.

Oh, my Elizabeth! How remarkable you are. With that thought, Darcy set the empty coffee cup down, slid his journal atop the calendar, and opened at the marked page for last night's entry.

Once again, she defied my direct order, proving, as she undoubtedly did when confronting Lady Catherine, that she is fearless. Brave and bold, perhaps more so than I. She refused to leave the bedchamber as I commanded, charging toward me until nearly nose to nose for a scathing rebuke I shall never forget.

"Tell me truthfully Fitzwilliam Darcy. Am I to conclude that our mutual love and desire are emotions to be disdained and ashamed of? Is this contempt and repugnance to continue after we wed? Or is it that you honestly reckon you are such an uncontainable beast that you would hurt the woman you love? Or do you have so little faith in my self-control that you assume I would willingly allow you to ravage me like a bought woman?"

Hurt Elizabeth? God no! The very thought brings me to my knees. Had my actions unwittingly given her the impression that I distrusted her virtue and strength of character? Had I shunned her affections to the point of damaging our future marital relations? Suddenly my fear of losing her respect and love was far greater than my ridiculous physical struggles. Then, with her next words, I abruptly comprehended that fear was the true root indeed, just not the fear I had surmised.

"William, listen to me carefully. I do not believe any of the questions I asked are true of you. What I do believe is that you are afraid to express your emotions freely. You are wrapped in an inflexible cocoon of discipline and righteousness, terrified that if you loosen one single cord, you will unravel completely. You love me and desire me,

yet resist showing me how much because you fear I will be disgusted or disappointed if I discover you are not this towering paragon of virtue and excellence you deem yourself."

Ah, such truth. Indeed, I, Fitzwilliam Darcy, a man forever prideful of his intelligence and clarity, have been stupid and blind. Elizabeth pierced through every facade. She saw the truth of my fears and laid them bare. Elizabeth, who faces me boldly as few can, knows of my weaknesses yet loves me for them and still trusts me with her entire being. How can I not trust her with the same? There is an amusing irony to the charade when viewed in light of our past. Fearing to release my "inflexible cocoon of discipline and righteousness" and fearing the free expression of my emotions at this point in our relationship is nonsensical when it is exactly those negative traits that caused Elizabeth to refuse my first proposal of marriage.

"Do you not yet comprehend how deeply I love you?" This singular question, uttered with raw emotion, was alone adequate proof of how wrong I was to judge her feelings as being of a lesser intensity than mine. If I needed additional validation, her subsequent words—her endearment, her touch—were amply sufficient to lift the yoke from my shoulders. My dearest Elizabeth shall forever be my sufficiency.

This was the extent of his entry. Volumes more could have been added, but chronicling every impression was unnecessary. Darcy would eternally remember the whole of last evening's conversation as vividly as he would their argument after his horrendous first proposal. Thankfully, the aftermath of this most recent confrontation was encouraging, rather than the heartbreaking outcome from last April.

Minutes later Darcy entered his dressing room whistling a jaunty tune. His valet, Samuel Oliver, greeted him politely and commenced the routine morning toilette as if Mr. Darcy whistling was normal.

Nearly laughing aloud, Darcy suddenly realized that whistling *had* become a normal activity—whistling, along with humming and involuntary smiles. Extraordinary!

Samuel's natural reticence and impassive expressions gave no hint as to his opinion regarding Darcy's unusual mannerisms of late. Based on Samuel's reaction to his master's engagement news, Darcy doubted his severely proper valet dwelt upon the matter beyond the professional regard for which waistcoat, cravat knot, or cologne selection was best for the planned activity of the day.

A month prior, on the afternoon of his engagement to Elizabeth, Darcy had informed his valet, as calmly as possible, "We shall be staying in Netherfield for an indefinite period."

Samuel had nodded once and replied with a simple, "Very well, sir."

When no further questions were asked, Darcy pressed on, "As it happens, I have asked for the honor of Miss Elizabeth Bennet's hand in marriage, and she has accepted my proposal."

Expression unchanged, the valet had given a second nod identical to the first and continued brushing Darcy's coat without the slightest falter in rhythm. "Congratulations, Mr. Darcy," he had offered in his typical bland tone. "Will you need particular wardrobe requirements for the weeks ahead? I can send a footman to Pemberley or London for additional supplies and garments."

In the weeks since, wardrobe and grooming concerns were still the main topics of their conversations. Clothing selection and a detailed awareness of Mr. Darcy's daily schedule was the closest

Samuel came to touching upon the subject of his master's upcoming marriage. For twelve years Samuel Oliver had been in Darcy's employ, inarguably familiar with his physical person above anyone in the world. Regardless, as two men with similarly introverted personalities and strict adherence to protocols, conversations beyond the business at hand were rare and always had been. Darcy preferred it this way and was unfazed by Samuel's indifference to his engagement.

Exiting his suite, Darcy went in search of his sister. Too often over the past several years he and Georgiana had not resided in the same house at the same time. Usually, this was the result of her remaining at Pemberley while he was away in London or elsewhere. Rarely were they at Darcy House together, and he suddenly saw the error in eating from a tray at his desk rather than meeting her in the breakfast room to share in the morning repast.

Old habits die hard, he thought. Then, smiling, he realized that with his marriage there would undoubtedly be a long list of "old habits" needing to die, like it or not.

Georgiana was in the parlor, as he expected, but not playing the pianoforte, as was typical. Instead, Darcy heard the murmur of voices rather than music and, before reaching the half-open door, distinguished his sister's dulcet tones from Mrs. Smyth's gruff accent. It only took a minute to ascertain they were discussing the luncheon scheduled for the following day.

Much to Darcy's amazement, at some point during the evening dinner with the Bennets two nights ago, his shy sister had invited Jane and Elizabeth Bennet to Darcy House for an afternoon of female gossip and food. Based on her terrified expression when she told him of it, Darcy deduced her invitation wasn't the result of extended forethought. With his own emotions in turmoil after his passionate exchange with Elizabeth on the terrace, he hadn't been in the proper state of mind to ease Georgiana's concerns. Fortunately, yesterday had changed everything, enabling him to soothe

Georgiana's fears over hosting a party solo for the first time in her life.

Still, aware of Georgiana's timidity, and equally aware of Mrs. Smyth's bossiness, he listened from behind the door for a few more minutes, feeling not at all guilty to be eavesdropping. Once assured Georgiana was holding her own well enough, Darcy decided to leave them be. Later he would talk to the housekeeper privately, adding a handful of his own requests for the party, but primarily to clarify that Miss Darcy had his unwavering support and was ultimately in charge. From time to time Mrs. Smyth needed to be reminded that he was the master of Darcy House, not her.

Another reason to postpone what could be a lengthy conversation with Georgiana or Mrs. Smyth was his eagerness to embark upon his quest for the day. He was determined to unearth the perfect wedding gift for Elizabeth.

Attacking the job with his thus-far-reliable logic and superb organizational skills, Darcy climbed into his waiting carriage at nine o'clock sharp. With most of the elite still abed or barely sitting down to breakfast, the street traffic was thin as the hordes had yet to descend upon the shops, which were just opening their doors. Additionally, Darcy wanted to make sure he completed his mission before Mrs. Gardiner and the Bennet brides-to-be commenced their planned shopping day. Running into his betrothed with her gift in his hands would not be ideal.

All in all, his ideas were solid—the execution of them was not.

The first indication of poor preparedness was deciding upon Conduit, Bond, and Savile Streets for his shopping destination—force of habit, as this is where Darcy's tailors were located and where he acquired the bulk of his personal items. After more than a decade, how had he never noticed there literally was not a single store selling products for the female gender?

On the heels of that failure, Darcy directed the driver to Oxford Street. Multiple stops later and long before reaching the last business

—presuming there was an end to the row of merchants—Darcy was grasping his second error. By the time the carriage traversed a third of Piccadilly and Pall Mall, his predicament was glaringly obvious. In contrast to the precinct dedicated to men's requirements, these shopping zones were primarily dedicated to women. While this might sound like a boon, where does one begin when the possibilities are endless and, quite frankly, every retailer looks identical?

For most gentlemen, buying a gift for a lady was a straightforward task. Jewelry is always a safe bet, so Darcy had been told, as was perfume or anything made of fur. Unfortunately, this was the extent of what Darcy had learned from those scarce occasions when he had paid attention to what his friends said about their ladies. Only in recent weeks had the folly of his indifference occurred to him.

Nevertheless, surely it could not be that difficult to find a necklace or broach worthy of his future wife. It sounded simple enough until faced with a half dozen jewelers on one block alone, each with hundreds of gorgeous pieces to choose from. And who knew there were scads of perfumers and furriers? If that had been the end of his options, maybe he would have muddled through and settled on something. To his dismay, there were milliners, haberdashers, hosiers, hatters, cobblers, and innumerable other specialty stores.

Three hours later, with not a single object purchased, Darcy was beginning to fear he had discovered the one challenge destined to be his defeat. The breadth of his ignorance was boundless. He painfully admitted this to himself, but the embarrassment of confessing his inexperience publicly and ask for help was a blow his ego couldn't take.

Then, amid his self-pity, Darcy remembered a conversation several months past. One night, while dining at the Matlock residence, he overheard a conversation between his aunt and another guest. This was during the period of Darcy's despair over losing Elizabeth Bennet, so while he recalled the guest was a woman, he drew a blank on her name or face. At any rate, the pertinent point for his current dilemma was that the topic involved shopping.

"Harding and Howell is by far the best London shopping mall," Lady Matlock had gushed. "It has everything one needs all in one central location, and as a mall, it is much nicer than the Pantheon Bazaar. Unless you are shopping for an exotic product or specialty children's item, of course. Then the Pantheon is preferred. Otherwise, I save my efforts and patronize Harding and Howell."

It was worth a shot.

A short time later, Darcy paused on a walkway across the busy street from the massive building with windows spanning the entire front facade. An enormous sign nearly the width of the building declared in bold lettering: Harding, Howell & Co. Below the sign and between the expanse of clear glass panes stood a gaping portal where a veritable sea of people poured in and out.

Perhaps that is a slight exaggeration, he thought, *although not by much.*

The bustling throngs were reminiscent of the Royal Exchange. However, at the Exchange men were the predominant sex and the seriousness of financial business yielded an air of hushed solemnity, no matter how large the crowd. At Harding and Howell, the swarm of shoppers were principally female, although there were enough males mingled in to prevent him attracting undue attention. The chief difference was the audible gay chatter and laughter, and kaleidoscopic colors from the variety of garments worn to the brightly decorated boxes and bags carried by trailing servants.

So much for missing the hordes of shoppers. Flipping open his pocket watch, Darcy noted the hour hand closer to the one than the twelve. Time was ticking away. *Get on with it already. How bad can it possibly be?*

Inhaling deeply, he squared his shoulders, stepped off the curb, and marched across the street toward the doors.

Once over the threshold and into the entrance foyer, he halted in stunned awe as waves of sensation deluged his senses. First was the steady rumble of hundreds of voices from every direction, at times ringing and then dropping into a constant hum. Wafts of smells pricked his nostril, the majority pleasant, such as the aromas of perfumes and clean fabrics, though interspersed with the intermittent stench of perspiration, dust, and other scents best left unnamed.

The greatest assault to his faculties, however, was the profuse array of merchandise lining every inch of available space. Wall to ceiling, case upon case, stretching on with no end in sight. With a one-hundred-fifty square feet interior, the mall was gigantic by any standards. The mathematical computation of how many items it was possible to fit into a building that size was beyond his capacity.

How will I ever find the perfect wedding gift for Elizabeth?

Scanning the quantity of furs and fans proudly displayed in the partitioned section closest to the main entrance—a mere drop in the bucket—Darcy felt the edges of panic creeping in.

It will take me weeks to search the entire store. Why have I paid scant attention to the unique requirements for a woman?

As if by chance, his gaze was captured by an exquisite ermine muff and stole paired together on a wooden mannequin. A sudden epiphany restored clarity to his jumbled mind.

Why limit himself to purchasing only one gift for his beloved Elizabeth?

Until now, he had resisted showering her with presents, aware that outward displays of his wealth made her uncomfortable. He had vowed to wait until after they married and she had adjusted to a higher standard of living before letting loose his innate desire to express his love and appreciation through gift giving. After all, he had it on good authority—his sister—that all women adored jewels, dresses, and other pretty accessories. Anything he purchased now could be sent off to Pemberley to await his new wife, thus not breaking his self-imposed vow.

In a flash, his mindset shifted. He no longer wondered why inclusive shopping malls existed. In one afternoon, he could acquire an abundance of women's accouterments certain to please Elizabeth, and surely one would speak to him as the ideal wedding present. Also in his favor were the dozens of knowledgeable salesmen and milling women, any of whom could remedy his pathetic lack of education, provided he bravely risked embarrassment or being branded a fool for asking imbecilic questions. For Elizabeth, he would gamble his reputation.

Based on a fair amount of experience buying furs for himself, he started with the ermine ensemble. No sooner had his hands touched the muff before the clerk swooped in, as expected. Bartering with salesmen was familiar territory, his success in obtaining the pair at a fair price establishing the firm footing necessary to bolster his confidence. Breathing easier, he was about to move on when a musical voice stayed his steps.

"Excellent choice on the muff and stole. I can guarantee she will adore both of them."

Darcy swung his gaze toward the beautiful, elegantly dressed woman in her early forties standing by a rack draped with assorted fur tippets. "I beg your pardon?"

"Mr. Halleck"—she bobbed her head toward the merchant who had taken the muff to be boxed—"is aggressive and annoying, but he is the finest furrier in Harding and Howell. His prices reflect this, of course, and in his case are acceptable. Now, if you are in the market for gloves for your wife—"

"Fiancée."

"Ah, I see. Congratulations are in order then. Your impeccable taste in fur bodes well for marital felicity, trust me. For gloves, you want those sewn by Mrs. Viceroy. Some will direct you to Mr. Dicey, and his work is stellar to be sure. The prices, however, are outrageous compared to Mrs. Viceroy's. Clearly this is not an issue for you, as it is not for me either, but I despise being overcharged if it is merely a blatant gouging. Do you not agree? Mrs. Viceroy's gloves are extraordinary and a third the price."

"Thank you, madam. The information is tremendously

appreciated." From the moment he had laid eyes upon her, Darcy felt a jolt of recognition yet doubted his good fortune. Attempting to verify what he hopefully suspected, he bowed gallantly and inquired, "May I have the honor of your name, to express my gratefulness specifically?"

She inclined her head, smiling as she extended her gloved hand. "Mrs. Kemble. Maria Theresa Kemble."

"Mrs. Kemble." Darcy respectfully bestowed a glancing kiss to her hand. "Mr. Darcy of Pemberley in Derbyshire, at your service. Indeed, this is a singular honor. I've had the privilege of watching you perform several times at Covent Garden. In fact, the first play I attended in London was *Tom Thumb* at Drury Lane. You were phenomenal."

"It is a pleasure to meet anyone who attributes 'phenomenal' to one of my performances, Mr. Darcy. I appreciate the praise, as all egocentric artists do no matter how humble they profess to be. However, I was not searching for a complimentary theater habitué. I must confess I have a soft spot for rescuing lost gentlemen in shopping malls."

"Was I that obvious?"

"Gaping while blocking the doorway was the first clue. What truly gave it away, Mr. Darcy, was not knowing what a tippet is."

"And here I was congratulating myself on bluffing convincingly when Mr. Halleck mentioned them."

"Take my advice—do not play cards for serious money."

Despite his embarrassment, he had to chuckle at that. "I have heard the warning before. Numerous times."

"While we cannot improve upon acting skills when none exist," she jested, "we can impart our vast knowledge of what women desire."

Mrs. Kemble's shift into the plural was a mystery for mere seconds. Circling from behind him were two women as lushly beautiful as Mrs. Kemble. They walked with a graceful poise wholly

22

unique and captivating to behold. Darcy recognized them instantly, awestruck as he bowed reverentially to each in turn as Mrs. Kemble formally introduced her companions.

Maria Theresa de Camp had made a name for herself as a dancer and actress years before her marriage to acclaimed actor Charles Kemble. As Darcy had said, she was the first starring actress he had seen perform, and while he would never confess it, his impressionable sixteen-year-old heart had fallen madly in love with the glamorous starlet. Long over those youthful passions, he still admired her talent, seen most recently the past December in *Smiles and Tears, or the Widow's Stratagem*, a comedy play she wrote.

To Mrs. Kemble's right stood Maria Davison, celebrated for creating the role of Julianna in *The Honeymoon* at the beginning of her career. Currently a principal actress at Drury Lane, Darcy had delighted in several of her fine portrayals over the past ten years.

Standing beside Mrs. Davison was none other than Sarah Siddons, preeminent *tragedienne* of the eighteen-century stage. Born into the Kemble acting family—Charles Kemble was her brother— Mrs. Siddons had acting in her blood and entered the profession during the 1770s when female actresses were on the cusp of attaining respectability. Her brilliance on the stage escalated her to a celebrity status of mythical proportions and had elevated the prestige of actors and actresses as a whole.

Born during Sarah Siddon's reign as queen of Drury Lane, Darcy had missed the acclaimed performances at the height of her career. Fortunately, he had attended every Covent Garden appearance of Mrs. Siddons in her later years, before retiring, including her extraordinary farewell performance as Lady Macbeth in 1812. On that night the applause had been thunderous, Darcy vigorously contributing, and she delivered the most incredible farewell speech in theatre history.

Meeting dignitaries was not unusual for a man of Darcy's station in society, but being introduced to luminaries of the London stage in the middle of a shopping mall was an entirely new experience. He was quite overwhelmed!

"Mrs. Siddons," he greeted the eldest of the three before turning to the youngest of the renowned actress trio. "Mrs. Davison. Indeed, my great fortune has multiplied exponentially. I am overwhelmed."

"We view it as a service to humanity, Mr. Darcy," Sarah Siddons assured in her famed voice. "Teach a gentleman the critical importance of costly trinkets to spoil his lovers, sisters, aunts, etcetera —of which he shall profit in unmentionable ways—and he will pass the information to his male friends. Rumors spread and our sex reaps the bounty for generations."

Mrs. Davison bobbed her head in agreement, and verily before Darcy blinked his eyes the three prima donnas of the London stage had "taken him under their wings" as they put it. For the better part of an hour they personally escorted him to the best merchandise in Harding and Howell and, with such illustrious women at his side, attention was inevitable.

Darcy intensely despised being stared at and fawned over, yet there was no denying the benefits in this instance. The news rippled through the mall with male and female customers flocking to meet the famed actresses. This didn't surprise Darcy. What did surprise him was the plethora of ladies who joined the noble cause of educating him. Universally, they delighted in imparting their perspectives on the products for sale and gushed endlessly about ways to "make his beloved happy."

The assistance continued long after Mrs. Kemble, Mrs. Siddons, and Mrs. Davison reluctantly departed. At the milliner and draper department every woman present—customer and sales assistant, young and old—held up gowns and donned hats to model for him. Never in his life had Darcy been surrounded by a surfeit of females parading and posing as they invited him to ogle brazenly. Only the humor in the situation inhibited his utter humiliation.

After three exhausting hours and more purchases than he had

ever made in a single day, Darcy was desperate for freedom. The crowds had thinned, and fewer helpers were dogging his steps, so when an extradition route presented itself, he grabbed onto a minute of distraction among his followers.

Ducking into a partitioned area selling perfumery and toilette articles, he hid behind a series of display cases taller than he. While used as an escape stratagem, Darcy's cloaking tactic was providential. Absently scanning the products on the shelves, his eyes slid past a box, only to jerk back. There it was! The perfect gift for Elizabeth that had stubbornly eluded him despite the massive pile of boxes and bags collecting at the porter's desk.

Lying on a cushion of dark-blue velvet inside a lacquered cherrywood box was an exquisite vanity set consisting of a brush, comb, and mirror. Stupendously crafted of silver with inlaid mother-of-pearl bordered by a raised ridge of emerald-green enamel, he had never seen another as superlative. Unfamiliar he may have been with the components of a lady's toilette, but Darcy knew silver artistry and masterful construction when he saw it, no matter the object.

Envisioning Elizabeth opening this priceless gift once they were alone on their wedding night was a superb vision. Picturing himself standing or sitting behind her while brushing her lush, long, wavy hair as the aroma of lavender rose into the air sent tingles of extreme pleasure flittering through his body. The reality was sure to surpass his imagination.

Shoving thoughts of Elizabeth and intimacy aside—a wise move if he wanted to keep his dignity intact—he motioned to the shop owner.

"I wish to have each of these pieces engraved in the finest script." Darcy paused, deliberating. Formally, his wife would be addressed as "Mrs. Fitzwilliam Darcy." These items, however, were personal, an intimate gift for their eyes only and mutual enjoyment. Coming to a decision, he smiled at the patiently waiting merchant. "Along each handle engrave *Elizabeth Darcy*."

His mission having been accomplished and exceeded his wildest expectations, Darcy was more than ready to call it a day. After checking with the porter's desk to ensure his purchases were accounted for and prepared for delivery to Darcy House—they were —a famished and weary Darcy hastened toward the exit with the securely wrapped vanity set inside the lone bag he carried.

The prospect of a restorative brandy had never sounded more appealing. So much so that he barely stifled a curse when his name was shouted from some distance away.

"Mr. Darcy, is that you?"

He instantly sifted through a dozen excuses to avoid conversation, not even caring if his abruptness came across as rude. A rapid assessment of the distance to the door revealed that he could make a run for it. Between preoccupation and overall irritation, no attempt was made to identify the voice. Then, in the split second before settling on a plausible evasion, the woman—that fact had unconsciously registered—answered her own question.

"Oh! It is Mr. Darcy! See, Lizzy, I told you I glimpsed him from afar while we were in the haberdashery."

For several seconds, Darcy froze in place. Shaking off his astonishingly bad luck, he forced a pleasant smile and turned around. Mrs. Gardiner, wearing a beaming grin, was bearing down on him fast. Flanking her, a step or two behind, were Elizabeth and Jane.

As instant as his annoyance over being waylaid it disappeared, to be replaced by happiness flooding his soul. Elizabeth's eyes sparkled with delight as she focused on him to the exclusion of everything surrounding, a radiant smile curving her luscious mouth. The crystalline image of her visage never faded from his mind, yet when he saw her in the flesh, especially after nearly a full day apart, he was struck anew by her breathtaking beauty and the effect her very presence had upon him.

"What a delightful surprise, is it not?" Mrs. Gardiner's question was a vague hum. Darcy could not tear his eyes away from Elizabeth.

"In a city the size of London, the odds of encountering a friend or acquaintance are remote. Yet here we are! And not merely anyone, but your betrothed. Quite fortuitous and extraordinary, would you not agree, Lizzy?"

"Indeed, I do agree. It is immeasurably fortuitous and supremely extraordinary. How are you, Mr. Darcy?"

"I am improving by the moment, Miss Elizabeth." Pausing to clear his bone-dry throat, and belatedly remembering his manners, he shifted his gaze to Jane and Mrs. Gardiner. "I pray the three of you are equally as well and enjoying your afternoon?"

Mrs. Gardiner and Jane responded in the affirmative, as did Lizzy, after which she inquired, "What brings you to Harding, Howell, and Company on this fine day, sir? I never conceived of this being an establishment you frequent."

The tease was not lost on Darcy, nor was the hint of acrimony. Honestly perplexed by what would cause the latter, and therefore concluding he must be mistaken, he shrugged nonchalantly and replied in a lighthearted tone, "I endeavor to retain a bit of mystery, Miss Bennet, but shall enlighten since you have caught me in the act. I have discovered the supreme benefit in enlisting the aid of other women when acquiring objects explicitly created for the fairer sex. Far more efficient and wise, as it turns out, than trying to judge for myself what is best for a lady. The women at Harding and Howell are surprisingly willing to assist."

"I *see*," she stressed, the teasing tone disappearing in favor of the acrimonious. "The error is in my assumptions, obviously. Are you *intimately* familiar with the mall then? Perhaps your superior knowledge of where to obtain feminine products will benefit us as well, Mr. Darcy, if it isn't too much trouble to share your accumulated wealth of information?"

Elizabeth's smile remained but with a stiffness to her lips that corresponded with the sharp undertone of her outwardly cordial words. Her eyes, Darcy noted with increasing mystification, had taken on a hard glint. Confused, he looked to Jane and Mrs. Gardiner for a clue. Each woman wore an expression of suppressed amusement. Mrs. Gardiner shook her head slightly and swiveled her eyes pointedly toward a cluster of attractive young women standing not too far away who were quite blatantly admiring his figure. Darcy frowned, then looked back at a pursed-lipped Elizabeth. Abruptly the pieces fell into place.

She is jealous—positively green with it!

The possessive fire within her lovely eyes loudly proclaimed the degree of her sentiments toward him, and perhaps it was an unattractive reaction, but his spirit soared. As pleasing as her jealousy, in one respect, decency demanded to disabuse her of the notion that he was a seasoned expert who frequently bought trinkets for women.

Then again, what harm was there in a brief bit of fun?

Darcy stepped closer and spoke softly. "My knowledge is not overly vast, but one does overhear conversations that often prove valuable. Harding and Howell has a well-earned reputation. However, you are correct, Miss Elizabeth, in believing I avoid such places unless forced by necessity to enter them."

"Is that so? And what *necessity* was it that *forced* you this time, Mr. Darcy?"

Mrs. Gardiner and Jane were still struggling not to laugh and had taken several steps backward to stay out of Lizzy's vision. The latter was too intent on boring a hole of shame through her fiancé to notice. Darcy bent until inches away from her irritated face and whispered, "This is my first time at Harding and Howell, my dearest love, and the purpose was a wedding present."

"For me?" she gasped, her eyes popped open wider and body relaxing. A flush spread across her cheeks, and Darcy had to exert all his control not to kiss her.

Instead, he arched one brow and grinned. "I believe it is customary. Besides, I did warn you that gifts from me would be a common occurrence once we were married, and I intend to begin as soon as possible. But for now"—he captured her hand and pressed a fleeting kiss onto her knuckles—"you are forced by necessity to wait in anticipation for another month."

~

*T*he unplanned encounter at Harding and Howell was not the disaster he had feared after all. Following his tease regarding the gift in his hand, Elizabeth dropped the subject entirely, to Darcy's surprise. Georgiana was worse than a buzzing pest when it came to presents, and he thought this was the natural female attitude. Other than two or three glances at the bag, Elizabeth expressed no interest whatsoever. Darcy fervently prayed it was a ploy of indifference, particularly in light of the massive quantity of merchandise soon to be on its way to Pemberley, as well as gift giving being one portion of his agenda for later that night.

He invited the ladies to join him for a light refreshment at the coffeehouse across the street from Harding and Howell. Their company, particularly Elizabeth's, had revitalized his lagging energy and suddenly coffee sounded better than brandy. They did not tarry overlong, as it was late in the day and everyone needed time to clean up and dress for dinner. Departing from his beloved on this occasion was a painless ordeal, knowing he would soon again be in her presence.

As he had for the past two nights since their arrival in London, Darcy and his sister welcomed the Bennets, Gardiners, and Mr. Bingley to Darcy House for dinner. While the first night had contained extremely pleasurable moments—Darcy did not think he would ever look at the rear terrace without feeling the bliss of Elizabeth in his arms—it had also been a trial and strain.

Last night—in the wake of Elizabeth forcefully setting him straight while in his mother's bedchamber that afternoon—the awkward tension had thoroughly disappeared. One and all had enjoyed a delicious meal and delightful fellowship. What he had not managed was a second alone with Elizabeth, not even to press a light kiss on to her cheek or brush his fingertips over her creamy skin.

Tonight, their third night in Town and after more than twenty-four hours of nothing beyond one kiss to her hand, Darcy determined to arrange matters to suit his desires. Besides, he did have a legitimate reason to sequester his fiancée, one that did not directly have to do with his ardency.

With this foremost in his mind, Mr. Darcy and Miss Darcy greeted their guests as they arrived with the standard pomp and circumstance. Retiring to the parlor while the servants finished preparations for dinner, Darcy drew Mr. Bennet to the side as soon as the opportunity arose without attracting undue attention.

"Mr. Bennet, sir. If I may request it of you, I would appreciate a private audience with Miss Elizabeth at some point this evening. After dinner, of course. I have a gift for her, something quite special that belonged to my mother, which I am anxious for her to have but prefer not to reveal in public. We would only be in the foyer area, so not too far away from oversight."

"I can find no fault in the request, Mr. Darcy. Even if I did, Lizzy would scold me most vehemently for impeding the giving of a present. A scolding by Lizzy is a rather fearsome thing, as I suspect you know. A rousing challenge, most of the time, but I'm not up to it tonight."

Indeed, Darcy knew of Elizabeth's temper all too well! And, like her father, he wasn't in the mood to fight tonight either. Far from it. Emboldened by Mr. Bennet's approval, he decided on the spot to seek helpful illumination on a nagging anxiety.

"May I ask a question, Mr. Bennet?" At the older gentleman's nod, Darcy forged ahead. "Miss Elizabeth has expressed her reluctance in receiving gifts from me. We have discussed the topic, and to a degree, I understand her rationale in preferring to wait until after we are married. However, what I am uncertain of is if her very nature is such that she is disinterested in gifts overall. Or is it that she would only want books or similar items, which I am delighted to bestow, as reading is a passion we share. Would jewelry, perfume, and…other feminine wares offend her in some way?"

Mr. Bennet chuckled. "Don't let her fool you, Mr. Darcy. Lizzy may not be as outwardly effusive about gifts or enamored of pretty trinkets as some, but she isn't blasé either. I am completely confident that anything you choose to give her, tonight and in the years to come, will be abundantly appreciated and cherished. Lizzy is surprisingly maudlin underneath her prickly exterior."

He clapped Darcy on the shoulder and started to turn away. Then he paused, adding almost as if an afterthought, "The foyer is fine, if you wish, but you might consider the terrace. Lizzy has a fondness for starry skies and fresh air. You may have learned that already."

Mr. Bennet winked, and then, with a grin in place, he moved to join the others, leaving Darcy practically gaping. All throughout dinner he felt as if Mr. Bennet was secretly laughing at him. About the time he concluded it was his overworked imagination, he'd catch Elizabeth staring at her father speculatively.

Did the older gentleman know of the liberties he'd taken with his daughter?

The question lingered in Darcy's mind, but he relinquished dwelling upon it. His impatience to be alone with Elizabeth overrode everything. After interminable hours at the dining table, then the gentlemen in the library, the regathering of the genders in the parlor for socializing, and then the ascension to the first-floor game room for entertainment, Darcy reached the end of his endurance.

Casually strolling to where Elizabeth sat beside Georgiana, he ignored the manners he'd had ingrained in him which taught never to interrupt two women sharing a hushed conversation. Standing behind them, he leaned down and touched Elizabeth lightly on the shoulder. She startled but smiled when she gazed upward to meet his eyes.

"Eavesdropping, Mr. Darcy?"

"Not this time," he responded blandly, smiling when she chuckled. "I wondered if I could steal you away from the riveting conversation with my sister."

Elizabeth's eyes widened and dropped to his mouth. It was a mere flash, followed by a rosy flush tinting her cheeks. "As you wish, sir."

Addressing the group as Elizabeth rose, Darcy informed, "Please excuse us. I have been granted permission to speak with my betrothed privately for a matter of some urgency. I promise not to keep her for too long." He inclined his head in Mr. Bennet's direction, the older gentleman absently returning the gesture from his chair at the chess table. Mr. Gardiner didn't even look up from his serious study of the pieces.

Satisfied, Darcy offered his arm to Elizabeth, but they were halted before reaching the door. "Take the time necessary to complete the business properly, Mr. Darcy," Mr. Bennet said while staring at the chessboard. "I am confident *all of us* can entertain ourselves in the interim, securely within the walls of this well-appointed room. I can think of no reason to bother you."

"What did he mean by that?" Elizabeth asked once they were outside the room and descending the stairs.

"I am beginning to suspect your father is not as oblivious as we have surmised. He may become distracted by my library, and he clearly has a soft spot for his favored daughter which leads him to turn a blind eye and trust implicitly. This does not, however, mean he is unaware of moonlit terrace embraces, solitary dalliances in the private rooms of the townhouse, or the host of stolen kisses and caresses at Longbourn."

"Oh my! I thought we were so clever."

"Apparently not. Fortunately, Mr. Bennet does not seem to be overly disturbed and may be encouraging the activity. Speaking for myself, this is tremendously relieving and gives me all sorts of brilliant ideas. Does this suit you as well, Miss Bennet?" The rosy blush spreading over Elizabeth's cheeks was utterly delightful, as was the frankly welcoming expression on her face. Darcy steered her to a bench in the foyer, waiting until she sat. "Hold that thought for now," he quipped, touching one fingertip to her nose. "Don't move an inch. I will return momentarily."

Hurrying to his office, he retrieved the two boxes sitting on his desk and hastened back. Elizabeth hadn't budged, as commanded, her eyes trained on him as he approached and brows lifting at the sight of the boxes in his hand.

"I thought I was forced to wait until our wedding night."

"You are, for the gift I bought today. These are something else. Here, come." He extended his hand, Elizabeth taking it and rising. "The terrace is an enchanting location for our discussion. Today I was informed that you have a fondness for starry skies and fresh air. Who knew?"

"I shall never be able to face my father again."

Laughing, they exited through the double door onto the wide terrace. The fountain bubbled musically, drowning any sounds coming from the townhouses surrounding. It was a chilly evening, but the sky was clear and air fresher than usual for London. Darcy selected a table and chairs directly in sight of the patio doors, which he left wide open. The terrace torches had been lit per his directions, so between those and the lights inside the foyer, there were no immediate shadows to hide them. While this did fulfill Darcy's promise to Mr. Bennet that they would be within eyesight, another purpose was to reveal what was inside the boxes, both of which he set on the small table.

Clasping her hands, he scooted his chair until their knees were touching. "I have two special items to give you, Elizabeth. First, I must apologize for the delay in bestowing them. Both have been kept securely locked at Pemberley, requiring two trusted staff members to deliver safely. They are priceless in several ways, as I shall explain. Then, I wanted them cleaned, polished, inspected for any damage, and resized in the case of one. You see, they have years of wear but also many years of sitting undisturbed, so I was unsure of their condition."

Pausing, his fingers traveled to the ring on her left hand. The gold band with the seven gemstones spelling out the message "dearest" had been given to her three weeks ago, and he had never seen it off her finger. Smiling, he went on, "If you recall when I gave this to you, I said it was not the betrothal ring I most desired to bestow." He pulled it from her finger, noting the involuntary flinch and breathy gasp with pleasure, and swiftly slipped it onto the ring finger of her right hand. Kissing the skin above the sparkling band, he murmured, "I trust this ring will always hold a special place in your heart, as it does in mine?"

"For all of my life."

The catch of emotion in her voice was nearly his undoing. Only the task he needed to complete stopped him from drawing her into his arms. Taking the smaller box into his hands, Darcy peered intently into her love-drenched eyes. "This is the ring that has waited, patiently, for me to place on the finger of the woman I promise to love, cherish, and be faithfully devoted to for as long as I draw breath."

Slowly he lifted the lid, watching as her eyes reluctantly left his face to peer downward. Her gasp was sharp and loud this time.

"William! It is exquisite!"

Inside the box was a ring of shiny gold, the narrow band adorned with a one-carat star sapphire of vivid blue, centered between two round half-carat diamonds.

Inhaling shakily, he explained as he slid it onto her finger, "My father designed this ring for my mother. As the story went, he searched far and wide across England for the most perfect,

34

magnificent sapphire. It was her favorite jewel, you see. Each time he told the story to me and Georgiana the search took longer, and the traveled miles grew."

Darcy laughed softly in remembrance. "We know he exaggerated, but also know the basics are accurate. He waited four years to marry Lady Anne Fitzwilliam, until she was of the proper age, according to the rigid rules of old Lord Matlock, Colonel Fitzwilliam's grandfather," he clarified. "My parents were passionately in love, and nothing but the very best was good enough for her. This is how my father felt about my mother, and why I have dreamt for the same passionate love."

Kissing the skin above the ring, as he had on her right hand, he then enclosed both hands between his palms. Pouring every ounce of his adoration into his gaze, he proclaimed confidently, "Giving you this ring, Elizabeth, isn't just my personal wish. My mother wanted you to have it. She, and my father, may not have known you, but at various times before they passed, each of them assured me that their heart's desire was for me to find a love like the one they shared, and when I did, this was the ring that woman should wear."

Tears were swimming in Elizabeth's eyes, and after twice parting her lips as if to speak, Darcy smiled and reached for the other box. Sliding it to the edge, he attempted to ease the overwhelming emotions they were both experiencing by making a joke.

"Might as well move on to the next part so we can completely lose all ability to verbalize."

She released a tremulous laugh that was equally an emotive sob, so his jesting worked a little. Palm atop the flat, wide box, Darcy launched into the second bit of family history.

"This belongs to you, Elizabeth, as will all the jewels at Pemberley. For reasons you will understand in a moment, this was one of my mother's favorite pieces, although it has been in the family for I honestly have no idea how many generations. My reason for gifting it now isn't out of extreme sentimentality or as a request from my mother, as it was with the ring. This wish is all me, and simply because I have always loved it. It is also important for me to stress that while I would greatly adore seeing you wear it on our wedding day, I do not want you to feel obligated to do so if you have a Bennet family heirloom or if this does not properly match the gown you have chosen, or—"

He stopped talking when she pressed two fingers against his lips. "William, I am honored to wear this on our wedding day. Whatever it is. To please you and express my incredible happiness in becoming your wife, I…would do anything."

Slowly grinning, he asked, "What if it is hideous?"

Laughing aloud, she shook her head. "Somehow I doubt that is possible."

"I wouldn't be too sure," he warned with mock severity. "There is a certain brooch I recall in one case that should have earned the jewelry maker a trip to the gallows. Or maybe my taste in jewelry is frightfully bad."

"Just open the box! The suspense is now killing me."

Suddenly feeling rather giddy, Darcy opened the lid dramatically slow. No heightening theatrics were necessary, however. Nestled on a thick pillow of white velvet was a stunning necklace of sapphires and diamonds in various shapes and sizes, masterfully crafted and woven into a spiraling arabesque style. The lights bounced off the polished metal and gemstones as Darcy lifted it off the velvet.

He draped it over his palms, Elizabeth reverently brushing her fingers across the sparkling stones. After a minute of awed inspection, he slipped it around her slender neck. Securing the clasp, he gently laid his hands on either side of the necklace, fingers caressing the nape of her neck.

"Beautiful. Almost as beautiful as you."

Elizabeth was staring at him, her glowing eyes round as saucers and teeming with emotions almost too intense for him to bear. With her left hand, she nimbly stroked the teardrop sapphire lying below the hollow of her throat. Her right hand floated upward, making contact with his chin as her thumb traced a lazy circle, before gliding up to his lips. The pressure was light, yet it sent rivers of fire over the surface of his mouth. He parted his lips, tongue moving toward the sensitive pad, but her thumb was gone, brushing across the corner of his mouth before drifting up toward his cheek.

The warm splay of her entire palm against his face intensified the delicious sensations racing through his skin. Darcy instinctively tilted his head to increase the pressure. Doing so, he realized how far he had already unintentionally leaned toward her. Her luminous eyes were inches away, still open although her eyelids had grown heavy. In the remaining seconds, before he bridged the gap to kiss her, Darcy noted everything. The eager lifting of her face, the tongue sweeping between parted lips to moisten, the sound of rapid breaths, the rich flush infusing her cheeks, and the increasing heat burning the hands still resting on the curve of her neck.

Then, an inch from the paradise of her mouth, she whispered, "I love you."

He groaned, the sound low and guttural yet surprisingly loud in the silence, and without knowing who closed the final distance, they were kissing. Considering the ardency he was fully aware they both felt, the kiss was astonishingly delicate and tender. Pervasive and passionate, yes, yet, with a controlled tempo. He wanted to enjoy every second, cognizant that the interlude could only last for a short time. The temptation to draw her to his body and repeat the wild embrace from two nights ago was difficult to resist, especially given Mr. Bennet's oblique jesting about it. Nevertheless, Darcy didn't think it wise to test the limits of what Elizabeth's protective father would allow.

A small part of his brain—a teeny, tiny sliver—stayed focused and clear. One kiss was permissible. A fiery, inclusive, protracted kiss...but still just one kiss. He even managed to keep his hands in a safe place, cradling her swanlike neck and delicate shoulders, and going nowhere near the swell of her breasts.

All in all, a job well done, he thought, as they gradually lessened the kiss before pulling apart. He was rather proud of his regulation and gratified that their sweet intimacy—while far, far from the level he hungered to reach—would tide him over. For a few hours, at least.

Elizabeth appeared to be of the same mind. For want of a better phrase, she looked as if she had been kissed quite thoroughly and thrilled in the experience. Apparently, he must have presented a similar picture, based on the smug smile curving her plump lips as she studied his face.

"I needed that," she blurted, dropping her eyes for an embarrassed second before joining Darcy in soft laughter.

"As did I, my love." He drew in a rasping breath. Pulling away from her enticing lips, he turned his contemplation to the stars. "We should return, although waiting a few minutes more is probably a wise idea, particularly for me."

To his amusement and relief, rather than blushing over his remark and the obvious meaning, she covered her mouth and burst into muffled laughter.

2

UNFORESEEN COMPLICATION

$\mathcal{T}$he following morning, Darcy left his quarters whistling lowly. As on the previous day, he sought out his sister and found her in the parlor playing the pianoforte. For several minutes he stood in the foyer listening. Georgiana's nimble fingertips glided over the ivory keys, the music issuing forth in a lyrical cascade. Her skill never failed to amaze him, and pride swelled his heart.

Then, he detected a subtle imperfection in the familiar piece written by Mozart, and a peek past the jamb revealed her posture abnormally stiff. Chuckling, Darcy strolled into the room.

"Brother!"

"Blessed morning, my sweet. As always, I appreciate being greeted with your talent. What better way to begin my day?"

"Better than coffee and eggs?"

Darcy bent and kissed her rosy cheek. "Indeed, it may be a draw between coffee and your playing. I cannot decide." He playfully pinched the tip of her nose. "Now, answer truthfully. Am I correct in my assessment that Herr Mozart's concerto lacked your usual precision? Can it be you are distracted by nervousness?"

Georgiana bit her lip. "I know very well I should not be nervous, yet I am. Please do not lecture."

Darcy feigned astonishment and pointed at his chest while mouthing *Me? Lecture?* His drama worked. Georgiana smiled, if a bit wanly.

"I have never hosted a tea party all on my own and admit that doing so unnerves me. Why I initiated the idea is unfathomable! What if I spill hot tea on Miss Elizabeth? What if I drop a blob of jam onto Miss Bennet's dress? What if I embarrass us by saying something inappropriate? Or what if my tongue refuses to move at all and I stare dumbly for hours? What if I—"

"At the present, I have difficulty giving credence to your worry over your tongue refusing to move," Darcy interrupted.

Georgiana clamped her lips tight.

"As for your other concerns, you are far too graceful to spill anything on anyone, and I can assure that any embarrassing utterances by you will never trump the ones already delivered by me. Have no fear, Georgie. If I were to wager, my money would be on the three of you laughing away the afternoon with gossip and whatever else females blather on about."

Delivering another tweak to her nose, he turned away and walked toward the servant's bell. Georgiana jumped up, suddenly cheerful.

"Then I suppose I can enlighten Miss Elizabeth about you when younger, yes? Should I tell her about the time you were half carried into Pemberley by Mr. Vernor because you stumbled on the carriage steps and twisted your ankle? Why again was it that Father said you were 'pickled enough to feel no pain'? And I am sure she would be amused by the time you and Cousin Richard lost your way while hunting in the woods a mile from Rivallain. Or should I start with describing the tragic outcome when you attempted to fashionably curl your hair?"

"That depends on how badly you want new gowns or music sheets—or food," he growled with mock severity. "Perhaps I was hasty in my assurances. Let us save the worst of my youthful mishaps for after Miss Elizabeth has married me. You do want to have a sister, do you not? Ah, Mr. Travers. Perfect timing. You have saved me from further rehashing past follies."

"I do my best, Mr. Darcy. How else may I be of service?"

"Please pass the message to have my carriage readied in one hour. I have an appointment with my tailor."

The butler gave his assurances and then briskly departed the room.

"Will you be gone all day?"

Darcy turned back to his sister, torn between amusement and sympathy by the strain in her voice and creased brows. Pretending he misunderstood the concern behind her question, he answered, "I will be away all morning. Beyond that I am unsure. No need to fret, Georgie. I promise not to interrupt your afternoon engagement."

"I was rather hoping you would join us," she mumbled, staring at her slippered toes.

"You do not need me for moral support, nor, to be frank, would I particularly enjoy sipping tea while three ladies gossip and share fashion advice." Darcy patted her cheek and switched to a tone of authority, as he knew she needed in times such as this. "You are Miss Georgiana Darcy of Pemberley, the daughter of Lady Anne Darcy and niece of the Countess of Matlock, and as such will perform brilliantly. Never forget who you are. Perfection as a hostess is in your blood, my dear."

Pleased at the confidence straightening her spine and lifting her chin, Darcy continued in the same Master of Pemberley pose. "I took the liberty of requesting orange pudding and sugar cakes be added to the menu since Miss Elizabeth and Miss Bennet expressed particular delight in each. I have also instructed Mrs. Smyth to use the Compagnie des Indes tea set"—Darcy ignored Georgiana's gasp —"and the Würth cutlery."

41

"Oh, William! Are you sure? I know Miss Elizabeth deserves the best, but what if—"

"Indeed, Elizabeth deserves the best and always shall have it. That, however, is not why I specified the two." Clasping both her hands between his, Darcy bent until at her eye level. "They were Mother's favorites when entertaining, so fitting for today. Most importantly, I knew you would be nervous and this, more than my words, proves my trust in your capabilities. Be placated, dearest."

He kissed her forehead and then straightened. "Now, I have a bit of work to attend to before my appointment. Have an enjoyable day with my beautiful future wife and her sister."

Confident that Georgiana would overcome her nervousness, especially once in the presence of the always-effervescent Elizabeth and soothing Jane, Darcy exited the room, once again whistling.

⁓

*L*ike all gentlemen of wealth and station in society, Darcy had his garments created by the best tailors, hatters, and boot makers in the business. Even with the plethora of possible choices in London, certain craftsman gained preeminence, with competition to be on their client list quite stiff. Fortunately, Darcy had access to three of the top tailors in London, thus having a choice when it came to selecting who would sew his wedding ensemble. Nevertheless, he hadn't needed to contemplate the matter.

Jonathan Meyer, the renowned Austrian tailor who serviced Beau Brummell and the Prince Regent upon occasion, was famous for his impeccable workmanship and unique designs. For an event as important as his wedding, Darcy insisted on something special, and there was no doubt that Mr. Meyer would deliver.

Standing before the tall mirrors lining one corner of the secluded fitting room suites at Thirty-Six Conduit Street on the northern end of Savile Row, Darcy examined the black woolen broadcloth trousers and jacket sewn precisely to his measurements. Not a flaw was found to any seam or hem, not that he expected any. Whether sewn by his hand or by one of his skilled assistants, nothing passed beyond the front doors of Jonathan Meyer's shop without his final inspection.

A young apprentice tailor materialized to Darcy's left, the final garment necessary to complete the suit hanging from his outstretched arm for full display. "Here is the waistcoat, Mr. Darcy. The embroidery is complete as per the agreed upon design. With your approval, and Mr. Meyer's,"—he bobbed his head toward the tailor quietly standing nearby—"we can sew the lining."

Darcy slipped the jacket off and into the waiting hands of a second attendant, his expression neutral as the unlined waistcoat was gingerly pulled over his shoulders to test for fit. A full minute passed with Darcy calmly turning side to side as he lightly ran his fingertips over the creamy ivory satin with polychrome silk floss delicately patterned into a scrolling floral motif along the edges up to and including the high collar. The cloth-covered buttons were also embroidered and positioned to blend perfectly into the design. While not as ornate as the handful of waistcoats he owned to be worn exclusively for official Court events, this one came close. Unlike those gaudy, old-fashioned suits that Darcy abhorred wearing, this modern-cut ensemble with the contrast of ivory and splashes of color against the midnight black was visually stunning.

Glancing toward the tailor, Darcy wasn't surprised to see his triumphant expression. Mr. Meyer was familiar enough with his client to detect Darcy's delighted approval with the waistcoat, despite the practiced noncommittal cast to his face. Mr. Meyer's smile of satisfaction, Darcy knew full well, was in part the result of another superbly crafted garment, but primarily about proving his stubborn client wrong.

Meyer's insistence that a fancier style was essential for his wedding had taken some convincing. Even after seeing the sketches, Darcy hadn't been one-hundred percent sure he would like something so different from the simple prints he preferred. His trust in Mr. Meyer's skill and experience in such matters had paid off to be sure. Somehow he knew that Elizabeth—who had never said a word about his wardrobe—would be delighted.

Approval rendered without hesitation, Mr. Meyer nodding once and saying nothing.

Darcy was still in a state of partial undress when Peters, one of the Darcy House footmen, arrived with a folded note. Emergencies or critical messages were rare, yet Mr. Darcy never left the townhouse without Mr. Travers being aware of Darcy's agenda. The habit had been put to the test infrequently, and if not specifically instructed by the sender of this note to immediately place it directly into Mr. Darcy's hand, the butler would have simply set it on his master's desk and thought nothing more about it.

Darcy broke the blob of red wax imprinted with a crown over a lone star. The single line was unsigned, but between the seal insignia and the scrawled message itself, Darcy knew it was from his cousin, Colonel Richard Fitzwilliam.

York's. 1pm. Usual table. I have news.

"Typical," Darcy mumbled.

Well versed in Richard's penchant for mischief and rattling his somber cousin, Darcy did not anticipate the "news" being anything of significance. It was more probable that the intriguing summon was a ploy designed to force a lazy afternoon upon him. Nevertheless, his interest was piqued and, he admitted, hot coffee, friendly male conversation, and lounging sounded far more appealing than the ledger waiting on his desk.

ork's Coffeehouse, located across from Green Park on Piccadilly Street, was a favorite place for Darcy and his cousin to meet. The address was a rough halfway point between Grosvenor Square and the townhouse of Lord Matlock on Saint James's Square, but easy access was only one reason the two men had chosen York's years ago.

First, the coffee was excellent. All the beverages and meals served were superb, in fact. Many coffeehouses in London could boast the same, yet few claimed a comparable atmosphere. Urbane and elegant was York's, with an air of casual comfort elusive in a pretentious gentlemen's club, such as White's where Darcy and Richard were members.

The black-brick building sat on the corner, the windows providing adequate lighting and a spectacular view of Green Park. York's spanned the entire ground level and two-thirds of the first storey. Unlike the majority of the coffeehouses scattered about the city, seating places were distributed spaciously rather than crammed into every available inch of space. If greater privacy were desired, it could be arranged—for a price—in the upper room, where thick walls separated the booths. York's was the perfect establishment to relax, drink, and converse freely without fear of eavesdropping or having one's behavior censured.

A smiling Darcy crossed the threshold, ascended the stairs, and headed directly to the booth next to a south-facing window.

"You are late," Colonel Fitzwilliam noted.

"You are fortunate to have me here at all. A servant had to hunt me down at Meyer's. Next time, send your order for my appearance earlier. Now, scoot over and remove your dusty boots from my bench."

"I will scoot," Richard drawled, "but I am terribly comfortable stretched out, so you will have to suffer the boots. I wiped the muck off, and a little dust will not kill you."

"If it does, I vow to haunt you." Darcy slid into the bench across the table from the colonel, then motioned to a passing waiter. Once placing his order, he bobbed his chin in Richard's direction. "No uniform today. Did they finally discover your limitations and toss you out of the army?"

"I am incognito. Actually, I am a notorious spy blending in with the common folk for an ultra-secret mission for the Crown. Quite heroic and dangerous. Are you impressed?"

"Exorbitantly. I always suspected York's a hideout knee deep in traitors of the king."

"The world is a strange place, Darcy."

"Is this drivel practice for captivating women? Or is your 'news' that you are fully delusional?"

"Neither, although the women angle has potential. Thanks, Cousin!"

Darcy laughed and shook his head. The waiter brought his coffee, Richard grinning while Darcy prepared the hot beverage to his taste. Once the first gulp was swallowed, he changed the topic.

"What have you been up to these past few days? Georgie said you delivered her safely to Darcy House without sparing a minute to steal my whiskey. Then, when no answer to my alert of arriving in Town came, I began to wonder if you were working, as astonishing as that possibility is."

Richard shrugged, unperturbed by the playful insult. "Nothing too taxing, although I did have some colonel-type business to finish after letting my duties languish while I attended to your request."

"You have my utmost appreciation for escorting Georgiana, Richard. I owe you for that."

"You owe me nothing," Richard asserted with a firm shake of his head. His voice was sincere when he added, "The pleasure of my little mouse's company is payment enough. And, of course, I know where you hide the whiskey at Pemberley too." He lifted his coffee mug as a salute and winked.

Darcy again shook his head but matched his cousin's grin. "So aside from informing me of the need to replenish my liquor stores, is there another purpose behind this meeting? Your note was typically vague."

The colonel's grin faded, and he put the mug down. "The pleasure of your company and sparring with your rapier wit was one draw. I do, however, have news. Good and bad. What do you want first?"

"I prefer to forego the bad news altogether, thank you very much. I am to be married in a month to the most marvelous woman in all of England, if not the world. Shockingly, I have discovered I like being giddy with happiness."

"If I were not truly delighted for you and Miss Bennet, I would jump on that 'giddy' comment with glee. I shall resist and save the taunting for later. I believe your positive attitude will serve in this situation. Last night, I was finally able to get away and have dinner with my parents——"

"So, they are in Town," Darcy blurted, cringing faintly. "I confess my sin in not taking the time to inquire."

"I am not a priest so save your confessions of sins. Besides, absolution is assured considering the purpose bringing you to London, and trust me that it is better to talk to me first. The main topic of conversation was your engagement."

"Is that the good news or the bad?"

"Depends, I suppose. They are dismayed, or perhaps confused is the better word, over your engagement to Miss Bennet."

The furrows between Darcy's brows deepened. "I cannot imagine why they are confused. I wrote to Lord and Lady Matlock not long after Miss Elizabeth accepted my proposal. I was forthright about her family, station in Society, and modest dowry while extolling her myriad virtues. I was also abundantly clear that I love her and that the feelings are reciprocated. Uncle's reply was reserved but not unfavorable. He expressed the desire to meet her, and Aunt Madeline's paragraph was congratulatory."

"That was nearly a month ago. What you do not know, Darcy, is that while blissfully living in giddy happiness, our dear, sweet Aunt Catherine has been busy."

Darcy's face darkened with the anger perpetually simmering under the surface when it came to his other aunt. "How do you mean?"

"You really need to pay more attention to gossip. I have been back in Town for less than two weeks, spent half of that time running an errand for you to Pemberley, and still managed to get an earful. Maybe I *should* become a spy."

Richard's levity was appreciated, but it failed to alleviate Darcy's foreboding. Hoping he was wrong, he smiled and forced an amused tone into his voice. "Listening to gossip is rarely beneficial, Richard, especially when I can readily imagine what is said."

"What you imagine is the anticipated chatter heard whenever a wealthy, handsome, eligible bachelor gets taken off the market. And do not let the fancy words go to your head. They are not mine, God knows. The blather is juicier because no one has ever heard of Elizabeth Bennet. Speculation is rife, as expected. It was when I detected certain facts mingled within that my suspicion mounted."

"Explain what you mean. What facts?"

"Details about her appearance, where she lives, her family—that sort of thing. Details difficult to discover unless one searched for them. Worse yet,"—he placed his booted feet onto the floor and leaned over the table—"there was an emotional tone tied to what was said. In truth, I *have done* some spying and collecting of intelligence in my time, so I know the difference between bare facts and those rendered with motive. Cousin, some of what I heard was, for lack of a better term, vicious."

Darcy listened as Richard imparted a sampling of the rumors disseminating through the *ton*. The scandal of Lydia and Mr. Wickham. The crassness of Mrs. Bennet and Elizabeth's lack of proper connections or money or education. Theories that the Bennet girls used unsavory manipulation to ensnare the first two wealthy men to ever appear in Meryton and the degradation of close relatives in trade. These were merely the tip of the iceberg.

The kernels of truth were exaggerated and painted bleakly, and most of the rumors were blatant lies. Far too many, however, included detailed information few people should logically know. It was the latter that was particularly noteworthy to Colonel Fitzwilliam.

"At first I suspected Caroline Bingley as the source. To a degree, this may be true. She has been in Hertfordshire for the most part and is now off in Bath, but has friends she may have vented her anger to in a letter. I know people, though, and despite Miss Bingley's general nastiness, she's not overly creative. It was the story of Lydia Bennet and George Wickham—God help that poor girl—and your supposed involvement that captured my attention. At first, I assumed the tale fabricated, and if so was too cleverly crafted to come from Miss Bingley's limited intellect. So I zeroed in on that, asked careful questions—in my capacity as a spy, you see. Before long I uncovered it was based on truth—how much I do not know, nor do you have to enlighten me—but significantly I learned that the story originated directly from Lady Catherine de Bourgh."

Darcy's entire being was bathed in cold fury. Anyone other than Richard would have stuttered to a halt in terror at his expression. Richard did hesitate, in fact, but he who was Darcy's oldest friend and close as a brother felt that Darcy deserved to be fully informed.

After a gulp of coffee, Richard plunged on. "I tried to deny it, William. I am less fond of our aunt than you are, but I would not have believed her capable of this. For no other reason than to preserve family honor and reputation, I could not believe what I was hearing. Then again, in her strange mind, she probably believes she's preserving family honor and..." Richard stuttered to a momentary halt, brows wrinkling. "What is it? A second ago you looked ready to kill someone. Now you are white as a ghost."

"Where have you heard all of this disgusting information? From whom?"

"Here and there. Assorted people."

"Now is not the time to be vague! I need to know!"

"What difference does it make?"

"Because, you imbecile, Elizabeth, her sister Jane, and Mr. Bennet are, right this minute, in London!"

"Oh! Well, yes, I see the problem." Richard glanced around the room, Darcy following his gaze and knowing what was coming next before his cousin spoke the warning. "First, calm down, Darcy. Don't make it worse by showing your emotions where people can see, not even here. Second, while I can appreciate your concern, I doubt the Bennets will—and don't take offense—be shopping at the high-end merchants where the gossipy women are. Nor will they be socializing with the crowd at Almack's and the like."

At Richard's warning and rationale, Darcy relaxed partially. He leaned back into the seat and drank his coffee as casually as possible though his insides churned.

True, they had no plans to attend any society functions and considering Mr. Bennet's modest finances they probably would not visit the exclusive, priciest stores. Nor were Elizabeth or Jane apt to engage in random gossip with strangers or draw attention to themselves by bragging over their fiancés are.

Still, London could be a surprisingly small town. Women reveled in chatting with other women, particularly when partaking in an enjoyable activity, and even if not involved in the conversation it was easy to overhear when in a small room.

"I'm not entirely placated, but for the moment there is nothing I can do about it. Might as well tell me the rest. I assume there is more?"

"Afraid so. I didn't tell you everything I learned from my parents last evening." The colonel paused for another swallow of his cold coffee, grimaced, and waved for a fresh pot.

"I might need something stronger than coffee before we are

through here." Darcy tossed back the last bit of his coffee like it was a shot of whiskey. "What did your parents have to add?"

"In a nutshell, Lady Catherine has been writing to my father. Often. He did not share the letters, but what he related to me matched the rumors. He is...upset."

Darcy winced.

Richard reached over and covered his hand in a comforting gesture. "Now, let me impart the good news, Cousin. As I said to you when you announced your engagement and expressed concern over my parents' response, my father is a fair man and he cares for you. Mother too. Hell, she was Lady Anne's dearest friend! Additionally, Father is not naive regarding his sister. My parents are aware that Aunt Catherine has what she deems a valid reason to ruin your relationship with Miss Bennet. Of course, if she had ever bothered to recognize how pigheaded you are, she would not be wasting her time. Oh, quit glaring at me! You know very well you are the most stubborn man on the planet. Once you make a decision it takes a visitation from God to change your mind. Lady Catherine, no matter what she may think, is not God."

A short laugh passed Darcy's lips. Richard smiled and leaned back against the bench. "Obviously, she is trying to shame you among your peers and pressure Lord Matlock to intervene. My father tolerates much from his sister, but being pressured is not in his makeup. Still, from his perspective—"

Richard fell silent while the barmaid placed a new pot of coffee and a heaping plate of food on the table. After pouring fresh cups, Darcy waved his scone toward Richard. "Dare I pray this is all of the bad news?"

"I suppose that hinges upon your point of view. Father wants to talk with you and meet the mystery woman causing all the uproar. The subpoena, I mean, invitation"—Darcy grunted—"to dinner tomorrow night is probably already on your desk. Just remember, Cousin, that while Father can be stern and take the whole 'I am an earl' stuff quite seriously, he does know you *very well*, and he truly loves you. Uncle James was his oldest friend. Personally, I am of the opinion Father would be way more upset if you had succumbed to Aunt Catherine's demands about Anne. Family inheritances and all that rot are important to him,"—Richard rolled his eyes—"but not at the expense of your happiness."

"Once they meet Elizabeth, their concerns will disappear."

"That is what I told him! You can thank me later, maybe let me win at billiards just once or buy me something special." Richard grinned. "I sang Miss Bennet's praises—not a trial in the least—and they were visibly relieved. Elizabeth is a good match for you, William. I am very happy for you, truly. I am confident my parents will agree."

They sipped and ate in companionable quiet for several minutes. Darcy absorbed all that Richard had revealed, sorting through the specifics. Anger at Lady Catherine's vindictive scheming lingered, but willfully suppressing those feelings was accomplished with minimal effort.

As for the rumors circulating through the high-and-mighty of London, it disturbed him only for the sake of protecting Elizabeth. Rumormongering was one of many reasons he despised London society and one of the main reasons he loved Elizabeth's unique, artless honesty. In every way, she was an invigorating breath of fresh air into that stifling world.

"Dinner tomorrow night should be doable. I was planning to host dinner at Darcy House, as I have thus far, so some rearranging will be needed. Mr. Bennet will accompany us, of course. What are Lord Matlock's intentions for the guest list? I would rather not subject my betrothed to an inquisition from the *ton*."

"Jonathan and Priscilla will be there. They are staying at the townhouse, so their attendance is probably for the food rather than curiosity about Miss Bennet or your dazzling company, no offense."

"None taken." Darcy refreshed his coffee, then topped off Richard's cup, asking as he poured, "Why are they staying at the

Matlock townhouse? Did something happen to their house in Berkeley Square?"

"It is being redecorated. Again." Richard shook his head in disgust. "Why do women deem it of the utmost importance to change furnishings and upholstery on a yearly basis?"

"Lord and Lady Montgomery?" Darcy asked, offering no opinion on redecorating advantages or disadvantages.

"Don't be ridiculous! My sister, the esteemed Lady Montgomery, is far too vital to the very fabric of society to be bothered by a measly family gathering. Perhaps it is some small comfort, William, that your choice of bride is not the juiciest gossip in town. If it were, I could safely wager a tidy sum of cash on my sister changing her schedule, even if it meant postponing dinner with the prince himself."

"You have a point," Darcy acknowledged. "Knowing Annabella, that is a comfort. You will be there, I presume?"

"I would not miss this for the world!" Richard grinned. "Besides, you need me. My presence will guarantee an entertaining evening."

Darcy grunted a rude retort out of habit and expectation, which Richard gleefully countered. Strangely, that served better than any heartfelt verbalizations of appreciation.

"Dare I hope that is the complete company?"

"That is all my father mentioned. Georgiana's name did not come up, although I assumed her inclusion, so perhaps he did as well."

"Under the circumstances, I think it might be best if Georgie stayed out of it. She will be happier not to attend, to be honest. Just to be on the safe side, would you be so kind as to pass on my request for no others?" Richard readily agreed, but Darcy was frowning and shook his head. "On second thought, as soon as I return to Darcy House I'll send him a message with my request. While I am at it, I'll ask for an audience earlier in the day. Best to get most of the questions answered and any unpleasantness resolved before Miss Elizabeth and Mr. Bennet arrive."

For the remaining time they passed at York's Coffee House, the cousins reverted to their standard male discussion topics. Darcy unabashedly spoke of Elizabeth with phrases of gushing praise so laced with romantic sentiment that eventually even Richard ran out of ways to harass him. Little else was said about Lady Catherine, the rumors circulating, or the impact of Lord and Lady Matlock's opinion. By the time Darcy bid adieu to Colonel Fitzwilliam and mounted his horse for the ride back to the house, his gay mood was restored and lips were pursed for whistling.

3

INVIGORATING INTERACTION

*M*r. Gardiner's carriage halted before the blue door of Darcy House on Grosvenor Square promptly at one o'clock, as the invitation for Jane and Lizzy Bennet detailed. Cheeks rosy and hands fidgety, Georgiana stood in the foyer as Mr. Travers successfully gathered doffed bonnets and cloaks.

"Miss Bennet. Miss Elizabeth," Georgiana greeted as she rose from a graceful curtsy. "I am so pleased to welcome you to Darcy House. Thank you for graciously accepting my invitation."

"An invitation to pass the afternoon in your company, Miss Darcy, is an honor. Jane and I can conceive of no greater delight. Can we, Jane?"

Jane affirmed this as sincerely as Lizzy, causing Georgiana's blush to spread to her temples. "You are both far too kind. I know London boasts innumerable entertainments more fascinating than a luncheon at Darcy House. Why, you could be shopping, for heaven's sake!"

Lizzy laughed gaily and laced her arm companionably through Georgiana's. "Frankly, I am sick to death of shopping." Lizzy steered them gently toward the parlor, emphasizing when Georgiana gawked incredulously, "Indeed I am! After a while, all the fabrics and lace look the same, and I can no longer distinguish between sable or fox. On top of that, I am quite certain my feet shall never be the same after walking miles over rough stones. It is tragic."

"Now I am positive you are teasing me, Miss Elizabeth. I am suspicious of your claiming sore feet, given how often my brother has mentioned your fondness for walking. However, the evidence of jesting is that *everyone* knows the difference between sable and fox."

Amid the three women's laughter, they sat on the settees surrounding the low table already laden with a three-tiered silver plate rack and two porcelain salvers piled with an assortment of edibles. Decorative plates and shining silver cutlery pieces sat atop a crochet-edged linen tablecloth. The housekeeper Mrs. Smyth trailed behind them, delivering a tray with three porcelain cups on saucers, a steaming teapot, and sugar and cream in matching servers.

"Shall I pour, Miss Darcy?"

"Thank you, Mrs. Smyth, but I wish to attend to my guests."

The housekeeper gave a single nod and silently exited the room without acknowledging Lizzy or Jane in any way. Lizzy's brows lifted, and she shared a startled glance with Jane, but neither said a word. Georgiana's concentration was on the precision pouring of the hot tea into the cups, either heedless of the housekeeper's lacking manners or accepting it as normal. Shrugging it aside as unimportant, Lizzy replied as to tea-drinking preferences and helped herself to the snacks.

"May I ask if Mr. Darcy is at home?"

"Not presently, Miss Elizabeth," Georgiana answered without glancing up from her task. "He left early for an appointment with his tailor. I suspect by now he is either fencing at Angelo's or the track riding his horse. He mentioned needing exercise, and those are his preferred choices to expend energy. I am not sure when he will return. Oh!" Concern etched upon her face, Georgiana jerked her eyes to Lizzy. "How inconsiderate of me! Naturally, you wished to see my brother! I do apologize for not being clearer in my invitation and causing your disappointment."

"Miss Darcy, it is I who should apologize. Your invitation was perfectly clear, and we accepted for the sole purpose and pleasure of your company. I asked of Mr. Darcy merely out of curiosity. In truth, it is a boon that he is elsewhere. Female conversation is far more interesting, to my way of thinking, and having a man about would only disrupt. Is that not so, Jane?"

"Absolutely. At the first mention of gowns or hair accessories he would run screaming from the room."

"I will take your word for it since my experiences are minimal, although William made the same claim this morning. It is true that his eyes glaze over whenever I mention garments or the like. He immediately sends me to Mrs. Annesley or Lady Matlock."

"As I suspected." Lizzy nodded sagely before biting into a sandwich wedge.

"To be fair," Jane added while Lizzy chewed, "my mind wanders the second the topic of cigars or firearms is broached."

"Oh! How true that is! You have sisters, but I only have my brother. Visitors to Pemberley are predominantly male, such as my Cousin Richard, Mr. Bingley, and other gentlemen friends of William's. Not that I am often present at their private gatherings, mind you. Nevertheless, a lone female adolescent is easily forgotten when sitting silently in a corner. Despite my disinterest, I probably know more about popular sporting events, the top horses on the racing circuit, and strategies for winning at billiards than most females do."

"Think what an advantage this will be, Miss Darcy, when the time comes for you to find a suitor."

Rosiness once again touched Georgiana's cheeks, but she laughed at Jane's comment. "An advantage or disadvantage, depending on the man, I suppose. If I unearth one who likes what I do, such as music, dancing, and ladies fashion, we would be an anomaly to behold!"

"Something to toast too, I say." Lizzy held the delicate china cup in the air. "To Miss Darcy someday finding her male anomaly!" Ringing clinks and sips followed, along with laughter. "See, we are having tremendous fun and have barely started!"

Jane leaned forward to brush a finger over the teapot. "This is a beautiful tea service, Miss Darcy, and these tarts are exquisite."

"Credit for the food I cannot claim, nor the tea set since it has lived in this house longer than I have. But I am gladdened to hear you are satisfied. I confess to being quite nervous." She peeked at her guests through her lashes, murmuring, "This is the first tea party I have hosted myself."

The sisters shared a smile, Jane assuring, "I am stunned to hear this, Miss Darcy. You are an excellent hostess. My guess was years of practice."

"You are most kind to say so, Miss Bennet. I assure you that is not the case, although I have attended numerous social gatherings, mostly small ones," Georgiana disclosed in a firmer voice. "I have assisted my aunt frequently, that is Lady Matlock. She has taught me the proper etiquette, of course, yet the greater benefit is in observation. She is elegant, confident of hand, and immensely skilled in the art of casual conversation. Wait until you meet her, Miss Elizabeth, then you will know of what I speak."

"You are fortunate to have a gifted, and willing, relative living near you, Miss Darcy. Her influence shows."

"Indeed, Jane is correct." Lizzy patted her sister's hand. Then she cocked her head and smiled archly at Georgiana. "On the other hand, Miss Darcy, think how improved the fortune of your education if you lived closer to Lady Catherine de Bourgh. She is prodigiously knowledgeable on every subject, you know, and by her admission greatly accomplished. Oh! To be frequently exposed to a grand house decorated with imposing sophistication and refined style. Rosings Park, where quality is visible even in the windows and glazings. Just imagine how improved your manners as hostess and stimulating our conversation if she were the aunt fate settled nearer to you."

"Lizzy," Jane softly admonished.

Georgiana, however, had pressed the back of her hand against her mouth and her shoulders were shaking with silent laughter. Lizzy winked over the rim of her teacup.

"Indeed, it is quite all right, Miss Bennet," Georgiana finally squeaked out. "Surely William would scold me for unkind thoughts, but I confess my sentiments refuse to behave properly where Lady Catherine is concerned. She has terrified me since I was a child!"

"Mr. Darcy would scold because that is what responsible, grown brothers are required to do. I can almost guarantee his heart would not be fully engaged in the reprimand, Miss Darcy. As for me, well surely you have gleaned by now that I tend toward impertinence as a general attitude? I did warn Mr. Darcy of the risks involved in allowing me to corrupt your gentle nature." She sighed and set her face into an overblown mournful expression. "Alas, he did not heed my warning."

"I daresay he would not, Miss Elizabeth! There is not a risk of corruption but rather hope for improvement. Your impertinence, as you name it, my brother defines as boldness and confidence, both of which I need more of."

"I do confess that our time together, Miss Darcy, is insufficient to render a verdict as to the levels of confidence and boldness you own. My preliminary judgment, however, is that you are better disposed to each than you warrant. As for Lady Catherine, I suspect impertinence is a foolhardy maneuver while being terrified is an indication of good sense."

"Perhaps." Georgiana bent to pour fresh tea into their cups, eyes on the task as she talked. "My father was neither foolhardy nor terrified, yet he hated Rosings. He rarely visited, the last time when I was very young. My last memory of the manor is a vague one of dim corridors and frightening tapestries. One of the few times I recall

Father angry was when Aunt criticized me about something. I no longer remember what, but he was furious. After that, on those occasions she visited Pemberley, he never forced me to interact beyond the basics of hospitality. William has never asked me to accompany him to Rosings."

"So he frequently travels to Kent?"

"At least twice yearly since our Uncle Lewis passed on. My brother is acutely loyal to family and friends, Miss Elizabeth. I am sure you have learned this yourself."

Lizzy nodded and took the cup from Georgiana's hand.

"In the case of Rosings, my brother's loyalty was first to Sir Lewis de Bourgh. He was a nice man. Very gentle and warm. And of course, my brother is immensely fond of Cousin Anne. Not as he is fond of you, Miss Elizabeth. Never was it like that!"

Lizzy laughed and waved away Georgiana's wide-eyed concern. "No need to worry, dear girl. Mr. Darcy has unraveled the misunderstandings on that relationship with extreme clarity. I envy you both, if you must know. Jane and I have few cousins our age, and none live close to us."

"Neither do I. Cousin Richard is the only one, really, but he is older still than my brother. I have no female friends my age."

Georgiana handed the cup to Jane, speaking without sadness or rancor in stating the facts as they were. Her nonchalance struck Lizzy harder than if she had whined pitiably about the loneliness of her childhood. Guiltily Lizzy thought of all the times she had wished there were fewer flighty females crammed into Longbourn annoying each other. How many hours had she spent away from the manor for no reason other than to gain minutes of peace? Only in the past weeks as she prepared to leave Longbourn, and especially now, with Georgiana's youth in mind, did Lizzy begin to recognize how blessed she was to have four sisters.

"Soon that will change, Miss Darcy," Jane stated.

Georgiana looked at Jane with creases of puzzlement marring

her brow.

Jane smiled and patted Lizzy's hand, speaking tenderly, "In a matter of weeks you will have a sister."

"Absolutely!" Lizzy fervently concurred. "And one who comes with an army of sisters in tow! Jane you already know is wonderful"—Jane blushed and demurred—"and I am certain you will like Kitty and Mary too."

In truth, she was certain of no such thing. Best to be positive at this juncture, however. Not that it appeared to work.

Georgiana's expression was equal parts hopeful and alarmed by the prospect. Probably not wanting to dig further into the subject, she rapidly changed the subject. "How was your tour of Mr. Bingley's townhouse at Berkeley Square, Miss Bennet?"

"Delightful, thank you. It is an excellent house with generous proportions to the rooms, tall windows, a pleasant garden, and a parlor on the uppermost floor with a superb view of the square. The location is fortuitous as well."

"It is within blocks from Darcy House, which will surely be advantageous. How did you find the decor?" Georgiana's seemingly innocent query and serene gaze at Jane were almost convincing—if not for the lips twitching as they fought a smile.

Lizzy hid her smirk by sipping slowly on the hot tea.

"The decor is…unique," Jane stammered. "There are *plenty* of furnishings, no doubt of that. Some are not quite my taste."

Lizzy burst out laughing. "Some? What my sister is too polite to say, Miss Darcy, is that aside from Mr. Bingley's specific rooms, it was garish and cluttered. Miss Bingley has been mistress of the house for some time now, has she not?" Georgiana affirmed with a single nod. "Oh, my dear Jane! I foresee endless fun and challenges ahead! Do not fret over my sister managing, Miss Darcy. We are quite familiar with Miss Bingley's peculiar personality."

Lizzy went on to amusedly describe the Bingley townhouse decor as Jane had revealed to her in shocked dismay. Jane added the random comment, always with a tone of kindness even when reporting something ghastly, and soon all three of the women were laughing.

"I must beseech you to change the subject or I shall surely say something unkind, earning more scolding from my brother! Tell me about the wedding plans. That should be a safe topic, yes?"

"You would think so, yes." Lizzy wiped at the tears pooling in her eyes. "Then again, you have yet to meet our mother."

"Now, Lizzy," Jane began, but Lizzy forestalled her by clasping her hand.

"I am teasing. Mama has been surprisingly reserved, once she finally accepted that neither Mr. Bingley nor Mr. Darcy intended to apply for a special license or insist on being married in Winchester Cathedral."

"There was no need for the expense of a special license, of course," Jane added, ignoring the Winchester Cathedral nonsense. "Plenty of time to announce the banns. In fact, the first call was this past Sunday in Meryton, as I presume it was at Saint George's for Mr. Bingley."

"I cannot say on that, but the first banns were called by Reverend Bertram two Sundays past." Georgiana pressed her palms against her chest, smiling radiantly at Lizzy. "Oh! I cannot begin to express my joy at hearing them read. 'I publish the banns of marriage between Mr. Fitzwilliam Darcy of Lambton Parish, and Miss Elizabeth Bennet of Meryton Parish. If any of you know cause or just impediment why these two persons should not be joined together in Holy matrimony, ye are to declare it. This is the first time of asking.' And of course, no one had a word of objection, only delight. I was overwhelmed with congratulations and thankful Cousin Richard was at my side to assist."

"Well," Lizzy murmured, feeling fairly overwhelmed herself, even hearing of it second hand. "I am pleased to learn that the local citizens enthusiastically greeted the news of Mr. Darcy's betrothal."

"Indeed so! Stability and continuity of the Darcy family are essential for so many who depend on us. Granted, they are probably not as concerned about my brother's personal happiness as they are the technicalities." Georgiana reddened, belatedly remembering certain aspects of the "technicalities" involved with family continuity, then rushed on. "You will adore living at Pemberley, Miss Elizabeth, I know you will. Now you must describe your wedding gowns. Is the train four feet and of the spun silk you wanted?"

Lizzy snorted a laugh, nearly spewing a gulp of tea. "Mr. Darcy told you about that? Oh my!"

"He was utterly amused, of course. As he is with everything you say."

Lizzy blushed and, once she caught her breath, went on to describe her gown. Jane did as well, Georgiana as interested in her details as she was with Lizzy's. This surprised Jane, and when she obliquely remarked as such, Georgiana was swift to reassure.

"Indeed, I am very interested, Miss Bennet. Mr. Bingley has been our friend for over five years now. More a friend to my brother, naturally, but I defy anyone not to like him immediately."

Georgiana proceeded to recount her first meeting of Mr. Bingley. The high-spirited, gawky nineteen-year-old university student from a family one generation past actively engaging in trade had astonishingly gained favor from the stern, humorless Mr. Darcy, already Master of Pemberley at twenty-three. Not too long after their fledgling friendship began, Darcy had invited Mr. Bingley to dinner at Darcy House, and it was then that Georgiana met him. She vividly described the initial introduction and her impressions with a hitherto unknown wittiness and dramatic skill that had Jane and Lizzy breathless with laughter.

Into this near hysteria, Mr. Darcy returned from his visitation with Colonel Fitzwilliam. Attempts were made to halt the laughter long enough to listen attentively to his formal welcome, but mirth had taken root. He finally bowed and, with a shake of his head and resonant chuckle, left them to their madness.

For over an hour more they chatted as only females who are wholly at ease with each other can. Topics ranged widely, serious at times but mostly gay and trivial. Lizzy was impressed by the intelligence Miss Darcy hid behind her shy exterior, and with each passing minute, her delight in acquiring such a sweet young lady as her new sister grew stronger.

Amid the casual conversation, she and Jane learned innumerable tidbits about the men soon to become their husbands. Innocent comments about Georgiana's brother revealed a wealth of information Lizzy tucked away.

Georgiana's suggestion to leave the stuffy parlor for a stroll about the rear yard was latched onto enthusiastically. Crossing the broad foyer toward the wide corridor leading to the terrace doors, the trio encountered the butler Mr. Travers carrying a tray upon which sat a silver pot and lone cup.

"Ladies," he greeted, managing to perform a stately incline of his head while holding the tray steady. "A walk in the garden appears to be on the agenda?"

"It is a fine day for it," Georgiana acknowledged.

"Indeed, it is, Miss Darcy. Carry on, and call if you wish for a cool beverage after ingesting pots of hot tea." After another polite nod toward each of them, he resumed his careful trek toward the side of the house where the library was located.

"My brother has tea in the afternoon if he is at home. He is such a creature of habit."

Lizzy glanced away from the retreating butler, the placid smile on her lips slipping upon encountering the surprisingly calculating expression Miss Darcy wore.

"I think you should deliver his tea, Miss Elizabeth."

"Oh no! I could not impose upon him uninvited." Even as she spluttered the negation, her eyes swung back to the butler.

"He will welcome the interruption from you, trust me."

Jane's subtle shrug decided the matter. Dwelling on the idea no further, Lizzy scurried after the butler and ignored the giggles floating behind her.

"Mr. Travers?"

"Yes, Miss Bennet?"

Suddenly feeling utterly ridiculous, even with his calm face and the faint smile, she pointed to the tray and stuttered, "Is this...I understand this is for Mr. Darcy? In his office?"

"Indeed, Miss Bennet. He always has tea this time of the day. And I am always the one to deliver it. An expectation he has undoubtedly grown weary of. Might I impose upon you to tend to the task for me? Just this once, of course."

His expression had not changed one iota. Releasing held breath, Lizzy bobbed a curtsy. "It would be my pleasure to relieve you of this duty, Mr. Travers. Just this once."

"One knock," he instructed, transferring the tray carefully into her hands, "then wait for his permission to enter. Mr. Darcy prefers to serve himself, although in this case, he may make an exception to that rule."

She swore he winked as he turned away. *What a nice man. I believe we shall get on fine. As for Mrs. Smyth, I am not so sure.*

Leaving musings of future servant relationships aside, she concentrated on the heavy tray and approached the door. Pausing to take a deep breath, she knocked one hard rap.

"Enter," came his voice, muffled through the solid wood.

The stout door swung open easily on well-oiled hinges, Lizzy crossing the threshold with words of welcome tingling her lips.

"Sit it on my desk, Mr. Travers. I will manage myself. That will be all."

Mr. Darcy sat beside his desk, the tall back of the leather-and-wood chair ending exactly along the line of his shoulders so that all she could easily see was the back of his head. One hand waved over his shoulder, vaguely in the direction of the desk, and his tone was distracted more than harsh, but the dismissal was obvious.

Whatever sunny greeting she might have extended was forgotten, and for several seconds Lizzy stood frozen in the doorway. The weight of the tray restored enough clarity for her to gingerly enter the room, each step closer to the sleek surface of his desk bizarrely mixing her emotions.

Darcy's head was bent slightly, and Lizzy suspected he was listening to the murmuring voices of Jane and Georgiana drifting through the open window he faced. Fleetingly wondering if he listened for her voice, she soon realized all his focus was on a thick book propped in his lap. It was a ledger of some kind, and he traced one finger down a line of sums written in penmanship Lizzy knew not to be his. He had removed his jacket—a glance noted it on a coat rack in the corner—loosened his cravat, and sat with booted feet propped onto a large ottoman. It was the most relaxed pose she had ever seen him in, despite the fact he was attending to business.

Abruptly, all traces of enthusiasm for her surprise interruption vanished. The sense of imposition compounded. For a panicked moment, she almost dashed from the room, tea tray still in her clutches. Mastering the impulse, she placed the tray quietly on the corner of his desk—praying he did not choose that instant to turn around—and took one step backward before freezing once again.

Mr. Darcy had blindly reached with his free hand to nudge a sovereign-sized wooden ball on his desk. The ball rolled across the flat surface some four inches, smacked into the base of the unlit lamp, ricocheted, and rolled back into his waiting hand. Never glancing away from the ledger in his lap, he repeated the maneuver several times in rapid succession.

It was astounding! Lizzy stood mesmerized for six or seven precision rolls before the realization that she was engaged in active voyeurism woke her out of the daydream.

A decision was required. Her options were to either slink out the cracked open door or speak up. The urge to do the former remained, yet felt a cowardly move now that she had mastered her initial panic. Elizabeth Bennet was rarely intimidated. After all, she had boldly accosted Mr. Travers with the intent to enter her fiancé's sanctuary unbidden. If she backed away now, how would she explain it to Miss Darcy and Jane? Or Mr. Travers? The butler was unlikely to inquire directly, but if he saw her scurry away, then he would assume the future Mrs. Darcy was a milksop. That was unacceptable!

The speaking-up option would, of course, prove that she had been spying on him. Being a private, reserved man, Lizzy was honestly unsure how he would react to such an intrusion, even from her. At the end of the mere seconds it took for these thoughts to race through her mind, she observed him in unguarded repose, and it was the returned yearning to be alone with him that impelled her to action.

Dwelling on the possible outcomes no longer, she slipped behind him, squeezed both shoulders, and whispered close to his left ear, "Any guess who this is?"

Perhaps she should have given the matter a tad more thought, she later confessed.

Mr. Darcy jerked violently, the book tumbling to the carpeted floor with a dull thunk and the wooden ball shooting off the desk. She was fairly sure he swore too, but the precise curse was lost amid her instant laughter and gasping attempts to apologize.

Adding to the ridiculousness, he precipitously swiveled around. Lizzy emitted a squeal along with the gasping giggles, caught utterly off guard by a chair that moved. Still in a bent posture, her jolt of surprise pitched her forward until their noses bumped together, falling into his lap prevented when she locked her elbows and splayed her hands on his chest.

A dozen exclamations, curious questions, and justifications for her behavior skipped across her tongue. None of them were uttered or involved what she impulsively did instead.

She kissed him. Hard.

As her eyes slid shut, she saw his flare wide open. Caught up in the throes of an unexplainable impulse, Lizzy grabbed ahold of the slim lapels on his waistcoat and tugged with astonishing vigor. As insistent and strong as she was, Lizzy could not have propelled a man Darcy's size out of his chair alone, however.

His compliance to her entreaty to rise was voluntary, but he lurched upward unsteadily. Off balance, and locked at the lips, he clasped onto her waist with both hands in, perhaps, a vain attempt to gain control.

Lizzy's back contacted the firm surface—the edge of a picture frame digging into her left shoulder blade—and her front collided with his solid torso when he stumbled and squashed her against the wall. Air whooshed from both their lungs, but their mouths miraculously stayed connected in a kiss that was growing remarkably tender considering the circumstances.

Darcy pressed his palms into the wall on either side of Lizzy's waist, restoring stability, and then eased his weight off her body. She rather missed the feel of his muscled chest but did appreciate the ability to breathe freely, especially when he took advantage of the space to part her lips with his tongue. Sighing, she slipped her arms over his shoulders and welcomed him in.

Within seconds Lizzy sensed an incredible difference in this kiss compared to the others they had shared.

Darcy's mouth was relaxed, his lips nuzzling hers with soft, sweet pressure. The tip of his tongue teased, gentle touches applied playfully. There was a purpose, control, and no hesitation. He was clearly enjoying himself and willing to do so without fear of overstepping a line or distressing her.

Liberation was the word that popped into her head, and seconds later she knew it an accurate term when he withdrew a scant hairbreadth and spoke in a steady whisper.

"I believe you frightened a year of life out of me."

Lizzy smiled but did not open her eyes or move. "I do apologize."

"There is no need to apologize. This makes up for it. Trust me."

"Does it make up for disturbing your work and bending the pages of your ledger?"

"Bent pages can be unbent," he murmured between featherlight kisses across her jaw. "The work will wait. It was not a vital task anyway," he assured from the slope of her neck.

"My distraction has kept you from your tea. It is now probably cooled."

"Cooled tea is easier to drink. Besides, after the quantity of coffee I consumed today, and more importantly the current alternative, I am not interested in tea."

Lizzy could think of nothing more to say—she could barely think period. Darcy's kisses had reached her right shoulder and were beginning a lazy descent along the lacy edge of her décolletage. Her dress was modestly designed but the bodice dipped low enough for each stroke of his lips to spread fire through her bosom. Every shallow pant lifted the swell of flesh closer to his mouth, her back reflexively arching as if to force the desired contact. And then there was the startling hardening of her nipples and the exquisite pleasure when he inadvertently rubbed against them. She truly wondered if it was possible to faint from nothing more than scattered kisses.

Perhaps he wondered the same because he completed his circuit, engaged her mouth in another delicate exchange, again clasped onto her waist with both hands, and in a smooth maneuver unlike the tottering steps that got them to the wall, drew her against his body and walked backward toward a nearby sofa.

The graceful, calculated relocation to the comfortable, solidly supportive sofa probably would have ended with them sitting on the cushions with finesse—if either of them had done something similar before. Instead, the edge connected with Darcy's legs sooner than his desire-hazed brain expected, and Lizzy missed his tactile cue to rotate her body to sit down beside him. The result was Darcy dropping onto the sofa rather abruptly, with Lizzy falling into an odd straddle over his lap, skirts bunched and legs bent awkwardly. The absurd humor of the situation overcame any embarrassment, both laughing helplessly.

"Stand up, Elizabeth, and let us try this again," Darcy directed, once he'd regained a modicum of control. "Now, sit on the sofa next to me, close," he hastily insisted, patting the space next to his right thigh. Lizzy complied. "There, is that not better? Comfortable, and without the shattered dignity of being sprawled across my lap, as pleasant as it was."

"Better…yes," she concurred between giggles further instigated by his comment and his awkward assistance in smoothing her skirt over her legs. "You really are terrible at this, you know."

"If by 'this' you mean being scared out of my wits by skulking women who then manhandle me into a kissing dance across the room, I admit you are correct. I guess I should have practiced previously."

Lizzy grunted and gave a hard tug on the dangling end of his cravat. "I was referring to your lack of skill in rearranging fabric. It is muslin, for heaven's sake! Imagine the consequences if I were wearing silk."

"Either would be attached to your body, my dear, and likely to have lacy layers or sashes or some other adornment I am unsure of the proper placement for."

Turning to gaze upon him full in the face for the first time since entering the room some fifteen minutes prior, Lizzy instantly understood what he meant. She absorbed the picture of her handsome betrothed in his shirtsleeves with neckcloth untied just enough to expose the hollow at his throat and several dark hairs. Merely imagining her hands coming into close contact with his body to retie his cravat or slip on his jacket made joyful flutters dance in her belly. Noting how his hair was delightfully disarrayed, and that his facial expression was one of amusement and simmering desire increased the tingling sensations.

Then he dropped his gaze to linger upon her recently kiss-smothered chest.

"On second thought," she blurted, "you being clumsy and inept has a certain charm I rather like."

"I pray you are not describing the kiss itself?" His resonant purr and smoky-blue eyes made her shiver. He pressed one hand to her cheek, fingertips embedding into the curls by her ear, and drew her close. "I cannot claim great practice in that activity either, but have been under the impression we were doing well. Was I mistaken?"

"No, you are not mistaken at all. Although I do anticipate we will improve with practice."

"I, for one, will greatly enjoy testing that theory." And before she could manage a nod of agreement, he was proving how true this was. He kept the kiss short—much to Lizzy's chagrin—pulling away to settle casually into the sofa corner. Grasping onto her hand, he smiled and asked, "Did you bribe my butler, or was he a willing participant in this deception?"

"The latter. I could be mistaken, but I sense a cheekiness hidden under the proper exterior."

"You are not mistaken. He has served as my butler for over a decade, and as underbutler prior to his advancement for longer than I can remember. He is an excellent manager and a good man. His air of humor is familiar and comfortable, having known him for so long. He is professional, yet, unlike Mr. Taylor at Pemberley, Mr. Travers has a lighter side that the staff responds well to. They appreciate his humor—except for Mrs. Smyth," he confided with a mischievous chuckle. "It drives her insane. Not that she has ever said a word to me against him, but I detect the currents."

"You surprise me, Mr. Darcy."

"In what way?"

"I would not have suspected you to be tolerant of anything less than strict discipline amongst your staff. I mean no offense yet must confess my image was of you as more controlling. Now I see clearer what Mrs. Reynolds meant in her exalting praise of you as a master."

"She is a kind woman," he replied in an embarrassed mumble. "No, I am not offended, my dear. I suppose if not for my grandfather I probably would be more controlling. His leadership style and belief were that, in general, servants and tenants want a master who sets the rules, listens to their concerns, assists when necessary, but otherwise leaves them alone to do their jobs. What do I know about being a butler? Or cook? Or farmer for that matter? Even in those areas I do have more knowledge, specifically our horses, I respect the experience of the grooms and breeders who live and breathe thoroughbreds. Hire capable people, my grandfather said, then you can sit back and relax. Not that he ever relaxed."

"Nor do you, I suspect."

He shrugged. "Too much relaxation makes one fat and dulls the wits. My expectations for my sex are more stringent than those for yours, if you can believe it." Lizzy laughed as she nodded. "On the subject of accomplished women, did my sister perform brilliantly as hostess today?"

"Beyond brilliant." Lizzy described their afternoon, up to and including Georgiana's humorous remembrance of meeting Mr. Bingley for the first time. "She is a dear girl, William. Truly. I am grateful for today's opportunity to know her better."

"Georgie was nervous. We share the common flaw of not easily conversing with unfamiliar people. As you have wisely noted numerous times, practice is the key to improvement." His salacious grin let her know he was not referring only to conversation. "This afternoon provided an opportunity for my sister, as well as for me."

"I detected scant nervousness and conversation was never a problem." Lizzy wisely left the kissing-practice reference alone. "My conclusion is that neither of you is as flawed as you think."

"I will concede this is partially true. Except for when around beautiful women I want to impress."

"Women?" She stressed the plural and raised one eyebrow.

"Yes, sadly. Although with you I was especially tongue-tied and horrid when I did speak."

"Well, you are managing quite capably now, Mr. Darcy, and since you no longer need to impress other women, future interactions promise smoother sailing."

If he discerned the sharp edge to her tone, he did not comment on it. Instead, he slapped one hand onto his thigh, declaring as he rose from the sofa, "Speaking of impressing people and ease in conversation, I have an invitation to share. My uncle and aunt, Lord and Lady Matlock, are lately arrived in London and have expressed a desire to meet the woman who has captured my heart. They have invited us, and Mr. Bennet, of course, to dine with them tomorrow. They have a townhouse on Saint James's Square..."

He rambled on, Lizzy watching him sift through several papers on his desk before selecting a folded foolscap with a broken wax seal. Presumably it was the invitation, but Lizzy's attention wandered to the view of his backside, as it was the first time she'd seen it uncovered by his jacket.

She had never exhibited interest in a gentleman's posterior and, like many revelations during the past weeks, was amazed how enticing the angle. Even as she lost herself in the emotions stirred by her fiancé's masculine figure, an academic portion of her brain analyzed whether it was his form causing her heart to pound or merely maturity and awakening desires in a general sense.

Then he bent over to grab the ledger off the floor, the fabric tightening and outlining his firm buttocks and muscled back in a highly pleasant manner, and the answer was immediately clear. Realizing how ridiculous the question was in the first place, Lizzy nearly laughed aloud. She did not have to clinically line up a dozen jacketless men bending at the waist to know that none of them would affect her as William did.

The direction of her gaze did not shift speedily enough when he pivoted about, so her expression undoubtedly revealed at least a portion of her musings. Darcy's commentary—which Lizzy had not heard a word of—faltered slightly and a faint rosiness spread across his cheeks. He said nothing about her intimate ogling, thankfully, handing the invitation to her while resuming his report.

"Colonel Fitzwilliam plans to join the party. Thus, the group will consist of only eight. Hardly an intimidating number for one with your dexterity in social situations."

"Eight?" Lizzy blurted, perceiving when he lifted one brow that, by asking, she revealed her previous inattention. Warmth flooded her cheeks, the heat rising at his amused reply.

"Did you arrive at a different calculation? I believe I correctly applied the mathematics, but perhaps I was mistaken. Let's see, the list includes you, me, Mr. Bennet, and Colonel Fitzwilliam. That is four. My cousin Annabella and her husband have a prior engagement, so we cannot count them. Lord and Lady Matlock make six, and with my cousin Jonathan and his wife the number rises to eight. Yes?"

"I think I like the taciturn, humorless Mr. Darcy better."

Laughing, Darcy crossed to the corner coat rack. "He is still here, trust me, and you shall see him often enough if that is any consolation." Jacket donned, he set to retying his cravat, doing so deftly while stepping to his desk. "Additionally, I received a missive from Mrs. Reynolds today. Included in her report were specificities I am to obtain directly from you to ensure meeting your needs."

Rifling once again through the stack of papers until he found the one he wanted, Darcy then turned back toward her. "I do pray, Miss Elizabeth, we can supply the information for Mrs. Reynolds without fretful expressions of inconveniencing the Pemberley staff?"

Noting his smile and glittering eyes, Lizzy lifted her chin and crossed her arms. "That depends, Mr. Darcy. Is this a ploy to uncover personal details you are too polite to ask or I refuse to divulge?"

"Not this time. My housekeeper acted on her own, I promise, and you can write directly to her with your responses—those you wish to divulge, that is."

He handed the folded paper to her, maintaining his hold and bending closer. "Besides, if I really want to know your foot measurements," he whispered, the reference to a tease from Kitty regarding Lizzy's not-so-tiny feet that had embarrassed her profoundly, "I would simply ask your mother." Briefly glancing down at the slippered toes she rapidly tucked behind the hem of her dress, he added, "I am sure Mrs. Bennet has a wealth of fascinating minutiae about her spirited child and would not hesitate to enlighten me. Luckily for you, my love, I prefer the adventure of self-discovery." And with that, he winked.

She was so surprised at the atypical gesture that she missed responding to the soft kiss he delivered to the tip of her nose and nearly dropped Mrs. Reynolds's letter when he let go of it.

"My," she stammered, "you are quite the imp today."

"Being diverted pleasantly from dull paperwork and columns of mathematics is a surefire way to improve my temper."

"Here I thought you lived for paperwork and excelled at mathematics. Shocking."

"I am brilliant at mathematics," he declared pompously, "but that does not mean I enjoy them. Frankly, they give me a headache. At any rate, passing the time with you is far superior to anything else. That unquestionably clarified,"—he extended his hand—"I must reluctantly return you to my sister. Suffering her verbal irritation for stealing away her guest will also give me a headache."

Lizzy took his hand, standing as she asked, "You will walk with us for a while? Or must you return to your ledger?"

"A stroll about the garden sounds utterly delightful, and it gives me an opportunity to remain in your company. I am far too selfish to give Georgiana all the joy, especially since I shan't see you again until late tomorrow."

SHARON LATHAN

He linked her arm with his and steered them toward the library door. "Thank you again, Elizabeth, for understanding why I cannot dine with you tonight."

"Well, it is unfathomable that you have friends beyond me and those in Hertfordshire. Who would have thought?"

Darcy smiled at her tease. "Once we are married you will socialize with more of my friends and acquaintances than you will probably want to. Even then, anguishing through an evening with a couple dozen men smoking smelly cigars and talking of nothing but horses will never intrude upon your pleasanter agenda."

"Thank the Maker! I would either fall asleep from boredom or faint from the fumes. No, you have your fun at the Jockey Club, William. Besides, in light of my big reveal to Lord and Lady Matlock, a night of rest and quiet may prove beneficial. I am joking!" she laughed when he lifted his brows. "A lady needs her beauty sleep, to be sure. Nevertheless, whether I sleep deeply or fitfully, I promise to be presentable by tomorrow evening. If it takes me all day to erase the horrid sight of droopy eyes, tangled hair, and pillow creases on my face, it shall be done."

Darcy had paused by the door and was staring at her with an odd expression as he slowly shook his head. "Horrid? I must disagree. The vision of you upon waking in the morning is one I constantly dream of and long to see with my own eyes, pillow creases included. I can think of nothing more beautiful."

So enraptured was she by his face that the intimacy of his declaration did not even raise a blush to her cheeks. Later, she would marvel at how rapidly his countenance could shift into smoky desire, and how the obscurest reference to an insignificant thing could arouse his ardency. Not for several weeks into their marriage would she fully comprehend the depth of his hunger for her, and that she would fully reciprocate.

For the present, she ceased to think, giving in to the thrill of his burning gaze sweeping across her face and lush lips slowly parting as he bent his head toward her. With one hand, he warmly caressed the right side of her face, tenderly drawing her closer, while his right hand slid over her hip until it rested on the small of her back.

Then, as the gap narrowed till their lips were inches apart, both of his hands tightened and he pulled her forcefully against his body. She barely managed a swift inhale before the blissful invasion of lips and tongue consumed her.

God, what is happening to me?

The thought screamed through her mind, yet not as a plea for help but rather as an exalting declaration. Indeed, there was no fear or confusion in her reaction to William's touch. Quite the opposite. She felt vibrantly alive—as if every moment of her life, prior to the day her betrothed kissed her for the first time had been drab and blurry. Now her vision was crisp, the colors vivid. In truth, all of her senses enhanced.

More remarkable than sensations being in sharper focus than ever before was the recognition of a purpose to her existence. A vital importance infused her being, an explicit reason to rise in the morning and anticipate the weeks, months, and years ahead with a previously unimaginable joy.

Joy.

Such a small word to encapsulate such a profound message. And, as astounding as it seemed, the embodiment of her joy was the man in her arms. A man she had once believed was the last man in the world she would ever marry. Those harshly spoken words were now incomprehensible to her, and if not for delirious distraction of his ongoing kiss and the resulting rapture infusing her head to toes, she would have laughed aloud.

Time completely lost all meaning. Fused together from lips down, she never wanted this embrace to end. Later that evening, when alone in her bedchamber reliving the experience, Lizzy admitted that if William had returned to the sofa and taken their wild passion to the ultimate conclusion, she would not have fought him. In fact, every fiber of her soul longed for him to make love to her right then, consequences and rules be damned. Even if not rationally understood in the heat of the moment, her desire was so intense that she moaned in despair when he loosened his grip and withdrew from her lips.

Resting his forehead on hers, he said nothing and kept his eyes closed for a very long time. Finally, although still breathing in harsh gasps, he spoke. "I hope you do not want an apology Elizabeth because I cannot in honesty give one. I…" He paused to gulp, only then opening his eyes. "I want you…immensely. As we established previously, if I am to retain my sanity between now and our wedding night, these interludes are essential."

The seriousness of his claim was without argument, yet there was a trace of humor to his tone that brought a soft smile to her lips. "I shall risk being branded as a wanton woman and assure you, my love, that I echo your sentiments with equal fervor."

It was an admission delivered honestly, albeit in a somewhat halting, embarrassed mumble. Warmth rose to her face, and she struggled not to look away from his eyes. It didn't help that a significant portion of her mind was stuck on the vivid picture of their bodies entwined on the nearby sofa.

As if reading her mind, Darcy flicked his eyes to the cushioned surface steps away, the action so swift she almost missed it. Then, he slipped the hand still resting on her back down lower until it was splayed over her rear, pressing her firmly against his pelvis. For a second—an exquisite, rousing second—Lizzy held her breath in anticipation.

"Those words I shall remember and cherish forever," he pledged. Releasing his adamant grip on her body, he grinned in a way that could only be described as smugly satisfied. "And now I must delay no longer in returning you to the others, ere they send in the hounds."

4

ILLUMINATIVE CONVERSATION

*A*s it happened, Lizzy's evening was not as relaxing and restful as anticipated.

Mr. Darcy passed a delightful evening in horse-centric conversation with his fellows at the Jockey Club. He missed Elizabeth, of course, but if being truthful, not too much until back at Darcy House. And even then, between a rich dinner and far too much fine wine, he slipped rather quickly over any sensations of melancholy and right into dreams of his beautiful fiancé.

Mr. Gardiner and Mr. Bennet also spent a marvelous evening away from the house. The two gentlemen accepted a last-minute invitation to join Mr. Bingley at a boxing match, followed by who knew what manner of entertainment, and did not return until nearly midnight.

As a result, Lizzy dined alone with Jane and Aunt Gardiner. For a treat, their nieces and nephews joined them for dinner and then for a rowdy interval of family fun in the parlor. Eventually, the nanny came to collect them for bed, and after the obligatory moans and protests, the ladies were left in peaceable solitude.

Curled in chairs close to the fire, they each pulled out their needlepoint projects. For a time, Lizzy concentrated on the bookmark she was creating, but because it was a planned present for William, her mind continually drifted to him and their passionate exchange in his office. She wasn't aware that she was staring into space or that she had sighed for the fifth time in a half hour.

"What has you pensive and distracted this evening, my dear?"

Mrs. Gardiner's question pierced the silence, jolting Lizzy visibly despite it being asked in her aunt's normal subdued voice.

"Nothing at all," she hastily replied only to stutter into a convicted silence when her aunt quirked one brow in an obvious *I know you are lying* message.

Speaking from where she sat placidly sewing by the fire, needle flashing without pause, Jane spoke up. "She has been in a mood since we departed Darcy House and refuses to confess the truth or the cause. I believe it has something to do with the private audience Lizzy had with Mr. Darcy while at his townhouse today. A *lengthy audience*, I must add——"

"Must you *really*?" Lizzy interrupted. She wasn't sure whether to laugh, snap irritably, or roll her eyes at the merciless teasing at her expense.

"I am glad to hear of it, Lizzy. Long private audiences during one's betrothal period are necessary for a happy, fulfilled marriage. A new bride should not be wholly surprised on her wedding night. A bit of prior knowledge and practice is most beneficial for early and lasting pleasure with your husband in the bedchamber. Make sure you arrange a few private interludes with Mr. Bingley, Jane dear."

Mrs. Gardiner had resumed her needlepoint after speaking matter-of-factly and was, at least outwardly, oblivious to the dropped jaws and flushed cheeks of her nieces. Then she peered at them over the top of her glasses, a sly smile spreading.

"Now, I wonder, which has you two the most shocked? That I would approve of such scandalous behavior before marriage? That an old woman like me still engages in and enjoys bedroom antics? Or that I would openly broach the topic in the first place?"

Not too surprisingly, Lizzy had regained her composure sooner than Jane, who was still scarlet and staring into her lap. "You are far from old, Aunt," Lizzy observed, "and with four young children, it isn't a revelation that you engage in…"

"Bedroom antics," Mrs. Gardiner supplied when Lizzy faltered.

"Yes…that." Lizzy swallowed, glancing away from her aunt's amused smirk toward an even redder-faced Jane. Seeing no help forthcoming from that direction, Lizzy stumbled on. "It isn't so much the encouragement to practice, as you put it, before our wedding, although that is…irregular. For me, and perhaps for Jane, it is the implications of enjoyment and…pleasure."

Lizzy didn't think her face was quite as red as her sister's, but it was a relief when, instead of teasing further, her aunt assumed a serious expression. "Is the idea of felicity in the marriage bed an unfathomable concept? Surely you have both experienced the delight in your young man's touch? His kiss? The feelings provoked inside of you? All teasing aside, a proper lady should not take matters too far until wed, but to feel nothing would be a poor sign indeed."

"No…that is, yes, I do feel…something, but do not…" Tongue-tied, Lizzy stuttered to a halt.

Still staring into her lap and voice barely audible, Jane explained, "What I believe has Lizzy and myself shocked is that, until now, our only reliable source of personal, experienced information has been our mother."

"Ah! I see. This is unfortunate. Well"—Mrs. Gardiner set her needlepoint onto the side table—"we must remedy this dearth in your education before it is too late. Where shall we begin?" She stared at each of them in turn. Jane finally lifted her eyes for a moment, but when neither offered direction, she crisply, and rather business-like, resumed speaking. "It appears 'at the beginning' is the answer, although I can't believe neither of you understands the basic mechanics of the mating process. Surely your studies included biology and anatomy, and you do live on a farm, for heaven's sake."

"We aren't that ignorant!" Lizzy blurted, feeling a tad offended.

"I did not think you were, my dears. Although, it is best not to assume anything. However, the pressing issue at hand is creating an environment of ease, now and later. You are grown women soon to be married. If the remotest reference to intimacy brings on blushes and stammering, how will you ever communicate openly with your husbands? Whatever their prior experience, they are not mind readers. A healthy, mutually satisfying relationship requires wives who will talk to them freely."

Suddenly, as if a door in her mind opened, Lizzy saw the value in a frank discussion with someone who obviously enjoyed a physical relationship with her spouse. Thus far, all they had gotten from Mrs. Bennet was one rambling dissertation containing a smattering of valuable details amid the bizarre euphemisms and placations that they would somehow survive the ordeal! Their mother had not once mentioned pleasure or enjoyment, nor hinted that such was possible. Considering how a simple kiss made her feel, Lizzy had instinctively known her mother had been missing something.

Additionally, Lizzy believed that with greater intimacy, the delightful sensations thus far experienced with William would multiply. Merely thinking of him gave her tingles! After the interlude with William that day, and her wild desire to have him make love to her on the sofa, there was no denying the obvious. He had said, "I want you," and she knew precisely what he meant.

Mysteries remained, however—and a fair amount of fear. Now, finally, the answers were within her grasp. Shaking off the uncomfortable visions of her aunt and uncle engaged in the act itself —no less nausea inducing than envisioning her parents—Lizzy vowed to overcome her embarrassment and take advantage of her aunt's willingness to enlighten.

If only I could shake off the disquiet caused by the "whatever their prior experience" comment.

"Your admonition is received, Aunt. We must cease being silly girls. If we cannot speak of intimacy with another female, one whom we trust, then how will we do so with our gentlemen. Right, Jane?"

Jane had gathered herself, her face once again composed with only a faint rosiness remaining. Her hands clenched into tight fists upon her lap, the knuckles blanched from the strain of bravely facing an awkward topic, but her voice was steady. "I agree with Lizzy. Mr. Bingley deserves a wife who will know how to please him."

Mrs. Gardiner chuckled softly. "Oh, trust me when I assure that a man is easy to please! A woman does not have to do all that much. Nevertheless, there are ways to improve the experience, for both of you, and the results are worth the effort. Being in love, as each of you is with your intendeds and they with you, is an incredible benefit. Mr. Gardiner and I did not have that in our favor in the beginning, yet we managed quite capably. As time passed and we grew to love each other, our intimate relationship improved profoundly."

"You and Uncle have always been so affectionate," Jane said. "I am quite astonished to hear it was not always so."

"We were fond of each other, but our marriage was one of convenience and mutual necessity more than affection. Have I never told you the story?" They shook their heads in tandem. "Well, my word! It isn't all that exciting, but may prove helpful to the subject."

She explained how her father had endured a chronic illness, and after her mother died and siblings had left the house, she, as the youngest, assumed his care. "It wasn't a sacrifice in truth. I had no suitors, loved my father dearly, and was overjoyed to run his business with him. In time, I was keeping the shop on my own while nursing my father, and I thrived on the pace."

Her father, she explained, despite being forward-minded enough to include her as an equal in business, was old-fashioned in other ways. Primarily, he worried for her future as a spinster once he passed on. No matter how capable she was, a fact he was immensely proud of, or that her siblings were nearby and supportive, to his reckoning, a woman simply could not survive in the long term without a husband.

"He fretted over it so, bless his heart," Mrs. Gardiner remembered, a warm smile on her lips. "To ease his heart, I bowed to his wishes."

She recounted how Mr. Gardiner, and his father, had known the girls' aunt's father for decades. They were friends and occasional business partners in various ventures, and their shops in Cheapside were on the same street. "I had known Mr. Gardiner for years, of course, although not well. He is quite a bit older than me, as you know, and I was nearing thirty at the time. Now we can laugh at never considering the other as a prospective mate, but we simply never did! Even when my father expressed his preference, after talking to Mr. Gardiner about the arrangement first, I was stunned."

"Was Uncle stunned too? Or did he secretly fancy you?"

"I must disappoint, Lizzy dear. There was no fancying on either side. He was as stunned at the idea as I was. Yet he saw the advantage in securing a wife, for all the typical reasons men want a wife, and not having to bother with wooing one was fortuitous." Mrs. Gardiner paused to laugh aloud, the girls joining in. "Best of all, I possessed a sound head for business. Always practical, your uncle!"

"How romantic," Lizzy intoned drily.

"Indeed," Mrs. Gardiner laughed again. "I insisted on marrying only after my father passed on, which we knew was imminent. A year later, we married, without having done more than sharing a handful of chaste kisses. I was a decade older than you two are, probably more innocent, not in love, and not particularly interested in being a wife. Strangely, those physical urges which plague the young seemed to have skipped past me."

She paused for a moment, gazing seriously at her nieces. "This brings me to the main point in sharing this ancient history. I suspect, with this bleak and decidedly unromantic set up for our marriage, it would be logical to deduce our consummation and subsequent intimacies empty, unfulfilling, and maybe downright painful. Yes?"

Lizzy didn't know quite how to respond, and a glance at Jane showed the same uncertainty. On the one hand, Lizzy could not fathom marrying a man she had no feelings for, not only because of her strong love for Mr. Darcy, but also because she had vehemently rejected marriage twice to men she held no affection for—that one of those men happened to be the man she later did fall in love with was an amusing piece of irony!

On the other hand, as she was beginning to realize, she was much like her aunt in not hitting puberty and instantly becoming obsessed with flirting and seductive ploys to ensnare a husband. Thus, while she loved William deeply and unquestionably responded as a female ought to her lover's touch, did her years of indifference to the male populous carry a negative foreboding?

Waiting no longer for a comment from the silent duo, Mrs. Gardiner continued, "You would be mistaken to think so. We were quite compatible, in fact, and enjoyed the physical aspects of our marriage tremendously. This pleasure we experienced despite not being in love. A few years later, our children came along in swift succession after nothing happening for a while, and during this period, our fondness and affection for each other evolved into love— a strong, abiding, spiritual love. Neither of us spoke of it. We simply knew our relationship had altered. Now, ask me how it was we knew."

Jane was smiling dreamily, her countenance revealing her understanding. It was Lizzy who answered, however, growing bold in her enthusiasm. "Your lovemaking had changed. It was even better than before. Am I right?"

"Spot on! You see, my dears, the physical act, as designed by God, is meant to bring the greatest of joy. In part, this is achieved merely by how the body was created. Certain areas of the male and female body will respond to certain stimuli. Under the proper circumstances, as long as both persons are willing, the act will culminate in passionate release regardless of the emotions between the two. You would need to be utterly blind or a mental deficient not to recognize this truth.

"Tragically, too many women fall into the role of servicing the physical needs of those males who seek such pleasure outside of marriage. In some cases, such women enjoy the activity and have chosen this lifestyle. Personally, as a woman of faith, this is abhorrent to me, yet I cannot deny the reality of it, mainly because it is a fact that our bodies are designed to respond and seek pleasure. What these situations lack, as did my marriage for a time, is the other part to the equation. Love. Degrees of affection enhance the experience, but when deeply in love, the affinity of heart, soul, and mind will lift the physical pleasure to a heavenly realm."

At this point, both Jane and Lizzy were mesmerized. Embarrassment was forgotten, although it would resurface in small increments with spoken graphic words and phrases. Largely, however, they listened raptly as their aunt proceeded to elucidate in both clinical and erotic verbiage on the mysteries of lovemaking.

By the end of that long evening cloistered in solitude, it was safe to say that there were no mysteries remaining other than crossing the line into personal application.

~

*J*ane and Lizzy did not speak as they climbed the stairs to their bedrooms. Their silence was not the result of lingering bashfulness or unease over the subject matter covered in precise language, but due to distracting imagery and emotions that inhibited mundane talk. They parted, after perfunctorily murmuring their good-night and sleep-well wishes, each entering their own chambers and setting to the process of preparing for bed as if automatons.

For Lizzy, all that her aunt had spoken of could be summed up in one word: revelation.

She now comprehended every sensation she had experienced in the past weeks with William as she never had before. Granted, she had known on an elemental level, as well as intellectually, what the feelings meant. With the mind-opening revelation of exactly what the marriage bed fully entailed, she was not afraid—quite the contrary.

She now fathomed, with improved clarity, just how fantastic the act of lovemaking would be. She, a maiden whose experience was limited to gentle, pleasurable stimulation from a kiss or passionate embrace, had fervently yearned for more. The desires increased daily, so how strong would they be after another month has passed?

The crazed vision from earlier that day, of William loving her in his office, was more vivid.

It also raised the question: Would she *really* have crossed the forbidden line of losing her virtue before exchanging vows? Just a few days ago she had quite vehemently assured William that she would never allow such a thing. Today? If William were to walk through her bedchamber door right now, with her concupiscence at an all-time high, would she send him away?

Lizzy gazed at her reflection in the mirror. A flushed face with bright eyes stared back.

It is fortunate he is miles away, she thought, sighing forlornly.

Lizzy reflexively began removing the pins from her hair, plopping each one onto the table sightlessly, her musings continuing.

Another aspect of the revelation from today, both from Aunt Gardiner and the passionate exchange with her fiancé at the townhouse, was greater sympathy for Darcy's struggles.

Surely, a mature man Mr. Darcy's age had been aware of his carnal lusts for a decade, if not longer. If her sexual awareness, so recently awoken, could lead to such intense temptations, it logically followed that he faced a far stronger temptation. Furthermore, distressing as the thought was, Lizzy doubted his experiences in this area was limited to only her or to simple kisses and embraces. Presuming this was the case—the details of which she hoped never to learn—when he imagined loving her, the visions must be crystal clear and explicit.

However, he had not loved any of the women he may have entertained in the past. Only she held William's heart, of this fact she was positive. This amazing man she loved was a person of deep emotions, loyalty, and faith. Lizzy believed William was already cognizant of the God-ordained plan that made lovemaking exponentially rapturous when between two who were bonded soul and spirit—in this, she was confident.

The conclusion to all of this being, his restraint was more remarkable than she had credited.

"This is going to be a long four weeks," she declared aloud to her reflection in the tall mirror she stood in front of. Dreamily, she nodded and then smiled bemusedly upon noting that, while lost to introspection, she had changed into her bed clothes, unpinned her hair, and was now brushing the long locks which fell in a wave down her back, the ends almost reaching her bottom.

William adores my hair.

The thought came unbidden, and her brushing rhythm faltered. Only once, that she was aware of, had he seen her hair down. The day she walked to Netherfield to attend to a sick Jane, she had hurried out the door, not bothering to pin it. She would never forget his face when she walked into the breakfast room. Not for many months would she comprehend the emotions and thoughts behind his dumbfounded expression or the other countless times he had stared at her in frank appreciation.

Oh yes, he adored her hair, but that was not all. Examining her familiar facial features with recent revelations in mind, Lizzy focused on altering her perceptions. How did William view her?

His "barely tolerable" remark at the Meryton Assembly—the result of frustrated moodiness and trying to keep Mr. Bingley from playing matchmaker—had long ago been discounted. There was no question William considered her beautiful. The only surprise in that statement was that *Lizzy* had never considered *herself* particularly beautiful. *Honestly, tolerable is an apt word. Perhaps a bit more than tolerable, but not the beauty of Jane or adorable, dimpled cuteness of Kitty.* Nor was she lushly provocative, like Lydia. Not being unkind but merely honest, of the five Bennet daughters, Lizzy ranked her looks above only Mary, who was the plainest.

Of course, as the ancient saying maintained, beauty is in the eye of the beholder. William beheld the woman he loved, and in his estimation, she was the most beautiful woman alive—his words, not her prideful imagination. On the handful of occasions when he had relaxed his guard enough to touch her face, she readily recalled how his fingertips would sensuously brush over her skin from feature to feature, his passion-glazed eyes following and conveying without a single word his fervid attraction.

His actions and expressions vivid in her mind, Lizzy lifted a hand to her face. Tracing a similar trail as he, she swept her fingers across her forehead, brows, nose, cheek, and then down to rest on her lips. Her mirrored image faded, shimmering into his form and his eyes hungrily, reverently staring back.

She didn't realize how rapidly her heart was beating and how shallow her breaths until, in the same mesmerized manner, her fingers glided along her jaw then down her neck to rest lightly in the hollow of her throat. No longer was her fevered mind envisioning his fingertips. Instead, she felt his lips as they had traversed the sensitive flesh of her shoulders and bosom earlier that day. The sensations coursing through her body from the memory were nearly as intense as his tangible mouth had aroused. *Perhaps the intimacy of the current setting contributes*, she thought dazedly. After all, she was alone, steps away from a bed, and wearing nothing but sleeping garments.

For the first time, she deliberately contemplated how it would be on her wedding night. William, for the first time, would see her as she is now. Hair tumbling down her back, feet bare, and a loose gown of thin material the only barrier to her naked flesh.

Lizzy emitted a breathy sigh as tingles cascaded over her skin. Shivering, she instinctively crossed her arms over her chest and hugged her shoulders.

Not even when purchasing the filmy nightgowns and robes for after her marriage—at the insistence of her aunt—had she dwelt upon his reaction to seeing them on her. "Such garments are not designed to be worn for long," her aunt had quipped, causing both Lizzy and Jane to blush furiously. All five of the hastily selected, delicate and lacy sets were packed away, out of sight. Lizzy hadn't braved looking at them again.

Suddenly, Lizzy heard her aunt's words from just a few hours ago, but with another application.

"… the pressing issue at hand is creating an environment of ease … If the remotest reference to intimacy brings on blushes and stammering, how will you ever communicate openly with your husbands?"

The concept did not apply only to verbal communication, she now saw. She must learn to overcome her modesty, to be open, at ease, and unafraid when exposing her body to her husband. If she blushed at the very *idea* of wearing a semi-revealing gown, would paralysis ensue when he asked to see her naked? Or worse, would she do something utterly stupid, like run from the room?

Vexed at herself for being such a ninny, Lizzy released her arm and peeled the robe off her shoulders. Seconds later, the nightgown lay on the floor, and there she was, naked as the day she was born. Forcefully tamping the hesitancy and lingering twinges of embarrassment, she assessed the familiar figure reflected in the glass from the perspective of the man who loved her.

An episode from some two years ago came to mind.

One afternoon she and her sisters were sitting in the Longbourn parlor, each attending to a task of some kind, while their mother hummed a soft tune as she sewed. Mary was reading the Bible, and at one point asked, "Mama, what does Solomon mean by saying her 'two breasts are like two young roes that are twins.'?'"

Mrs. Bennet nearly suffered apoplexy on the spot! Not attempting to answer, she snatched the book from Mary's hands and forbade her from reading the Song of Solomon. This reaction only confused poor Mary, made Jane blush, and Lizzy stifle giggles, but Lydia instantly perked up. For probably the first time in ages, she'd grabbed another Bible off the shelf and scoured the poetic book of romance for anything remotely sexual, which she then recited for the whole room. Kitty was swiftly caught up in the frenzy, although she probably didn't understand most of the language and meaning. Their poor mother retreated to her bedroom, not seen for the rest of the day.

Mrs. Bennet's overreaction to a simple fact of life made the situation far worse, not that this was unusual when uncomfortable topics came up. Lydia and Kitty soon grew tired of the game, but Lizzy had been left intrigued. Rereading the Song of Solomon—done privately later that night—with more mature eyes was enlightening. Without a doubt, God intended for men and women to delight in each other, in every way, with the visual certainly being an important aspect. For a young woman nearing nineteen, this wasn't a major epiphany, of course. No matter how innocent one is, recognizing a handsome man and presenting oneself in an attractive light are as natural as breathing, even if not taken all that seriously most of the time.

As the memory and subsequent ruminating filtered through her mind, Lizzy continued to study her reflection. Then she lifted her arms over her head, twirled around a time or two, bent at the waist to touch her toes, and performed a few dance steps and other such freeing movements. Primarily, her goal was to grow comfortable being unclothed. If she could watch herself, knowing she was far more critical of her flaws than William would be, then perhaps the transition to exposing her body to him would be easier.

It was amazingly liberating! Laughing aloud, she continued the experiment while imagining William in the room. Her husband, sitting on the chair and laughing at her antics, lying on the bed watching with his intensely passionate gaze, and then standing near her. His handsome face, his gentle hands, his soft lips—even his velvety tongue—were distinctly imagined.

With every illusionary touch, caress, and kiss, her excitement increased. The visions escalated, enhanced by the vividly remembered incidents of being held tightly in his embrace, firm chest muscles pressing against her breasts, and him cupping her buttocks to draw her against the steely length of his arousal. The picture remained somewhat hazy, as her knowledge was not complete enough to fabricate an unclothed version of him. What her ingenuity could create, however, was sufficient to ignite her passion.

Lizzy never knew how long she stood still with eyes closed and arms crossed over sensitized breasts. The sizzling of the candle flame as it hit the melted wax, seconds before extinguishing, broke the spell. The room was cold, goose pimples had risen on her arms, and she shivered.

Yet her tremors were not from the cold. Inside, she was on fire, alive with sensations evoked by the fantasy dance with her lover. She was lightheaded from panting breaths and rapid heartbeats, and her loins ached excruciatingly in a way she'd never experienced. She felt exhilarated and empty at the same time.

In a daze, she donned her gown and crawled between the cold sheets. She fell asleep almost immediately, slipping into a dream of William. Interestingly, her subconscious miraculously filled in the blanks her conscious mind could not. This dream—the first of many more to come—was incredibly detailed, realistic, and most decidedly erotic. It was, by far, the best dream of Elizabeth Bennet's entire life, and she woke the next morning astoundingly refreshed.

5

ARISTOCRATIC RECEPTION

*L*ord Matlock agreed to meet with his nephew at noon. The earl's response to Darcy's request had given no hint as to his frame of mind. Despite the lack of positivity, Darcy wasn't worried about the eventual outcome.

All that he and Colonel Fitzwilliam had discussed regarding Lord Matlock's character—the fondness for his nephew, abiding affection for the late James Darcy, and keen awareness of Lady Catherine's acerbity—was accurate. Lord Matlock was quite formal and not overtly affectionate, as was Lady Matlock, so Darcy could not claim to possess a deeply personal relationship with his uncle. Nevertheless, he trusted the older man's wisdom and decency would overrule his adherence to social status and protocol. More importantly, he believed in Elizabeth Bennet's ability to charm and impress.

While sure of these facts and confident that they, as a family, would arrive at a place of accord, he was firm on other truths as well.

Darcy had asked for this audience with his uncle, yes, but not out of fear or weakness. In reality, if not for the earl's divisive sibling, Darcy would not have been *having* a discussion with his uncle about

Elizabeth. Lord Matlock was the one who somehow deemed it within his purview to evaluate Darcy's choice of wife, pass judgment, and bestow his approval. It was an authority Darcy unequivocally did not grant him. Frankly, the presumption made his blood boil.

Lord Matlock's invitation, or "subpoena" as Richard had half-jokingly called it, forced Darcy to enter a conversation he found abhorrent. He will defend Elizabeth to the death if need be, of that there was no question. The problem with this defensive situation was that the woman he loved—a virtuous, honorable woman of strength and intelligence—was under a vicious, unwarranted attack. It was grossly unfair, yet rather than enjoy familial support, Darcy had to counter poisonous lies, explain his heart, reaffirm his mental acuity and independence, and who knew what else.

Being on the defense, as opposed to the offense, was not an acceptable position for Darcy of Pemberley. Not ever.

With all of this at the forefront of his mind, Darcy followed the butler into the library where Lord Matlock sat in a leather chair close to the fire. A low table was already laden with a tray, upon which sat a glass decanter and one glass. The other glass was in the earl's hand, half-filled with liquor, and used to indicate the identical chair across from the table as he said by way of greeting, "Have a seat, William. Help yourself to the brandy, or, if you wish, Mr. Willis can fetch something else."

"Brandy is fine, thank you, my lord." He sat in the chair, pouring a glass and taking a sip before meeting his uncle's unreadable eyes.

For a full minute neither spoke, assessing the other in silence instead. Finally, Lord Matlock smiled, albeit somewhat grimly. "I see how it is to be then. I expected as much. You may not realize how similar you are to your father. I rarely won an argument with James, especially if his dander was up." He paused, but when Darcy merely took another sip, he continued, "Lower your guard and smooth the hackles, Nephew. I've known Lady Catherine far longer than you have. Trust me when I tell you I could share stories that would curl even your hair."

"My father shared a few," Darcy offered when his uncle once again paused. "Yet here I am, the one on trial, so it seems."

"Dramatic like James too. Or worse, like your Uncle George." Lord Matlock grunted. "You aren't on trial, for heaven's sake!"

"Is Miss Bennet?"

Lord Matlock returned Darcy's harsh glare. "William, I cannot fault your loyalty to Miss Bennet. This is admirable and as it should be if you marry her."

"*If?* There is no *if* about it, my lord."

"I know you are a mature, capable man. Never have I doubted your sense or worried over your choices in life. These facts, along with Richard's assurances, go far in easing my mind regarding Miss Bennet."

"I suspect a caveat is coming," Darcy interjected, aware of his rising irritation and gruff tone. "And I reiterate my objection, strenuously, over the use of a subjunctive word. Miss Bennet and I *will marry* within a month."

Sighing, Lord Matlock relaxed his face and softened his tone. "You are a man of honor, Darcy, and I applaud this. You are also a man of rational sense. Logically, you must know you would not be the first man to fall prey to a pretty face. Men, since the dawn of time, have lost their heads when love, or more typically lust, clouds their judgment. And I know you will fume to hear it, but women down through the ages have used their charms to manipulate rich men. Huff at me all you want. It's still the truth."

To his surprise as much as Lord Matlock's, Darcy began to chuckle. *Ah, the ridiculousness of Elizabeth's marrying him for his wealth!*

"Allow me to set the record straight on any rumors or assumptions regarding both of those statements." He leaned forward to emphasize the seriousness of what he was about to demand. "May

I first have your promise, as a peer of the realm, that the words spoken today stay between us?"

As anticipated, the earl bristled at having his honor questioned, his face hardening and spine stiffening. Since Darcy's honor being questioned was what led to this absurd circumstance and conversation, his stare was intense and unrelenting.

"You have my promise, of course," Lord Matlock agreed tersely.

Darcy acknowledged this with a quick bob of his head and then sat back in his chair. "Miss Bennet and I met last fall, and to be blunt, she despised me. My first opinion of her physical appearance, as told to Mr. Bingley, was less than savory. I'd rather leave it at that."

Revisiting his harsh, ungentlemanly words was painful, even in an obscure reference. Swallowing a gulp of brandy, he went on, "My opinion changed over time, after my comprehension of Miss Bennet's intelligence, personality, and character. I fully understand now that I had fallen in love with her, but I denied the sentiments and left Hertfordshire. Forward to this spring and unable to forget her, I traveled to Rosings for the express purpose of proposing marriage."

Lost to terrible memories, Darcy stared into the glass, absently swirling the rich caramel-colored liquid. Inhaling, he mentally shook off his preoccupation with the past.

"She refused me. Quite vehemently, I must add. I was, and I quote, the last man in the world she could ever be prevailed upon to marry. Hardly the actions of a female using charms to manipulate a rich man. To this day, and I mean that literally, Elizabeth refuses to accept a single pence from me. Not one present either, other than her engagement rings. Trust me, your worries over Miss Bennet's motives, and my judgment, are unfounded."

Lord Matlock was gazing at him in wonder as if a light shone within his mind. "Is this why you were acting bizarre all summer?"

Wincing, Darcy nodded.

"Lady Matlock was deeply concerned. In fact, I now recall she speculated if a woman was involved. I disregarded the notion. It seemed incredible to me that any woman would refuse you, or that you had entertained a lady since we heard nothing of it. I see now how wrong I was. Frankly, knowing how James felt for my sister, I should have suspected it possible for you."

Speculative silence fell for a time. Darcy waited, not sure what else to say. If those were his uncle's two main concerns, then he had clarified the issue, and they had nothing more to discuss. It would suit Darcy just fine not to talk about Lady Catherine or the swirling rumors. The private matters he had just divulged crossed a line he was already uncomfortable with. The thought of delving further made his skin crawl. Alas, dashed were his fervent hopes of a closed topic seconds later.

"While my curiosity remains as to how Miss Bennet went from hating you to accepting the second proposal, I know you well enough to conclude it shall stay a mystery."

When Darcy ignored his uncle's pleading expression, the earl laughed resignedly.

"As I thought. Very well then. I am appeased that your relationship with Miss Bennet is genuine. Perhaps this will surprise you, William, but this troubled me more than the rest. I want you to know"—the earl shifted in his chair and cleared his throat, eyes sliding away from Darcy's face to focus on the fire—"that my affection for you is also genuine. In large part due to James, who was a brother to me, but equally because of who you are...as a person. When James...died, I keenly felt it was my duty to...I guess watch over you is the best way to put it. Be a mentor or guide or perhaps simply a respected friend—whatever else you needed from me. You see, your happiness and well-being, and Georgiana's, are of paramount importance to me...to us. Your aunt's sentiments are as intense. As she delights in pointing out to me, she is far better at expressing them."

Of that there can be no argument, Darcy thought as he felt his lips twitch in a fight not to smile or laugh. His uncle's commentary, mumbled at points and laced with contemplative lulls, was as amusing as it was informative.

As a startling aside, amid this supremely bizarre and awkward discourse, was Darcy's epiphany that he was like his uncle in many personality traits. He always presumed his aloof, introverted attributes—alien to both his parents—were inherited from his grandfather. Now he gleaned that the genesis likely filtered down from both sides of his family. A double punch!

"I said all of that drivel, badly as it was delivered," Lord Matlock continued in a firmer tone, "was an effort to convey that while I freely admit my choice for you would be a lady of elevated station, wealth, education, and so on, I do not discount the importance of affection. Love, that sentiment lacking in most marriages, is the best formula for success."

Lifting his glass in a casual toast, which Darcy returned, the earl tossed back the last swallow. Looking at the glass and then the decanter, he hesitated. Then, mumbling "What the hell," he poured a generous amount into the empty glass, topping off Darcy's right after.

"For that reason, I never gave my full approval to Catherine concerning you and Anne. In fact, you may not know this, but I agreed with James when, long ago, she first brought up the idea of a union. God, I think you two were still in diapers!" He laughed wistfully. "I remember James laughing, almost hysterically. Then he realized she was deadly serious, even wanting documents drawn up. I'd rarely seen James so angry. Your poor mother was trying to play peacemaker between sister and husband, with no luck, so I stepped in. Forcefully. It was months, maybe a year and a bit, since inheriting my title, so I didn't carry much clout in her eyes. She did let the matter drop though, for years." He shrugged, then his eyes widened. "Come to think of it, Sir Lewis was there! He always could handle Catherine in ways we never comprehended. Ha! Yes, that must have been it."

"Thanks for whatever persuasion you, Sir Lewis, and my father managed at that time. Unfortunately, she did not let the topic drop forever."

"Indeed. Which is why we are sitting here, isn't it?" Lord Matlock directed his authoritative gaze toward Darcy, once again all business. When Darcy did not answer, the earl resumed. "I am pleased you have found a woman who loves you, William. I do not have tremendous issue with her modest means, informal education, and whatever social skills and status she lacks. I trust you, and Richard as well. Additionally, I know very well what my sister is trying to do. The truth is, her verbiage in describing Miss Bennet was too outrageous. No one as awful as she depicted could have ensnared someone like you, not even with the aid of a gypsy or druid witch. Keep the lie simple is a principle Catherine never understood."

Darcy smiled at his uncle's dry humor, although his words were a reminder of the gossip disseminating around town, all thanks to his aunt. Speaking from the heart, he said, "You will see the truth tonight, my lord, and readily give your blessing. Of that, I have no doubt whatsoever. My only serious concerns are the damage Lady Catherine has caused. As we sit here, these lies are bandied about, taking hold and enhanced as gossip inevitably is. Because of Lady Catherine de Bourgh, my future wife, the woman who will soon be Mrs. Darcy, the Mistress of Pemberley, is having her name sullied. The darkening of the name *Darcy* is occurring in the process. But honestly of the deepest distress to me, is that Miss Bennet is right now in the shops of London where she could easily be subjected to ridicule or overhear these heinous whispers."

Lord Matlock was frowning, his countenance troubled. "What are you talking about?"

Surprised, Darcy answered with a question of his own, "Did not Richard tell you of the gossip?"

"He made a vague reference or two, yes, mixed in with his usual jesting. I recall a mention of my sister. Perhaps I should have paid closer heed to my son's news, but I admit to being focused on Catherine's alarmist letters. Tell me what he failed to report."

Darcy did as asked, leaving nothing out. The earl's face grew grayer and angrier by the minute. "Richard probably figured you were upset enough without making matters worse," Darcy placated. "Now, with all the facts laid bare, I hope you see where the real problem resides."

"Indeed I do. This is grave. Very grave. Unfortunately, malicious talk once started is impossible to stop. Fortunately, I am no longer a fledgling nobleman attempting to govern a strong-willed older sibling. Rest easy, William. I will deal with Lady Catherine. I cannot promise my influence will bring total acceptance of your marriage on her part. What I can promise is she will cease any direct interference."

Darcy remained dubious as to just how much control even the Earl of Matlock had over Lady Catherine de Bourgh, but he nodded. All the drama and nastiness made him ill, and his longing increased to be married to Elizabeth and safely sequestered at Pemberley. Suddenly desperate to end the discussion, he set his empty glass onto the tray, saying, "So! If we have finished, Uncle, I do have business elsewhere, and a special evening engagement to prepare for."

To his dismay, he got no further than placing his hands onto the chair's arms.

"There is the situation with George Wickham and one of Miss Bennet's sisters," Lord Matlock gently reminded. "What I have been told is unsettling, even if only half is factual. A scandal like that is not to be taken lightly, William. Is there any truth to it?"

Of course, Darcy had not forgotten that incident. Nor had he honestly believed Lord Matlock would not address it, so he had prepared for the probability.

"Yes, there is truth to the story. How much, I will not say, and you must trust me enough to leave it be. I request this not just for myself and the Bennets, but also *for another whom we both love.*"

Other than Elizabeth and Colonel Fitzwilliam, Darcy had vowed to tell no one about Wickham's planned seduction and elopement with Georgiana. He wasn't about to break that vow. Whether close friends and family suspected something had happened in Ramsgate, he did not want to know, especially now that it no longer mattered. It was a dead topic best left in the past.

Lord Matlock's eyes narrowed, but he said nothing. Darcy held his gaze. "The only pertinent truth for the present is that Wickham and Lydia Bennet are legally married. Wickham is serving in His Majesty's army, in Newcastle. Whatever 'scandal' there may have been was minor to begin with, unproven, and now resolved. In the past week, a dozen sensational scandals far more fascinating than this one have occurred within the highest members of the gentry and aristocracy. No one in Society knows who George Wickham and Lydia Bennet are and no one cares. A week after my marriage their names will be forgotten, if they haven't been already."

For a good two minutes, the Earl of Matlock stared silently, his expression bland. Then, slowly, a smile curved his lips. "You practiced that whole speech, didn't you?"

Darcy nodded once, determined not to return the smile yet.

"Well, it worked. Quite persuasive. I am greatly impressed. You know, William, I have friends in Parliament who could easily get you a seat in the Commons. Interested?"

～

*O*f the four carriages housed in the mews behind Darcy House, the double-bench coach chosen for this evening was the largest and grandest. It was not yet two years old and designed with luxury and comfort in mind. Sturdily constructed, spacious, and outfitted as completely as a modern conveyance could be, Darcy reserved it for long-distance travel or special occasions. In his estimation, this night was a significantly special occasion.

Even before his conversation with Lord Matlock, Darcy had

chosen the new coach to transport his betrothed and future father-in-law from the Gardiner residence in Cheapside to the Matlock townhouse in Saint James's Square. Primarily this was due to the interior roominess and the smooth travel over rough patches on the streets.

Additionally, he wanted to show his respect for Elizabeth and Mr. Bennet by providing the best he had to offer. After the chat with his uncle, the stately coach emblazoned with the ancestral Darcy crest would serve as a bold declaration regarding the occupants, which no one could ignore. Prideful ostentation was not Darcy's character generally, but this situation called for a grandiose spectacle and an undeniable message for curious onlookers who may have heeded nasty gossip.

What he had not anticipated was the reception upon seeing the coach parked majestically on the curb at Cheapside. The Gardiner townhouse occupants, all of them, had stopped abruptly on the entryway steps, mouths falling open and eyes widening in stunned awe. Slightly embarrassed at what outwardly appeared to be braggadocios flaunting of his wealth and station to the modest citizens of Cheapside, Darcy hastened to explain his reasoning, emphasizing the comfort aspect and leaving out the rest. Whether they bought his excuse or not, he was unsure. It didn't help matters when seemingly everyone on the street paused to stare with the same expressions worn by the others minutes ago.

It was a relief to reach Fleet Street and then the Strand where imposing carriages were common. By the time they traversed the twists and turns merging onto Pall Mall, the three were relaxed and engaged in casual conversation.

Mr. Bennet wore a new ensemble tailored to fit his physique and of a style closer to current fashion trends than his typical garments, which mostly dated to the past century. How his daughters had talked him into it, Darcy was not about to ask. Whether the fresh haircut and shave were his ideas or the result of badgering by Jane and

Elizabeth would also be left unanswered. In any case, Mr. Bennet was the model picture of a respectable country gentleman.

Elizabeth, as always in Darcy's eyes, was stunningly gorgeous. She too wore a new ensemble, each item from the glittering jeweled pins holding her dense curls in place down to the white kid slippers on her feet, had been recently purchased. Per her taste, the gown and accouterments were modest and simplistic, yet fashionable. She was a vision of pure loveliness, and he could not remove his eyes from her.

The Bennet pair sat on the plush-cushioned, velvet-covered bench across from Darcy. It would not have been proper for Elizabeth to sit beside him, and for the present, he was perfectly content with the arrangement. She was delightfully gawking at the scenery passing outside the carriage window, and his vantage point allowed him to observe her movements unencumbered. It was fantastic! She was childlike in her curiosity and enthusiasm, her face radiant and voice animated.

"The gaslight is beautiful! See how the window glass sparkles? Just think, Papa, someday every house will be lit as brilliantly. It shall be as bright as daylight at midnight."

"Pitfalls come with progress, but in this area, I can rejoice. If only to save my eyesight for improved reading, I will embrace a modern invention with potential disaster."

If Elizabeth heard her father's comment, it was not apparent. She had already continued her lively commentary about the people, architecture, foliage, and whatever else caught her fancy. For not the first time, Darcy wondered at her incredible ability to be at ease in any situation. The momentary stupefaction evoked by the coach had long since faded, replaced by keen interest and innocent appreciation for everything. If she felt out of her element, there was no hint of it. She noted the exclusive businesses along south Piccadilly and Pall Mall for their unique merchandise and elegant shoppers. The increasingly palatial townhouses did not faze her though she did marvel at their beauty.

"Will we pass by the palace, Mr. Darcy?"

Pulled out of his reverie with a start, Darcy shook his head. "I am afraid not. I initially instructed the driver to take the circuitous route past Saint James's Palace. Alas, as we discovered on our way to fetch you, His Royal Highness is in residence and hosting a fete of some sort. Hence the reason I was a bit late. By this time, it would add another hour onto our journey to go that way."

"A shame, but there is plenty of time for sightseeing later. The palace isn't going anywhere—at least not that I've heard."

Darcy laughed. "Not in the near future. Perhaps the day after tomorrow we can spend the afternoon touring the city if you wish."

"I may need to do more shopping." At this, she flashed an impish smirk toward her father.

Mr. Bennet grimaced. "Whatever you wish, Lizzy. This trip is for you and Jane. I can be long-suffering and generous, especially knowing the two of you buying everything you lay eyes on will soon no longer be my problem. I wish you luck, Mr. Darcy."

Darcy merely smiled and inclined his head. Elizabeth had returned her avid gaze to the passing views, although she did add, "Look on the bright side, Papa. If we go shopping, you have another free day to explore Mr. Darcy's library. There must be one or two shelves you've yet to scour. So you see, everyone wins!"

"Except for me," Darcy contradicted. "Whilst you shop, I shall be adrift without the pleasure of your company, Miss Elizabeth."

Turning to face him, her lips curved into the sweet, secret smile he now knew was only for him. "I cannot have you being left adrift weighing on my conscience, Mr. Darcy. It would be unbearable! Papa"—she patted Mr. Bennet's knee—"you can still bury yourself in books while we, with Jane and Mr. Bingley, tramp about Town. This will save your pocketbook and your feet. A day of sightseeing does sound enjoyable. Besides, the night isn't the best time for viewing a palace, nor is that the objective for this evening."

"True on all points. Tonight is for my family to acquaint

themselves with the superlative woman who has honored me with her acceptance of my proposal, and her esteemed father."

Brows lifted and eyes wide, Elizabeth exclaimed with dramatic dismay, "Is that the purpose? I thought it was for me to learn more about the mysterious gentleman who honored me with a proposal. Why I have my list of personal questions that only kinfolk can answer to tucked into my reticule. Are you saying, Mr. Darcy, that I shan't have an opportunity to interview each person in private?"

"Private interviews are forbidden, Miss Elizabeth, for the sake of my sanity. However, if it is any consolation, between Colonel Fitzwilliam and Lady Matlock and, to some degree, Mr. Fitzwilliam, I fear the granting of a wealth of information designed specifically to embarrass me."

"Then I am cheered considerably, sir. Thank you!"

Darcy laughed, letting the topic go in favor of indicating which houses belonged to whom, as they had now reached Saint James's Square.

"Illustrious names familiar from newspaper gossip pages," she murmured at one point. "Do you know all of them...personally?"

Darkness had fallen, and Elizabeth was again turned toward the window, preventing Darcy from scrutinizing her expression. What he could see through the shadows was not a face exhibiting extreme anxiety. Instead, it was the slight stumble of her words and trace of tension in her voice which gave him pause. Taken alone, he likely would have shrugged it off as his imagination. Then he saw Mr. Bennet turn his head around, a flash of outside light briefly illuminating the furrows between his brows and pursed lips as he peered at his daughter.

Was Elizabeth nervous after all? Had she heard snippets of the drifting rumors? Darcy's stomach clenched and heart thudded.

In the few hours they had been together since the report from Colonel Fitzwilliam yesterday, Darcy had monitored her words and actions carefully, seeking nuances that might indicate she was aware, even if minimally. Thus far, he had detected nothing amiss on that front. There had also been no hint that she felt any anxiety about tonight. It was perfectly normal to be apprehensive when meeting unknown people, particularly his family. After the atrocious behavior of Lady Catherine de Bourgh, meeting two more titled nobles couldn't possibly be a delightful prospect.

Trying to ease whatever trepidation she may be experiencing, Darcy aimed for soothing teases as he answered her question. "I have met most of the residents hereabouts at one time or another. Thereafter, I promptly did my best to forget them. Few are as interesting as you, my dear."

"Heavens! They must be astoundingly unremarkable then. Are you sure this is accurate, Mr. Darcy?" she asked playfully. "How disappointing if it is. The papers must exaggerate terribly to write such fascinating stories and scandals about all these boring people."

Pleased to see her humor intact and her brief flirt with nervousness gone, Darcy continued the banter by describing one of his uncle's craziest neighbors. The short anecdote involved a greatly disliked yapping dog and a large alley cat, the latter decisively winning the animal argument. On the high note of gaiety, the carriage gently lurched to a halt, signaling their arrival at the London townhouse of the Earl and Countess of Matlock.

The foyer of the Matlock townhouse was larger than the Darcy House foyer by some four to five square feet, and was equally as impressive in fine furnishings. Throughout the house, Lady Matlock's sense of style was, like the late Lady Anne Darcy, elegant in a reserved, almost understated way. The decor was both grand and soothing, the combination brilliantly broadcasting the power and wealth of the Earl of Matlock while expressing warmth and welcome. Elizabeth and Mr. Bennet scanned the surroundings with interest, but neither appeared overwhelmed. If his beloved felt any return of nervousness, she hid it well.

Pride swelling his heart, he offered his arm, escorting Elizabeth into the drawing room where the butler, Mr. Willis, led them. Everyone was present and stared at the trio as they entered. Lady Matlock sat on the gilded settee facing the door, a smile already lighting her delicate face. The three men—Lord Matlock, Colonel Fitzwilliam, and Jonathan Fitzwilliam—stood in an arc between the settee and the larger sofa upon which perched Priscilla Fitzwilliam. Ever a house where formality reigned, the butler announced each of them in proper order and precision. Once completed, he bowed and left the room, at which point the stasis broke.

Darcy performed the less formal introductions, beginning with Lord Matlock. His lordship greeted Mr. Bennet first, naturally, and then bowed to Elizabeth. As Darcy expected, Jonathan Fitzwilliam was coolly proper, his tone perfectly civil yet lacking the genial undertone and measure of interest shown by Lord Matlock.

For easily the hundredth time in Darcy's memory, Colonel Fitzwilliam proved his talent for easing tense situations. He bowed with exaggerated flair and welcomed both Bennets graciously but with his unique puckish charm. Then, when Mr. Bennet diverted his gaze, the colonel winked at Elizabeth, as if they shared secrets. Darcy instinctively experienced a flash of jealousy and was unable to prevent a fleeting frown. Richard raised one brow and smirked.

Oh, how well my cousin knows me. Internally laughing at the ridiculous reaction, Darcy's frown turned into a smile, and he shook his head. Elizabeth laughed at the exchange her sharp eyes had not missed.

Priscilla Fitzwilliam's acknowledgment was almost identical to her husband's. Darcy had anticipated as much but was surprised when she did not assess Elizabeth's garments with disdain. Darcy thought his fiancée beautiful in any outfit, but he had seen enough wealthy ladies wearing the latest fashions to grudgingly admit Elizabeth's modest finances and limited experience were not on par with high society. Mrs. Fitzwilliam's gown alone undoubtedly cost four times what Elizabeth probably had paid for her entire ensemble.

Furthermore, his cousin's wife was an attractive woman with a slender figure perfectly proportioned to exhibit current designs, thus one of the leading mavens of the *beau monde*. Not wrinkling her aristocratic nose, at the very least, sent a message to Darcy, although whether that message was utter disinterest or an effort to be kind, he had no clue.

Saving the best for last, Darcy turned to his aunt. "Miss Bennet, Mr. Bennet, allow me the honor of introducing her ladyship, the Countess of Matlock."

Darcy had forever been in awe of his aunt. She was, without question, one of the most beautiful women he had ever laid eyes on, age only increasing her resplendency. As exquisite as her physical appearance was her poise. Cultured and graceful as a ballet dancer, she also possessed a heart of pure gold. A quick glance at Elizabeth and her father revealed the same awe he always experienced. Then she spoke, her voice as remarkable as her presence.

"Welcome to our home. We are delighted to meet you both. This is a precious moment long desired." She glanced at Darcy, smiled, then returned her gaze to Elizabeth. "Please, sit here by me, my dear."

Lady Matlock patted the cushion, Elizabeth doing as asked automatically. Her eyes widened at the gentle endearment, Darcy noted, and she trembled slightly. Then his aunt clasped onto one of her hands, saying gaily, "Oh, we have so much to talk about! I have known Fitzwilliam since he was born, you know? Just imagine the stories I have accumulated."

Richard burst out laughing. Darcy groaned and covered his face with his hand. Even Lord Matlock and Mr. Fitzwilliam snickered.

"It appears the questionnaire inside your reticule will be used after all, Lizzy." Mr. Bennet grinned at Darcy, who decided it was time to change the subject.

"My lady, I understand Lord and Lady Montgomery are attending His Highness's fete at the palace."

"Indeed, they are," Lady Matlock confirmed. Turning to Elizabeth, she continued, "It is requisite I extend the apologies of our daughter, Miss Bennet. She greatly desired to meet her cousin's betrothed. Alas, a commitment to the prince regent must take precedence."

Richard suppressed a cough at the "greatly desired" comment, Darcy nudging him with an elbow into the side. Luckily, no one seemed to notice, thanks to Mr. Bennet's question.

"Pardon me, but is your daughter married to Viscount Montgomery?"

"Indeed, Mr. Bennet," Lord Matlock confirmed.

"His speeches in Parliament are remarkably well penned and convincing. His recent arguments on the slave issue were excellently wrought. I daresay he rivaled the best by Wilberforce or Fox. I have often wondered if he speaks as eloquently when the setting demands extemporaneous commentary."

Lord Matlock's brows had arched in surprise and respect at Mr. Bennet's words. A short round of discussion on the slave trade and public speaking commenced, the two older gentlemen unconsciously strolling toward a portrait of the late prime minister William Pitt the Younger. Essentially, this single remark on Darcy's cousin-in-law's speaking style had launched a conversation that roamed from politics to world events, to changes in the university educational system with contrasts between Oxford and Cambridge, literature favorites, and eventually estate management and country living. As they walked to the dining room, and for portions of the dinner itself, Lord Matlock and Mr. Bennet were engaged in friendly discourse, often oblivious to the discussions or activity around them.

Frankly, Darcy was amazed. Familiar as he was with both men, he had trusted their inborn civility would override any clashes in their personalities. Neither were the type to ignore honor and the importance of the occasion simply because they irritated the other. Therefore, Darcy had not fretted over uncomfortable tension arising but had considered it probable that Mr. Bennet's wry jocularity and rustic, occasionally blunt manner of talking would not blend with his uncle's formal, devoid of humor, reserved style of speech. Shockingly, to him and his family—based on the assorted raised brows and shared silent communications—they smoothly slipped into friendly accord as if fast friends for years.

Lady Matlock had reorganized the entire dining room, including selecting a table sized precisely for eight diners. Elizabeth sat across the white-linen-draped, elaborately appointed surface from Darcy, both positioned on Lady Matlock's end. Mr. Bennet was wisely assigned to Lord Matlock's left, with Jonathan Fitzwilliam across, on the earl's right. Mrs. Fitzwilliam sat beside Darcy, and the colonel was between Elizabeth and his brother.

The arrangement and table size allowed easy conversation from end to end. Intellectual discourse absorbed the two older gentlemen and Mr. Fitzwilliam, leaving the others largely on their own. Not that this was a problem in the least.

"How are you enjoying your stay in London, Miss Bennet?"

"Tremendously so, my lady. We rarely come to Town, so this journey has been a wonderful treat, particularly due to the circumstances. My sister Jane and I are here, with our long-suffering father, expressly to purchase our wedding gowns and trousseau."

"Your sister is to marry Mr. Charles Bingley, is that correct?"

"It is. Are you acquainted with Mr. Bingley, my lady?"

"Not as intimately as my nephew, but we have met a handful of times. We also dined with him and Miss Bingley once, at Darcy House. He is an agreeable young man. A great friend to Mr. Darcy for some years now, and in this world that is an accomplishment worthy of rejoicing. What a fortuitous turn of events that two such worthy gentlemen found brides of quality hiding in out-of-the-way Hertfordshire. A double wedding must be the highlight of the decade. You must tell of the plans, starting with the wedding gowns."

"Females and weddings!" boomed Colonel Fitzwilliam. "A most

riveting topic of conversation! Please, do tell us all about the wedding gown, Miss Bennet. I can't fathom *anything* more fascinating. Can you, Darcy?"

Elizabeth laughed. "Have no fear, Colonel, or you either, Mr. Darcy. It is considered bad fortune for the groom to see the wedding dress before the ceremony. I am not sure whether describing the dress counts, but we shan't tempt the whimsies of fate. Thus, I shall save you from the agony. What I shall say is that we have reveled in the preparations. However, we have discovered it to be an exhaustive process."

"Yet marvelous fun, to be sure. Even old married ladies such as myself remember the joy of preparing to be a bride." Lady Matlock regarded her husband with fondness. "Of all the gowns one purchases in life, none are as special as the one worn when wed. Is that not so, Priscilla?"

"Absolutely! Mine was chiffon and silk, all in white, naturally, with lace imported from France. Pearl buttons on the cuffs, which were…"

Mrs. Fitzwilliam's lengthy description of her gown continued to an equally detailed visual of her accessories. Every last one! Her dreamy expression matched the worshipful tone, yet not once did she glance at her husband. Apparently, Darcy thought, clothing incited her passions above what Jonathon could manage, not that this was a shocking revelation. After a good fifteen minutes, Darcy felt his mind numbing, the only salvation being Richard's covert eye rolls and the comically feigned fascination on Elizabeth's face. Then, just when he felt tingles of horror that Priscilla's wedding undergarments were next up for illumination, Lady Matlock, bless her soul, took advantage of a minuscule pause to smoothly interrupt.

"Perfumes! That reminds me. Thank you for the timely remark, my dear daughter. Miss Bennet," she hurried on before Mrs. Fitzwilliam finished her inhale, "I have discovered a new fragrance at the perfumery in Harding and Howell. It is divine! I like it so much I bought three bottles. I shall never use it all, so would be delighted to gift one of them to you, if the fragrance appeals."

"Is it what you are wearing tonight, Lady Matlock?"

"That is correct, Darcy. I should have suspected you would take note. Not all men are as attentive to the ladies around them, a lesson I despair of teaching certain males present in this room." She peered pointedly at her sons. Jonathan had the good grace to blush, but Richard merely shrugged and swallowed his spoonful of soup.

Smiling, Darcy went on, "It is a pleasant fragrance, but am I correct in understanding that the chemicals comprising the perfume will react with some variance on each woman? Meaning this perfume may not smell as divine on Miss Bennet?"

"Now, this is a man who listens and learns. You see how exceedingly blessed you are, Miss Bennet?"

"I daresay awareness of my supreme fortune is growing on a daily basis." Elizabeth smiled at Darcy, a teasing glint in her eyes. "Why, just two days ago, we caught Mr. Darcy at Harding and Howell, where he declared his mission to educate himself on feminine requirements was so vital he sought assistance from any female willing and able to lend him a hand."

"Harding and Howell? You actually went *inside* that place?" Richard dropped his spoon with a clank, the gape directed at Darcy bringing smiles of amusement around the table.

"Don't look so aghast, Colonel. There may come a day when such knowledge will benefit you." At this Richard blanched and choked. Darcy grinned and passed the wine decanter—which Richard gratefully grabbed to refill his empty glass—and then turned to his aunt. "I have you to thank, my lady. I recalled a conversation from some months back, in this dining room, when you mentioned the mall as superior to the Pantheon Bazaar."

"Oh yes! Lady Hayes-Smithfield and I were talking about shopping. My word, I did not notice you listening. Impressive. My faith and hope in the masculine gender are restored. I pray you found what you were seeking?"

She glanced at Elizabeth and Darcy nodded. "I did, yes, even beyond my greatest expectations. Alas, Miss Bennet must wait an entire month to reap the benefits."

"It shall be worth the wait," Elizabeth assured. Her smile infused his heart with joy and rendered him momentarily speechless.

In fact, throughout the whole meal, Darcy struggled to interact coherently with the stimulating discourse or to remember proper eating habits. All he wanted to do was observe as Elizabeth dazzled his family. Her effortless ability to converse amazed him once again and was plainly pleasing to his aunt and uncle. The conversation was fluid and sprightly, the perfect mixture of inquisitive delving to learn more about his mysterious bride-to-be and the general topics suited for the dining table.

"William, you must extend my love to Georgiana and inform her I shall call upon her tomorrow."

"As you wish, my lady. She has been practicing a new musical piece and yearns to play it for you."

The countess chuckled and shook her head. "*Yearns* is perhaps too strong a word, don't you think? Do not forget that I am quite familiar with my darling niece. She is such a sweet-tempered girl, and with maturity, I believe she will overcome her shyness. Have you spent much time with Miss Darcy, Miss Bennet?"

"Since we have been in London, we have dined at Darcy House several nights now, and yesterday my sister and I passed the afternoon in Miss Darcy's company. She is an amazing young lady. So kind, witty, and prodigiously talented on the pianoforte."

"Georgiana is gifted," Darcy declared with brotherly pride.

"No argument on that front from me," Lady Matlock concurred. "We encourage her to practice and explore her passion, although I doubt our urging is necessary. I have seen her lost for hours at the pianoforte with the only 'encouragement' required a reminder for her to eat and drink."

"Miss Darcy's bashfulness is charming. I believe, as you noted, Lady Matlock, that she will conquer her reticence in due time. I sense a firmness and fire within her, which emerges when necessary and will grow as she leaves youth behind."

"I agree. Most astute of you to deduce after so little time in her company, Miss Bennet."

Elizabeth flushed at Lady Matlock's praise. "After passing the whole afternoon together, I noted similarities between Miss Darcy and my sister. Jane is quite reserved but possesses a strong spirit. The comparison is the extent of my astuteness."

"It is impressive nevertheless," the countess countered in a tone of finality.

"Then, if I may be so bold, perhaps it will please you to hear that she was the consummate hostess, of which she gave you the praise and credit. Her shyness disappeared. In fact, she kept us on our toes with her humor and excellent storytelling skills. There was nary a dull moment."

Lady Matlock was studying Elizabeth. "Now that I have met you myself, Miss Bennet, I can readily comprehend what my son"—Lady Matlock indicated Colonel Fitzwilliam with a loving glance—"meant in claiming you would be good for Georgiana."

Darcy's soul rejoiced at the approval in his aunt's eyes and tone. He knew he must have been beaming, based on the sensations swelling within his chest.

Elizabeth's rosiness increased. "I only pray to be a sister to her, my lady. Love and friendship reap bountiful harvests for all involved. In Miss Darcy's case, it is my pleasure, and I am blessed."

"Very well said. I agree one hundred percent." Lady Matlock smiled and then resumed eating.

The ladies chatter returned to shopping, with Lady Matlock and Priscilla Fitzwilliam heaping advice on the best shops for lace, flowers, clothing, edible delicacies, and more. As captivating as it was to observe the woman he loved forge a bond with his favored aunt, the subject matter was far down Darcy's list of interests.

Fortunately, Colonel Fitzwilliam inquired about his previous evening's appointment at the Jockey Club. A conversation on horse racing and thoroughbred breeding was much more to his liking. With Mr. Bennet, Lord Matlock, and Jonathan Fitzwilliam contributing, the remaining hour passed swiftly.

As they rose from the table, Darcy touched Elizabeth on the elbow, drawing her slightly to the side. "Before I leave you for the obligatory separation of the sexes, I wanted to tell you how proud I am, Elizabeth. You have utterly dazzled my entire family."

"Thank you, William. Although, let's be honest—is it truly possible to 'dazzle' Mr. and Mrs. Fitzwilliam? You know them better than I, so perhaps their bedazzlement is expressed in ways too subtle for my perception."

Laughing lowly, Darcy grabbed one of her hands. "My love, the desire to kiss your beautiful mouth is fairly overwhelming at present. It is taking a monumental effort, but I can resist the urge, provided I settle for a kiss to your hand."

When the men rejoined the ladies in the parlor an hour later, Mrs. Fitzwilliam was playing the pianoforte while Lady Matlock and Elizabeth were deep conversation on the sofa. The older woman was speaking of Derbyshire and the Matlock area she called home, and Elizabeth was listening intently. She was so engrossed, in fact, that she greeted Darcy with a quick smile and immediately turned her attention back to the countess.

"You speak so fondly of Derbyshire, my lady. Are you originally from the region?"

"No, Miss Bennet. My familial roots are Welsh and English, with estate lands near Shrewsbury and Rhayader in Powys. I married Lord Matlock and settled at Rivallain as a new bride. The countryside is vastly different, yet I soon fell in love."

"I have traveled minimally outside of Hertfordshire, so can only imagine the differences based on what I have seen on canvas or described in books."

Elizabeth's tone was wistful. Lady Matlock patted her hand and looked upward at Darcy. "In due course, you will visit much of the country. William is fond of travel, although not as fond as he is of staying at Pemberley."

"With a home as beautiful as Pemberley, I can understand."

Eyes widening in amazement, the countess exclaimed, "You have seen Pemberley? I was not aware! When was this?"

"In August," Darcy answered for her. "Divine providence brought Miss Bennet, along with her aunt and uncle, to my very doorstep."

"That is an accurate account," Elizabeth laughed, her gaze sharing in the joke with him. "Mr. and Mrs. Gardiner asked me to accompany them on a trip to the Lake District. At the last minute their plans changed, so we traveled to the closer Derbyshire instead. My aunt lived near Lambton when she was young, you see. Naturally, the draw to tour Pemberley was immense."

"I do believe the draw of the estate's fishing ponds were the enticement for Mr. Gardiner," Darcy teased.

"And I was drawn to the famed Pemberley library I had heard so much about from Mr. Bingley. It may well be that I fell in love with the library before its owner."

"Perfectly understandable." Lord Matlock intoned from the massive chair where he sat beside Mr. Bennet.

Mr. Bennet raised his glass toward the earl in an agreeing gesture, then addressed his daughter. "You also traveled to Kent. A most enlightening experience, I have gathered."

For the span of several heartbeats, both Darcy and Elizabeth froze. They exchanged an alarmed look, followed by Elizabeth shakily giggling. "I almost forgot. Thank you, Papa. Kent and Derbyshire I can boast, although neither holiday was extensive or involved high adventure. Is this sufficient to qualify me as being well travelled with worldly sophistication?"

"Perhaps not according to some," Lady Matlock amusingly admitted. "However, take heart, Miss Bennet. You have an advantage many new brides do not have, including me at the time. You have been to Pemberley, whereas I had never laid eyes on Rivallain. Who knew if the library was worth my leap of faith?"

Lord Matlock's eyes rested upon his wife, his countenance atypically unguarded to reveal his great affection for the countess. "Alas, the library at Rivallain does not rival that at Pemberley. I suppose this means I had only my attributes to recommend."

In response, her eyes as emotive, Lady Matlock disclosed, "Rivallain was overwhelming to me. Fortunately, I married a marvelous man who aided my adaptation to a new environment. Mr. Darcy shall do the same for you, I am confident—"

"Indeed I shall," Darcy inserted firmly.

"—but if he does not, alert me and I will take care of it." Lady Matlock peered at her nephew with a mischievous smile.

The colonel released a loud guffaw. "Trust me, Miss Bennet, if my mother says she will 'take care' of something, you can bet it will be done, painfully if necessary! You are warned, Cousin."

The other three listening gentlemen contributed their chuckles, but Darcy ignored them. Instead, he focused on the grinning colonel. "I shall heed the warning, Cousin, trusting your claim comes with a wealth of personal knowledge, considering how often your poor mother was forced to administer discipline."

Richard grunted, but did not deny the charge. Then, bowing in his aunt's direction, Darcy promised, "I vow to be extra cautious and diligent to my wife, your ladyship, giving you no cause to reprimand."

"Wise." Lord Matlock nodded sagely. "Very wise."

Lady Matlock also nodded firmly. Then she turned to Elizabeth. "In all seriousness, Miss Bennet, you have no cause to worry. Pemberley may seem imposing, but the Darcys have made it a home.

William is the soul of patience and kindness. I assure you, you will be most happy there."

"Thank you. I do not doubt that Mr. Darcy will lead me gently."

Colonel Fitzwilliam, wearing a sportive grin, contemplated his cousin. "Indeed, Mr. Darcy is patience personified, as all can attest. Even his horses declare it so!"

"Sadly, a lesson I could never impart to you, Richard. Your horses habitually choose to throw you rather than listen to instruction."

"That happened *one* time, I was fifteen, and the horse refused to jump that creek!" Richard turned to Elizabeth, pointing at Darcy with his thumb. "This braggart was twelve, rode a horse larger than mine, and jumped cleanly over the creek without hesitation." He shook his head in mock dismay, then groaned dramatically. "Very well, I concede. You are the superior horseman. Just never forget that I trump you at dancing and witty conversation!"

Lady Matlock said, "Miss Bennet, you have now seen what shall henceforth torment your existence whenever these two inhabit the same room. Their supreme entertainment since childhood is in baiting the other. Presumably, it will continue into their senility. God help us all."

"I only relate the truth Miss Bennet already knows, having confessed to me the dreadfulness of William's dancing and conversation in Hertfordshire."

"Colonel! You tease as well as color the truth," Elizabeth laughingly accused. "I said Mr. Darcy *refused* to dance, not that he danced poorly. He proved his skill at the Netherfield Ball, dancing with the grace of a gazelle."

"Grace of a gazelle? High praise indeed. Is this true, Darcy?" Lord Matlock grinned up at Darcy, who was now the center of attention. Even Mrs. Fitzwilliam had stopped playing and was watching him with an amused gleam in her eyes.

Darcy coughed. He felt heat flooding his cheeks, but Elizabeth's gay expression relieved his embarrassment. "Miss Bennet is generous, as always. I managed to avoid stepping on her feet and making a total fool of myself. In my particular case, it remains fortunate that dancing proficiency and engaging repartee are not the only inducements to affection."

"Quite so," Jonathan Fitzwilliam agreed. "I abhor dancing and socializing more than you, Darcy, and that is saying something, yet my wife tolerates me. One's beguilements and personality can be hidden secrets for only select individuals to divine."

"I concur, Mr. Fitzwilliam. Thank you." Elizabeth bowed her head gratefully—Mr. Fitzwilliam inclined his head to acknowledge— and then swung her eyes back to Darcy. Again wearing the secret smile imbued with love, she spoke in a hushed pitch that somehow grabbed attention better than if she shouted. "Some people are rather like a fine bottle of aged red wine. The cork must first be removed. The wine is then poured and allowed time to breathe. One must wait patiently for the aroma to rise and captivate those who wish to partake of its delights. The wine warms in the glass, aided by the touch of a hand, as the flavor softens and mellows. Slowly, gradually, the wine's true essence is exposed." She paused, adoring eyes locked onto Darcy's. Concluding in a whisper, "Some people are structured so, and they are abundantly worth the wait."

Everyone in the room was mesmerized by her impromptu speech. For at least a minute, the only sound was the ticking of the mantel clock.

"Superbly spoken, Miss Bennet." Lady Matlock's murmured comment broke the spell. Darcy could not pull his eyes away from Elizabeth but peripherally noticed the pointed non-verbal exchange between his aunt and uncle.

In time the evening came to an end. As Elizabeth was retrieving her redingote from the footman while talking with Lady Matlock, Darcy and Lord Matlock casually stepped a bit away.

"I like her, my boy, enormously. There is absolutely no question that she loves you. Her father is a gentleman, intelligent and humorous. Both have impeccable manners. I can find no faults."

"Thank you, sir. Your opinion means a great deal to me."

Lord Matlock's eyes narrowed as he peered intently at his nephew. Cocking his head, he asked, "What would you say if I did not approve? She is, after all, manners notwithstanding, not quite in your class. What if I agree with your Aunt Catherine?"

Meeting his uncle's gaze with the same intensity, Darcy answered, "Sir, it would grieve me, as I grieve over Lady Catherine's attitude. However, my choices are just that. Mine. Elizabeth is my life. I am nothing without her."

"And Pemberley?"

"My lord, I understand what you are asking and why. All my adult life I have placed Pemberley's needs before my own. I believe I have been a worthy Master of Pemberley and that I carry the Darcy name proudly. Years have I searched for a woman of quality, someone strong and brave, intelligent and wise, empathetic and giving. All the characteristics the Mistress of Pemberley must have. I am not a blind fool, Uncle. Elizabeth possesses these attributes, amongst a host of others. I have fallen in love with a woman my equal, if not superior. As remarkable as all of this, it is inconsequential compared to the fact that she loves me. Her paramount value to me, and to Pemberley, is in this truth."

The warmth and emotion in Lord Matlock's voice were more than Darcy could have hoped. "Your father would be very proud of you, Fitzwilliam, as would your mother. James and Anne loved each other, as you know. It is an emotion uncommon in our society, sadly. They were better human beings because of it, and Pemberley thrived. I do approve of your Miss Bennet, wholeheartedly. You have my approval and blessing…for what *that* is worth."

The earl clapped Darcy on the shoulder as the two turned around. Instantly, Darcy's eyes veered to where Elizabeth had last been standing, but to his surprise, she was a mere three feet away. A rosy blush covered her cheeks, and she ducked her head, but not swiftly enough for him to miss seeing the moisture in her eyes.

She was eavesdropping. Rather than feeling irritation, Darcy wanted to laugh aloud.

Instead, he crossed the short distance and clasped both hands. "Are you well, my dearest? You are flushed. Have we overtaxed your strength tonight?"

"Tease," she mumbled, staring at her toes. "You caught me listening, I know it." Lifting her eyes, she smiled. "Guilty as charged, I confess. Now it is I who wants to kiss you. Desperately. You had to suffice with my hands, but I shall toss caution to the wind." Rising onto her tiptoes, she pressed her lips firmly and lingeringly against his cheek. Then, while still inches away from his face, she breathed, "I love you. With all my heart and for eternity."

He was so startled and overwhelmed that she had pivoted about and was nearly to the door before he recovered.

6

CAPITAL EXPLORATION

*T*rue to his promise, Mr. Darcy partnered with Mr. Bingley to escort Miss Elizabeth and Miss Bennet for one whole day of blissful togetherness.

The enormity of London prevented a comprehensive exploration within a day, no matter how long they stretched the hours. When asked for sightseeing preferences, Lizzy and Jane declined to offer any guidance. They contentedly announced that whatever the gentlemen decided would be fantastic. As nice as it was to be trusted implicitly, neither lady realized how challenging the task was for their eager-to-please fiancés.

For over an hour Darcy and Bingley deliberated over which places provided the highest intrigue and entertainment, while also being best suited to the personalities and interests of their respective ladies. They also considered which were open for public viewing on a Thursday and possible to adequately canvas in a few hours.

The last two stipulations eliminated several options immediately, yet the list remained long. It came down to bargaining and veto power.

Darcy began by voting for the British Museum, knowing Elizabeth would adore the wealth of history and ancient artifacts. Bingley yawned at the very mention of a museum, effectively striking off a half dozen similar destinations Darcy had as alternatives. Bingley favored visiting an art exhibition and specifically mentioned his favorite: the Society of Painters in Watercolours. Darcy adored art and could understand Bingley's desire since Jane painted in both oils and watercolors. Elizabeth, however, while appreciative of art, was not a talented artist or passionate about the subject. Using his veto, Darcy crossed artistic options off the shrinking list. Turning again to historic places, Darcy proposed Old Bailey and Newgate. Leaving no doubt as to his vote, Bingley dramatically rolled his eyes before pretending to fall asleep, loud snores included for emphasis.

Swinging the other direction, Bingley suggested Astley's Amphitheatre, the Royal Menagerie, or the horse races. All of these options and others of a similar bent were favorable for the excitement aspects to be sure. They analyzed each at length, yet the more they discussed the pros and cons, the prevailing negative was the noise and potential for large crowds. Indeed, it was long past the height of the Season, but London never completely emptied or slowed down, particularly at the prime spots for lively entertainment. Escorting their beloveds to places teeming with overzealous people crammed into tight spaces with enclosed animals resulting in swirling dust and odiferous stenches did not appeal.

These were the sensible excuses to avoid the popular London destinations, of which both gentlemen concurred. What Darcy did not add to the argument were his fears of Elizabeth encountering those amongst high society. Cognizant of how gossip circulated faster than lightning, the odds of meeting a single person ignorant of the rumblings spread by Lady Catherine were not in his favor. Staying away from the choicest areas people of his class frequented decreased the chances of overhearing whispers or being boldly confronted. Frankly, since his precipitous offer made in the carriage on the way to the Matlock townhouse, Darcy had mentally cursed himself as a fool dozens of times.

It figures that the one occasion I behave spontaneously may well prove the importance of regulated speech and careful forethought!

At this point in the planning process, Bingley reminded Darcy that the day of exploration was born out of Elizabeth's interest in Saint James's Palace. True enough, Darcy admitted, whereupon Bingley suggested driving around town to view all the grand palaces, stately mansions, and other noteworthy buildings. Darcy was aware that Bingley's rationale in this idea was to stare at his "angel" Jane from his carriage seat across from her—understandable to a degree as Darcy could easily stare at Elizabeth for hours on end—but the prospect of being confined to a vehicle fighting traffic all day sounded more nightmarish than fun.

Darcy countered with a compromise to launch the expedition at the palace and limit the visit to two or three of the historic locales London had to offer. Bingley reluctantly conceded, the debate then turning to which two or three. By the end of the session—with several brandies consumed—they settled on a flexible itinerary of places located within a reasonable proximity of the palace to save travel time and allow leisurely strolling while exploring.

Lastly, at Darcy's suggestion, Georgiana was enlisted to play the part of chaperone. His reasoning was admittedly multifaceted. For one, he sensed that poor Mrs. Gardiner was exhausted—although she would likely never admit to it. A day of rest was much needed and deserved. Using the pretext of desiring his sister to spend time with Miss Elizabeth and Miss Bennet, and elaborating her yearning to explore the city, Darcy convinced Mrs. Gardiner to relinquish her self-assigned role. What Darcy also suspected, not that he would verbalize the bonus reason, is that Georgiana would be even laxer as a monitor than Mrs. Gardiner often was.

While Mrs. Gardiner as chaperone purposefully turned a blind eye to the sly caresses and brushing kisses the lovers shared,

Georgiana would be innocently oblivious to most furtive demonstrations of affection. Those she did notice would either make her smile happily or blush, with scolding never crossing her mind. Undoubtedly, the Gardiners and Mr. Bennet were aware of this fact, but thankfully no one argued over the idea. As both gentlemen eventually discovered, the change in chaperone was supremely beneficial.

⁓

*M*r. Darcy and Miss Darcy arrived at the Bingley townhouse near Berkeley Square bright and early that Thursday morning. Already transported via the Gardiner carriage, the Bennet sisters were waiting with Mr. Bingley. After a hearty breakfast, the group of five was ready to begin their day. The temperature was cool, as typical for late in October, but the sun shone brightly with few clouds to obstruct, and there was no wind, allowing the landau hood to be folded down. The coachman slapped the reins as soon as they seated comfortably, and off they went.

Mr. Bingley interrupted the gay chatter a few minutes later, just as the driver turned onto the main street past the townhouse. "So, here we are, in the carriage, heading south on Bond Street toward Piccadilly. Now, I wonder if our two clever ladies have deduced our immediate destination?" His question met with neutral expressions, placid smiles, and no verbalized replies. Grinning, he continued, "The next question is, do we enlighten you as to the day's activities? Or do you wish to remain in the dark? What do you think, Darcy?"

"I am entirely at the pleasure of our ladies. It shall be a test as to how fully they delight in being surprised, or if mysteries are a cause of displeasure. Such information may well prove useful in the future."

Darcy's reply to Bingley's question was delivered while holding Lizzy's gaze, his eyes sparkling with mirth. Smiling, she responded, "I am willing to play the game of mystery, noble sirs. After all, I heard a tale of excessive, dramatic plotting and scheming for this one small day of adventure"—Georgiana's flush and averted eyes revealed where that information came from—"so I could not live with my guilt-ridden conscience if we spoiled a single moment."

"Nor could I," Jane agreed in her soft voice. "Additionally, it may be fun to see just how clever we truly are, by gleaning hints along the way."

"Oh yes! A guessing game! What a great idea, Jane." Lizzy patted her sister's hand. "We shall see how well Mr. Darcy and Mr. Bingley can keep secrets and maintain the suspense. Who shall break first? Can we successfully read their thoughts, or will they slip? Who will win the prizes, them or us?"

"If one or both of you make a correct guess, what do you want your prize to be?"

"A kiss!" Georgiana's blurted suggestion to Bingley's question elicited laughter and a few blushes, although not enough to quell the gaiety.

"A fair prize indeed, dear Sister. That way both parties win, no matter what. Now, as neither lovely lady has voiced a guess of our destination, and we are here"—Darcy pointed in the direction over the women's shoulders—"that means the first-round score goes to the gentlemen."

Twisting in their seats, Jane gasped. "I did not realize your townhouse is so close to the palace, Mr. Bingley. We could have walked and saved the horses."

"A trick, Jane, to maintain the mystery," Lizzy said. "Take the carriage to insinuate a long trip. Oh so sneaky, Mr. Darcy."

Chuckling, Darcy countered Lizzy's teasing assertion. "I wish I could claim foresight and deviousness, Miss Elizabeth. Alas, we were merely saving our ladies' feet at the outset of a long day. Additionally, we will require the carriage throughout the day. Besides, the game was a recent challenge, was it not?"

"Very true, I admit," Lizzy murmured, her eyes on the palace.

"The gauntlet tossed recently or not, we shall not forget the win is ours."

Jane turned around to meet Mr. Bingley's eyes, her cheeks rosy. "The count has begun, sir. However, if I may suggest, perhaps it is best to mentally store the tally and save for a future time of privacy to collect?"

Laughingly agreeing that this was indeed a logical choice—no one stating aloud that it was also beneficial to ensure the kisses were more than chaste cheek pecks—the group gave their full attention to the looming redbrick gatehouse and crenelated turrets of Saint James's Palace. The carriage slowed to a crawl, pedestrians and wheeled vehicles crowding the terminal end of the street bearing the royal residence's name where it abutted Pall Mall. Darcy instructed the coachman to halt, and the small group disembarked onto the cobblestoned walkway.

As Mr. Darcy and Mr. Bingley conversed quietly with the driver, Lizzy, lost in admiration of the palace, stepped away from her sister and Georgiana. She did not hear Mr. Darcy approach, jolting when he spoke from close behind her right shoulder.

"Do not be ashamed if your opinion of Saint James's Palace is less than favorable, Elizabeth. You would not be the first person to lay fresh eyes upon the palace and note its appearance as rather mundane, particularly in comparison to royal castles on the Continent."

"I can't argue from the standpoint of comparing to the elaborate palaces of France or Germany, at least based on paintings I've seen. But we have our history to be proud of, which transcends grandeur or opulent construction. I rather like that we are a country of understated aesthetics."

"I agree, although I doubt anyone would deem baroque or gothic as 'understated' design aesthetics. My knowledge of architecture is minimal yet enough to comprehend the superb Tudor styling of Saint James's Palace. The designers and engineers employed by King

Henry built a solid structure expressing the artistic philosophy of the mid-sixteenth century. Thankfully, with few exceptions, subsequent additions and repairs, such as after the horrific fire seven years ago, have maintained the Tudor influence."

"Yes, they have. It is precisely like the paintings and etchings I've seen. And, now that I am here, I believe my father took us past the palace when I was too young to appreciate the significance. It is a hazy memory. In any case, I am not disappointed."

Before more could be said, Mr. Bingley, with a sunny Jane holding his arm, drew alongside. Flipping open his pocket watch, he lifted it up for Darcy to see, and both men nodded.

"More mysteries, Mr. Darcy? Are we on a tight schedule?"

"Only for the present, Miss Elizabeth." Darcy offered one arm to his fiancée and the other to his sister, both ladies accepting. Following behind Bingley and Jane, he clarified in a pitch loud enough for the duo to hear, "We have fifteen minutes to elbow our way through the loitering onlookers and costermongers taking advantage of the event to sell their wares. By eleven o'clock promptly, we must be in place."

"Is guessing the event part of the challenge, Brother? I would hate for either Miss Bennet or Miss Elizabeth to miss an opportunity to secure a win."

"My, aren't you the cheeky imp today!" Darcy laughed at his sister's belated flush. "The question is a valid one, however. Should we allow a guess, Bingley?"

Before Mr. Bingley could answer, however, Lizzy proclaimed with mock imperiousness, "I shall claim ignorance. Whether true or feigned to swell your confidence and lead to further slips of the tongue, I shall not say."

"An interesting tactic, Lizzy," Jane tossed over her shoulder, "but since I know a fact of history to boast of, a rarity for me, I shall make a guess. At eleven o'clock is the Changing of the Guard Colour Ceremony. Am I correct?"

"Ha! The score is even! One kiss for the gentlemen, and one for the ladies. Well done, my dear Miss Bennet."

Lizzy could only see a portion of Mr. Bingley's face as he gazed upon her sister, but the adoration was easily discernible. Smiling, she squeezed Darcy's arm tighter against her side, using the excuse of another pedestrian for the improper closeness. Their adventure was just beginning, yet already it was marvelous!

"This is also Georgiana's first experience watching the Changing of the Guard ceremony," Darcy informed them, as they crossed the active intersection. "Thus, it is an occasion worthy of making special arrangements. Come!"

Walking briskly with a spring in his step, he led them directly to the main gate, above which an enormous triangular clock hung, marking the approaching eleven o'clock hour. Pausing only to release the light grip of feminine hands on his arms, Darcy stepped to a smaller portal to the left of the gate and spoke to the sentry inside. A few moments later, he gestured to the others, and together they entered through the opened gateway into a high-vaulted and arched tunnel with white plastered walls.

The armed guard who escorted them did not utter a single word, nor did the two stoic, immobile guards stationed on either side of the gaping entry. They may have been silent and impassive in appearance, yet no one doubted their alertness or capability to respond swiftly, and brutally if necessary, to any threat. It was a fact both comforting and unnerving, something Lizzy realized she was not alone in feeling when a trembling Georgiana pressed closer to her side.

Fortunately, the tunnel was lit with oil lamps, even in daytime, and not exceedingly long. The expansive courtyard beyond was readily visible, brilliant sunlight shining onto the gray-stone covered ground. Their escort wordlessly indicated the covered colonnade to their right, the wide sheltered piazza spanning the entire western wall of the courtyard. Some two dozen spectators were already present, a few politely greeting the new arrivals as they filled the gap between two of the thick pillars supporting the roof. There were no barricades preventing crossing onto the vacant courtyard, yet instinctively everyone knew to stay behind the pillars. Furthermore, while not completely silent, those who talked did so in soft tones barely above a whisper, including Mr. Darcy, who stood between Lizzy and Georgiana and bent slightly before launching into a murmured commentary.

"On the off-chance my sister's costly education has excluded this section of our history..." He paused to flash an amused grin her direction. "...allow me to elucidate on a few facts as we wait. First, we are standing in the Colour Court of Saint James's Palace, so named due to the ceremony we are about to witness wherein the regimental flags, known as 'colours' are exchanged. It is necessary to note that while formal, as all such procedures are, the purpose of the guard change ceremony is of vital importance. In brief, the old guard is being replaced by the new guard, that is the regimental troops incoming for the next twenty-four hours. Ah, here they come now."

Indeed, a line of guards was entering the courtyard via a corner archway. The only sound the rhythmic clap of booted heels on stone, they marched in a single file until standing in an exact square formation evenly spaced to cover roughly half of the open area.

As they marched in, Darcy again bent to deliver a hushed history lesson, as several others amongst the crowd were also doing. "The foot guard regiments that form the household division date to the 1660 restoration of Charles II to the throne, and, in fact, a bit before that, when he raised them while in exile. These designated troops have guarded the sovereign, the royal palaces, and other important places for nearly two hundred years. There are three or perhaps four regiments in the infantry—"

"Wait," Georgiana interrupted, a teasing lilt to her voice, "is there a fact my learned brother is unsure of? Say it is not so!"

"I confess my military knowledge is incomplete. I leave that field to your cousin, Colonel Fitzwilliam. Of course, now that you point it out, a dearth in education is a tragedy which should never be allowed to remain unchecked. Perhaps we should enter into a comprehensive course of study on military history, tactics, and ceremonies. We might as well include the major wars and battles also. How does that sound, Miss Darcy?"

His expression was utterly serious, his brow arched and lips stern, as he gazed down at his no-longer-jolly sister. Even Lizzy was unsure how much of his statement was a jest. Then, just when nearly all color had drained from Georgiana's face, a smile broke and he laughed. Tweaking her nose, he said, "I'll spare you the torture of severe lessons, my dear. I do, after all, have much better things to do with my time in the months ahead."

He glanced at Lizzy, warmth and renewed humor lighting his countenance. "However, if I may continue with the miniature history lesson, without further impertinent interruptions?" Georgiana hastily and vigorously bobbed her head. "I am *fairly sure* there are three foot-guard regiments in the household division. The Grenadier, Coldstream, and Scots regiments. There are also the household cavalry regiments, but we won't see those guards here today.

"Now, these regimental soldiers perform many duties, including fighting in times of war, but will always have a portion in London, or wherever the monarch and royal family members are. The primary royal residence was the Palace of Whitehall, of course, until a fire destroyed the bulk of it in 1689. Upon establishing the official royal residence here, the foot guards transitioned here as well, but the processional we are about to see has remained largely unchanged. Now, listen."

At that exact moment, the bell tower clock struck the eleventh hour, the clangs initially drowning out the sound of music growing louder. The enormous black doors of solid oak and metal marking the main entrance to the palace, which they had so recently passed by to access the Colour Court, were thrown open. The sounds of instruments and marching feet echoed down the tunnel, reaching the excited spectators long before they could see anything.

"The new guard musters in Friary Court, located to the south, on the other side of that building." Darcy pointed to the three-story high, red brick wing to the right of where they stood. "They march up the alley, past Marlborough House, around the corner, and along Pall Mall before entering through the main gate. They are, as you can now see, led by a contingency of the Coldstream Guards Regimental Band."

Indeed, all the spectators could now see the leader of the parade. Lizzy's breath caught as others released gasps and exclamations of awed enthusiasm for his august presence, as well as the personages immediately behind him.

The drum major wore a stunning uniform of scarlet and gold, his chapeau decorated with a profusion of feathers. Behind, in timed-step, were four musicians of African heritage, two with tambourines and two with cymbals. Exotic faces with skin and eyes black as night, they wore magnificent Turkish costumes of white and silver with billowing muslin trousers, vests in scarlet velvet adorned with fringe and tassels, and white muslin turbans festooned with red plumes and jewels.

The quality of their performance was equally as impressive as their appearance. While not a musical aficionado, Lizzy had seen enough minstrels and orchestras in her life to recognize something special was happening before her awestruck eyes.

The ability to play an instrument with skill was an essential factor that lifted one artist above another. However, transcendent mastery meant instrumental excellence in conjunction with an exceptional flair for performance. The Coldstream band was irrefutably in this category.

The tambourine players, for example, did not merely hit their hands onto the flat surface, but also rolled their fingers over the parchment and flicked the bells in varied tempos, all while whirling the instrument around and even tossing it into the air. Similarly, the cymbals of silver—polished bright as mirrors to catch the sunbeams and add glittering sparkles with each strike—were flourished side to side and above the musicians' heads. The quartet capered rather than marched, and their agility with fingers, arms, and legs was timed to the music.

"I have read of the Janissary percussionists," Lizzy whispered. "Introduced by the Duke of York some two decades ago, yes?"

"Correct," Darcy whispered into her ear. "For the guard change ceremony there are only a few, usually just two, so we are fortunate today. Someday, perhaps next spring when in Town for the season, we shall observe the Horse Guards' Parade, Trooping the Colour, or another performance with the household guards. Then you will witness the full complement of musicians. It is a sight to behold."

Lizzy could not fathom it and for the present just wanted to relish the extraordinary experience fast unfolding in the courtyard. The rousing martial song was accompanied by musicians playing bugles, trumpets, bassoons, oboes, and an assortment of drums. While marching in a proper formation and lacking the tricks employed by the fantastical percussionists, the artists were every bit as outstanding musically.

As breathtaking as they were, the band served the express purpose of setting the beat for the march of the Household Division of the King's Guards. The regimental soldiers, two abreast, trailed behind the musicians. Dressed in vividly scarlet coats, bleached white breeches and gaiters over glossy black boots, and tall, bearskin, plumed hats, they marched out of the arched portal in perfect configuration, bayonetted muskets held against their shoulders. As with the band led by a drum major, the guard was led by the commanding officer. The sun glinted off the mass of medals pinned to his broad chest and the gold tips of the lance he swung in time to the music's beat. This was the new guard, as Darcy had informed them, although aside from the slight differences in uniform and banner color, the men were as alert and rigidly postured as the soon-to-be-relieved old guard waiting patiently in the courtyard.

The newcomers lined up facing the outgoing guards, their square formation an exact duplication. The Coldstream Band had marched to the north wall of the Colour Court, standing nearest to the gateway tunnel, and continued to play for an additional fifteen minutes. Then, abruptly and with a crashing crescendo, the music ended.

Into the gradually receding musical echoes, brisk shouts of formal greeting and declaration burst forth from the lips of the two commanding officers. Saluting with their rifles, the captain of the old guard then stiffly extended his arm, the key to the palace gripped tight in his hand. The captain of the new guard grasped onto the key, his hold firm and secure, and only then was the key relinquished. Upon completion of this symbolic gesture, the transfer of responsibility for the palace's security, and by extension the safety of the reigning monarchy and royal family, was fulfilled.

The entire ceremony was conducted as if not a soul were around except for the musicians and guards themselves. Not a one of them glanced aside or acknowledged the existence of the witnesses. The soldiers of the new guard remained in a rigid pose until the old guard passed through the gates and out of sight, with the military band now trailing behind. In crisp military posture, the new guard scattered to their assigned stations surrounding the gate and elsewhere within and without the palace compound.

The awed spectators murmured if they spoke at all, and slowly moved through the tunnel and past the gate. Once outside, they joined the crowds who had watched the processional from the street. Darcy and Bingley subtly drew the ladies aside, close to the outer wall of the palace, allowing the people to disperse in varying directions rather than fight the press of bodies.

Finally breathing normally, Lizzy squeezed Darcy's arm to gain his attention, and then asked, "How is it that we were able to watch from inside the palace when so many were outside? Do they not know it is possible to come inside?"

Surprisingly, he appeared faintly embarrassed and stammered as he answered. "The guard is…particular in whom they allow inside. One has to be, approved, shall we say." At her confused expression, he sighed, then explained, "I made advanced arrangements, once Bingley and I decided on our agenda. It pays to have family in the aristocracy, upon occasion, at least."

"Oh! I see. Well, this time, *at least*," Lizzy laughed, "I am quite happy your relatives are lords and ladies. It was truly a phenomenal experience I shall never forget. A wonderful start to the day, perfect to inspire patriotism and pique interest in exploring more of the city's fascinating history. Thank you, William."

As Mr. Darcy would prove over and over during that day, his knowledge of London and English history was profound. It was somewhat daunting, in all honesty, to recognize the breadth of his education and the deftness of his mind. His ability to retrieve statistics, dates, and concise answers to nearly every question she asked was frankly mind-boggling.

Riveted to every word, Lizzy's respect for his intellect increased massively. Bingley, Jane, and Georgiana, conversely, often assumed the glazed, blank eyes of people fighting to appear interested.

In short order, the crowds cleared until average street traffic and pedestrians were all that remained. It was then that the women noticed Mr. Bingley's landau waiting next to the curb not far from where they had disembarked, only now facing east on Pall Mall

Whether designed for honest exploration or to cause disorientation, the subsequent thirty-minute circuitous ride was enjoyed by all. At a loss as to the carriage's destination, Jane and Lizzy accepted defeat in the guessing challenge for the next round. Instead, they studied the passing scenery and listened to Mr. Darcy's history lectures and fascinating insights.

"Charing Cross, the relatively open space where Pall Mall,

Whitehall, and the Strand meet, derives from the ancient village named Charing. It was a resting place between London and Westminster once upon a time, and indeed, there was an enormous cross built here by Edward I. Removed in 1647, according to records, the stones were used to pave the front of Whitehall Palace. Before removing the cross, the statue of Charles I was erected nearby."

As he spoke, the carriage turned right onto Cockspur Street. The bronze statue of King Charles I mounted on horseback rose high into the sky atop a pedestal of stone. Lizzy knew the history of the English civil wars leading to the abolishment of the monarchy and the king's execution in 1649, as well as how the statue was hidden away for nearly thirty years until miraculously being "found" after the restoration of Charles II to the throne. Regardless of her knowledge, it was a delight to listen to William's resonant voice as he recounted the dry facts of history, mingling then with humorous anecdotes and intriguing minutiae, and delivering it all with a storyteller's flair she hadn't expected.

The coachman, directed by Mr. Bingley, parked the carriage near the corner of Cockspur and Whitehall. From their comfortable seats, they could leisurely inspect the impressive statue and rows of handsome buildings fronting the bustling intersection. Darcy and Bingley took turns pointing out the various businesses and residences, such as Northumberland House, but of particular importance to Darcy was the Royal Mews.

"The current building houses the horses which belong personally to the king and prince regent. As such, it should more appropriately be called the Royal Stables. However, as the original area and structures were for the falcons and hawks kept by the monarchy for the sport of falconry, from as early as 1377, the term *mews* has remained. How I wish they were still intact and able to be seen with my own eyes."

His timbre carried a note of reverence Lizzy had never detected before, and his eyes glowed. Not until after they were married would she learn of his passion for falconry and the mews at Pemberley. At present it was a mystery to file away, the tour commencing with a sudden snap of the reins driving them back into the traffic heading east on the Strand.

Passing by the Savoy and Somerset House, Darcy and Bingley shared the history and personal perspectives of both. Moments later, the carriage turned left onto a narrow, unnamed street. This diverting was followed by a series of left and right turns, Lizzy struggling in vain to reconcile their location with the vague map of London in her mind. Thus far, the ladies were losing the guessing game. Not that they would truly be losers in the end, of course. Nevertheless, there was an element of pride attached.

"Are we to shop at Covent Garden, then?"

Jane's query was asked in such a calm, indifferent tone that, for a whole minute, no one said a word. Naturally, it was Mr. Bingley who rallied first.

"Outstanding, Miss Bennet! See that, Darcy? I knew we could not fool them."

"I am sincerely impressed," Darcy admitted. "Indeed, Miss Bennet, we are nearing Covent Garden."

Piping up from her cozy spot between Jane and Lizzy, Georgiana implored, "Praise God, a place to find food. I am famished!"

"I fail to see how you could be 'famished' so soon after breakfast, Sister dear, but you are correct that we did have the idea of a light snack of fresh fruit or whatever looks appetizing, with a beverage to quench our thirst."

For over an hour they explored the vast square containing rows of stalls selling fruits and vegetables, as well as the endless varieties of flowers the market was famous for. Darcy offered tidbits of history in between buying anything Lizzy or Georgiana showed the faintest interest in. As for the purchasing, Lizzy's embarrassment over his inexhaustible generosity slowly faded, primarily due to Georgiana, who was accustomed to her brother obtaining anything she wanted, so she didn't bat an eyelash. As for the history, while frequently interrupted and often difficult to hear over the clamor, Lizzy soaked it in, along with the exhilarating sights, sounds, and smells.

"The Earl of Bedford hired architect Inigo Jones to create an organized layout for the market. I believe that was somewhere in the second or third decade of the seventeenth century. Jones's design included the piazza you see along two sides of the square, the graveled central courtyard itself, terraces of impressive houses ringing the square, and Saint Paul's Church." Darcy indicated the colonnaded, distinctly Romanesque building in the precise center of the western side. "It holds the distinction of being the first new church built in London after the Reformation. Jones was inspired by Italian architecture, hence the Tuscan porticos and raised arcade. Fire has damaged the church once or twice, with reconstruction undoubtedly altering the original design, but it is still impressive."

"The whole square is quite lovely," Lizzy said. "I suppose it is unfair to compare a famed, city marketplace with the ramshackle, country equivalents I am familiar with. Covent Garden is a pleasant surprise."

"The Earl of Bedford was forward thinking, a trait I admire. Sometimes we forget that London was not always the modern metropolis which now surrounds us. In the era of Henry VIII, the lands separating the boroughs of London and Westminster were considerable. Vast acres of orchards, gardens, meadows, and farming connected to Westminster Abbey's Benedictine monastery. It is the latter wherein the name comes from, *covent* being an etymological derivative of the Latin and the ancient French words for a religious house. That random information aside, even a hundred years after King Henry, much of this area remained farmland. The need for a centrally located market for produce was a brilliant idea of the earl's, and Charles II agreed, with royal Letters Patent granted to him."

They had reached a large, low-gated patio attached to Evan's Hotel, located at the northwest corner of the piazza. Dozens of tables with matching chairs dotted the sizable space edged with potted bushes and trees displaying varying stages of autumn leaves. Situated roughly catercorner from Saint Paul's Church, the patio afforded an excellent view. It was here they rested for a spell, revivified with pots of coffee and tea, and a light repast of fresh fruit and baked pastries served by the hotel. For a while, they drank and ate in silence as they watched the endlessly fascinating sea of people out in the market.

Jane, her eyes scanning the many storied buildings bordering the marketplace, reinitiated the conversation with a question. "I imagined the Theatre Royal would have an elaborate entrance in keeping with its prestigious reputation. Yet I cannot discern which of these it is."

"None of them, Miss Bennet," Bingley replied. "The theatre entrance is on Bow Street, one block to the east. The rear abuts the houses along the eastern piazza, so it is quite close, hence the more common name of Covent Garden Theatre, though it's not technically accurate."

"The theatre was not built until 1731, Miss Bennet," Darcy added when Bingley said no more. "By then, the square was established with no room for a grand theatre. Plus—and this is my personal conclusion based on what I have read—I believe John Rich, the celebrated *harlequin* who established the theatre for his company and obtained the financing, mainly wanted to compete with Drury Lane's Theatre Royal. In his estimation, it was a bonus being a block separated rather than two or more."

"Ah, well that explains my confusion. Thank you. It also explains why the buildings are all so uniform. Excepting the church, of course."

"Precisely, Miss Bennet." Darcy leaned to pour more coffee into his cup, doing the same for Bingley, followed by topping off the cups of tea fir each lady, continuing his narrative as he served. "As I said earlier, the Earl of Bedford, that being the fourth to bear the title, was a man with modern sensibilities and foresight. He, with the help of Jones, was the first to create the concept of a town square with symmetry and similar architectural style as a hallmark feature. It is an ideal we now enjoy all over London. Originally, the buildings fronted by the piazza and those located on the secondary streets were residences of persons of title and high rank, as well as of men esteemed in the world of art and literature. Newer, fashionable areas arose to supplant Covent Garden, and by the middle of the previous century, all but a handful of the homes transformed into shops, hotels, coffee and oyster houses, and so on. As you can see."

Speaking with a tone of nostalgia common when remembering the past, Mr. Bingley divulged a personal perspective of the area. "I remember my grandfather's house on Maiden Lane, just one street to the south. We lived there for a short time, while my father and mother were renovating our townhouse. I was young, and the memories are dim images of our nurse walking to the market. She always bought us a piece of fruit, once even a banana, quite a rarity then, and a single flower for Louisa."

"Miss Caroline did not earn a flower?"

Mr. Bingley smiled at Georgiana's innocent question. "She was but a babe in a wheeled miniature carriage, Miss Darcy. Although, now that you mention it, I never recall nurse being as generous with flowers for my younger sister. Of the three of us, Caroline has always been the most…troublesome to love."

"Does your family still own the house on Maiden Lane?" Jane's sweetly voiced question diverted from further unpleasant comments about Caroline, a relief to everyone.

"Not too many years later he sold the house and moved in with us. In part, this was due to his failing health, but he often spoke of the changes to Covent Garden. His father had built the house, and my grandfather lived his entire life here. He watched unsavory ilk infiltrating. It was a distressing development which pained him greatly."

"Sadly, this is true." Darcy added, a hint of sadness in his voice. "The area has tremendously changed. For several decades, it became nigh impossible to enter the market without risking thievery or worse. Improvements are happening, slowly, and I believe the time will come for a complete revamping. Covent Garden is too important and too centrally located to ignore. Even now, it is not wise to stay past dark or stray off the main paths and open areas. When the crowds are thick, even in the broad light of day, one has to be particularly diligent guarding the pocket where their purse resides."

Cognizant of the day's ongoing agenda and the time rapidly ticking away, they finished their midafternoon meal. The men led the ladies down the Piazza arcade, leisurely strolling to Russell Street where the carriage waited. Encumbered with several bouquets of aromatic flowers and four baskets of assorted fruits and vegetables for the coachman to safely stow in the landau's luggage rack, they once again climbed into the carriage. With an improved grip on her directional bearings and the hint of passing through Charing Cross and then south on Whitehall, Lizzy was ready to guess the next destination.

"Is Saint James's Park next to be explored, then? Or are you two jesters leading us on another wild ride which will end on the opposite bank of the Thames or the East India Docks or Hampstead Heath?"

Gravely nodding, his face serious, Darcy proclaimed, "We considered the latter three, at great length, and the debate was intense. Alas, in the end, we settled on the more logical, and closer, Westminster Abbey. Thus, tragically, your guess is incorrect, Miss Elizabeth. Another win for the men."

"Darcy! You are a rascal!" Bingley exclaimed in between laughs. "Miss Elizabeth, I can assure that the docks were never a consideration, although Darcy did suggest Newgate, which I deem unpalatable. To be fair, as much as I would like to keep the prize tally in our favor, we do plan to walk in Saint James's Park as a twilight end to our day, so Miss Elizabeth's guess is correct."

Georgiana was shaking her head. "As the official arbiter, I call a technicality. Miss Elizabeth did say 'next' when guessing the park, after all. Hence, the score should, by rights, belong to the gentlemen."

Darcy's left brow lifted and his eyes widened in feigned perplexity. "I don't recall granting you the office of arbiter, Georgie. Although, you are the designated chaperone, so it makes sense. Moreover, being the only neutral person in the challenge gives you a clearer view. Hence, your conclusion to award the point to us is logical. However"—Darcy furrowed his brows and sighed dramatically —"Miss Elizabeth's guess is also correct, the sequence qualifier a minor detail. How shall we solve such a severe dilemma?"

Lizzy narrowed her eyes and pursed her lips, points of argument running through her brain, while Jane shook with silent laughter. Eventually, after further banter, they agreed to award each team a point. The tally tied at three each, the group exited the parked carriage eager to begin the late afternoon portion of the day. A church was not the place for encounters of a romantic nature, so the collection of kisses remained a pleasure to anticipate, the sensual sensations bubbling below the surface of the lovers' skin all day.

As with most of the significant places in London, Lizzy had seen dozens of paintings and drawings of the Abbey of Saint Peter at Westminster. None of them prepared her for the breathtaking reality. Standing on the Tothill Street walkway across from the enormous paved, circular concourse fronting the western facade to the church, the impression of holiness was already palpable. Lizzy gazed in awe at the incredible beauty of the structure, stunned by the magnificence of the twin towers flanking the main entrance rising two-hundred twenty-five feet into the heavens. In silence, Lizzy absorbed the majestic vision, spellbound as were the others, into a sort of paralysis.

Darcy's resonant voice gently broke the stasis, his subdued delivery of the expected historical background given as the group drifted toward the doors.

"The original church built on this site in honor of the Apostle Peter was ordered by King Edward I in the eleventh century. Tragically, the king died days after the consecration ceremony, which he was too ill to attend. The following year, in 1066, William the Conqueror was the first monarch to be crowned here. That tradition has continued without fail ever since."

Pausing a few feet away from the arched entrance, he continued, "After two centuries, Henry III decided to rebuild the church in the Gothic style sweeping Europe. As the location for royal coronations and the burial of monarchs, the king believed Westminster Abbey should be grander and comparable to a cathedral. The new church was consecrated in 1269 and is unchanged, other than some reconstruction as necessary over long centuries. There have been a handful of additions made to the church, primarily the stunning, Tudor-influenced Lady Chapel by Henry VII in the first decade of 1500, and the towers of Portland stone we see before us, completed in 1745. Truly a marvel to behold."

At that point, Darcy resumed the journey to the doors, and for the whole of their time inside the massive church, he offered no further history. In fact, he reverted to his typical taciturn manner. The reasons for his abrupt change became immediately obvious.

In the whole of Lizzy's life, she had only attended religious services in modest, country churches constructed with average-height ceilings, one or two small stained-glass windows, maybe a single carved arch or elaborate statue, and housing a basic organ at best. Nothing she had ever seen, whether a place of worship or other fine structure, remotely came close to the interior of Westminster Abbey.

In fact, the entryway leading to the ornately carved double doors was a cause of awed amazement. Wide and almost tunnellike, the gap between the pillars was recessed and arched to a high pinnacle. Engraved panels, small buttresses, and niched cornices adorned the walls.

Moving past the doors and into the nave wrest the remaining air from Lizzy's lungs, her mind instantly filled with profound wonderment and reverence. She felt her mouth drop open yet was powerless to stop the gawking action. It was the feathery touch of William's hand against the small of her back which restored her senses, heat rising to her cheeks.

How long have I stood stupefied, blocking the aisle? Was I, heaven forbid, emitting odd sounds or some other mortifying gesture in my abstraction?

Ripping her eyes from the spectacular vaulted ceiling, she rapidly scanned the people close to her, relieved to note no one was paying her any heed. Then she swung her gaze to Darcy's face, her mouth opening to whisper her apologies. Instead, her lips curved into a smile as misty tears coated her eyes.

Mr. Darcy was staring into the nave, his blue eyes gliding slowly over the interior from wall to wall, and the expression he wore was indescribable. His countenance was awash with transcendent joy and peace, amongst other unnamable emotions.

"Beautiful, is it not?" he asked in a hushed whisper. "One can feel God's Holy Spirit alive within these walls."

A host of emotions inundated his voice. Then he turned to her, smiling in a way she had never seen before. Suddenly, she understood.

Religion was a part of her life, as it was for most, but admittedly in a peripheral way. Lizzy believed in God and accepted His presence in her life as a matter of course. Beyond the obligatory Sunday attendance and other liturgical ceremonies, and her firm commitment to follow the commandments and rules written in Scripture to the best of her ability, Lizzy went no further. Biblical instruction had never interested her as it had Mary.

Based on offhand comments and almost-forgotten memories of his solemn attitude while attending church services during their stay in Kent, Lizzy suspected his devotion to the church was deeper than most, including herself. The depth of his piety was another matter, and one not broached by him or contemplated by her. Until now.

Lizzy observed the spiritual euphoria visible upon his face and the full impact struck her. For Fitzwilliam Darcy, faith was a wholly unique experience that was personal, intense, and absolute. At this epiphany, her heart was uplifted yet oddly, simultaneously dismayed. Knowing that her beliefs, while in line with his, were not as extreme was disconcerting. Would she ever be as religious as he? Would this disparity lead to his disappointment or displeasure? Would it affect their unity?

"Do not be concerned, Elizabeth," he whispered, somehow reading her thoughts. "Faith is personal and varies, but I know you are a believer. More importantly, I know that God's Hand rests upon our relationship. The miracle of bringing us together, through all the odds against us, is the only proof I need. Trust in that, as I do."

He said no more, steering her with gentle pressure to her back, where his hand rested, to commence a thorough exploration of the church. His words soothed her overactive mind in a way she could not explain. Considering where they were, it was sensible to give the credit where due, her silent prayers of thankfulness offered in a continual litany as she walked closely beside the man she loved more with each passing hour.

For over two hours they drifted from one awe-inspiring view to another, separately and sometimes together. The wealth of beauty, history, and spiritual imagery overwhelmed. Lizzy knew she would never sort through all the mental pictures or remember the poetic writings, inscriptions, and famous persons entombed. In fact, after a while, she stopped trying to maintain order in her mind or read the monument engravings. Instead, she opted to bask in the glorious atmosphere and delightful impressions.

Eventually, they wandered outside via the great north door, the need for fresh air and space winning over the desire to investigate every inch of the interior, which was impossible to do in one visit anyway.

Immediately beyond the door stretched a grassy expanse in the shape of a rough triangle, with the stone street called Broad Sanctuary to the left, and Saint Margaret's Church to the right. Darcy identified the avenues after one massive inhale and cleansing exhale. leaving his solemnity behind.

Walking briskly toward the intersection of Broad Sanctuary and King's Street, the others skipping to keep up with his long-legged gait. As they crossed, Darcy gestured at the visible spires of Westminster Hall, the Parliament buildings, and Saint Stephen's Chapel in the near distance.

"I wish we had time to tour the plethora of buildings in the area or to view the cloisters, monastery, Jewel Tower, and Chapter House located on the south side of the abbey. Another time, I suppose."

"Another appointment, Mr. Darcy? Should we try guessing?"

Darcy grinned and pressed the hand resting on his forearm. "You already have guessed, Miss Elizabeth, and scored the point. A leisurely sojourn in Saint James's Park as the sun sets will be our final destination for today. Then back to Darcy House for dinner and whatever entertainments we desire to engage in."

Lizzy peered upward, trying to decipher if a hidden meaning lay behind his last words. He was smiling softly, a definite glint in his eye, but he turned his head to check for traffic before leading across the street. A minute later they reached the carriage, which was waiting on the corner as close to the abbey as possible. Still wondering over his words, she did not immediately notice his subtle shift to the right and shortened steps until Bingley pulled into the lead, with Jane and Georgiana at his side. The purposeful maneuver became clearer when Darcy took advantage of the distraction of Bingley assisting Jane and Georgiana into their seats.

Leaning until his lips touched her right ear, he whispered huskily, "I have not forgotten the kisses to deliver and receive, my sweet Elizabeth. I will find a way to collect. Tonight. So be prepared."

Lizzy gasped, her heartbeat instantly accelerating, and if not for his arm slipping around her waist and hand holding hers, she surely would have stumbled on the carriage steps!

The guessing game had been ongoing all day, with kisses the stated prize. Still, amid the endless wonders and lighthearted teasing, the reality of collecting six kisses all in one sitting hadn't fully penetrated her brain. She wondered if it had occurred to Jane, or if Mr. Bingley had found a way to whisper a similar promise into her sister's ear. If either were true, they were doing a fabulous job at pretending to be unmoved.

Lizzy was the complete opposite of unmoved. All she could think about was William's whispered promise. She found it exceedingly difficult to focus on the natural beauty and fascinating history of Saint James's Park, a distraction Miss Darcy noticed and questioned. Cheeks flaming, Lizzy stammered something lame about being tired, unsure whether Georgiana bought the excuse or not.

It didn't help that Darcy spent most of the time at the park shooting her suggestive glances and touching her covertly. Strolling down the tree-lined avenue next to the Canal, he intermittently offered details of the park's stages of development and use by the successive monarchs.

Speaking did not stop him from sneakily using the spreading shadows created by the sun creeping closer and closer to the horizon. Few pedestrians were on the trail, and it was quite easy to lag behind or fabricate an excuse to pause next to a fortuitously placed tree or statue. He was, of course, always the gentleman, and Lizzy suspected he wasn't seriously trying to isolate her to deliver his kisses. Rather, the mild liberties taken were to heighten the anticipation.

Oh! How well it worked! The skin he managed to caress with brushing fingertips tingled and burned. The delirious three minutes he drew her back against his chest and spanned her waist with his hands left her lightheaded for a good fifteen minutes. The kiss he pressed onto her inner wrist—after murmuring, "This does not count. I shall claim my kisses on your lips."—left her knees so weak she thought sure she would be unable to make it back to the carriage.

It was a relief to once again settle into the cushioned carriage bench and no longer worry about tripping over her own feet. The landau's hood was unfolded and secured to protect from the fast cooling air of twilight, so she could hide her flushed face in the dim shadows. Plus, she could no longer see his penetrating gaze. Not that this prevented her *feeling* the intensity of his stare—or maybe this was merely her overactive imagination, because when they entered the brightly lit foyer of the townhouse, Mr. Darcy appeared perfectly serene.

⁓

*G*uest bedchambers had been assigned for each Bennet to rest in while the kitchen prepared dinner and they awaited the arrival of Mr. Bennet.

Mounting the stairs behind Georgiana and Jane, Lizzy looked back at Mr. Darcy where he stood talking to Mr. Bingley. He smiled at her, his blue eyes warm and peaceful. Then, just as she reached the upper landing, he mouthed *I love you*. Giddy, she returned the sentiment, his grin widening as he marched toward the corridor leading to his chambers.

Neither Lizzy nor Jane had thought ahead to the evening dinner plans, a belated realization causing some embarrassment. Georgiana, bless her sweet heart, waved her hand dismissively as she assured, "We are enjoying setting a casual table, to be honest. No need to dress fancy for dinner tonight. But, the servants will brush the dust from your gowns while you rest, and if you do not mind sharing, I have plenty of garments, jewelry, and accessories to fit for evening attire."

They could certainly not refuse such generosity. With swift efficiency, the maid helping Lizzy had her undressed down to her shift and comfortably settled in a beautifully decorated bedchamber in no time at all. Once left alone, Lizzy stood in the middle of the room and examined her surroundings.

The huge bed beckoned, so she climbed onto the incredibly plush mattress covered with a fluffy, down-stuffed duvet. Five minutes later, she bounded up from the bed. There was no possible way she could lay upon a bed without thinking of William. Vividly! Napping, or even relaxing, was utterly out of the question.

Giving up on that idea altogether, she explored the bedchamber, the tiny sitting room attached, and the small water closet hidden behind a folding screen in the far corner. Every item was of the finest material and exquisitely crafted. Ordinarily, her curiosity would have taken hold, but she simply could not stop thinking of him.

What was he doing, right now? Sleeping? Changing his clothes? Bathing?

Any of those possibilities involved some degree of nakedness and were a bit too intimate for her to imagine without worsening her jitters.

The speculation did lead her to ponder the location of his bedchamber relative to the one assigned to her. Rapidly analyzing the townhouse layout in her head, she concluded his suite might be almost directly below.

Dashing to the rear, alcove window, she jerked the curtains aside. It turned out her calculations were only partially accurate. Indeed, the master suite was below her, but farther to the right than she figured. In fact, if not for the light shining outward through what she assumed was a glass door, the low-walled stone patio would not have been visible at all in the darkness.

Sighing rather pathetically, Lizzy leaned her forehead against the glass. The cold was soothing to her skin. She closed her eyes and ever so slowly forced the coiled energy to ease out of her muscles. Relaxation took hold, and the prospect of falling asleep for the hour that remained until she needed to dress for dinner finally felt possible.

Opening her eyes, she released a second sigh before lifting her head from the glass and starting to turn away.

Just then, the light down below flickered, and a tall shadow waved over the stones. Instantly she was alert, eyes wide and face pressed into the cold glass.

Please, let it be him!

Seconds later, William walked out the door. The distance, shadows, and thick vines twining over a trellis obstructed her view, but she noted a tumbler in his right hand, and that he wore only his shirt and trousers.

This time her sigh was closer to a whine of longing.

Grasping onto the window latch, a crazed vision of throwing the window wide and shouting his name, as if a whimsical Juliet to his Romeo, whipped through her mind. Next came the insane notion of scaling the wall, climbing down the conveniently located trellis, and dropping half-dressed onto his patio. Covering her mouth to stay the giggles threatening to burst forth at such ridiculousness, Lizzy removed her hand from the latch as rationality slowly reasserted.

No. It is much preferable to enjoy this small gift of an intimate peek at the man I love.

For some minutes, she unashamedly watched from her cozy vantage point.

William stood in the middle of the patio with one hand on his hip, gazing into the sky as he sipped from the tumbler. Twice he glanced in the direction of her window, and each time her hand was halfway to the latch before she stayed the unconscious movement. The light inside his chambers illuminated him, whereas she was hidden in the window alcove behind thick curtains shielding the lone candle she had left by the bed. Knowing that he was thinking of her was enough for now.

Tossing back the last swallow of liquid, William returned to his bedchamber, at which point Lizzy accepted she would not be able to sleep. She called for the maid, requesting water and necessities for her toilette. Scrubbing her face and cleaning her teeth was amazingly invigorating. The maid returned with Lizzy's cleaned gown, and an armload of clean shawls, fichus, petticoats, footwear and stockings, over-dresses, and other accessories selected by Miss Darcy. The servant laid them in perfect order atop the bed, then moved to the mirrored vanity table prepping the array of items for dressing Lizzy's hair.

In a daze, Lizzy ran her fingertips over the costly fabrics lying on the bed, dreaminess flowing through her body as her thoughts swirled.

Very soon, this will be my life.

An army of servants to attend to her needs. Elegant and expensive furnishings wherever she looked. Garments of the finest quality and latest fashion professionally tailored. Days upon days of leisure, parties, and entertainment. A way of life foreign, for the most part, from her modest existence thus far.

I will have a husband who loves me and fills me with immeasurable joy.

Ah! The real treasure. She would become accustomed to the changes in her elevated status, especially with William beside her.

Less than a month away!

Inhaling deeply, she closed her eyes and savored the dreamy happiness. Submitting to the maid's skill, within fifteen minutes the woman styled Lizzy's hair into an arrangement impossible to manage herself, and she then transformed the simple day-dress into an elegant dinner ensemble.

Sincerely amazed, Lizzy thanked the servant for her excellent service, which seemed to surprise the young woman, and then politely dismissed her. There was still nearly thirty minutes until dinner at eight o'clock, and Jane had said she would come to her room so they could descend the stairs together. But, surely *someone* was in the parlor already. Had her father arrived? Was Mr. Darcy downstairs awaiting his arrival?

Might he be alone?

Decision made, she inspected her reflection one last time, adding a final pinch to her cheeks and dab of perfume to her neck. That should be sufficient, she deemed. Giggling and with an eager smile curling her lips, she turned away from the mirror. At that second she heard a faint tap on the hallway door in the adjacent sitting room, followed by the nearly inaudible creak of the door opening.

Stifling a groan of disappointment, she stepped toward the room while calling aloud, "I'm coming, Jane! You are early, but I am ready. We can head down—"

Lizzy froze on the threshold, the shock of seeing William, not Jane, immobilizing her tongue and limbs.

"I am early on purpose, am relieved to see you dressed or this risk might prove more than I can handle, but was rather hoping you were not overly eager to head down quite yet."

Laughing, she hastily dashed into his arms, gave him a hug, and emphatically assured, "I was only eager to see you, my love."

"Were you? A man can live on such sentiment. Dare I hope you wanted more than merely to see me?"

"Tease! I suspect you are not here merely to see me either. Who shall collect their prize first?" Rising onto her tiptoes, stretching to lessen the unwanted gap, Lizzy answered her question. "Honestly, I no longer care who won the game or claims their prize first. I just want to kiss you, William."

His smile was nothing short of radiant. He did not comment, bending his head until his lips were so close to her mouth she could feel the emanating warmth. Eyes closed and lifted lips parted, Lizzy was taken by surprise when his mouth pressed against the edge of her jaw. From there he traveled to the tender flesh below her ear, planting a series of firm kisses along the way.

"Remember, these do not count. Only kisses to your lips." Whispered huskily, he followed with an earlobe kiss. "Now, turn around."

If not for his hands on her upper arms guiding her into a pivot, her delirious brain never would have translated his verbal command into action. Then, with his hard chest in contact with her backside and his soft lips grazing over the nape of her neck, coherency rapidly disappeared until sheer sensation remained.

Perceptions which were raging, wild, and fiery!

Sensations that drove away interfering rationality but were alive and vivid. Lizzy felt, heard, and smelled with sharp clarity—the aroma of his musky cologne, the fibers of his jacket and the round buttons on his waistcoat, the slight rasp of his whiskers and lightly calloused fingertips, the rush of air with each increasingly harsher breath.

As had happened with their previous passionate interludes, pointless realities like the time or location no longer registered. Lizzy counted every kiss and touch, cataloging and storing for future retrieval when alone yet could not have said with certainty whether his exploration of her neck and shoulders lasted a minute or ten times longer.

Somewhere in that indeterminate span of time, his hands slid slowly down her arms, reaching her hands and entwining their fingers. For unknown minutes, he held her hands together with both of his—the brushing kisses ongoing and thorough in their quest to explore—and then, almost lazily, he transferred their grip into only one hand. His newly freed hand languidly stroked up her right arm, fleetingly brushed over her breast—an electrifying sensation eliciting a gasping moan—and across her chest until caressing the left side of her neck and jawline.

Helplessly, blissfully, she relaxed fully into his body. Her head fell back onto his shoulder, and with the hand splayed firmly over her face he tilted her head to the side. For a second their eyes met, his dark with raging desire, and hers, she hoped, expressing the same. Then he bent his head, eyes slipping closed, and captured her mouth in a gentle kiss. The angle was odd, and for a moment rather awkward, yet amazingly, they quickly adjusted to what was, for her certainly, a unique experience which escalated to euphoria when his left arm tightened, securing her in place as he deepened the kiss.

Whiskey. That was the liquor he sipped on the terrace. The taste was on his tongue, the flavor mingled with a hint of mint and the savory sweetness uniquely him.

The Biblical words from the Song of Songs flashed through her mind: "Let him kiss me with the kisses of his mouth! For your love is better than wine." Was it possible to exist on nothing but a lover's kiss? Perhaps not, technically, although her hunger pangs had stopped. More than willing to test the theory, she nearly burst into tears when he ended the kiss.

They were still standing in the middle of the small sitting room, William supporting her body with one strong arm as he stroked her neck with the other hand. He didn't immediately open his eyes, and Lizzy felt the tension in his body that was indicative of his struggle for control. Understanding, she gazed into his face and waited, fighting her own rushing passions. An infinitesimal relaxing of his muscles and a low groaning exhale indicated the shift, and he opened his eyes.

"On second thought, collecting one kiss at a time may be a wiser plan."

His smile was a tad strained and his voice rough, the comment half-tease and half-serious. Lizzy knew he was probably right. She simply did not care.

"You have collected one kiss, William. Now it is my turn to collect."

Twisting in his arms, she surprised them both at how easily she broke free of his grip. Clasping his face, she paused only long enough to be sure he saw her determination and ardency—of that there was no doubt. His eyes widened, then dropped to her mouth, and he inhaled sharply. The hands spanning her waist clenched almost painfully, then drifted upward, the action involuntary, until resting just under her breasts. His reactions, spontaneous and instant, fueled the fire within her.

Just a kiss. A simple kiss.

But the first she would deliver of her own initiation. Lizzy did not count her precipitous kiss in his office three days ago. Now, unlike then, she was thinking clearly—as much as possible, that is, when held in his arms—and while completely likely her control would be fast overwhelmed, she intended to prove she could be bold and take the lead.

Smiling, she slowly lifted onto her tiptoes, hands gliding to encircle his neck and twine into his hair. Perhaps comprehending her purpose, or maybe out of amazement, she was not sure, he held still, not even lowering his head.

For a fraction of a second uncertainty sliced through her. After his clever embrace and novel kissing position, a straightforward exchange seemed rather blah. Playing the seductress sounded easy until put to the test.

"Just one kiss," she murmured encouragingly, not aware she spoke aloud until he released his held breath and nodded.

Closing the small space to his mouth, she pressed her lips lightly against his—a gentle pressure maintained for several seconds before parting her lips. Yet rather than proceeding as typical, she touched the tip of her tongue to his upper lip, a glancing touch before delicately pulling it between her lips.

Galvanized by the increasing pitch of his breathing and squeeze to her ribcage, she repeated the action to his lower lip using a bit more intensity and drawing out the final sucking nibble. Then, a leisurely sweep of her tongue over the entire surface of his lips, mingled with feathery busses.

Truly, she had no clue what she was doing or whether a particular maneuver made sense. She was driven by instinct, whatever remote idea popped into her mind, and what she found pleasing. Bumbling as her kissing procedure may have been in her own estimation, it was absolutely crystal clear it had a dynamic effect on William!

His hands trembled, and a shudder ran through his body. The muscles in his neck and jaw clenched under her palms. Still, he allowed her to continue the lead, his mouth soft and responsive but not assuming control, even when she slid her tongue past his parted lips, delving into the crevice by his teeth and slick inner lip. At this, he moaned—a guttural growl, really—emanating deep in his chest, and the reflexive squeeze of his hands was painful.

Enough.

The word floated through her mind as if riding on a gentle breeze. Not a shout of command or scream of warning. No accompanied embarrassment or fear. Only a softly whispered advisement.

Wait, the still voice hummed. *Be patient. Now is not the time.*

Lizzy understood. Whether her own conscience or a divine message, she did not know, but the voice was correct. The fire between them, the passionate desire inspired by their love, was wonderful and beautiful. It was as God designed and therefore nothing to be ashamed of—but full enjoyment was meant for after they were married.

Obeying, she ended her claimed kiss as tenderly as she began, then pulled away. William opened his eyes sluggishly, the heat of his aroused state visible within the smoky-blue depths, as well as wonderment and profound adoration. They stood as they were, bodies touching and faces barely an inch apart, for several minutes. A million words passed through her mind, yet none of them felt as right as the honesty of silent contemplation.

Gradually, he relaxed, his hands slipping down to her waist and his breathing normalizing. When he spoke, however, it was mumbled through a tight throat.

"I'm certain my sister did not envision this when she suggested the prize for today's game. She better not have, I should say, or she has serious explaining to do!" He laughed, a hoarse barking sound, and swallowed before continuing, "On the other hand, I am beginning to believe innocent ladies have far greater imaginations and inborn gifts than we males give them credit for."

"Perhaps we are mysterious creatures blessed with unfathomable talents waiting to be discovered. Or possibly it is mere luck." She hesitated, then whispered, "Dare I presume that was a compliment for my kiss…for me?"

He frowned, cocking his head to the side, and peered closely into her eyes. After a seemingly endless span of intense scrutiny beginning to make her squirm, he shook his head, laughing with uncontainable mirth.

"Sweet Lord, Elizabeth, you nearly brought me to my knees! If that kiss was mere luck, then I am assured my wildest dreams will be fulfilled far beyond my feeble imaginations when your talents are let loose upon me. And I am not complaining in the least, trust me. The hunt of discovery will be highly enjoyable, my love. Of that I am sure."

7

SENSATIONAL REVELATION

*F*or the subsequent two days, the Bennet sisters barely had time to breathe, let alone sleep.

The day of touring portions of London, while a welcome break from whirlwind shopping, , had been as exhausting as it had been fun. Friday consisted of more shopping and the final wedding gown fittings. On Friday evening Mr. Bennet and Mr. Gardiner, in collusion with Mr. Bingley and Mr. Darcy, surprised the women with an evening at Vauxhall Gardens for a symphony performance.

The four young Gardiner children loudly expressing their dissatisfaction at spending so little time with Jane and Lizzy dashed any hope of relaxing on Saturday. The women happily consented to pass the day with their adored young cousins doing whatever their wee hearts desired. By unanimous agreement, the Royal Menagerie at the Tower of London was the choice, as much a thrill for Jane and Lizzy, who had never been, as it was for the children. While the women were occupied viewing wild beasts, the gentlemen, including Colonel Fitzwilliam, gathered together for the day. They visited White's Club, amongst other manly pursuits.

The Darcys hosted the group for dinner on Saturday, as usual. Returning to the Gardiner townhouse from the menagerie late in the afternoon, Lizzy had scant time to relax before needing to bathe and dress. All too soon she was wedged inside the coach making its way from Cheapside to the distant Grosvenor Square. Between the silence of her equally tired family, the twilight shadows, and the rhythmic swaying of the carriage, Lizzy came close to dozing. Jane's subdued voice pierced the calm as if she had shouted.

"Perhaps, in time, we will grow accustomed to the changing pace of our lives as the wives of important men. At present, however, I confess to being rather drained. London has much to offer, to be sure, and when I was here in the spring, I developed an appreciation for the city's charms. Of course, I was here for weeks and never engaged in the entertainments of high society. I was largely at my leisure. Frankly, I cannot fathom how the *ton* manages the endless dances, dinner parties, and theatre events of the Season! I feel a bit overwhelmed merely thinking of it. Not that I regret our time here, Papa, and pray I do not sound unthankful for this sojourn."

Lizzy and Mrs. Gardiner's amused chuckling caused Jane to fall silent. Mr. Bennet countered humorously, "I do not think it is possible for you to sound unthankful, my dear."

"Rest easy, Sister." Lizzy gave Jane a gentle hug. "I am confident we will adjust to our new lives, in due course. Remember that we have crammed much into a short period. Dwelling in the country where a walk about tiny Meryton can consume an entire day is ill preparedness for the bustle of Pall Mall shops. I say we have performed brilliantly under the circumstances."

Jane rested her head against Lizzy's, sighing. "We survived, I shall agree with that, and finished the mission."

"We have what we need for the wedding and beyond, and did so without depleting papa's pocketbook completely. Such bargain shoppers we are! You have taught us well, Papa, and must be bursting with pride."

"I am indeed," Mr. Bennet concurred, "particularly in light of the massive pile of boxes in the foyer of your uncle's house. It looks to me as if the two of you bought out half of London, so I am shocked to have any funds left at all."

"Only a third. We considered it polite to leave something behind," Lizzy teased.

Mr. Gardiner added his jesting. "The children are enjoying the maze created by the bags and boxes. They will be devastated to see the piles gone. Nevertheless, another day or two of shopping and we may not be able to enter the house through the front door."

"Oh! You two exaggerate," Mrs. Gardiner scolded.

Exaggeration or not, the bounteous purchasing extravaganza had created a problem, which Jane addressed. "We do face the dilemma of how to get all of it to Longbourn. Bless you, Uncle, for the lovely gift of new trunks, but we have stuffed so much into them already that we can barely secure the latches. Do you think we can manage the added weight and find the space in our carriage, Papa? Or have you come up with an alternative solution?"

"Your uncle did. He is conscripting one of the wagons he uses in his business to transport the precious cargo once the shopping is finalized, which, dare I hope, will be soon?"

"I believe our papa is homesick, Jane. Does the lure of Mr. Darcy's well-appointed library no longer placate?"

"Your Aunt Gardiner's generosity to serve as escort saved me from tromping behind the two of you, up and down noisy streets entering an endless number of bustling shops. Mr. Darcy's hospitality in sharing his outstanding collection of fine literature occupied my time in the best possible way. For both kindnesses I shall be eternally grateful. Nevertheless, this old country gentleman is only truly at peace in wide-open spaces where the air is fresh and natural sounds prevail."

"After just over a week doing the tromping, and scant time for the joy of solitary communion with Mr. Darcy's books, I admit to yearning for the pastoral quiet of Hertfordshire. I suppose we are, in the end, simple country creatures like our papa," Lizzy said. Jane murmured her agreement.

Clearing his throat,= and darting a glance to Mr. Gardiner, who nodded encouragingly, Mr. Bennet asked hesitantly, "Then, if we have accomplished the purpose of this trip, do we need to stay the full two weeks?"

After a startled minute, Lizzy answered, "Honestly, I do not see why we must. Our wedding dresses are unfinished, but we have had our final fitting, so Aunt can send them to us when the modiste delivers them. What say you, Jane? Shall we ask Mr. Bingley and Mr. Darcy if a Monday return to Hertfordshire is doable?"

What Lizzy did not add was that as the days ticked away, the realization that she would soon be leaving the only home she had ever known pressed upon her heart. Unlike any other period away from Longbourn, this week in London had aroused rare sensations of homesickness. At first, she had shrugged off the laughable feelings, but as they intruded stronger upon her consciousness, Lizzy was forced to evaluate the meaning.

Focusing on Mr. Darcy, the wedding, and the desire to be alone with him had overridden her emotions over parting from her entire family and moving out of Longbourn permanently. She was impatient to begin her life as Mrs. Darcy and trusted that the joy of being with William at Pemberley would soothe most bouts of sadness. Mostly, she was far too practical to dwell on the negative. Nevertheless, she planned to relish every moment of her current life, including soaking up each minute with her ofttimes annoying family. That meant departing crowded London on Monday.

As had become the routine, Mr. Darcy and Miss Darcy welcomed them in the parlor, joined on this occasion by Colonel Fitzwilliam. After proper greetings and brief conversation, they were escorted directly into the dining room. It continued to amaze Lizzy that no matter when they arrived, the table setting was complete, the butler was uncorking the wine, and servants were on their way from the kitchen with the first course of what was always an excellent meal. She fancied Mr. Darcy had a sentry posted at a top-story window whose sole job was to watch for their carriage. Whether this was true or not, she did not ask. It was more fun to live with the mystery.

Of no mystery was the strict adherence to dining formality standard practice at Darcy House, and at Pemberley, as Lizzy recalled. Precise to the last detail, from the rigidly poised footman in impeccable livery to the flawless execution of the meal service to the unblemished, and costly, tableware, it was a sharp contrast to a typical dinner at Longbourn. Or rather as evening dining was before Mr. Bingley and Mr. Darcy joining them.

Mr. Darcy, particularly, was a man of elevated rank with staunch protocol and exacting manners woven into the fabric of his character. His inclusion had affected the Longbourn servants and the family in a host of ways, the dining table only one of them. Lizzy had amusedly observed how her betrothed adjusted to the casual atmosphere and playful table conversation—to a degree, that is— while unaware of how his presence caused the household to improve its dining standards.

Once in charge and in his natural element, Mr. Darcy had instantly reverted to the rigid customs of dining in high society. That had lasted all of two days—a party including Mr. Bennet, Lizzy, Charles Bingley, the Gardiners, and the effervescent Colonel Fitzwilliam was doomed to backslide into frivolity.

Not utterly, of course. On this Saturday evening, the proper dinner topics and formality lasted for three courses. Then the women related the details of their menagerie adventure, accented with animal vocalizations and the expected hilarity consuming a bulk of the time. Mr. Bennet's opportunity to broach the subject of departing London on Monday arose between the fifth and sixth course.

"I need to make an announcement, of a sort, that I hope will not disrupt too greatly. Jane and Lizzy have informed me that the purpose of our trip to London has been adequately fulfilled, enough, at least, to indulge an old man's preference for his home. Additionally, while perhaps a flaw in my character, I have never delighted in city life, even as a young man at university. My dear daughters have graciously offered to sacrifice their fun and leave on Monday rather than later in the week, as initially planned."

"Of course!" Mr. Bingley exuberantly assured. "Monday is perfect! I understand completely, sir, as I too have grown fond of Hertfordshire. London is my home, so holds a special place in my heart, of course, but the country is charming. Is that not so, Darcy? You have long extolled the virtues of clean air and estate living, which I now can appreciate as never before."

Darcy gave the briefest of nods to Bingley's rhetorical question but said nothing. As the details for departure time, where they would meet, and the like carried on, Lizzy watched Darcy's face with growing unease. His expression was neutral, displaying no obvious hint to his thoughts or emotions, yet Lizzy sensed something was not right.

"William," she whispered as soon as the opportunity arose for a semiprivate conversation, "is something amiss?"

He swung his eyes to her immediately and then dropped them to his plate. "No! Nothing. That is, nothing to worry over. We can discuss it later."

"I would rather discuss it now, please. My overactive imagination will leap to all manner of ridiculous assumptions. You know it will. Do you really wish to be the cause of that, Mr. Darcy?"

His lips twitched, but he still evaded her gaze. Hesitantly, speaking so low she had to lean closer, he explained, "I do not wish to cause wild speculations but also do not wish to ruin your dinner."

"A dinner this superb will not ruin, I assure you. Now,"—she flattened her hand atop his, which was fiddling with the edge of his napkin—"look at me and speak plainly."

Sighing, he did as she asked. His eyes were faintly troubled but more sheepish than anything. "I regret to inform that I shan't be able to escort you home. I must stay in London on…business."

"Oh! I see. Well, this is disappointing, of course, but I understand. We have sprung the news suddenly and did plan to stay longer. What business do you have? Or is it more of your secret plotting for my grand entrance into Pemberley?"

"Perhaps," he hedged. "I have a meeting with my solicitor, Mr. Daniels, on Tuesday for various estate matters. On Wednesday I am meeting with a merchant at the Exchange who is…acquiring select items for me. No, do not ask," he added when her lips parted. "However, the main reason is…Well, to be frank, it is a bit embarrassing."

"Something embarrassed Mr. Darcy? Oh please tell me."

Smiling, he slid his fingers through hers, the napkin acting as a shield from the sharp eyes of Mr. Bennet at the far end of the table. "I may regret confessing this, but, as you are aware, I attended a meeting at the Jockey Club last week. It seems that in the excitement over our engagement, it completely slipped my mind that one of the horses bred at Pemberley is competing at Newmarket. I really should not miss… Must you laugh? Have you no pity for my predicament, Miss Elizabeth?"

"Forgive me, but I am imagining the consternation amongst your Jockey Club peers at having anything horse related 'slip the mind' of Mr. Darcy. Were they searching the sky for flying pigs?"

"Not that I noticed. Although, now that you mention it, Lord Westingcote *did* stare out the window for a long while. I thought that the result of Mr. Shelley's riveting dissertation on the benefits of blue banners over red. What do you think?"

"Of Lord Westingcote's inattentiveness or the banners?"

"Both."

"I cannot fathom how a discussion of the vital importance of proper banner color bored any one of sound mind, so his lordship must have been searching the sky for the flying pigs. And obviously red, always red. Unless they plan to invite bulls to the races?"

"We voted against that this year. It was a narrow margin, however, so perhaps blue banners might be safer, in case they revisit the inclusion of bulls another year."

Lizzy shook her head, laughing softly to avoid drawing undue attention, and squeezed his fingers. She adored bantering with him, the fun enhanced now that he had learned to relax and explore his surprising propensity to tease and outwit. "So, an important race is upcoming, and you wish to watch your exceptional Pemberley thoroughbred take the prize. I can find no fault in this perfectly reasonable excuse to stay in town, Mr. Darcy. I suppose if I must share you with other entertainments, horse racing is a worthy choice."

"Once we wed, you can come with me, Elizabeth. If you wish."

"I would like that very much. I've never been to a horse race, but it must be thrilling. Watching you race certainly is, when I am not frightened half to death by one of your daredevil exploits, that is. I look forward to sharing in those sports and activities you are passionate about."

"And I you, my dear. Who knows, I may even surpass your skills as a juggler, in time and with serious study."

Lizzy groaned. "I swear, from this day forward you are forbidden to listen to another word anyone in my family says to you regarding my youth. But, for the record, I did master three balls in the air at once."

"If only you had persevered, instead of diverting in your quest to conquer shovelboard and become the reigning champion in all of Hertfordshire. How did that endeavor go again?"

Lizzy groaned a second time and briefly covered her eyes.

Grinning, Darcy pressed on. "Imagine the possibilities. You might now be a juggling master performing at Astley's circus."

Further joking was interrupted by the next course, Lizzy

reluctantly removing her hand from Darcy's. Once they were served, Lizzy took advantage of the footman serving Georgiana, who sat beside her, and again leaned toward Darcy, whispering, "I will miss you terribly. No one can tease me as skillfully as you, William. But… that is not the main reason."

She held his gaze, ensuring he understood her meaning. His gaze softened and dropped to her lips, and a swiftly indrawn breath confirmed the message was received. Swallowing, he huskily replied, "I will return on Friday, possibly Thursday evening, if my business concludes. Being parted from you, Elizabeth will be agonizing, so be prepared to make up for the lost time."

Smiling dreamily, she reminded him, "We still have tomorrow, and for the sake of preventing overwhelming agony, I suggest it wise to find a way to create a stockpile, so to speak. What say you, Mr. Darcy? Does this sound like a feasible plan?"

"Darcy! I have told Miss Bennet of your idea for a walk tomorrow afternoon, and she is most agreeable. Capital, isn't it?"

Mr. Bingley's interruption was fortuitous. Lizzy and Darcy seemed to have some difficulty remembering where they were, and who was around them, a fact that must have been clear, as Richard Fitzwilliam was smirking and Mr. Bennet's face had a half-amused and half-scolding expression. Lizzy flashed an unrepentant smile in her father's direction before diving into her food. At the same time, Darcy answered Bingley's question in a steady voice, no trace of being taken unawares or caught in a mild impropriety.

"I thought it would be a nice outing, if the weather holds fair, as I suspect it shall," Darcy said. "Grosvenor Gate opens into Hyde Park and is only two blocks away. An easy walk and this area of the park is far less crowded than the Row and south of the Serpentine, especially this time of the year."

"Oh yes!" Georgiana enthused. "Mrs. Annesley and I walk into the park often, sometimes with a picnic basket and blanket. The trails are maintained, and it isn't far to the lake. The ducks have probably gone away by now, but the walnut trees lining Park Lane are brilliantly yellow in autumn."

"The air is fresher in the park," Mr. Bingley added. "Once past the fence and out amongst the trees, the city scape disappears from view and nature surrounds. A small slice of the country, as it were."

"I read that cattle and sheep still roam the grasslands. Is this true?"

"Yes, Miss Bennet, it is true. Not wildly or in vast numbers, so no need to worry. And they tend to accumulate in the northwesterly areas."

"I have seen a handful of cows, although Mr. Bingley is correct that they do not venture this direction often. Hyde Park has an ancient, fascinating history! My brother is knowledgeable of the past details, Miss Elizabeth, which I know will interest you."

"It does indeed interest me. Thank you, Miss Darcy. As I learned the other day, your brother is well educated on London's history and has a flair for imparting dry information compellingly. A pleasant surprise. Plus, it is always nice to know we shall have *something* to talk about if normal conversation lags."

Laughter erupted at this jest, in equal parts due to Mr. Darcy's well-known reticence, as well as for Lizzy's penchant for history lessons. Talk turned to organizing the Hyde Park agenda—which was to begin at two o'clock with a light lunch at Darcy House before setting off to explore—so it was not until the dessert course that Lizzy had another chance to engage Mr. Darcy in a quiet conversation.

"Are you and Miss Darcy attending church tomorrow morning?"

"We are. We usually do, unless a legitimate impediment arises. Do not worry, my dear. We shall be back at the townhouse well before our scheduled luncheon."

Amused, Lizzy assured, "I am confident you would never plan an outing if there were the slightest chance of you being tardy, William.

I asked about church because I greatly desire to accompany the two of you if the request is not an imposition."

In his surprise, Darcy swallowed his bite of lemon mousse a bit too hastily, coughing twice before being able to speak. "Nothing you request could ever be an imposition, Elizabeth. Having you join us would be a tremendous honor and joy, most assuredly. I only hesitate because I do not want you to feel obligated. Surely you would prefer to worship at the church where the Gardiners do? Is that not where you attend when in Town?"

"You forget that I can count on one hand the number of times I have been in London, and those were some years ago. Even at home, we do not regularly attend, I am embarrassed to admit. I have realized these past weeks, especially while at Westminster Abbey, that faith is of great importance to you, my love. As Mrs. Darcy, it will be my duty and honor to worship in the traditional Darcy family parish, here and at Pemberley."

Squeezing his hand for emphasis, she declared, "I want to be clear, however, that more important to me than duty is my immense desire to share in your interests because I love you and *want to be with you*. I long with all my heart to be your wife and partner, William. Standing beside you in church, I can, if only for a short while, feel as if I already am."

Once again, they lost themselves in a world of their devising. Eyes locked, Darcy said nothing for several seconds. Then, slipping his fingers under her palm, he lifted her hand to bestow a lingering kiss to her knuckles. "Thank you," he whispered, his voice rough. A next kiss followed, and then another, a bit closer to her wrist, before Mr. Bennet gruffly clearing his throat reminded them they were not alone.

Tragically, that brief interlude was the extent of the intimacy arranged that evening. Collecting the remaining kisses would have to wait.

⁓

*D*arcy stood before the parlor window with eyes fixed on the street entering Grosvenor Square. Barring a traffic mishap, which was not unusual in London, the carriage sent to convey Elizabeth safely should return any moment.

Mr. Gardiner kindly offered to provide a vehicle for his niece's transport to Darcy House, which Darcy appreciated but deemed too risky. If all the Bennets traveled together, Darcy acquiesced to the use of Mr. Gardiner's older but adequately maintained carriage. This time it was Elizabeth alone, however, and he could not permit her to travel without a trusted vehicle and the security of two strong footmen to escort.

Darcy had smoothly refused the generous offer so as not to offend and now waited by the window with bated breath. Despite his absolute trust in the chosen footmen, Hobbes and Peters, and in the coachman's superb skills, this *was* London. Reliable street conditions and policing—brigands were always around, even on a Sunday morning—meant that anything terrible could happen. Thus, he exhaled audibly when the familiar coach turned the corner.

"Are you going to dash outside and make sure she wasn't rattled about excessively?"

Darcy ignored his sister's teasing comment. The truth is, the idea had occurred to him. Instead, he remained at his post, feigning a calmness he did not feel.

Worry over Elizabeth's safety while traveling wasn't the primary cause of his roiling emotions. Aside from the excitement and intoxicating joy always felt when she was in his presence, he remained overwhelmed by her request to join him at church. Years before meeting Elizabeth Bennet, one of the deepest desires of his heart was to stand in worship beside the woman he loved. It conjured images of more than Sunday services, such as the reading of banns, their wedding, and christening babies. Another item to check off his list of long-held dreams. At times, the promise of fulfilled dreams seemed like a dream itself.

With these musings forefront in his mind, the carriage came to a halt before the townhouse and seconds later his soon-to-be wife was peeking out the door opened by the footman. Darcy's dreams were now a flesh and blood reality.

Dressed in a lovely, deep-blue gown and ivory velvet pelisse, her bonnet adorned with tiny white flowers and a ribbon matching her dress, Elizabeth was stunningly beautiful. More than her clothing, however, it was her bearing which caused his heart to soar. Her bright eyes scanned the townhouse top to bottom with warmth and admiration, a sweet smile curving her lush lips.

Taking Hobbes's hand, she alit from the carriage, her svelte figure gracefully descending to the walkway. She said something to Hobbes that made him crack a small smile, and then turned to Peters and the coachman, Mr. Anders, offering, Darcy presumed, her thanks or Sunday blessings or perhaps both. They looked rather startled, the gesture quite unusual, but politely responded in kind. Such a small thing, but to Darcy it was immense.

She practically skipped up the front steps, pausing to greet Mr. Travers, whom Darcy could not see from the angle of his window but knew to be the one holding the door open. Sure enough, less than a minute later the butler escorted her into the parlor.

"Miss Elizabeth! You are here! Such a delight, is it not, Brother?"

Understatement of the century. "Yes, indeed, a lovely delight. You are well this morning, I trust, Miss Elizabeth?"

"Quite well, Mr. Darcy." Her teasing tone and twinkling eyes expressed her amusement over the blandly spoken traditional greetings. "I trust you are well this morning, sir? And you, Miss Darcy? Yes? Fabulous! I am delirious with relief to discover we are all so very *well*."

"Oh, Miss Elizabeth. You do make me laugh! I will miss you awfully. Must you *really* leave tomorrow?"

Sitting on the sofa beside his sister, Elizabeth clasped the girl's hand. "I am afraid so, my dear Georgiana. Be cheered, as we shall see each other again in just a few weeks."

"Yes, but only for a day or two before I am forced to return to Town while William whisks you off to Pemberley. It may be months before I am in your company again."

Resisting an urge to scold her over her histrionics and impertinent liberties, Darcy settled for basic facts. "Pouting and whining will not change the plans, Georgie. Furthermore, you will be home by Christmas, so less than a month is the accurate interval. Surely you cannot begrudge my time alone with my new bride?"

She flushed and dropped her eyes. "No, of course not—"

"What your brother does not understand," Elizabeth interjected when Georgiana stammered, "is that women as close as sisters can be quite silly. Almost childish at times. A fault, according to some, perhaps, yet a truth we freely acknowledge as a divinely gifted characteristic of the fairer, gentler sex." She sighed, as dramatic as his sister, and Darcy half expected her to dab a pretend tear from her eye! Instead, she turned her face his direction, a saucy look warning him. "We must be tender with him, my dear, and ever strive to ease his severity with gaiety, as is our purpose in life. To be male has such heavy burdens and tragic deficiencies."

The sudden chime of the longcase clock striking the half hour distracted from the laugh he attempted to muffled behind a cough. The reminder that it was time to depart also saved him from enduring further feminine whining and dramatics.

Grosvenor Chapel was located on Audley Street a few blocks south of the townhouse. As Darcy explained to Elizabeth on the short ride, the chapel had been his family's place of worship when in London since shortly after construction in 1731.

"Most of the buildings in this area"—Darcy swept his hand toward the rows of grand townhouses passing the carriage window —"were developed in the early 1700s at the initiation of Sir Richard

Grosvenor, the fourth baronet. Our great-grandfather was Sir Richard's friend, one of the reasons he built the townhouse in Grosvenor Square for the Darcys."

"As I learned yesterday, it can pay to have connections in high places upon occasion."

Darcy laughed. "Quite so, Elizabeth. Whether gaining entrance to the palace or purchasing a home, knowing the right people is beneficial. As for the chapel, my great-grandfather was not a particularly religious man, or so I gathered from the stories. On the rare occasions he attended services with his family, he chose this chapel solely for its proximity and connection to Sir Richard. Our grandfather, however, had a different opinion, both in the application of his faith and reasons for choosing Grosvenor Chapel. Someday I will share more of my family history regarding the former, and since we are nearly there, I shall let you guess on the latter. Bear in mind that I am very like my grandfather in personality and beliefs."

"Another guessing game, Mr. Darcy? These are proving to be somewhat dangerous."

"Frankly, I quite enjoy the thrill of danger. It warms the blood and stimulates the...mind." He winked, satisfied to see a rosy hint touch her adorable cheeks. "However, we should be safe if the prize for this test is jewelry or some other tangible object less hazardous to give."

"We shall see," she demurred. Her cheeks were still rosy, but she flashed an impish smile before turning to look out the carriage window.

Oh yes indeed, my sweet. We shall see. I still have two kisses to collect and two to deliver. Nor do I intend for the prizes to be interrupted and delayed, as happened last evening.

Georgiana's gaze darted between the two, confused by the banter, to Darcy's relief. Then she shrugged, declaring, "I'll spare you guessing my favorite aspect of the chapel, Miss Elizabeth. It is the organ! A fabulous instrument built by organ specialist Abraham

Jordon of elegantly carved oak and brass pipes. It dates to 1732, and the sound is incredible. The rector let me play it once. Oh, it was such a thrill!"

"If only your recollection of and enthusiasm for historical dates and facts filtered to other subjects besides music." His tease was accented by a brotherly peck on her cheek and tweak to her nose before he opened the door and hopped out of the carriage. Assisting Georgiana from the carriage first, he then turned to Elizabeth, watching as she scrutinized the outside of Grosvenor Chapel.

"I can already understand your appreciation, William," she said after a few minutes. "It is the classical form and modesty of construction, as seen in the simple tan bricks and white stucco, and in the pediment gables which are bold and in the Romanesque style reminiscent of Pemberley. Even the bell tower, though shorter than I suspect you would prefer, is strong and beautifully ornamental."

Leaving off her visual inspection of the chapel, she looked up at him and continued softly. "You are a man of contradictions in many ways. The grandeur, dramatic beauty, and boldness of Baroque styling appeals to you greatly, I believe. Yet, when tempered with aspects of romanticism and the picturesque, a perfect balance is achieved for your sensibilities—an equal melding of the natural form and minimalism expressing harmony and reserve, with the intense contrasts and opulence declaring power and wealth.

"Your aesthetic style is a dichotomy, of sorts, as is your personality in many respects. The exception to this is in your relationship with God and how you believe it best manifested in a house of worship. My guess is that while you can appreciate the artistic beauty of ornate architecture, sculptures, paintings, and the like, you feel it subtracts from the purity and simplicity of the Biblical message. Hence, a plain chapel such as this is more to your liking, as it was, I deduce, for your grandfather."

This was not the first time Elizabeth had amazed him at her insights into his soul and mind, so perhaps he should not have been so stunned. Nevertheless, once again, he was flabbergasted. He could not recall discussing his personal religious beliefs with her beyond the most cursory of comments, and after touring Westminster Abbey, where grandeur and opulent architecture were prevalent, it would be logical for her to conclude that more to his taste. Instead, she somehow comprehended his feelings on the subject with absolute accuracy and summarized her conclusions in precise language.

"I can only attribute your remarkable insights to Him, Elizabeth. I swear you know me better than I know myself." He lifted her gloved hand for a light kiss, then placed it on his forearm. Offering the other arm to Georgiana, he escorted his two favorite women toward the small church.

The possibility of encountering people of his acquaintance who might have heard the lies disseminated by Lady Catherine de Bourgh had occurred to him moments after Elizabeth asked to accompany him and Georgiana to church services. There were much higher odds of it happening at the chapel attended by many of the families who resided in the Mayfair district, which included Grosvenor Square.

His joy over her request overcame the worst of his anxieties. Furthermore, as far as he was aware, over a week in London had passed without any confrontations or overheard whispers disturbing Elizabeth. Darcy was beginning to believe the gossip wasn't as bad as his cousin Richard had reported, had already faded away as gossip naturally did when unfuelled, or had given way to a more scintillating scandal.

Despite this, he was on alert as they entered the church. Being a reserved, closemouthed, and somewhat aloof man by nature, and with a sister who instantly reverted to her innate shyness when in a crowd, it was typical for the Darcys to nod noncommittally as they silently passed through. If there was one skill Mr. Darcy of Pemberley possessed that was as natural to him as breathing, it was the ability to exude imperious indifference and ignore anyone he chose to. With this tactic in his favor, and the fact that services were soon to begin, he adroitly evaded conversation. Even Elizabeth's sunny smile and openly welcome expression failed against the perfected aura of Darcy unsociability.

Darcy led his sister and fiancée through the chapel narthex, ascended the stairs to the upper gallery, and unlocked the door to the secluded box-pew long ago designated for the Darcy family.

Elizabeth's faint gasp and lifted brows indicated surprise over something. Confused, Darcy used his assistance in seating as a cover to whisper into her ear, "Is something amiss, Elizabeth?"

"Not at all," she quickly reassured him, smiling. "I've just never seen such plush seating and unique construction in a pew." She ran her hand over the lacquered mahogany paneling, then gently patted the red velvet cushions covering the bench seat. "I'm rather jealous, to be honest. These benches are molded into a curve befitting the human body to prevent the inevitable aching back. Furthermore, I'm lamenting the years of sitting on the hard pews in our Meryton church where, apparently, no one considered adding a cushion!"

"It is a toss-up, I suppose. Too comfortable and one may fall asleep, particularly if the priest is less than riveting in his delivery. Too uncomfortable and the soreness of one's buttocks preoccupies rather than the message."

"Indeed," she agreed, stifling a laugh. "Although, for me, it was the sharp edges digging into my shoulder blades that annoyed. Whichever Darcy ancestor came up with the brilliant idea of curved and padded backs has earned my undying gratitude."

"Alas, I doubt it was a Darcy invention, as all the pew boxes have them. However, it was my grandfather who increased the depth of this row and added the small footstools. He was taller than me, and legs our length quickly cramp up in tight spaces."

"Taller than you? My goodness, he must have been a giant."

"He always seemed so to me, for a host of reasons. I wish you could have known him, Elizabeth, and my father as well. They would have adored you."

The statement was true, Darcy knew it for certain in his heart, although why the sentiment chose that moment to slip out, he could not say. Her eyes grew slightly misty, and she swiftly caressed the top of his hand where it lay on his thigh as she glanced down into the nave.

It seems we are both easily affected by maudlin emotions these days, he thought, unsure whether this was laughable or alarming. The entrance of the choir as the organ sprang into life diverted further personal analyzing of his strangely unbridled sentimentality.

Upon later evaluation, Darcy would acknowledge the fault in averting the unpleasant after-service encounter lay solely upon his shoulders. Elizabeth's proximity throughout the worship and sermon gave him a taste of their future as one soul united in God. Blanketed in the warmth of his emotions, he exited the church with his guard lowered, mind numbed, and focus narrowed.

At the shouting of his name from amid the milling crowd of churchgoers, he stopped and turned, a bemused smile fixed upon his lips. Worst yet, upon seeing the two men hastening directly toward him with two finely dressed women trailing behind, his smile broadened.

Not a single bell of warning chimed.

~

*T*he only bells Lizzy heard were from the residual ringing song of the excellent church choir and organ.

Arm linked with Mr. Darcy's, she exited the chapel in step with him, but her attention was on the bubbly girl skipping to her left. Georgiana gushed on about the organ's tonal qualities, pipe speech, reed timbres, and other technical notations which were gibberish to Lizzy. This mattered not, of course, as Georgiana was precious in her joyful enthusiasm, and Lizzy was far too happy to be perturbed by anything.

In truth, her mood was remarkably similar to Mr. Darcy's. For starters, she had never enjoyed a Sunday service to the extent she had this one. The music truly was as fantastic as Georgiana claimed, and the priest spoke his message in a voice both pleasant in tone and lively in elocution. The latter was a rarity, Lizzy unable to resist whispering a comparison with Mr. Collins into Mr. Darcy's ear, his chuckle thankfully unheard from their sheltered pew in the upper level.

Jesting at her ridiculous cousin's expense notwithstanding, Lizzy's present disposition arose in part from the service itself, but not as the primary source. Unlike her serious, religiously inclined betrothed, until recently Lizzy had never envisioned standing in worship with a future spouse.

The night before, when requesting to join him, she had said, "I long with all my heart to be your wife and partner, William. Standing beside you in church, I can, if only for a short while, feel as if I already am." Though spoken with sincerity, she had not expected how real the illusion of being his wife would feel. An ordinary, weekly ritual engaged in more times than she could count had today become a momentous experience.

Thus, between listening to Georgiana's effusive praise of the organ music and the warmth of her emotions, Lizzy did not hear the shout of her future husband's name. Rather, it was his unexpected halting and pivot about—her hand losing contact with his arm in the process—which alerted her to anything.

Pressing a hand to Georgiana's arm in silent communication, she peeked from behind William's back just as a rotund, older gentleman boomed out, "Darcy! Well met, indeed! I was hoping to see you here! Based on your high breeding standards and promises, I will be placing a hefty bet on Bathsheba Fire to win at Newmarket. I best not be disappointed!"

From her partially hidden vantage point, Lizzy observed Darcy inclining his head respectfully. Then, in a warm tone edged with humor, he greeted, "Good Sunday to you, Lord Westingcote. I have the utmost confidence in Bathsheba Fire. She is an excellent filly. However, you know as well as I that one can never promise how a race will end. If it is some assurance, I intend to wager a substantial sum upon her myself, so we shall both face the outcome, whether grievous or celebratory, together."

Lizzy instantly remembered Lord Westingcote from their dinner conversation the previous night about the Jockey Club and flying pigs, the name recognition causing her to speculate if the distinguished gentleman walking a step behind the generous-bodied lord was the banner-obsessed Mr. Shelley. What a coincidence that would be!

The unidentified second gentleman, whoever he was, wore an amused grin. In a timbre almost as resonant as Darcy's and with matching warmth, the dignified man bobbed his head toward Lord Westingcote as he warned, "Don't let him play upon your pity, Darcy. The old schemer will place more than one bet at the Newmarket races, increasing the odds for a winning day in the end."

"Your Grace." Darcy bowed deeply, his bearing and reverent inflection announced the speaker's elevated rank even if Lizzy had not caught the term of address. "The information is appreciated, although I suspected as much, largely because I will do the same. Besides, Lord Westingcote is not unique in spreading bets, now is he, Your Grace? I've yet to attend a horse race where you have not done the same, even in the same race."

The duke shrugged, his smile broad. "It is prudent to spread one's wagers far and wide. A lesson I taught you long ago, my boy!"

Based on the casual teasing and social reference, the nameless duke and her fiancé were well acquainted. It was so unexpected Lizzy barely stifled an involuntary squawk of amazement and was thankful her position behind Mr. Darcy concealed her dumbfounded expression.

An actual duke! Despite William's elevated position in society and kinship to an earl, the possibility of standing face to face with the highest-ranking peer of the realm, one of a handful of titled dukes currently in all of England, had never crossed her mind. It was staggering.

Thankfully, Lord Westingcote's boisterous laugh jerked her back into awareness before she succumbed to the nervous flutters threatening to burst forth. She had no idea what had been said to create such hilarity, but Darcy and the duke joined in the rollicking chortles so it must have been a riot. Clapping a big hand onto Darcy's shoulder, Lord Westingcote declared, "Excellent news, Darcy! I am delighted you can attend the races and insist you join us. You have room in the box for another, do you not, Your Grace?"

"Absolutely. There is always room for Darcy of Pemberley. We can celebrate Bathsheba Fire's win together. I will not take no for an answer, Darcy. You know where it is after all," he finished drily.

At his lordship's zealous hand gesture, Lizzy gingerly hopped to the right, instinctively avoiding his hand connecting with her face. No longer shielded by Darcy's broad shoulders and height, her view of the scene improved, while also revealing to the men that Mr. Darcy was not alone.

Two sets of eyes swiveled her direction, the appraising sweep head to toe—as men typically did when first encountering a woman —swift and thorough. Determined not to flinch or glance away, she endured the assessment, even managing to smile. The unnerving, sharp gaze of the duke rested upon her for several seconds before he shifted his focus to Georgiana, who stood in bashful silence a foot or so to Lizzy's left.

Exhaling in the momentary respite, she peripherally took note of the two women near Lord Westingcote. Neither appeared to be paying any attention to the conversation on horse racing, so she paid them scant heed. Besides, the duke was talking, his firm baritone as captivating as his physical presence.

"Ah! I see you are not alone today, Mr. Darcy. Neither are we, as it happens. Our preoccupation with horses derailed properly attending to our venerate ladies. Ignoring such loveliness borders on being unpardonable." Maintaining eye contact with Lizzy, the duke pressed his right hand over his heart and inclined his head. "Please accept my sincere apology. May I be so bold as to request introductions, Darcy?"

"Forgive my lapse in manners, Your Grace. The fault is entirely mine." Beaming, Darcy turned toward Lizzy and Georgiana. "Ladies, it is my pleasure and honor to present His Grace the Duke of Grafton, the Viscount and Viscountess Westingcote, and their esteemed daughter, Miss Pratt. Sirs and madams, my sister, Miss Darcy, and my betrothed, Miss Bennet of Longbourn in Hertfordshire."

The standard greetings ensued, accompanied by the befitting head bobs and curtsies. Lizzy noticed that Lady Westingcote and Miss Pratt's air of indifference only disappeared at the mention of her name, a bewildering oddity she shrugged away. Of much greater interest to her were the effervescent viscount and the charming duke, both of whom were quite loquacious.

"Miss Darcy, I suppose you hear it frequently, but you uncannily resemble your honorable mother, the Lady Anne. She was a remarkable lady and is greatly missed by those fortunate to have known her."

The Duke of Grafton's sincere testimonial touched Lizzy, as it did the shy Georgiana, who murmured, "Your Grace is most kind."

The Duke directed his attention to Lizzy, undoubtedly to Georgiana's immense relief. The Duke of Grafton was handsome for an older gentleman, and his face kind and smile warm. There was an aura of power emanating from him unlike anything she had ever felt, and his eyes seemed to pierce into her soul. For one of the few times in her life, she experienced profound awe and bashfulness, suddenly empathizing with her soon-to-be sister.

"Miss Bennet, a pleasure to meet you and to hear of Mr. Darcy's engagement. I now comprehend why he was distracted to the point of forgetting a Pemberley thoroughbred was racing at Newmarket this week. Causing a man as focused as Darcy into forgetfulness, particularly regarding horses, is a feat only a woman of unique qualities could manage. Well done, madam!"

"Thank you, Your Grace. I shall accept the compliment." Lizzy jauntily bobbed a curtsy, her smile impish. The gestures, forced a bit, helped overcome her timidity. "I do pray, however, that no one at the Jockey Club was overly disturbed by Mr. Darcy's unusual behavior. One can only imagine the speculations wildly running amok."

The duke chuckled. "Here is a secret and a warning, Miss Bennet. When men are chattering about horses and racing, they pay little attention to anything or anyone else. Something to bear in mind after you are married."

"I shall tuck that information safely away, sir. Thank you."

The bantering was cut short by the appearance of two new horse enthusiasts. Properly introduced to Lizzy and Georgiana, Lord Ailes-Combe and Mr. Crannick offering nothing beyond the formalities before launching into an intense discussion about, naturally, the upcoming races.

Half-amused and half-peeved, Lizzy muttered, "I see what the duke meant. We have apparently become invisible."

Georgiana squeezed her hand reassuringly. "I can't lie and tell you William isn't passionate about his thoroughbreds to the point of obsession. I have suddenly become invisible a number of times, but it never lasts too long. Besides, he now has you in his life, and trust me, Miss Elizabeth, he is far more passionate about you."

Blushing, she squeezed Georgiana's hand gratefully, the reassuring words flooding her with contentment. Unfortunately, seconds later the happy sensations were doused.

"So, this is the Miss Bennet we have heard so much about."

Lizzy jerked her eyes toward Lady Westingcote and Miss Pratt, unsure which woman had spoken. After the initial introductions neither had added a single syllable to the conversation and aside from the eerie sensation of disapproving scrutiny, Lizzy had almost forgotten they were there. Being directly addressed was surprising. Stranger still was the comment itself, but most bewildering of all was how the women were looking at her.

The Viscountess Westingcote wore an expression of thinly veiled distaste, her dark eyes hard and lips pinched. It brought to Lizzy's mind how one reacted to a noxious smell, repulsed but striving to control the reflexive retch. Miss Pratt made no attempt to conceal her dislike, or she was a pathetically mediocre actress. Lizzy could not imagine peering at a filthy street beggar with such repulsion, yet there was an underlying glint of grotesque delight within the young woman's brown eyes.

Lizzy could not stay the involuntary shudder or make her numbed lips lift into a neutral smile. Confused, a bit alarmed, and prickled with pangs of unaccountable mortification, she stared at the duo blankly.

This reaction seemed to increase Miss Pratt's perverse pleasure. "You are famous, Miss Bennet," she sneered. "Or is *infamous* the proper term for a woman from a scandalous family? Either way, I am somewhat disappointed. Based on the story Lady Starkley conveyed, I presumed your physical appearance to be remarkable at the very least."

Lady Westingcote sniffed. "Nothing of worth has ever come out of Hertfordshire. Indeed, a fine family is to be polluted by inferior stock, just as Lady Catherine de Bourgh claimed. It is a travesty!"

"True, Mama. Still, I thought sure there would be some glimmer of a reason as to how she ensnared a gentleman of Mr. Darcy's prestige. Alas, her wits are as dull and unattractive as her figure, increasing the mystery."

"I suspect she has talents of a particular, unmentionable nature. Even the best of men fall victim to a skilled temptress," the viscountess spat as her gaze pointedly dropped to Lizzy's pelvic region.

Lizzy stood, paralyzed, the thudding in her ears so loud and painful that she truly believed she might faint. The insults slammed into her one after another, registering brutally even though the internal chaos prevented effective assimilation.

Whether it was Georgiana's gasp of shock, the mention of his name, or something else which alerted Mr. Darcy, she had no idea. She feared she might have fallen if not for his strong arm suddenly clenched tightly around her waist. Dimly she felt the rigid tension hardening his muscles and heard him harshly snap a vicious rebuke.

As William drew her closer into his protective embrace before steering her away, she caught a glimpse of Miss Pratt's gaping mouth and blanched face. This was followed by a swift view of Lord Westingcote's red cheeks and furious eyes as he grabbed his daughter and wife by the arm. Their squeaks of pain were audible.

A sensation of fervent satisfaction rippled through Lizzy's gut, but she was too distraught to relish the moment. Focusing on not collapsing as she mechanically placed one foot in front of the other took all her energy. Not quite sure how he managed it without raising a fuss or drawing attention from the groups of churchgoers still socializing on the walkway, Darcy had them safely inside the carriage in what seemed like a matter of seconds.

No one said a word on the short ride back to Darcy House. Lizzy stared out the window, vaguely aware of Georgiana soothingly holding her hand and William's steady gaze. She could not bear to look at him, however, fearing she would detect traces of the same disgust shown by the women in his eyes.

Once at the townhouse, he proved once again his remarkable ability to take command and act calmly under the most distressing circumstances. Speaking in a normal tone, he politely ordered the housekeeper, Mrs. Smyth, to fetch hot, strong tea from the kitchen and then turned to instruct Mr. Travers to escort Miss Bennet to the library.

Touching Lizzy gently on the arm, he leaned close to her ear. "I shall join you there momentarily, my dear. I need to speak with Georgiana for just a moment." He planted a tender kiss on her cheek before pulling away.

Glancing up, she met his eyes for the first time since the debacle at the church. The rush of relief in only seeing intense love and concern was immense. Smiling, wanly but still a smile, she nodded.

Darcy's combined office and library were organized, plushly appointed, clean, and spacious. It was the exact opposite of her father's office and library at Longbourn. Nevertheless, she felt the same sensations of comfort now that she had felt in her father's office since her earliest memory. It was being surrounded by books, which she adored passionately, but instinctively she knew the solace, then and now, came from being in the sanctuary of a man who loved her wholeheartedly.

Strolling along the aisles of varnished oak cases stuffed with dust-free books, the turmoil in her mind began to ease. She remained confused by what had happened after the service and cringed contemplating the meaning of the spewed slurs, but the fog was clearing and the feeling of shame was disappearing.

Then why do I want to scream and cry at the same time?

The door opened, William entering with Mrs. Smyth carrying a tea tray close behind. "Set it on my desk, Mrs. Smyth. That will be all." He gave the command curtly, his eyes darting around the room until finally spying Lizzy where she stood at the far end, between two tall bookcases. She could hear his sigh of relief, and immediately he marched toward her.

"Stop!" She held her hand out, palm forward. "Wait. I need you to hold me, William, but not yet. If you do, I will cry, and I must talk through it first. Please."

He slowed but did not stop until within touching distance.

Troubled eyes searched her face, the war to disregard her request visibly fought as she pleaded silently for him not to. Finally, after a second sigh, he spread his hands open at his sides. "As you wish, Elizabeth. Can we sit at least? A cup of tea will do us both good."

She hesitated; then, remembering the last time they sat on the library sofa, she shook her head. "No. Standing is better. For now. I… I presume Georgiana told you what…they said?"

He clamped his lips into a thin line, grim expression growing angrier by the second, and bobbed his head once.

Glancing away from his evident fury, she blindly peered at the nearest shelf. Inhaling, she stammered, "I'm not sure where to start. Apparently, I'm famous…or infamous. Me, a woman of scandal! Who would have thought?" A harsh, humorless laugh burst from her dry throat.

Darcy impulsively leaned toward her, but she again halted him with a hand gesture.

"Lady Catherine was mentioned," she murmured, still staring at the row of book spines, "and someone named Lady Starkley."

"The Countess of Starkley is related to Lady Westingcote. She is a notorious gossip and one of my aunt's oldest friends. I should have known she was the one sent to do Lady Catherine's dirty work. I'm surprised Richard didn't figure that out, not that it mattered after the deed was done. No doubt she enjoyed every minute of telling fabricated falsehoods to her captive audiences. The old crone! I could happily wring both their necks!"

It was neither the vehemence in his voice nor statement of violence that caused Lizzy to swing her eyes to his face. Frowning, she stepped back a pace. "Wait a minute. Did you… Are you saying that you *knew* these things were being said about me?"

"Richard heard the whispers before we arrived in Town. He has a certain talent for collecting information."

"And you didn't think to mention it to me?" Ejected shrilly, it wasn't a question as much as a condemnation.

Darcy, to her amazement, cocked his head and furrowed his brows in honest confusion. "Whyever would I do that? My fervent hope was for you to *never* learn of it. My duty is to protect you, Elizabeth, above all else. I shall always avoid telling you something that I know would cause you pain unless it is necessary. This was inconsequential."

"Inconsequential? You call this inconsequential?" This was definitely shrieked louder than warranted, but she was swiftly losing control. "Maybe if I was aware such tales of my infamy were being bandied about I could have prepared for a confrontation! Did you consider that, Mr. Darcy, when you were imperiously deciding what is best for me? I can make my own decisions, you know! I do not need some hulking, domineering...man—"

"If it helps to unleash your frustration upon me, Elizabeth, then shout away. This hulking, domineering man is strong enough to withstand the tirade. When you finish, perhaps we can then discuss this nonsense calmly, rather than irrationally." He hadn't moved an inch, yet somehow loomed larger in the space between the bookshelves. His eyes were dark and nostrils flared with each rough inhale.

"Nonsense, is it?" Lizzy was still lashing out, although her words lacked the same vigor as before. "The same 'nonsense' that had you ready to strangle two old women with your bare hands? It does not sound inconsequential to me."

"Anger directed at the source is warranted and justified. Even so, I would not *literally* strangle either of them—at least I don't think I would. Perhaps a good horsewhipping is a better compromise." He grunted a half laugh. Closing his eyes and pinching the bridge of his nose between two fingers, he breathed deeply for a minute or so.

Lizzy watched him in silence. Rational thought, usually one of her greatest virtues, had eluded her. William was right in that accusation. Was he right about the rest?

"Elizabeth, listen to me."

The gentleness in his voice matched the tender way he encircled her cold hands with his. Tears prickled the insides of her eyelids, but she blinked them away. It was past time to regain her senses, and blubbering like an infant was counterproductive.

"Perhaps you are correct that a warning may have prepared you," he continued in the same soothing tone. "However, in my judgment, it is more likely that you would have been on edge this whole week if you had known of my aunt's lies. Despite what happened today, I stand by my decision not to tell you. Your time in London, our time together, would have been tainted, and for what? Gossip. Mean spirited and ugly, yes, but gossip just the same."

"How can you be so angry one minute, and then in the next minute brush it off as just gossip? *Inconsequential* gossip, no less? I do not understand!"

"My dearest, I am furious at my aunt for her persistent refusal to accept the fact of our betrothal. Mainly, I am furious for her unconscionable actions which have now caused you pain. I do not believe anyone is without forgiveness, but God help me, Lady Catherine is skirting the edge in my mind and heart! This is where my anger lies, not on the specifics of the rumors. You must trust me, Elizabeth, when I assure you that in the grand scheme, it does not matter."

"But…those women today…what they said and how they acted toward me was…vile. How can this not matter, to you and to us? Is not reputation and proper behavior everything within society?"

"Consider what they said and how they acted, and tell me who is truly most vile? It assuredly is not you! Lady Westingcote and her pernicious daughter are prime examples of how people in society often behave. They preach a moral and ethical high ground, and all the while they are debauched, shallow hypocrites. Not everyone, of course, although far too many for my taste. The majority are decent people who only possess the typical, largely harmless faults and sins that plague all of humanity. The point is, as much as I hate certain aspects of that world, I comprehend the intricacies. Therefore, you must believe me when I assert that while I do not for a second minimize the pain such words have caused you, they are, indeed, inconsequential."

He drew her hands to his lips, kissing each with a firm pressure before laying them against his heart. "To be clear, I owe much of this revelation to you, Elizabeth Bennet." He smiled at the questioning cast to her face. Lizzy was sincerely perplexed as to his meaning. "I hesitate to bring up past confrontations we have sworn to leave alone. However, not too long ago, you sternly pointed out my prejudices and ridiculous arrogance. It was your moral character, your confidence and boldness, that forced me to hearken to your words. As I have already revealed to you, I spent months reevaluating my actions and thoughts, seeking to improve my character. I hope I have succeeded in that endeavor, at least to some degree?"

The droopy mouth, sad eyes, and overblown expression of supplication was impossible to resist. Lizzy shook her head and giggled breathily.

"Ah! A laugh! Much better. I shall take that as a yes." He kissed her lightly on the forehead before guiding her toward the sofa. He still held tightly to her hands and did not ask if she was wanted to sit, but Lizzy discovered she was more than ready to relax beside him. Plus, suddenly a cup of tea sounded fantastic, even if cooled to lukewarm.

He poured two cups and added the exact amounts of sugar and cream she preferred to one. Watching quietly, she waited until he joined her on the sofa before responding in a jesting tone. "It is a yes by the way. You have improved, although you never were *quite* as defective as I first thought."

"Good to know. Thank you." He lifted his cup as if toasting, flashing a grin before taking a sip.

"And I am sorry I called you hulking and domineering."

"Oh, no need to apologize for that. I *am* hulking and domineering. And a man. So, guilty as charged."

Mutual laughter eased most of the remaining tension, and the amazingly still hot tea played a significant role as well. They drank in silence for several minutes. Lizzy realized she was feeling almost her old self—a remarkable recovery, really, considering the extreme chaos of her emotions mere minutes ago.

Then again, being close to William was inevitably comforting and joyous—and more than a little arousing. Even when not touching or looking at each other, those internal sensations she now identified as desire were kindled into flames. It was an elemental, visceral reaction that she no longer denied or tried to suppress. So when she had the last swallow of tea, she planned to set the cup aside and kiss him… but he spoke.

"Maybe I should let the topic go, but I fear you may later, in your quiet moments, revisit what happened today and begin to doubt." He looked up from his empty cup, serious eyes scanning her face. "Elizabeth, your words…before…did more than cause personal introspection. I removed the blinders installed by my upbringing and opened my eyes, as it were, to the world I was born into, assessing it honestly."

Cups relegated to a nearby table, he scooted closer until their knees bumped and he clasped her hands. "I've often felt… uncomfortable in society, as you know, but I was never so naive that I did not to see how people could be. It was all I had ever known, and I suppose it is normal to make excuses or pretend. I wanted to believe in the exalted ideals of our class structure, in elevated rank and superior breeding, the duty to family and ancestry. I still do, to be honest. Only now I know the limitations and the failings. I know that for all the positives there are negatives, and this isn't any different wherever one falls on the social ladder."

He paused, face tight and deep creases marking the space between his brows. Finally, after a huge sigh, "What I am trying to explain, not very well I think, is that within the somewhat indistinct group known as 'Society' there is a hierarchy with rules and standards. This is true. There is also corruption. Into this comes rampant gossip typically forgotten for the next round of rumors. Upon occasion, sadly, the gossip can lead to real damage, depending upon the persons involved and the degree of truth to the scandal. However, overriding any of this is rank, wealth, and power. Simply put, if one has the latter in large quantities and is well connected to others who do, no amount of scandal, even if extreme, can seriously harm them in the long term."

Peering intently into her eyes, grave and with the self-assured nobility of his station firmly settled upon his countenance, he asked, "Need I elaborate further? You will soon be Mrs. Fitzwilliam Darcy of Pemberley, my wife. Do you now fully comprehend why I am absolutely certain none of the lies matter?"

It fleetingly crossed her mind to tease a bit for the arrogant boast. In reality, his supreme confidence wiped out any remaining negativity from the ugly encounter at Grosvenor Chapel. Furthermore, the blatant authority heard in his resonant voice and seen in his autocratic features heated the simmering desire until all she wanted was for him to kiss her.

A slow smile spread over her lips and she bobbed her head once.

"Good, it is settled. Now, although I suspect the others to arrive any minute, if not already here and being entertained by Georgie, I am not letting you leave this room, Miss Bennet, until I kiss you thoroughly."

And then he did. Quite thoroughly indeed.

8

FESTIVE COMMEMORATION

On the tenth day of November, Darcy greeted the dawn precisely as he had each morning since his engagement. With eyes still closed, he woke in languid stages as his vivid, erotic dreams of Elizabeth slipped smoothly into conscious visions of being with her in some capacity that day. What they found to occupy the hours never mattered to him, except for ensuring they managed at least a few minutes alone for shared kisses and caresses.

As the days counted down toward the wedding, solitary interludes were becoming easier to arrange. Darcy suspected Mr. and Mrs. Bennet would not be quite so trusting if they knew his "rigidly proper gentleman" pose was largely a ruse. He felt a bit guilty for the minor deception. Then he would take Elizabeth into his arms and kiss her delicious lips…and the guilty feelings scattered into the wind.

Anticipating more of the same, he was halfway done with breakfast before a glance at the calendar on his desk reminded him of the actual date.

Today is my twenty-ninth birthday! Why do I continue to forget?

The main reason, as he well knew, was because observing his

birthday had not been a major event since his youth. Since his mother's death twelve years ago, and indeed for a time before that, festive celebrations of any sort were rare. If not for some well-intentioned loved one remembering, Darcy strongly believed his birthday could come and go without him marking it at all. This wasn't implausible, having forgotten until just now after being reminded two days ago!

That past Friday morning, as he'd prepared for his return to Netherfield, Mrs. Smyth had greeted him with, "Good morning, Mr. Darcy. As you are leaving today, I shall extend my wishes for a joyous birthday now." As he'd stood there stammering his thanks, Georgiana had bounded down the stairs with a wrapped gift in her hand that she insisted he open immediately.

All in all, he had felt extremely foolish, even if the scene was a near repeat of his birthday for the past ten years plus.

Georgiana always remembered the date, bestowing a colorfully wrapped present along with an exuberant hug and well wishes. Maybe four times in the past decade, his cousin Richard had tossed him an unwrapped gift—always some sort of liquor that Richard drank half of—along with a birthday wish inevitably including a mention of advanced age and senility.

If Darcy happened to be at Pemberley, and he usually was by November, Mrs. Reynolds would warmly extend her blessings and ensure dinner included all of his favorite dishes. Never one to relish being fussed over, even when young, the minimal attention suited him just fine. Who wanted to be reminded that another unremarkable, lonely year had sped by?

Of course, this birthday differed greatly due to the blissful addition of his beautiful Elizabeth. She was, no argument or competition, superior to any gift received, past and future. He neither needed nor wanted anything else. Regardless of his current happiness, nothing had changed as far as his tendency to forget the date itself and his preference to forego any fanfare when forced to acknowledge he was another year older.

These truths notwithstanding, on the carriage ride from London, Darcy had pondered several birthday-related questions he worried may cause a problems. Should he announce his upcoming birthday to Elizabeth as soon as he arrived? Doing so went against his natural reticence and humility. But if he said nothing, how would Elizabeth feel when she discovered his birthday had passed? Would she interpret his silence as withholding a portion of himself from her? Would she be more distressed at not having an opportunity to honor him and celebrate a special day or at having a mere two days to find a gift?

Perhaps such mundane calendar events are unimportant to her, as most of them are to me.

Deep in his gut, Darcy knew better. Elizabeth was practical, more so than many women, but also extremely romantic and thoughtful. Women were particularly sentimental regarding birth anniversaries— understandable since females are the ones who bring new life into the world—and held high expectations regarding their own. The latter had more to do with the gifts, he suspected, based on his sister's zestful delight over the smallest trinket garnished with a bow.

Additionally, while not quite as animated when presenting a gift as she was when receiving one, Georgiana adored expressing her love for him by finding special objects befitting his personality and hobbies. Her birthday gift this year, an exquisite cravat pin crafted to match his wedding ensemble, was proof.

Long before reaching Hertfordshire, Darcy had decided to remain silent on the subject. Aside from his indifference toward observing his birthday, upon further reflection, he concluded Elizabeth was probably long ago aware of his birthdate. For one, she simply wasn't the type of person to overlook what most people considered an important detail. Second, he recalled a dinner conversation which had taken place shortly after their engagement, while dining at Longbourn one evening.

Amid the disorderly and frequently too-loud discourse Darcy found highly irregular and irritating, Kitty had launched into a fretful whine over her early December birthday being forgotten due to wedding aftermath. Not in the least interested in Elizabeth's younger sister's petty concerns, he was grateful for the topic as it provided a sensible opening for him to ask Mrs. Bennet when Elizabeth had been born. Even he, avowed loather of his own birthday, appreciated that this was of vital importance to females. Tremendously relieved that he had until the following May to figure out how to properly honor her special day, his much-sooner birthday never crossed his mind.

What Darcy did recall was that he had directed his gaze toward Elizabeth where she sat at the opposite end of the table near her father chatting with Mary. Seconds later, she had lifted her eyes and smiled at him. Whether she had overheard his hushed, brief exchange with Mrs. Bennet hadn't concerned him at the time, but in retrospect, he believed it possible.

She had never asked him directly, but there were any number of people who could have enlightened her, Georgiana or Charles the probable culprits. Therefore, odds were good that she was aware of the date and, worse yet, she might be planning a major celebration.

Standing at the window of his Netherfield bedchamber and staring at the light dusting of snow upon the ground, Darcy had a sudden horrific vision. In sharp detail, he imagined an elaborate gathering with half the citizens of Hertfordshire hoisting him into the air while toasting his health and singing, "For he's a jolly good fellow!" He honestly preferred torture with hot brands than to suffer such a fate. The joy of Elizabeth's company was barely enough incentive to keep him from crawling back under the covers and claiming a deathly case of the plague.

Bravely deciding to face the day, Darcy headed toward the

main parlor, as he did each morning, to meet Bingley before driving to Longbourn. The younger man was already there, staring out at the landscape with a happier expression than Darcy had directed at the dreary gray clouds and snow. Charles appeared quite delighted, in fact, and a suspicious Darcy found this annoying.

Steeled for a boisterous happy birthday hail, he was taken aback when Charles gestured to the scene outside the window and boomed, "Look at it, Darcy! Quite stunning, I daresay. Although a bit more snow to completely cover the ground would have been nicer. Either way, it is colder, and that is excellent. Don't you think?"

Bingley's bright smile was completely at odds with the weather.

What did the sneak mean about the snow and cold being excellent? Moody and on edge, Darcy scanned his friend's face for any clue that secret birthday plotting was afoot.

"I am fond of the cold and snow," Darcy admitted, narrowed eyes scrutinizing, "but did hope the temperate weather would hold for a bit longer. Frozen or muddy ground is not promotive for long, solitary walks."

"Ah, but for a carriage ride snuggled close under blankets and furs, it is perfect! Or have you forgotten my Jane's suggestion for today?"

He had forgotten, in fact. Apparently, the curse of poor recollection was becoming an epidemic. While at dinner the previous evening, Jane had innocently inquired of her fiancé, "Mr. Bingley, am I mistaken or does the garage at Netherfield house two phaetons?"

"Indeed, it does, Miss Bennet. Why do you ask?"

"Well, I was thinking, if we do have snow tonight, and it isn't a significant amount, as Papa ensures it will not be, perhaps we could take a drive on the morrow? Nothing is as lovely as freshly fallen snow blanketing the open meadows."

Elizabeth had immediately added her exclamation of approval, her eyes sparkling so captivatingly in the candlelight that Darcy's murmured agreement could have been for plans to feed wild lions for all he knew.

"I know you too well, Darcy," Bingley said, interrupting Darcy's revisit of the previous night's dinner conversation. Turning from the window, smug grin in place, he walked across the parlor toward the door. "You would no more miss an opportunity to be alone with your betrothed than I would mine. If Mr. and Mrs. Bennet interpret two open carriages driving together as allowable under the rules of propriety, who am I to argue? Besides, we both have excellent vision so can see the other carriage even if little more than a dot on the horizon. If asked, we can swear we were within eyesight the whole time."

Pausing on the threshold to the foyer, Bingley winked and then laughed.

Instantly in a jolly disposition, Darcy hastily followed, forgetting all about birthdays and the rather bizarre case of forgetfulness too. His thoughts had already skipped ahead. After all, a couple in love could enjoy all manner of tender liberties when bundled under concealing blankets on a deserted country road!

~

*D*arcy and Elizabeth were closing in on six weeks since she had accepted his second proposal of marriage. Of all the remarkable developments between them during those weeks, the most surprising to Darcy was how incredibly close they had grown. He had anticipated complete accord to evolve *after* they exchanged vows, with the weeks of courtship establishing foundational stones to build upon later.

Instead, he often found it necessary to remind himself that they were not already wed. The degree of comfort he felt with Elizabeth was extreme, and he knew she felt the same. Conversation, no matter the topic, was as spontaneous as breathing. Good-natured raillery and private jokes flowed. Best of all, or worst of all depending on the place or people present, was the intensity of their mutual attraction and how natural the expression.

He had lost count of the number of times he caught himself before caressing her cheek or even planting a soft kiss while in the middle of a crowded room. Probably a few more than the times he *hadn't stopped* the impulse, but not by a wide margin. It was quite alarming how rapidly his restraint, the product of nearly thirty years of harsh discipline, was disappearing.

Then, he would receive a spontaneous peck on his cheek or firm squeeze of his hand, gaze into her love-filled eyes, and any concerns would flitter away. What was the worst that could happen? A disapproving glare he would not notice anyway? A stern rebuke he would apologize for and then promptly disregard? The world would not screech to a halt if Darcy of Pemberley broke a rule or acted in a less-than-perfect manner.

The second he drove the phaeton off the busier thoroughfare connecting Longbourn to the village of Meryton, he scooted closer to Elizabeth until they were pressed together hip to toe. She welcomed the maneuver by ensuring the woolen blankets draped over their lower bodies weren't caught in between them and then rested one gloved hand just above his knee. The sun was shining between the wisps of clouds, so while colder than it had been thus far that November, the air temperature was rising. Then again, even if it had been arctic out, the heat of her touch would have been more than enough to ward off the deepest chill.

Between the distraction of her fingertips lazily stroking tiny circles and his own searching for the side road he intended to take, Darcy belatedly realized what Elizabeth was chatting about.

"Where did you learn of a new publication upcoming from Lord Byron? I hadn't heard that news."

"Really? It was listed in the 'Literary Intelligence' section of this month's *Gentleman's Magazine*. You do not subscribe?"

"I do, but it was just published and I have been rather occupied of late, in case you had not noticed." She nudged his side, laughing. Continuing in as serious a tone as he could muster, he said, "I am surprised a genteel lady such as yourself, Miss Bennet, would waste her delicate intellect on a magazine primarily intended for the male mind."

"Well, naturally I first scour through *La Belle Assemblée* and the *Lady's Magazine* until they're memorized. I only flip open the *Gentleman's Magazine* to read the recipes and domestic articles Mr. Urban has included. It isn't my fault if my eyes accidentally fall on the latest news from Parliament, crime reports, and literature reviews."

"Yes, I see. Indeed it is the editor's fault." Darcy winked but kept his focus on the road as he made the tight turn onto the narrower lane. "Now that we have cleared that up," he resumed once safely heading straight, "I thank you for the information. I shall send a note to Mr. Hatchard in London, asking him to procure a copy of Lord Byron's poems as soon as it is available. In December, you say? He can send it to Pemberley, then. It shall give us something to do on those long nights."

"Ha! If I have my way, sir, reading will be the last activity on your mind, particularly at night."

Darcy nearly choked and had to swallow several times. Despite their comfort with each other and their mutual passionate desire, bold references to lovemaking still surprised him!

"While you are making requests, William, if you do not mind, there were a couple of other titles I am also interested in."

"Of course, Elizabeth. Anything you wish. All you have to do is ask. If they are already released publications, I can check with Mr. Leonard at the book shop in Meryton. He seems competent."

"You can ask and may have influence where I don't." At his frown, Elizabeth shrugged. "Both titles I want are written by women. Mr. Leonard is old-fashioned about such things. Your jesting a moment ago would be a fervently held opinion of his, trust me. I rather doubt he allows Mrs. Leonard to read a lady's magazine, if she can read at all."

"Such attitudes are outrageous," Darcy fumed. "Never mind then. I'd just as soon not do business with him. Mr. Hatchard usually has new books on hand anyway, so can have them delivered to you at Longbourn."

Pleased at that report, she said no more. Bobbing her chin toward the approaching end of the lane. "We are to visit the bluffs?"

Snickering, Darcy nodded. "We are, although I cannot help but laugh at the local moniker for what barely constitutes a hill being 'the bluffs.' I've seen fairy mounds that were higher."

"Allow us deprived flatlanders our delusions, please. We aren't blessed to have the majestic Peaks in our backyard, rising to uncharted elevations. Why I heard intrepid climbers are giving up on scaling the Himalayan heights in lieu of challenging the Derbyshire Peaks!"

"Ha-ha, very funny. But, the point is valid. It is a matter of perspective in the end. I will concede the view from your revered bluff is an impressive panorama. Bingley and I thought that with the snow, the view should be lovelier still."

"Ah, yes. The view. *That* is why you chose this destination. What other reason could there be?"

Darcy's answer was a lusty grin and penetrating leer from her mouth to bosom. Her instant reaction was a bright flush to her cheeks and averted face. One minute saucy and alluding to bedroom activities, the next blushing and struck with shyness—oh, how he adored his Elizabeth's mix of brazenness and innocence!

Moments later, they reached the wide clearing of the so-called bluff. Darcy steered to the right, a quick glance noting Bingley driving his phaeton to the left. Directing the horses into a slight angle, he reined them to a stop and set the brake. Another swift inspection revealed Bingley doing the same, the two open carriages within eyesight of each other, and within hearing if one shouted, but aligned so unable to peer directly into the hooded seating area. Securing the reins before taking off his gloves, Darcy turned toward Elizabeth.

A playful smirk curved her lips, and one brow was lifted, and her brown eyes sparkled naughtily. She didn't need to comment on the parking arrangement for him to know she understood completely. Quite sure his own expression was similarly naughty and playful, he slipped his right arm over her shoulders and drew her into his body. The shift in position slid her hand higher up his thigh until dangerously close to his groin—a pleasant relocation that raised his internal temperature.

"So, Miss Bennet, shall we enjoy the view?"

"I have seen it before, with more snow than this, in fact. I doubt much has changed."

Needing no further encouragement, Darcy lifted his hand to her face and lightly stroked her delicate skin. There was no need to rush this sweet interlude. He and Bingley had agreed—in halting and cryptic verbiage, as neither was comfortable discussing matters of intimacy—to limit their time at the bluff to thirty minutes tops. Without expressly saying it, each man comprehended the hazards in pushing boundaries. They were, after all, only human!

Cradling Elizabeth's jaw in his palm, he drew her tighter into his embrace while bending to meet her upturned lips. As always, that initial moment of contact, whether gentle or firm, took his breath away. A muffled sigh caught in his throat and a sizzling current of heat rushed through his body. Instantly, his groin stiffened, and a harsh mental rebuke was necessary to deter a full-blown arousal that would rob him of the last shreds of coherency.

Instinctively intensifying the kiss, one thought screamed through his mind: *Dear God, how desperately I want to make love to her!*

As if one of his nighttime dreams were invading his waking mind, Darcy could see himself loving her right there in the carriage. More than that, *he could feel it*. Vividly. He had never conceived of doing such a thing, yet his mind's eye effortlessly provided step-by-step, full-color, moving illustrations! He'd start by running his hands up her legs while lifting her skirts until her lower body was bared. Then, he'd pull her onto his lap so that her lean, silky legs straddled his thighs. A simple twist to the buttons on his breeches, as he'd done thousands of times, would free his swollen member. Clasping his hands onto her firm, rounded buttocks, all it would take is a hoist upward followed by a smooth thrust to be buried deep inside of her. Ah! To be joined as one with the woman he loved—exquisite bliss transcending all imagination!

Shuddering, he withdrew from her lips with a gasping groan and dropped his head onto her shoulder. Inhaling slow and deep, he blocked the visions and willed the seething sensations to subside.

"What is it, William? Is something wrong?"

There was some consolation in hearing her husky tone and breathlessness. He wasn't the only one physically affected by an impassioned kiss.

"Nothing is wrong," he finally managed to hiss through a clenched jaw. "Except, perhaps, for the timing."

She said nothing for a minute at least, holding still as if in thought while Darcy collected his scattered wits. What was intended to be a playful, temperate interlude of kisses and maybe one or two borderline-indecent tactile inspections, had gone wildly astray within five minutes, leaving him quite rattled. Then, when he was almost entirely in control, it was Elizabeth who moved first.

Removing her hands from where they lay on his right thigh under the blankets, she encircled his neck and laced her fingers into his hair. Tugging gently, she drew him up until able to look into his eyes.

"I am not sure what you mean by that, although I have my suspicions. What I do know is that we must soon leave for lunch at Netherfield. As I see it, the timing is perfect for what we can safely do right now. I do not intend to waste a single second." She paused only long enough to smile, vibrant and confident, and then took the initiative.

Darcy wondered if those occasional bouts of acute lust were critical in the long run. It wasn't the release he desperately needed and wanted, not by a long shot, but letting loose his pent-up sexual energy in small measures aided in preserving his sanity and maintaining restraint over the remaining days until they married. Today, as had happened before, once past the violent, spontaneous reaction, he was able to calm—comparatively, that is—and enjoy the sweet pleasure of tender kisses and caresses.

Following her lead, he returned the kiss, and both regulated themselves as they explored with tongues and lips. With a tug, he untied the laces of her brocade cape, eased the fabric aside, and slid his hands into the warm pocket surrounding her upper body. She wore a collared spencer of thick woolen flannel over a high-bodice gown, understandable with the colder weather, so unless he went as far as partially undressing her—a tempting but ill-advisable action— over-the-clothing fondling would have to satisfy his need to touch her.

Elizabeth apparently came to the same conclusion. With a surprising degree of deftness, she unbuttoned his overcoat and jacket and, after briefly toying with one waistcoat button, contented herself with leaving two layers of garments under her exploring palms.

The game was rather humorous. In those scant occasions when they had managed to be alone long enough to touch each other, it was as if they strictly delineated their bodies into safe zones and taboo territory. The permissible areas were from head to naval— except for Elizabeth's breasts—and the stretch from knee to mid-thigh was harmless.

Darcy freely admitted riskily trespassing into forbidden regions more often than wise or proper, mainly by cupping her buttocks and pressing her body against his throbbing hardness. Once, completely on accident, he had brushed over her breast, searing into his brain the titillating sensations of round, soft flesh and pebble-hard nipples.

Yet every kiss and caress increased their comfort with each other, deepened their connection, and furthered their mutual trust. Darcy was convinced that these periods of intimacy would benefit them on their wedding night particularly, and in their relationship as a whole.

Everything was as Elizabeth had forcefully proclaimed a mere two weeks ago in his mother's bedchamber. Heeding her advice, he had surrendered to his passionate nature and freely expressed his love —within reason, of course, which is why the body boundaries and the unstated but bilateral agreement to pull away after a delightful fifteen minutes. Breathing a bit too heavily and heart rates significantly faster than normal, they cuddled close and passed the remaining time staring out at the landscape.

Whether either of them actually *saw* the scenery is doubtful.

~

*W*ith the carriage interlude foremost in his mind and conflicting mightily with competently driving the phaeton, Darcy suspected absolutely nothing when they arrived at Netherfield. He could barely keep his eyes off Elizabeth's glowing mien to pay attention to the footman who was attempting to assist him with doffing his overcoat, gloves, and hat. Then his beloved linked her arm with his, and the duo following behind Bingley and Jane automatically.

Not an inkling of aroused suspicion, even when he noted bypassing the dining room. Bingley's cheery assurance that they were to dine in the second parlor, that one smaller and facing the rear of the house so not as often used, was shrugged off as well. It wasn't until the door was shoved open with a bit too much vigor and Bingley danced aside, so that Darcy, still paying minimal attention, walked over the threshold first, that he finally recognized the truth.

Two steps into the room, Darcy was struck dumb. He could not believe his eyes.

The parlor had been converted to a ceiling-to-floor, wall-to-wall party suite. Ribbons in a rainbow of hues draped over the windows, the twisted yards of fabric pinned to the ceiling crisscrossing the whole expanse with numerous streamers dangling and swaying in the air. Covering the opposite wall was an enormous banner, upon which were painted in bright colors the words: "Joyous Birth Day!"

In the middle of the room were two tables. One was elaborately set for four diners with a single chair, presumably for the guest of honor as it was decorated with a massive red ribbon tied into a bow. A smaller table practically sagged from the weight of presents and a huge cake the likes of which Darcy had never seen before. Round and frosted white, it was adorned with real flowers and leaves, and in the center was a tall, thick, flaming candle.

Elizabeth wrapped her arms around his waist, lifting on tiptoes to whisper in his ear, "Are you pleased, my love?"

Bingley and Jane walked into the room, pausing only to smile and extend their wishes. Turning his attention back to Elizabeth, he noted the mixture of pleasure and anxiety in her expression.

"I am quite speechless, to be honest. You planned all of this?"

"With the help of Jane and Mr. Bingley, of course."

"Who gave me away?"

"Georgiana told me weeks ago. I know you are not fond of surprises, William, especially for your birthday, but I had to do something. I do pray you are not too upset over the fuss. Are you pleased, at least a little?"

"Yes! Yes, I am!" Embracing Elizabeth and squeezing her tight, he bestowed a tender kiss. "Rather shockingly pleased, I have to say. To be honest, I kept forgetting myself. When I did remember, I hoped you had no idea of the date although I figured you probably did."

"I suppose you feared an outrageously ostentatious fete with all of Hertfordshire in attendance."

Laughing, he nodded. "You know me remarkably well, don't you?"

"More each day. This is a simple celebration with just us. I didn't tell anyone else. Goodness knows what my mother might have done with the information!"

"I owe you for that kindness," he remarked earnestly. "And, truly, this is wonderful. Thank you, Elizabeth. I love you for remembering me."

"I wanted to surprise you. It is more fun that way. But I was worried you might feel hurt that I had said nothing or asked outright when you were born, as you did my date of birth. I am sorry if you thought I did not care."

The sadness in her voice broke his heart. "My dearest Elizabeth, never could I doubt how much you care for me." He kissed her again, a bit deeper, and caressed feathering fingertips over her cheek. "As for my birthday, I haven't honestly cared about it since my youth. This is quite unexpected, but pleasantly so."

"Excellent! We do have all sorts of festivities on the agenda. However, another thing I know about you, Mr. Darcy, is that about now you are starving, so we shall begin with luncheon. Come!"

If Darcy had been forced at pistol point to plan his own birthday party, that afternoon's entertainment would have been unchanged. The day was perfect from the start to the finish, many hours later.

As Elizabeth rightly conjectured, Darcy was famished so beginning with luncheon was an excellent way to launch the fun. The Netherfield cook was skilled, and today she and her helpers had outdone themselves. The delicious menu included turtle soup, a salmagundi of mixed greens and vegetables with seasoned vinaigrette, Scotch quail eggs, beef a la mode, spinach soufflé, stewed oysters, and a salver of assorted fruits.

Then, no sooner had the table been cleared than a servant entered carrying a tiered server upon which were an array of sweet and savory treats. In step with the first servant was a second bearing a tray upon which sat a silver gilt pot and four cups. Quite replete, Darcy was eyeing the piles of ratafia cakes, coffee wafers, lemon biscuit, and fruit fritters with a mix of delight at seeing his favorites and dismay at how he could not eat another bite after the fabulous luncheon. Sincerely hoping the idea was to leave the treats on the table to be nibbled on at leisure, he gave no thought to what he assumed was a pot of brewing hot tea—not until the tray was set onto the table centered between the two settees did the aroma catch his attention.

"Hot chocolate!" he exclaimed, instantly looking at Elizabeth, who was beaming. "You remembered."

Bingley laughed. "Darcy, when will you finally accept the reality that our lovely ladies have us completely figured out and will forever strive to please us?"

"As will we for them," Darcy confirmed, also chuckling. "Of course, you are correct, Bingley. Thank you, Elizabeth. I'm sure tea can be brought, if preferred over chocolate."

Jane leaned to pour the thick beverage into the waiting cups. "Lizzy and I can count on one hand the number of times we have tasted hot chocolate. No offense, Mr. Darcy, but this is the part of the day I have most looked forward to." Smiling, she handed him a steaming cup.

"None taken, I assure you." As soon as the foursome held their filled cups, Darcy lifted his into the air. "A toast to friends who are soon to become family."

"And to Mr. Darcy, whose fortuitous day of birth has given us an excellent reason to indulge in chocolate and much more," Bingley added, with rousing cheers of agreement from the others.

Silently sipping the sweet drink and chewing a pear-and-apple fritter, Darcy peered at the cake. Unsure how he was finding room in his stuffed stomach for the fritter—even as he finished it and reached for a jam-smeared lemon biscuit—he prayed the afternoon's program called for slicing into the cake after hours to digest what he had already consumed.

"The cake"—he gestured with the biscuit—"is fascinating. I have never seen one with a lit candle. Is there a purpose?"

"Lizzy read about it," Bingley answered. "A German tradition, is that correct?"

"It is." Elizabeth bobbed her head, then setting her cup down, she clasped onto Darcy's hand. "You will appreciate this, William, as you love historical tidbits. A few years ago, I read the English translation of Andrew Frey's interaction with the Moravians in Germany. He wrote in detail about the birthday celebration for a Count Ludwig von Zinzendorf, which included a cake that had one candle for the years of his life. Over fifty! The imagery intrigued me and stayed in my mind. I've seen references since, scattered here and there, primarily German. They have for centuries celebrated birthdays as an important rite of passage, as we do not tend to do in England. The candles are an old tradition. Typically one is inserted into the cake for each year that has passed, with a single candle in the center representing continued life in the year ahead. Hence the name 'light of life' for the main candle. A lovely custom, I think."

"We opted for just one candle to avoid risking the house burning down," Bingley joked.

Once the snickers passed, Elizabeth elaborated, "Per tradition, the candle must stay lit all day and be blown out at dusk. One big candle is easier to maintain and extinguish. Making a wish before blowing out the flame ensures its granting."

Darcy smiled softly and squeezed her hand. "All my wishes have already come true. Nevertheless, while I am not one to lend credence to silly superstitions, this one is harmless fun, so I shall play along."

On schedule for the remainder of the afternoon were a series of parlor games. Not a huge enthusiast of group games which inevitably involved acting silly and being the center of attention, Darcy was less than thrilled at the prospect. Being an intimate quartet eased his qualms, as did the choice of charades as the first game and being paired with Elizabeth. While still not overly comfortable having all eyes upon him, the game of acting riddles required a fair command of language and some skill at dramatic performance. Aware that his capability with the latter would come as a shock to the watching trio, he volunteered to go first.

Running through the charades he had memorized, he settled on one he could alter slightly. A tad suggestive, true, and sure to raise a rosy blush to Elizabeth's cheeks.

Hiding a smug smile, he rose and stood at the designated spot for a solid minute of theatrical caesura. Then, eyes locked with Elizabeth's, he abruptly broke the silence with exaggerated resonance accompanied by impassioned facial contortions and melodramatic arm gestures.

"When night brings on her moonlit hour,
And stillness holds her magic power,
All mortals to my arms repair,
To bid adieu to toil and care.
I am for various ends designed,
Yet often love… you there will find.
Within my vaults you seek repose,
In joy, and peace, find *release* from life's woes."

From the corner of his eye, Darcy noted Bingley and Jane reacting to his charade technique with expressions of astoundment. Elizabeth's face had initially shown a similar cast, but she swiftly overcame her amazement to listen carefully to his riddle. Eyes followed his hand movements, tiny creases between her brows as she filtered through the words and relating gestures.

"Shall I repeat the charade? We are on a time limit for the point," he teased.

She didn't answer immediately. He could almost see the wheels turning as she pondered the riddle! After a full minute, she opened her mouth, Darcy thinking she was about to ask him to repeat the charade when suddenly her eyes widened. The flush he anticipated spread across her cheeks, but she also grinned saucily and didn't glance away.

"Bedroom. The answer is bedroom."

Bingley burst out laughing and Jane blushed scarlet.

Darcy inclined his head respectfully. "Excellently done, Miss Elizabeth. First play score is ours. Next turn is yours, Bingley. Try to top that." He murmured the last as Bingley passed close by, adding an amused chuckle.

Charles merely shook his head.

Resuming his seat beside Elizabeth, Darcy was content to say nothing and simply enjoy the pleasant sensations swirling between them. All in all, a fantastic beginning for the entertainment portion of the day!

At the completion of eight rounds of charades, Darcy and Elizabeth were declared the winners. Next on the agenda was twenty questions. Being a game of intellect alone, Darcy was thrilled. Per the request of Jane and Elizabeth, Mr. Bennet had selected the mystery objects for the guessing game. To ensure fairness, his choices were written upon individual slips of paper and sealed in a thick envelope opened only when they were ready to start playing. Deducing the correct answer in under twenty questions proved to be a challenge even for Darcy's superior education and mental capacity. Mr. Bennet's objects covered a range of topics, with the difficulty levels running the gamut from a handful of moderately easy ones to several brain twisters.

For the final parlor game of the day, the party plotters had agreed upon blindman's bluff. In any other situation, participating in a game which required stumbling blindly about the room to chase after and then touch a person's body was too horrific for Darcy to fathom. On the maybe two or three rare occasions in his social outings when someone broached playing the game, he had politely but vehemently refused to join in.

Today, with these close friends, or more specifically with Elizabeth as his intended prey, the concept wasn't quite so unpleasant. The choice of blindman's bluff rather than the dozens of alternative options had been favored precisely because of the physical contact necessary. One must follow the rules, after all. If the game requirements failed to stipulate that kisses and embraces were not allowed, well, the fault was with the creators of the game pamphlets, right?

With their lithe figures and experience as dancers, the ladies were naturals at evading capture. Jane employed her innate talent to be quiet and calm as a sort of shield from detection, almost as if she faded into invisibility from all the senses. When someone came close, she silently sidled away. It was fascinating to observe. Elizabeth was agile and speedy, traits that aided her in rapid direction changes and skipping out of reach.

Darcy was the worse player by far. Between being a complete novice at a game the others had played numerous times before and his body being larger than the others, he was greatly disadvantaged. He suspected Elizabeth permitted him to catch her, enjoying the resulting kisses. Besides, as they all quickly discovered, there was no question who the victor would be. Bingley excelled at the game. He was quick on his feet, for one, but he also possessed an uncanny ability to home in on a person's location and anticipate their movements. It truly was remarkable.

After several rounds, they no longer bothered to keep score. Bingley was the obvious winner, as far as points went, but they were all winners in the ways most gratifying.

They collapsed onto the sofas, winded from the exercise but in high spirits. The sun was low on the horizon, the colorful sky visible through the windows as a lovely background to the happy emotions they were each experiencing.

"I can't believe we ate all of those." With the hand not clutching Elizabeth's, Darcy indicated the tiered tray now empty but for crumbs. "And we drank through…was it two or three pots of hot chocolate?"

"Just two, I'm fairly sure. Shall I call for more?"

"Thank you, Jane, but no. Even I have had my fill." Darcy smiled at his future sister. "I think tea would be a nice change, and it would complement the cake. Did you not say I must eat cake before dusk?"

Elizabeth shook her head, eyes glittering as they always did when about to tease him. "What I said, Mr. Darcy, is that you must make your wish and blow out the candle by dusk. When we eat the cake is optional. Are you considering the vital importance of adhering to the superstition? Or is your empty stomach the primary concern for the timing?"

Darcy feigned shocked concern, complete with a hand upon his heart. "I would never place my selfish needs over the sacred rituals of the universe, Miss Bennet."

"Good to know." Her solemn expression and grave tone were as overblown as his mockery. "With the fate of the universe at stake, I guess we better hasten to fulfill the tradition."

Bingley stood and headed toward the servant bell. "I'll call for tea and request they hurry. After all, we haven't a moment to spare, or Darcy's light of life candle will lose its magic. God only knows what that may portend!"

As a matter of course, Darcy disregarded anything remotely hinting of the occult or mysticism. Perhaps it was a newfound appreciation for frivolity on the whole, or merely the pleasure of being honored with a birthday celebration which opened his heart to the harmless fun. There was no guarantee his willingness to engage in similar superstitions would last, but his beloved Elizabeth and dear friends had labored to ensure his birthday was special. Therefore, it felt right to show his appreciation by embracing the silliness and doing all he could to amplify the entertainment.

Once again calling upon his newly revealed mastery at theatrics, Darcy drew out the birthday wish ceremony.

Pretending to strain at what to wish for, all the while peering at an amused Elizabeth, he finally bowed his head to deliver a solemn, protracted monologue.

"I, Fitzwilliam Darcy, do humbly entreat the gods of birthday-wish bestowment to attend to my forthcoming request, secretly spoken within the depths of my mind, and do trust they shall hold to the immutable laws of metaphysics by honoring the wish, blessing me with the profound desire of my heart."

How he made it through that drivel without falling into helpless laughter was a miracle. Somehow he remained in character and proceeded to dramatize the candle-blowing procedure, first by positioning his body at "the perfect candle-extinguishing angle" with fists planted securely on the table. This he followed with three slow, cleansing breaths before a last mighty inhale and forceful exhale. Amid the laughter at his farce, the trio added cheers and clapping.

Elizabeth rounded the table and clasped his arm. "Fantastic! I was going to play the strict mother hen and make you wait until after dinner for dessert, but you have earned a hefty slice with that performance."

Jane handed him the cutting knife. "You may have missed your calling, Mr. Darcy. I never would have guessed it, but you would shine on the stage."

"I fear my talents are meager and only revealed in intimate company. The compliment is kind, but I shall stick with being an estate owner and horse breeder."

The cake was delicious, of course. Satisfied beyond description at what was, no debate, the best birthday celebration Darcy had enjoyed ever, the phase of present opening boosted his joy to immeasurable levels.

The first box Elizabeth plopped onto his lap was narrow and

long. "This is from Georgiana. She gave it to me before we left London."

"But she gave me a gift on Friday before I left."

"Yes, the cravat pin. Isn't it fabulous? That was her gift for the wedding, she told me. This gift falls into the useful category, and she wanted you to have one from her to open at your party."

Nestled on a bed of cloth was a shiny leather riding crop. "Useful indeed." Darcy flourished it in the air. "I have several, but a horseman can never have enough riding gear."

Bingley's gift was a pocket watch. "I know how you like old watches, Darcy, and antiques in general. God knows we tramped through enough museums together to etch that into my brain! This one is a Flemish watch by clockmaker Michael Nouwen, dated before his death in 1613."

"Charles, it is astounding. I truly cannot thank you enough. Yes, I do adore old watches, probably because my grandfather was fascinated by the technology. This one is a gorgeous specimen, and probably older than any others I have, or close to. It will sit in a prominent place in my display cabinet, I assure you."

His gift from Jane was a set of six silk handkerchiefs, each embroidered in the corner with his initials. "I am sincerely touched, Jane, that you would go to so much trouble for me," he said with feeling, as his fingertips stroked the fine fabric. "These are precious, and I shall handle them carefully if I use them at all. Thank you."

Jane's blush and murmured reply warmed his heart—so much sentimentality and heightened emotions! No wonder he shied away from fussing over his birthday. And it was only going to get worse because it was Elizabeth's turn. She handed him a flat present wrapped with burgundy silk and tied with a blue ribbon. It was obviously a book, but he was stunned at which one.

"*Paradise Lost* by John Milton. Unbelievable!"

"You did say you were searching for that one to add to your collection. I hope you haven't found one."

"No...I...Elizabeth, I cannot believe you remember me saying that! You were at Pemberley, in the library, when I mentioned it in passing, more to fill the air and overcome my nervousness."

"But you were serious, weren't you?"

"Yes! Yes, I was. This is marvelous, and no, I haven't yet found one myself, so this is a true prize. I'm just...shocked at your recollection."

She reached up and gently touched his cheek with her fingertips. "William, I vividly remember every moment and word of our day together at Pemberley. It was a special day for me."

Vaguely Darcy was aware of Bingley rising and silently escorting Jane from the room. Taking advantage of the privacy, not that he would have been able to stop his actions had the other couple remained, Darcy clasped her hand. Bringing it to his lips for a series of kisses, he then leaned over and kissed her mouth.

"Have I told you lately how utterly amazing you are? I love you with all my soul, Elizabeth. Finding this is a serious coup. How did you manage it?"

"My father," she laughed. "I believe he spent the vast portion of his time at Oxford in the library. He is well acquainted with the head librarian, who specializes in finding sought after volumes. Papa is forever adding old and rare books to his shelves. Would you believe the Oxford man had three first editions of *Paradise Lost?* Now, open the book. There is another gift tucked inside."

"I'm not sure my heart can take any more emotional surprises."

The declaration was a partial tease, but upon spying the object lying on the title page, he wondered if his heart would burst from the overwhelming emotions. Inside was a bookmark sewn of the finest silk, the back lightly quilted. Onto the silk, she had embroidered two intertwined hearts in red with his name in one and her name in the other. Above the linked hearts was a verse from Genesis.

"The two shall become one flesh," he read aloud, the words barely audible. Tears welled in his eyes, and further speaking was impossible. Gathering Elizabeth into his arms, he embraced her for a long while. He prayed the wild beating of his heart would convey his immense thankfulness for the gifts and her presence in his life. Though not yet wed to her, he already felt more complete than he ever had.

Releasing his tight grip, he gazed into her eyes and brushed his thumb across her cheek. She was smiling and so beautiful. No power on earth or in Heaven could have stopped him from capturing her mouth in the wildly passionate kiss that followed. In seconds, they were lost to raging sensations.

Forgetting the taboo zones, Darcy slid his palm down the leg she had conveniently lifted and draped over his knee. At the same time, Elizabeth somehow managed to loosen his cravat enough to glide the slim fingers of one hand down his neck until almost touching the bend at his shoulder. The other hand was far from idle, starting on his chest and steadily creeping lower and lower, until lingering just below his naval—too near the one part of his body that, if touched by her hand, would be his undoing.

The words of the scripture on the bookmark rang within his mind. He was consumed by a yearning to engage in the physical act of love, fulfilling the Biblical promise to become one flesh. Some shred of awareness as to their location was the only deterrent to the force of his desire. Even then, taking control of the precarious situation required a monumental act of strength.

Eyes closed, he clasped her face between both hands and rested his forehead against hers. His ears burned from the clamor of his harsh, erratic breathing and the pounding of rushing blood. "I want you desperately, Elizabeth. Waiting to be with you, completely, as your husband is agony. God help me to be strong."

"Only two more weeks, my heart."

"Eighteen days, unfortunately."

Elizabeth leaned away and opened her eyes. Darcy could discern the heat of remaining passion in the brown depths staring up at him, a truth confirmed by her next words. "You are not alone in wanting to be with you intimately or in the agony of waiting. Saying two weeks sounds better."

"To me, they both feel like an eternity." After a huge inhale and exhale, he kissed her lips tenderly. "Elizabeth, this has been an incredible birthday. The absolute best of my entire life. How can I ever thank you adequately?"

"You have until next May to think of a way. You are quite clever, sir, so I am sure your endeavors for my birthday will tip the scale back in your favor. But for now"—she slapped his knee playfully and scooted over—"did I say we were done for the day? Indeed not! There is plenty of cake left to eat, of course, and we still have dinner."

"Dinner? You didn't invite... That is, please tell me there is nothing major—"

Laughing gaily, she stood and offered her hand. "You should see your face! Breathe easy, love. Dinner tonight shall be as it is most nights, that is the four of us and my family. Having each other as chaperone only goes so far, even with my tolerant, somewhat oblivious parents. Charles feared if we were gone the whole day and into the night they would suspect we had absconded to Gretna Green."

"Now that would have been an even better birthday gift!" Darcy said enthusiastically. "I could have a carriage ready in minutes, avoiding the dinner portion of the day altogether and lifting this birthday to rapturous heights."

"Silly man! Don't worry, William. Papa swore not to tell anyone it is your birthday. It is entirely your choice to reveal the fact or not."

Naturally, his choice was to pretend it was just another day ending with just another dinner. Therefore, naturally, the specialness of the day somehow spilled out roughly five minutes after they sat down to dine. To Darcy's immense relief, none of the Bennets, not even Elizabeth's excitable mother, said more than the obligatory best wishes.

Breathing easier, Darcy passed the final hours of the day he turned twenty-nine in pleasant company. He ate a second spectacular meal, consuming not one but two generous slices of birthday cake, and finagled a good-night kiss from Elizabeth.

Darcy's final birthday task was completed after the Bennets departed and Charles had gone up to bed. Descending the stairs to the dimly lit, empty kitchen area, he saw what he had come for. While unbeknownst to him on this tenth day of November, Darcy would reveal the full extent of his sentimentality to his new bride that upcoming Christmas when he shared his collected boxes of mementos from significant events in his life. One of those objects was the light of life candle from his cake, which the butler had saved for him as requested.

The candle was lying on a clean linen napkin in the exact center of the long cooking prep table. Right beside it was a fork and a plate with a big slice of cake. Apparently, his birthday celebrating would continue a bit longer after all.

9

RELATIVE TRANSITION

*W*hen not otherwise preoccupied entertaining their handsome fiancés, the brides-to-be had begun incrementally sorting through their possessions in preparation for relocating to their new homes. Jane would be moving a mere three miles away, making the job easier for her on several counts. Lizzy, conversely, would be at Pemberley in Derbyshire, a nearly two-day journey to traverse the one-hundred-fifty miles. Not an impossible distance to send anything she might forget, but assuredly life would transition smoother if her belongings were readily available from the start.

Jane and Lizzy had shared a bedroom for the bulk of their lives. According to their mother, she and the girls' old nurse had tried to make them sleep in their respective beds, going so far as to punish them in various ways. Jane remembered refusals of late-night snacks and water, while Lizzy recalled employment of the switch a time or two. Nothing worked. Inevitably, the siblings, born a bare year apart, would tiptoe through the dark, always ending up in the room assigned to Lizzy.

Mr. Bennet had, in a rare episode of inserting his will into a childrearing matter, finally called a firm halt to the separate-bedchamber endeavor. It helped that Lydia was born at about that same time, giving Mrs. Bennet and the nurse something better to occupy their minds. From then on, Jane's bedroom, while technically still belonging to her, was set aside for guests. Though rarely slept in, the bedroom had become an overflow for the amassed belongings of both Jane and Lizzy, which now meant that despite sharing a sleeping space, the oldest Bennets had more to sift through than initially believed.

Over the weeks, some headway had been made in discarding old garments and other items deemed no longer necessary. After twenty plus years living in the same house, both had accumulated an outlandish quantity of what was, if honest, primarily junk. To a degree, it was relieving to have a concrete reason to dig through stored boxes and crammed trunks. Lizzy gave up counting after the tenth time she examined some object with a deeply significant meaning to her and asked, "Does anyone remember where I got this or who gave it to me?" All of those ended in the pile thrown out with the refuse or the one for charity, depending upon its condition. So far, the pile for the garbage was winning the game.

It was a plodding process. In part, this was due to handsome fiancés consuming their time and thoughts. Laxity in a chore as boring and labor intensive as cleaning closets was understandable when the alternative was so much pleasanter.

Primarily, as they admitted to each other when alone, dawdling at the job was a way to postpone facing the inevitable. The sisters were overjoyed to be married, naturally. At times they were unable to think of anything else but the future with the men they loved. They were also cognizant of the fast-approaching day when their lives would irrevocably change. Their emotions were an odd combination of nostalgia for their childhood home and hesitation to relinquish their familiar lives.

Nevertheless, one cannot procrastinate forever. Two days after Mr. Darcy's birthday celebration, the opportunity to put a large dent into the project came along.

Mr. Darcy and Mr. Bingley had ridden north before daybreak that morning for a two-day shooting party at a university friend of Darcy's. As explained in animated tones to the politely listening females, the man owned an estate renowned for large quantities of pheasant, grouse, and mainly, migrating woodcock. As Lizzy and Jane now knew in more depth than ever dreamed of, the woodcock was a highly prized bird not readily found during the shooting season.

"They rarely remain in Derbyshire," Darcy had explained with genuine vexation, "even with Mr. Burr trying to entice them." Clearly, the invitation to hunt the elusive woodcock was too compelling to resist.

The gentlemen would return before dinner the following night. Seizing the occasion as much to sidetrack themselves from missing them, they rose early and set to it.

For close to three hours, they managed to maintain an organized process with delineated, tidy stacks. If left to their own devices, the lofty goal of completing the task that day might have been attained. That dream perished when Mary, Kitty, and their mother arrived to help, using the word in the loosest meaning possible.

By noon, the shared bedroom looked as if the wardrobes and bureaus had violently regurgitated their contents! Strewn across every available surface were gowns, undergarments, stockings, hats, gloves, shawls, coats, and more. It was a sea of lace and fabric verily surging as a tide, heaped upon the boxes filled with books, treasured possessions, wall hangings, needle crafts, and the like.

Initially vexed at the assistance and ensuing chaos, Jane and Lizzy soon recognized the underlying motivation. While struggling to reconcile their own mixed emotions over the radical changes happening in their lives, neither of them had paused to consider how their younger sisters and mother would be feeling.

Lydia's marriage and departure had occurred unexpectedly, allowing no time to prepare. The strained circumstances inhibited talking openly about her situation, the loss of a beloved sister keenly felt but unable to reconcile. With only one correspondence received, it was as if Lydia had disappeared or never existed.

Then, barely a month after that fiasco and still reeling from the effects, Jane and Lizzy had become engaged days apart. Two more gulfs in the Bennet family loomed in front of them. Evidently, the unspoken consensus was to embrace the weeks they had together. Doing so turned a straightforward operation into an opportunity for female camaraderie.

"Oh! I've just had the most marvelous idea. Lizzy and Jane should put on their wedding dresses."

"Kitty, it is bad luck to wear one's wedding gown before the day." Lizzy snatched her gown out of Kitty's hand.

"Pooh!" Kitty snorted. "Such nonsense. You of all people would never believe that."

"Not normally, true. But when it comes to my marriage and future, I am not about to tempt the temperamental fates. Besides, it is too risky. I inevitably muss my garments ten minutes after donning them."

Kitty rolled her eyes. Turning to Jane, she set her face into a pleading expression. Jane's firm shake forestalled a whined entreaty. "Don't ask, Kitty. Customs are to be respected, no matter how silly, nor do I want to risk a tear or stain."

"Ha!" Lizzy exclaimed from deep inside the wardrobe. "When have you ever torn or stained a dress?"

"I have…a few times…I am sure of it…" Jane stammered to a halt, rosiness highlighting her cheeks as three pairs of dubious eyes swiveled her way. "Well, if you didn't run across dirt fields and help feed the barn animals, your clothes might stay cleaner and in better repair, Lizzy."

Content that her wedding gown was stowed safely, Lizzy backed away from the wardrobe. "Guilty as charged," she sang. "I suspect the Pemberley gardeners and groomsmen would frown at their mistress treading into their designated areas, so shall necessarily forego digging in the dirt or helping care for the rabbits, if they even have rabbits."

"Who cares what the outdoor staff thinks, Lizzy? Mr. Darcy enjoys your outside activities, that is for sure. He stares at you with an intense expression when your cheeks flush from the brisk air. And if tendrils of hair have escaped your bonnet, well, he becomes especially animated!"

"Kitty! My word!"

"Well, he does, Mama. I'm not an idiot. I know what he is thinking. So does Mary."

Mary pressed her lips primly together and continued to fold Jane's shawls into precise squares, but her cheeks pinked and eyes faintly twinkled. Lizzy had again busied herself inside the wardrobe, hiding her dreamy smile and trembling hands. If any of them knew *just how animated* and intense Mr. Darcy truly was...

"Men are always thinking about...that." Mrs. Bennet stumbled on the last word and fluttered her hand nervously in the air. "This is part of the problem with the male gender if you ask me."

"Doesn't seem like a problem to me," Kitty objected.

"Oh! How innocent you are, my Kitty. Jane and Lizzy will soon learn how it is—"

"Mama, could you help me with these stockings? Your method of rolling saves space, and you always manage a tighter bundle than me." Jane's casual interruption had the immediate desired effect. Whether Mrs. Bennet giving her opinion was terminated altogether or merely delayed was another question.

Muffling her groan within the folds of hanging garments, Lizzy fervently beseeched the heavens for help. With increasing frequency, she and Jane were subjected to oblique insinuations of the "discomforts of the marriage bed" with the inevitable advice of clever ways to avoid "a man's persistent urges."

Is it too much to ask, she prayed to any listening angels, *for the topic to pass and not spark another annoying diatribe?*

Unfortunately, the angels must have been busy elsewhere.

"Why are your new shifts and other undergarment made of such thin fabrics and adorned with lace and ribbon accents?" Mrs. Bennet held up one of Lizzy's new shifts, the supple cotton so finely woven as to be semi-sheer, and sewn with pale-blue ribbons in a braided pattern under the bodice. In her other hand, she brandished a corselet made of silk taffeta. "Why, this stay is barely boned at all! And it is pink!"

"I believe it is more of a lilac color, Mama." Mary's technical correction was ignored, thanks to Kitty's outburst.

"Did you see their new nightclothes?" Grabbing one of Jane's flimsy nightdresses off the bed, she held it against her body and began prancing about the room in what she deemed a seductive manner. "Ooh! Mr. Bingley, look at how pretty I am! Now, Mr. Darcy, stop staring at me like that! Oh la la!"

Lizzy gave up hiding in the wardrobe. Figuring it was impossible to postpone the inevitable, she widened her eyes in mock innocence and directly addressed her mother.

"Our Aunt Gardiner was of the opinion that undergarments should be visibly appealing, especially for a new bride. In fact, she spoke at length and in meticulous detail of the positive reception derived from wearing them. It is, as you have taught us, Mama, our duty to be obedient wives and please our husbands. Thankfully, we now know, with Aunt's adamant assurance and education, that we too shall reap the rewards. Something to anticipate, I think. Don't you?"

Jane's mouth dropped open and face flushed a magnificent shade of red. Kitty collapsed onto the floor, laughing but also watching for Mrs. Bennet's reaction. Even Mary was captivated, her eyes uncharacteristically soft and fingers absently stroking the silk chemise lying in her lap.

To their surprise, Mrs. Bennet did not launch into a contradictory lecture. Instead, her cheeks tinted pink and her eyes grew misty, as one hand tremulously patted the skin over her heart. Mouth opening and closing several times, she finally murmured, "Well...I daresay, my sister is a wise woman. It was kind of her to offer advice in...this area. Yes...I... Well now, look here, we have filled most of the boxes! I shall see if we have more...and perhaps some refreshments as well? Yes, and tea, strong tea, would do me...us, good. Indeed..."

Whatever else Mrs. Bennet had to say was inaudible as she scurried from the room. Oh, how difficult it was not to burst into laughter! Avoiding eye contact, each of them called upon inner stores of restraint. A handful of breathy snickers was the only sound for a while as they attacked the project with fresh vigor.

The conversation gradually resumed, starting with a few questions regarding a particular article of clothing or which box to use. Soon the foursome veered into silliness and laughter augmented by the frequent finding of a long-forgotten, buried object sparking remembrances of youthful shenanigans. Intermixed with the merriment were the inevitable discussions about the wedding and future lives of the engaged pair.

"Has Mr. Darcy's aunt found a lady's maid for you, Lizzy?" Mary asked at one point.

"Ooh la! Fancy Mrs. Darcy to have a fancy lady's maid." Kitty mimed fussing with her hair, face set in a comically arrogant expression. "Shall I wear the taffeta or the silk? The mink or the ermine? Oh! And what jewels shall I choose?"

Laughing, Lizzy tossed a pillow at Kitty's head, for all the good it did. Kitty brushed the projectile aside without the slightest hiccup in her improvisations. Ignoring her, Lizzy addressed Mary. "Lady

Matlock received the names of three experienced maids from women of her acquaintance, all with excellent recommendations. Mr. Darcy has instructed Mrs. Reynolds, the Pemberley housekeeper, to interview each one. I shall leave it up to Mrs. Reynolds to decide. The whole procedure is alien to me, and a bit uncomfortable, to be honest."

"Mr. Bingley suggested I do the same. I would prefer keeping Betsy with me, as she is skilled at coiffure, but she would be miserable away from Longbourn. I have asked Lady Lucas for advice in the matter." Jane spoke in her usual imperturbable manner, but her downcast eyes and the pinch of pink to her cheeks were revealing.

Assistance in dressing and styling one's hair was a necessity of life, of course, so employing a lady's maid was not the cause of their disquiet. Rather, it was the significance in facing another major change. For as long as they could remember, the Bennet females had primarily relied on each other to lace stays, fasten the unreachable buttons, fix unruly hair, get advice for which shoes or bonnet matched best, and so on. Even with Betsy's talent with hair, and the maid Kay's eye for fashion, it was to a sibling they typically turned, never realizing how the daily routines tightened their bonds of unity.

Pausing in her theatrics, Kitty asked Jane, "Did Lady Lucas have any suggestions? If not, Tilly Watson told me that she heard the draper's daughter, Gertrude, say that Mrs. Goulding is unhappy with her personal maid. You know how *she* is, complaining loudly the whole time she was in the store, Gertie said, and then never did buy a thing! The poor servant is probably a delightful person who would jump at the chance to escape that harridan."

"Kitty, for once I shall not scold for your bad judgment in listening to village gossip."

Beaming at Lizzy's praise, Kitty then turned to stick her tongue out at the frowning Mary.

Ignoring that exchange, Lizzy went on, "Jane, if half of what

Kitty said is true, and knowing Mrs. Goulding it is, you would be performing a service to humanity by snatching the maid away."

"You have a valid point," Jane hesitantly agreed. "I can ask Lady Lucas if she is aware of the situation." Lizzy lifted her brows at Jane's generous statement. Lady Lucas was renowned as the worst gossip in the area. Not a whisper of local news escaped her hearing. "How about the choices on the list from Lady Matlock? Any whom strike your fancy?"

Lizzy smiled, aware that the question was more to divert the topic away from gossip or Lady Lucas. Indulging Jane's need for politesse, even as she darted a glance toward Kitty, weighing what response there would be from her, Lizzy admitted, "All three have impeccable references and considerable experience, but my interest was piqued by the one William also favored. A Frenchwoman named Marguerite Charbaneau."

Predictably, from Kitty, "Ugh! The French. They are so pompous. I can't imagine this Marguerite would be any fun."

"A lady's maid is not there to be entertaining, Kitty." Mary shook her head, then reminded her, "The French design the clothing you fawn over the most. Why you have plates from *Costume Parisien* plastered all over your wall, most so scandalous I cannot bear to look at them! Like it or not, the French are the reigning masters of both fashion and cuisine. Does Mr. Darcy employ a French chef, Lizzy?"

"I honestly do not know. I've not asked. The food was delicious, I can attest to that. The best I've ever tasted, in fact."

"Mr. Darcy probably insisted on the very best dishes while you were there, no matter who the cook is. After all, he was in love with you already. If Lydia hadn't gone and tried to elope, you would probably already be married to him."

Kitty's offhand comment was truer than she knew, and a topic best avoided. Jane apparently agreed, hastily but smoothly interjecting. "Lizzy, that reminds me. Did you finally finish the questionnaire from Mrs. Reynolds that Mr. Darcy gave you?"

Laughing, Lizzy nodded. "I did. It wasn't an intensive interrogation as much as a welcome letter expressing her pleasure at our engagement and promise to aid in my transition into the household. The questions were basic queries about my food preferences and aversions, any specific requests to improve my comfort, favorite flowers, that sort of thing. She is so sweet to be concerned."

"There! I believe those are the last, Lizzy, unless you have others stashed in unusual places." Mary stepped back from the empty bookcase and gestured toward the five large boxes stacked in front of her. "I never noticed that your book collection was so huge. Do you really need to take all of these? I thought the library at Pemberley was enormous and well stocked."

"Oh, it is, believe me. In fact, there is more than one library at Pemberley." At the intrigued expressions worn by Jane and Mary— Kitty was paying no heed to what was, in her mind, a boring subject —Lizzy elaborated. "The main library is, indeed, enormous and two-stories high. There is a curving staircase at either corner of the far end, and access doors from both levels. It is…" She sighed dreamily, her eyes faraway. "…absolutely beautiful. Oh! How you and Papa will love it, Mary!"

While not the passionate lover of all books, as Lizzy and Mr. Bennet, Mary read steadily, albeit with a narrower scope of interest. She would greatly enjoy exploring the Pemberley library, of that Lizzy was confident. The unknown was when her family would make the journey to her soon-to-be residence.

Preferring to remain in the present, Lizzy went on, "Attached to the main library, on the first-floor level, is the second library. The Darcys have been collecting books for generations, meaning some are of inestimable worth. For this reason, they are segregated, and the door is kept locked."

"Did you see inside?"

Lizzy smiled at Mary's awe and enthusiasm, remembering that

she had felt the same when Mr. Darcy had shown her the room while visiting that August past. As captured as she had been by the rows upon rows of books, many so ancient they were under glass, she had been acutely aware of his warmly glowing blue eyes resting upon her. The memory brought tingles to her skin.

"Yes, I did. It was a profoundly moving experience, like being in a museum." Shaking off the memory, which naturally made her think of William, whom she missed terribly, she cleared her throat and resumed the narrative. "I also was given a tour of the library located off the music room where are keep the volumes dedicated to musical theory, composition, and history. I never imagined so many books were written on the topic! Of course, all the sheet music is stored there as well, some of those quite old as well. Of no shock whatsoever, it is Miss Darcy's favorite library. Then—"

"There is another library?"

"My tone carried a similar note of amazement when Mr. Darcy spoke of it. I believe it to be the last library, although I could well be wrong. I did not tour it when I visited Pemberley, but near his office, or perhaps directly attached, is a library exclusively for the family histories and journals, estate records, and business related books. Apparently, many Darcys kept journals, the oldest, he said, belonging to Frederick Darcy, the Irishman who established Pemberley in Derbyshire during the early fifteenth century. Can you imagine? The value of such a thing is incalculable. No wonder those priceless books are separated. I am unsure if this one room stores all the historical family documents, although William intimated as much. After nearly four hundred years, it must be a sizable room to hold them all."

"Where will you put your books, then?"

Lizzy shrugged. "I am not sure, to be honest. Ideally in our bed— that is, my bedchamber." Instantly blushing at the slip revealing her secret wish to share sleeping quarters with her husband, Lizzy shot her gaze at Kitty. Thankfully, she was contentedly humming to herself while packing the London purchases into Jane's new trunk.

Dashing a silent prayer heavenward for her younger sister's book indifference preventing her latching on to the last remark, Lizzy added, "Outside of the designated libraries, I saw cases of books in several rooms. Aware as I am of Mr. Darcy's passion for reading, I would be very surprised if he does not have a case or two in his private chambers. I am sure I can have the same, if I request it."

"I have sent a servant to fetch more boxes," Mrs. Bennet announced from the doorway as she breezed back into the room carrying a tray of sweet snacks. Mrs. Hill followed behind bearing the heavier tray with a pot of tea, five cups, and containers filled with cream and sugar. Dropping whatever was in their hands, the four sisters gathered around the table. Tea and snacks were a welcome break from work.

Cups poured and small plates piled with the treats, they relaxed into the cushioned chairs and sofa. Lizzy surveyed the room, rather amazed to discover they had made significant progress. Most of the floor was clear, the scattered heaps now stowed in the appropriate box, luggage case, or trunk. Those boxes and furniture pieces to be shipped to Pemberley were in Jane's unused bedchamber, lined orderly against one wall. The trunk set aside for Lizzy to take on her honeymoon was, thanks to Mary, packed tidily with plenty of free space available. All in all, a good day's work!

Between bites, Mrs. Bennet informed them, "While I was downstairs a message arrived from Mrs. Filiatreau. She reports that the florist in Derbyshire can send Jacob's ladder blooms as you requested, Lizzy."

"That is excellent news! They were plentiful in Derbyshire, including in the gardens at Pemberley. A beautiful flower with a lovely fragrance. They will blend well with the lavender and honeysuckle, in both fragrance and appearance, to create a fabulous bouquet."

"Bluish-purple flowers, is that right?"

"Yes, Jane. I saw some that were bluer than purple, the hue varying. Hopefully, the ones Mrs. Filiatreau sends are blue."

"To match the necklace Mr. Darcy gave you! Oh, it is divine. Can we see it again, Lizzy?"

Lizzy shook her head, Kitty immediately pouting. "Sorry, but I asked Papa to keep it locked in his desk. I cannot fathom its worth, even without taking the sentimental value into account. Frankly, having possession of such a necklace is a frightening responsibility."

"Might as well get used to it. Imagine the jewels you will have as Mrs. Darcy." Flipping from a pout to dreaminess, Kitty sighed. "I bet there are cases and cases of diamonds, rubies, emeralds—"

"Precisely why the wedding must be perfect," Mrs. Bennet interrupted. "Two Bennet daughters marrying wealthy, respected gentlemen of Society. We shall be the talk of the county for ages!"

Jane met Lizzy's eyes, the sisters sharing a tolerant smile. Their expressions were amused, a contrast to the contortions of dread and embarrassment perpetually worn during the initial weeks of their engagements. Harnessing their dramatic mother was a feat they had found impossible to do anyway.

Moreover, after discussing it privately, the brides-to-be had a revelation. The near-fatal disaster of Lydia's actions resulted in a hasty wedding none of them had been informed of in time to attend, even if they had wanted to. Despite Mrs. Bennet's brave face and boasting of Lydia being married to a gentleman officer, they saw her pain. She had been robbed of her honorable, rightful place as a mother, unable to participate in any way. Therefore, while a tendency to roll their eyes remained and they did from time to time need to pull on the reins, they had agreed to concur with whatever she wanted.

"The flowers are arranged for, even the yellow flowers you wanted, Jane. Roses should not be a problem, and Mrs. Filiatreau has connections that may have late-blooming dahlias or peonies."

"Thank you, Mama. I am content with whatever she can

manage. I am still amazed you talked Reverend Jenney into placing ribbons and flowers on the pews. He is a dear man, but a stickler for traditions."

Mrs. Bennet looked slightly offended. "He understands what an important wedding this is! Besides, I can be very persuasive."

"Mr. Darcy spoke to Mr. Jenney, requesting the inclusion as a personal favor."

Lizzy's teacup hit the saucer with a sharp clink. "He did? How do you know that, Mary?"

Mary flushed and dropped her eyes. "I was at the church when Mr. Darcy came in. I was in the back pew, praying, so do not think he saw me. I did not mean to overhear, but they were standing a half-dozen feet away!" Finally convinced that no one thought her an active eavesdropper, she explained, "Mr. Darcy specifically noted that allowing modest decoration inside the church was his request as a gift to Mrs. Bennet for her kindness. Is that not kind of him? I do not think he wanted you to know, Mama, so do not make a fuss over it. He does not like undue attention."

Lizzy was unsure what shocked her more—Darcy's thoughtfulness toward Mrs. Bennet, whom he pretended fondness for but Lizzy knew he barely tolerated, or Mary's astute observations of Mr. Darcy's character. Lizzy honestly could not recall Mary and Mr. Darcy speaking a single word to each other outside of the obligatory greetings.

As they enjoyed the repast, Mrs. Bennet prattled on, methodically enumerating upon the church decorations before moving on to the wedding cake and breakfast menu. They had heard the reports a dozen times, but what bride doesn't adore discussing her upcoming wedding? Just as the sweets were almost gone, the butler interrupted with a letter for Jane.

"It is from Caroline Bingley."

"Another one? That makes, what is it now? Three in as many weeks? What is she up to?"

"Now, Lizzy," Jane said as she tore the seal. "Perhaps her time away has given her time to reflect. Her correspondence has been quite pleasant. She expresses her delight in my marriage to her brother, and her professions of regard toward me are civil and suggest sincerity." At the impulsive snorts, snickers, grunts, and huffs, Jane primly rebuked. "Remember, Caroline is to be my sister. I know she is not entirely trustworthy, and we may never be friends. However, nothing is gained by unkindness."

"Of course, you are correct Jane," Lizzy offered, straining for a goodwill tone. "Maybe if you share Caroline's words, we will improve our opinions and feel the same kindness toward her."

And then the sun shall turn into a huge block of ice.

Jane narrowed her eyes but, after studying Lizzy's neutral face, read the letter aloud as requested. Blessedly short, there was only one valuable detail that Lizzy gleaned from the phony, saccharine-laced sentences.

"So, Caroline and the Hursts are to leave Bath this week, returning to London, and are planning to come to Netherfield sometime during the week before the wedding. Oh joy."

"We knew they would be coming, Lizzy. So will others who are attending the wedding, meaning we may as well accept the onslaught. On the positive, with lots of visitors, you won't be obliged to spend large quantities of time with Caroline."

Jane had a point, not that it completely alleviated the queasiness in her stomach. Worse yet, the mention of wedding guests reminded her of news she had been loath to impart. Anticipating her mother's reaction increased her nausea.

No time like the present, she thought, putting the uneaten scone back on her plate. Opening her mouth to speak, Lizzy got no further than taking a breath, upon which she was hit with a coughing fit thanks to her mother's next words.

"I do wish my Lydia was one of those attending. Alas, none of my letters have been replied to, so I can only assume she and Mr.

Wickham are not coming. It is a very long way and with his position in the army... Gracious me, Lizzy! Take a drink of tea, for heaven's sake!"

"Mama," Lizzy squeaked after gulping from her cup as instructed. "Am I understanding you correctly? Did you invite Lydia to our wedding?"

"She *is* your sister, Lizzy. Oh, I know you said there was some issue between Mr. Darcy and Mr. Wickham"—Mrs. Bennet waved her hand, the gesture conveying her apathy—"but how serious could it be? Besides, what better way to heal past transgressions than at a wedding?"

Truly dumbfounded, Lizzy gaped at her mother. Kitty frowned but was feeding pieces of a biscuit to her puppy and paying minimal attention. Mary flicked her eyes between the two, clearly troubled and confused. Jane was the only one in the room who knew the truth, and her countenance was as gloomy as Lizzy had ever seen it.

"Mama, I am quite vexed with you, I must confess."

Four sets of brows arched as four sets of eyes widened. Coming from sweet, perpetually unruffled Jane, this was as rough as it got.

"Mr. Darcy's reasons are his own to keep but should not be minimized or disregarded. He is an upstanding gentleman deserving the utmost respect. We miss Lydia but must never pretend she did not make wrong choices which nearly destroyed this family. Remember too that Papa has declared, most emphatically, that neither Lydia or Mr. Wickham are welcome at the wedding. He barely welcomed them to Longbourn after their wedding and only at our behest, relenting for that one short visit only. Therefore, I strongly suggest you pen another missive immediately, uninviting the Wickhams in language without ambiguity, and send it by courier to Newcastle posthaste."

The speech, a long one for Jane and delivered in a firmly disapproving tone, left all of them too stunned for a swift response.

Struggling to contain her vexation, as Jane had understatedly put it, Lizzy finally felt able to speak without screaming. "Please, Mama, take Jane's advice. Either of them at the wedding, especially Mr. Wickham, would be an unmitigated disaster. It simply cannot happen, not under any circumstances."

"Oh very well! Quit badgering! I shall write to Lydia. It isn't probable she would travel the distance. Newcastle might as well be the Americas it is so far away."

Tension remained thick, despite a handful of half-hearted attempts to interject with something frivolous. They rose from the table, slowly resuming the packing and organizing project. Gaiety restored little by little, although not quite to the level it had been. Lizzy missed William, and then there was the news she needed to impart. Groaning inwardly, still not keen on facing more of her mother's nervous hysterics, she decided to try again.

Inserting cheeriness into her tone, Lizzy turned from the bureau. "My word! I almost forgot. Mama, the letter from Miss Bingley reminded me of something else. I fear that with all the wedding excitement, it slipped my mind to tell you that Mr. Darcy has three additional guests coming to the wedding."

Mrs. Bennet, who was standing at the side of the bed and folding a stack of lightweight summer gowns, and straightened with a jerk. At the instant look of panic crossing her face, Lizzy hastened to her side. "No one to accommodate at Longbourn, Mama. Netherfield has plenty of room and is a more convenient location since the wedding feast is to be held there anyway."

"Oh my! We will need to adjust the amount of food! Why did you not tell me sooner? Is this in addition to his sister, Miss Darcy?"

"The food will be quite sufficient, Mama," Jane assured hastily. "We have an abundance purchased as it is and shall be eating off the remains for a week. Three additional mouths will not be a burden."

"Indeed," Lizzy nodded, squeezing her mother's hand. "Naturally, you needed to know, and I apologize for not telling you sooner, but it is nothing to concern yourself with."

"I hope it isn't that horrid aunt of his that Mr. Collins toadies to. Frowning, churlish old people should not be at a wedding," Kitty muttered absently as she inspected the array of perfume and cosmetic containers on the vanity.

Mrs. Bennet gasped, her hand pressed against her chest. "Lady Catherine de Bourgh? Oh, goodness gracious! I never imagined! Oh dear, oh dear—"

"Mama, calm yourself. I can assure you that Lady Catherine has not been invited to the wedding and if she had the nerve to show up would be thrown out. I am speaking of Mr. Darcy's other aunt and uncle." Eyes darting to Jane, who nodded encouragingly, Lizzy inhaled deeply. Still holding on to her mother's free hand, she continued. "This would be the Earl and Countess of Matlock, and their youngest son, Colonel Fitzwilliam."

After the briefest of pauses, Lizzy and Jane steeling themselves for the histrionics, Mrs. Bennet pressed a finger to her lips and asked, "A colonel, you say? Mr. Darcy's cousin is a colonel? And he is coming to the wedding? Well, well." Mrs. Bennet swiveled speculative eyes to the impervious Kitty, then back to Lizzy. "Would this officer and son of an earl be a bachelor by chance?"

How in the world had Lizzy not anticipated this reaction? In all the worried discussions with Jane over how to break the news of an earl and countess attending the wedding without their mother fainting, never had raptures over Colonel Fitzwilliam occurred to them.

In a blink, the tension over Lydia, worries over wedding decor and meals, and even concerns about the marriage bed and scandalous undergarments faded away. The thrill of a flesh-and-blood army officer overruled them all.

Should I tell Mama he is a confirmed bachelor? Quickly, Lizzy discarded that idea. This promised to be far too much fun. *Poor Richard! He has no idea what he is in for. Wait until William hears this.*

❧

"*T*hese are the last two, Mr. Hill." Lizzy pointed at the boxes stacked by the door. "Be careful with your back. They have books inside, so are extremely heavy."

"I can manage, Miss Elizabeth, but thank you for the warning."

Holding in her smile, Lizzy nodded, then turned away. The elderly Longbourn butler was a dear man, and quite proud. Never would she wish to embarrass him by watching him struggle to lift the weighty boxes. Ignoring the grunts and muttered curses, she pretended absorbing interest in the open portmanteau on her bed.

It had taken a week to thoroughly go through every nook and cranny of the two bedchambers and for the rest of the house to be searched for anything belonging to Jane or Lizzy. The wedding was still over a week away, so it hadn't been critical to rush the job. However, they both discovered an urgency to finish once the cleaning, sorting, and packing enterprise had begun. Now, finally, it was complete. Or mostly so, that is.

Jane's boxed items were stowed in her unused bedroom. They would be carted to Netherfield later in the week. The proximity to Longbourn meant that Jane hadn't needed to pack as tightly and carefully as Lizzy. Nor had Jane needed to plan carefully for what to stow away and what to keep at hand. The balance of what to send ahead to Pemberley and what to carry with her in the carriage after the wedding had been more difficult than Lizzy imagined.

Mr. Darcy requested transporting her things to Pemberley sooner rather than later, so the boxes containing the bulk of her possessions were, at that moment, being loaded onto a wagon parked on the front drive. "If it is not too much of an inconvenience," he had said, "to ship your possessions this week, the earlier arrival will provide the Pemberley staff plenty of time to unpack and organize. They can ensure the new Mrs. Darcy's personal effects are readily available when we arrive home."

Mrs. Darcy. Home.

The way he had said the words while gazing at her with his incredibly blue eyes awash with love and happiness, had filled her with a flood of emotions she could not begin to define. Remembering his countenance helped in easing the bouts of sadness.

When the butler's footsteps clunked down the staircase, Lizzy slumped onto the edge of the bed and closed her eyes.

The request had been logical, of course. Just not easy. The Darcy coach was spacious and sturdy enough to handle several trunks and a dozen luggage cases, but she only owned a few and wasn't about to mention this fact. She knew William well enough to be certain he would dash out and purchase a whole new set of the most expensive traveling paraphernalia on the market. Such extravagances would soon be a part of her life, but she wasn't Mrs. Darcy of Pemberley yet.

So, she had packed, unpacked, and repacked the baggage she owned a dozen times at least, making sure they could contain what she required for the next week. The lone trunk and three bags now waited for the final packing day. They were vivid reminders of the fast-approaching end to this period of her life.

Opening her eyes, Lizzy's gaze fell on the open trunk and then lifted to slowly scan the room.

Indeed, the reminders of her life changing were all around her. Or rather, the lack of them was the reminder. The once-cluttered bedchamber had been gutted. The walls were bare, not a trinket was in sight, the majority of the drawers were empty, and the back wall of the wardrobe was visible for the first time in well over a decade. Gaps amongst the furniture from those pieces Lizzy was sending to Pemberley made the room appear ravaged and uneven. It was her familiar sanctuary no longer, and the sensation was deeply unsettling.

Envision William's eyes and how he spoke of our home.

It helped, to a degree.

Standing, she strolled the room from corner to corner. Feeling sentimental, she brushed her fingertips across the worn furniture, stroked the dusty curtains, ran her palm down the faded wallpaper, and so on. All the while she scanned the shadows along the floor just to be sure a precious object hadn't fallen to the ground. A small portion of hers and Jane's personal belongings and clothing remained hanging inside the wardrobe, folded in the bureau drawers, and strewn atop the dressing table. Lizzy was thankful for the clothing and toiletries yet in place as they provided a semblance of normalcy. The contrast between their homey, lived-in abode and this far-too-clean, sparse room was stark, but if there were some personal effects, it wasn't too jarring.

A pair of slender arms slipped around her waist, squeezing tight as a chin rested upon her shoulder. As if reading her thoughts, a dulcet voice whispered near her ear, "There is no shame in shedding a tear, my Lizzy. I have shed my fair share, and I am not moving as far away. I can gradually adjust to being away from Longbourn. For you, the pain will be stronger, even with Mr. Darcy to comfort, as I am certain he will."

Lizzy brushed a tear off her cheek and attempted to laugh at her childishness. It came out as a choked squeak. Hugging Jane's arms tighter about her, she confessed, "I vacillate between feeling an utter fool, to telling myself mourning is healthy. Oh, Jane! I want to marry William with all my soul. I can think of little else, to be honest. Deep into the marrow of my bones, I know he is the perfect man for me, gifted by God. I am confident Pemberley will become my home, but I cannot relinquish the melancholy either. How does that make sense?"

"It doesn't make sense. How could it? Perhaps wise quotes of philosophy, the Bible, or a poet would instill some comfort. But, in the end, I believe we are normal soon-to-be-brides dealing with nervousness, as all brides have since the dawn of time. They survived, so I am sure we will too."

Lizzy turned and embraced Jane, the sisters holding each other in silence. Then Lizzy pulled away to kiss her beloved sister on the cheek. "As always, dearest Jane, your serene soul soothes me. What will I ever do without you to tame my tumultuousness?"

"Once, I might have submitted that Mr. Darcy, being the epitome of calm, disciplined logic, would replace me and be superior. However, I am no longer sure, in light of your vivid descriptions of his wild, passionate personality. Thus, I can extend no hope for you in that area."

"Then I am doomed," Lizzy sighed dramatically.

"That I seriously doubt. Now, I came upstairs not with the intent to cheer you or depress further, but to inform that Mr. Darcy has arrived. He expressed his desire to personally oversee the loading of your possessions before they headed to Pemberley."

And then it happened, as it always did—the mere mention of his name, particularly when said in conjunction with his physical person being nearby, was all she needed to zoom from sorrow to euphoria in seconds. The tears dried in an instant, the sulk replaced by a gleeful grin. Following Jane down the stairs, it was a challenge not to skip past her. At the landing, she resisted the urge no longer, swerving around the snail-paced Jane and dashing toward the door.

"Lizzy! Come here! You have to see this!"

Kitty was in the parlor, standing by the bank of windows overlooking the front drive. She vigorously waved one arm in a come-here gesture, mirth lighting her face and deepening her dimples. Curiosity winning over her yearning to greet her fiancé, Lizzy diverted into the room with Jane at her heels.

"What is it? Oh!" She took one peek out the window and clamped a hand over her mouth to stay the giggles.

Mr. Darcy was outside on the gravel drive, dressed as he always was in an impeccable suit probably costing more money than half her wardrobe combined. The surprise wasn't in his pristine ensemble, the precise cravat loops, and his boots polished to a bright shine. Rather, it was in what he was doing.

Circling the wagon, he was tugging on the ropes, adjusting the thick canvas tarp, and testing the packed boxes and furniture for security. One of the drivers followed alongside, repeating the same actions and responding to Mr. Darcy's instructions to tighten this or add more padding there. The second driver crouched in the bed of the wagon, doing much the same. All the while, the three men were laughing and chatting as if old friends.

"A moment ago," Kitty whispered, "I cracked the window wider and heard them talking about a sporting event in London. A pugilism match, I think. Mr. Darcy admitted to losing his bet on someone named Clubber Clyde. Then, that man"—Kitty indicated the lanky fellow trailing alongside Darcy—"his name is Mr. Hocking, or Tims, according to the other driver, who is Scotty, or Mr. Scott"—she pointed at a short man in the wagon bed—"told Mr. Darcy that he should never bet against Gentleman Joe. You should have seen the way Mr. Hocking was taunting Mr. Darcy. It was hilarious, but Mr. Darcy was giving it back good, which was even funnier!"

Lizzy's smile grew as she listened to the snippets of conversation audible through the narrowly opened window. The three men were discussing the laxity of police patrol at the docks, the topic itself not amusing, but the casual discourse and relaxed familiarity were fascinating. Just a few weeks ago Lizzy would have stood there in absolute shock and amazement to witness prim, aristocratic Mr. Darcy hobnobbing with rough working men. While still not the society he preferred to keep, Lizzy now knew the truth of why he could interact familiarly with such men, thanks to an enlightening conversation earlier that very week.

Since returning to the sedate country life of Hertfordshire—with birthday celebrating and successful shooting expeditions past—the engaged couples had greeted each day with nothing of import on the agenda. The snowy cold spell had lifted, but the weather remained too chilly and unpredictable for extended outdoor activities. Meaning, the bulk of the day for the past week had been spent lazing about the Longbourn parlor.

While it might seem a pathetically boring development, the lovers had discovered the inactivity to be advantageous. They had hours to do little else but relax together and talk. Even if playing a card or board game, or embarking on a short stroll about the garden, the pace was leisurely, and conversation was the highlight.

Mr. Darcy tended to prefer silence, unabashedly admitting to Lizzy that he often went days without saying more than a handful of words, and those only out of necessity to thank a servant or give a command of some sort. While not nearly as reticent, Lizzy was not a chatterbox either. Conversation came easily to her—a gift Darcy constantly marveled over—but she also craved solitude and tranquility. They equally split their hours together between silence and casual communication. Curiously, she learned as much about the man she was soon to marry in the nonverbal interludes as she did when they talked!

In small increments, he had begun to share more about his life at Pemberley. He avoided the past, Lizzy sensing the pain of lost loved ones weighed heavy on his heart. Instead, he spoke of his life as a landowner and horse breeder, Lizzy adoring how his eyes glowed and face relaxed. Passion and pride imbued his entire being, giving her glimpses of the confident Master of Pemberley she would learn to greater appreciate as time moved forward.

Hearkening to his words, she began to grasp the scope of his duties, which were essentially the same as those at Longbourn. Mr. Bennet was an indifferent estate manager, content to trust his steward and tenants. Darcy, however, was an enthusiastic participant in his estate's management, up to and including getting his hands dirty upon occasion. While a slight surprise, this hadn't shocked her all that much. What had been a huge revelation was to learn of his other business dealings.

"At some point after we are married, I shall take you to Derby," he had tossed out one afternoon while playing a game of backgammon. "It is the largest city close to Pemberley, not as metropolitan as London, of course, but clean and modern, excellent stores and historical places of beauty as well. We both appreciate history, so visiting will be a pleasurable diversion. Also, you can see the mill where I send our wool. Not that touring a wool mill or my cotton mill is riveting entertainment, but your curious mind would be fascinated—"

"Wait a minute," she had blurted, the badly lobbed dice scattering the flat discs across the board. "Did you say you own a wool mill and a cotton mill?"

"Not exactly. I invest in the wool mill and in a silk mill too, but those are merely financial deals. I have nothing to do with the running of them. The cotton mill I do own. Well, a third of it, that is." He had said all of this in the most offhand manner, his attention on the disordered game pieces and the double sixes she had thrown.

"But, isn't it…abnormal, even unacceptable, for a man of your station to be tied to such ventures?"

Still more absorbed by the game than the topic, he had nodded sagely and then shrugged. "You might be surprised just how many of the gentry, and even the aristocracy, invest in businesses related to trade. They will often deny it and pretend it is beneath them, but the fact is, a wise man with a head for business is prudent to seek ways to increase his capital. I will admit, however, that my insatiable curiosity inspires me to diversify more than most and to get personally involved, which is atypical."

At her silence, he had finally looked up, noted the ludicrous expression upon her face, and smiled. "Have I shocked you, my dear?"

Then, he had gestured toward the dining room where, visible through the open door, was the frame edge of a huge painting hanging over the sideboard. "If you recall, we Darcys have a long history of delving into various outside endeavors, Clara Steen being only one example. My grandfather tended to dabble in outside business, although not as much as me, whereas my father was totally uninterested. He said I was more like his brother George, my uncle the physician." Darcy had shrugged again. "Perhaps, but I don't see it. I've done my fair share of traveling abroad, but it isn't a passion as it obviously is for my uncle George. Then again, the trait is evinced in differing ways. For me it is the aforementioned insatiable curiosity. One curiosity leads to another and to another, and on it goes until now I have far too many financial fingers stuck into places that are taking up my precious time! Solving that is now my new priority."

Darcy had spoken a bit more on the subject, enough so that when he broached the prospect of transporting Lizzy's possessions to Pemberley, she wasn't at all taken aback when he insisted on utilizing the company he employed to carry cargo. Between Pemberley estate, the cotton mill, and the ships he shared ownership of—she learned about those in another conversation—readily available and reliable land transport was essential. He and his partners didn't own or invest in a cargo company, nor exclusively contract with a particular one, but they knew of the best wagoners in London and paid very well for their services. Hence his familiarity with the company whose wagon was now parked in front of Longbourn and his comfort with the drivers.

As he had said to her flabbergasted father, after sharing a truncated version of his business affairs, "It will ease my mind to use a wagon I know to be sturdy and have it driven by competent men I've personally interviewed and seen in action. There will be no doubt that Miss Elizabeth's prized belongings will reach Pemberley safely."

While she mused, the discussion around the wagon had veered away from London crime to the road conditions between Hertfordshire and Derbyshire.

Now kneeling inside the wagon bed, Darcy was frowning at something she could not see. "This padding is not thick enough for my taste. I can't risk this being harmed. Hand me one of those blankets, Mr. Scott. We can move it in between the boxes of books and wrap the blankets tightly around. Better stability and less space to slide around if items do shift from the bumpy roads. Do you agree?"

As the driver identified by Kitty as Tims lithely climbed into the wagon, Mr. Darcy lifted the canvas away from the object in question. Gasping, Lizzy saw the small curio she had received for Christmas nearly fifteen years ago. The poor old thing was cracked along the bottom edge and the door no longer closed straight. For days she debated bringing it, certain it would look even more pathetic amid the splendor of Pemberley's furnishings. It was perfect for her miniature teacup collection, however, and the sentimental value tugged at her heart, so in the end she had been unable to part with it.

Nevertheless, her cheeks flamed red to watch William fuss over it, as if it were the most precious object in the universe, when it probably cost less than a single china plate at Pemberley—even when brand-new. He was either the silliest man alive or the most thoughtful, wonderful, dearest…

Her heart touched, she pivoted from the window and dashed out of the room. Down the steps in a bound, she reached the wagon just as Darcy leaped over the side to land gracefully on steady feet.

"Miss Elizabeth! Excellent timing. I believe we have secured your belongings unless there is more we have missed?"

At her shaking head, he nodded. Smiling gaily, he indicated the two workmen. "Mr. Scott and Mr. Hocking are two of the most capable drivers I know. They promise with their lives to safely deliver every last hair clip and handkerchief to Pemberley. Is that not so, gentlemen?"

They bobbed their heads and offered their assurances, adding that they planned to drive through the night so as not to risk thievery at an inn. Lizzy stammered her thanks, which took a bit of time with the gregarious fellows, and then walked to the end of the wagon where Darcy had moved. He was bent over, inspecting the wheel or something underneath, and when he straightened, he took a step toward the far side. Grabbing his hand, he stopped and turned toward her, one brow lifted.

"This is all so very kind of you, William," she whispered. Feeling the heat spreading across her cheeks, she darted her eyes to the drivers, who were thankfully busy with the horses. "You are a dear man to exert yourself. I do hope you know how tremendously appreciative I am. But…these things are not worth fretting over or consuming so much of your time. Frankly, I am embarrassed to bring most of this into Pemberley."

Her gaze drifted to the dirt by her feet to avoid his penetrating stare, so she didn't see the arm bent her direction until his resonant voice made her peek upward. "Walk with me please, Elizabeth? Gentlemen, carry on. You are free to go whenever ready, but do not forget Mrs. Price has a basket waiting in the kitchen."

Holding onto his arm, they walked in silence around the corner to the sheltered garden where they had shared their first kiss a little over six weeks ago. Utilized numerous times since when wishing to be alone but within proper monitoring distance, leading her here was not at random. Only on this occasion, rather than kissing her, he gripped her upper arms firmly and looked down with a severe glower.

"Listen to me carefully, Elizabeth. My home will soon be yours. With very few exceptions, and even those are negotiable, every room down to the smallest closet will be under your jurisdiction as Mrs. Darcy, the Mistress of Pemberley. Foremost, you absolutely must be comfortable within your private chambers. Strip them bare, transform them into a replica of your suite here at Longbourn, furnish them with battered furniture, or decorate in Chinese or Egyptian motifs for all I care. As long as you are happy dwelling within, that is what matters to me."

He paused only long enough to slide his hands upward and cradle her face. He softened his expression but maintained a serious cast and a stern tone as he continued, "You are precious to me, do you not understand? By extension, your belongings are important to me, especially a treasured childhood cabinet. If it adds to your happiness, it will break my heart to see it harmed. Tell me now if you have chosen to leave anything else behind for fear it would somehow be at odds at Pemberley. I am emphatic about this. I shall be extremely vexed to learn you have done so."

He was so serious, as if the weight of the world depended on her answer.

"No, nothing else," she choked out, the sound a cross between a laugh and a sob. "I promise," she added when he cocked his head and arched a brow dubiously.

"Very well, then. I shall believe you, although I do think I will inform Mr. and Mrs. Bennet to keep an eye out for anything they think you might regret leaving behind."

Then he smiled, and she laughed. Steering her to their favorite bench, he clasped her hands and settled them upon his thigh.

"I suppose it is time to disabuse you of an erroneous conclusion. When you were at Pemberley, both on your tour with Mrs. Reynolds and later with me, you saw only the public rooms. Those are formal and thus furnished with the best. You have yet to see the private parlors, breakfast room, and, of course, the bedchambers."

Stopping, he pressed his lips together and glanced away. Speaking in a low tone, he explained, "You are not alone in having prized possessions from childhood, Elizabeth. Or in owning items worn from constant use that are too comfortable to part with. Honestly, I highly anticipate sitting together as you show me your possessions and recount any memories attached. It is a way to learn more of your heart. Mayhap you have gleaned of my sentimental nature, but you might be surprised to discover just how maudlin I can be. I've done my best to hide it, but hopefully, our engagement is too far advanced for this to frighten you away."

He flashed a grin, knowing the answer to that nonsensical statement, but with a hint of embarrassment and uncertainty in his eyes. In cases such as these, as they both had learned, words were not the best way to reassure.

Slipping her arms around his shoulders, she leaned in to deliver the kiss he was already bending to accept. Expressing her understanding and acceptance through kisses and caresses was not only more enjoyable, but it also conveyed a depth of emotion words never could.

Without any doubt, Darcy received the message loud and clear.

10

DRAMATIC INTERRUPTION

For the hundredth time in the past hour, Lizzy glanced away from the dress she was attempting to sew and peered out the window. A fragment of the main road connecting Netherfield with the thoroughfare leading to London was distantly visible through the trees and shrubs surrounding Longbourn. The sofa positioned by this window had been her favorite spot for years when doing any task that required unobstructed sunlight, yet until a few weeks ago, the fact that the angle afforded a view of the road had not registered as a noteworthy detail. This recent discovery had benefitted her enormously so she could see her beloved's arrival, providing some ten to fifteen minutes for ensuring she looked her very best. Today the awareness only brought sadness.

Lizzy glanced at the mantel clock. Since the last time she'd checked, the minute hand had inched another whopping two strokes.

It is after ten o'clock, she thought forlornly, *so surely he has already left for London.*

She was torn between disgust for wasting two hours trying to sew while pathetically riveted to a gap in the trees, and desolation for apparently missing the passing of his carriage during one of those brief minutes she completed a stitch.

As if a flash of horses and the Darcy crest would make me feel any better. What utter nonsense.

Cognizance of her idiotic actions and emotions did not prevent another pitiful sigh, probably the thousandth in the past hour.

"Try not to be too sad, Lizzy. I understand your feelings, but he will only be gone a few days."

"He said it might be a whole week." The correction to Jane's kindly meant consolation burst out as a plaintive whine. Cringing, Lizzy tossed the error-riddled gown into her sewing box. "Sorry, Jane. I am silly, I know. I shall try to exhibit calm restraint, as I know you would if the situation reversed. You would never stare out of a window for hours in the vain hope to glimpse Mr. Bingley's carriage passing by."

"Believe that if it helps. I shan't comment upon the numerous attempts to peer through the miles in the vain attempt to draw Netherfield into focus." Together they laughed at their joint whimsies instigated by hearts giddy with newfound love.

"I believe it is imprudent to squander the time God has given us in pointless anxiety. As the wise proverb of Solomon instructs, 'Whoever works his land will have plenty of bread, but he who follows worthless pursuits lacks sense.'"

Normally, Mary's pious lectures stirred nothing but annoyance within Lizzy. Perhaps it was her newfound appreciation for scripture, thanks to William, or maybe it was the truth of the words that pierced her heart. Whatever the root, Lizzy gazed at her sister seriously and nodded. "Thank you, Mary. While I do believe Mrs. Price would scream if I went anywhere near her garden or demanded to make bread, the metaphor is valid. I shall take it to heart."

"Might I suggest a visit to the Lucases? Kitty heard from Susie Ashe, who heard from Maria Lucas, that Mr. Collins has returned to

Hunsford, but Charlotte is staying to help her mother. Lady Lucas has the gout, you know."

"I think that was an excuse," Kitty piped up. She sat cross-legged on the floor, teaching her puppy to balance a treat on his nose, attention focused but never so much so that sharing gossip wasn't possible. "Susie and I saw Lady Lucas buying fabric from the draper yesterday, and she seemed fine to me. I think Charlotte wanted to be away from Mr. Collins and that horrid Lady Catherine. Who can blame her? And it was Mia Putman who heard it from Maria Lucas and told Susie, but I'm sure it is true."

"However the message passed along, it is good news." Rising from the sofa, Lizzy pointedly turned her aching back toward the window and stretched until her spine popped. Inserting vigor and positivity into her tone, she said, "The suggestion is a marvelous one, Mary. I haven't visited with Charlotte as frequently as I should have, I am ashamed to say."

"I am sure she understands, Lizzy," Jane said. "Not too long ago she was newly engaged so must know how it is to be centered on one's betrothed, romance, and future happiness together."

At this absurd declaration, hilarity erupted. Even Mary joined in, as well as Kitty's puppy if his spirited yaps counted. Lizzy's snort blended with a burst of uncontrollable laughter, the emitted sounds not at all ladylike. "Oh Jane! You are simply priceless! Bless your heart."

Into the bedlam walked the butler. No one noticed until he cleared his throat.

"Pardon the interruption to your entertainment, ladies. Miss Elizabeth, you have a visitor."

Before Lizzy had no time to run through the possible visitor's list, Mr. Hill stepped aside and in walked Mr. Darcy.

"William!" she exclaimed, shocked despite having done nothing but long for him all morning. They had said their emotional goodbyes last evening, so it had honestly not occurred to her to hope he would pause for a visit.

"Mr. Darcy!" Mrs. Bennet flew into the room, from wherever she had been, faster than the speed of light. "How absolutely delightful to see you! Oh my! I am all aflutter! We were not yet expecting guests. I am afraid you just missed breakfast, although I am sure Mrs. Price can prepare something in no time at all. We have fresh biscuits with strawberry jam made not a week ago, and coffee of course, with cream as you like it—"

"Please, do not trouble yourself, Mrs. Bennet," Darcy hastily interjected when she finally paused for air. Tearing his eyes away from Lizzy, who was literally breathless, he bowed respectfully toward her mother. "I dined well this morning, thank you. I apologize for calling unannounced and unexpected. I am, as you know, departing for a short trip to Town. However, as I approached Longbourn, I felt it my duty to pause and pay my respects, yet again, for your outstanding hospitality these past weeks. I also regretted not asking if you have need of anything from the city, Mrs. Bennet. It would be my greatest honor to acquire anything you may need or want. The same is true, of course, for all of your fine daughters."

"Oh, Mr. Darcy! You are so very kind!" Mrs. Bennet dabbed her teary eyes with her handkerchief. "My Lizzy is the most fortunate of women to have gained the notice of such a great man."

"Thank you, madam. I judge myself the truly fortunate one. With your permission," he said, rushing on before another word passed Mrs. Bennet's parted lips, "may I be granted a moment alone with Miss Elizabeth?"

"Mama." Jane gently clasped onto her mother's arm and steered toward the door. "I completely forgot that Mrs. Price wanted our opinion on the marzipan for the wedding cake. Safe travels, Mr. Darcy." At an added head bob to Kitty and Mary, they suddenly had vital duties elsewhere. In a matter of seconds, Lizzy and Darcy were alone, the women's voices drifting through the narrow crack in the door from farther and farther down the hallway until they finally faded into silence. Well before the last retreating murmur, Darcy had crossed the room in three long strides and enfolded her hands in his.

"I could not bear to leave without seeing you—"

"I am so surprised to see you—"

Soft laughter stayed their jumbled confessions. Apparently deciding to forego unnecessary explanations altogether, Darcy bent for a tender kiss. A mere brush of his lips sent a jolt of desire through her body. Instinctively leaning to increase the pressure and parting her lips invitingly, Lizzy released a whining moan when he stepped back a pace.

After drawing a shaky breath, he professed teasingly, "I do not trust myself with you, Miss Bennet. For some bizarre reason, I lose all sense of propriety when kissing you. The gentleman Mr. Darcy vanishes as if he never existed."

Smiling, he led her to the same sofa she had perched on for close to two hours that morning. "You appear amused, my darling. Then I haven't disturbed you by dropping in unexpectedly?"

"Don't be ridiculous. As if I would ever be disturbed to see you, William."

"Glad to hear it. Honestly, I did not plan to stop. I thought I had convinced myself that our affectionate parting last evening was sufficient to hold me for the days I shall be in London. Alas, as my carriage neared Longbourn, the vision of you here, perhaps yet in your bedclothes, was too tempting. It was quite simply beyond my capability to resist." Grinning, he reached up and tucked an unruly lock of hair behind her ear, his fingertips playfully tickling her lobe. Another tingling current cascaded through her until it created butterflies in her belly.

"So," she stammered, "the stalwart Mr. Darcy confesses to weakness, does he? Unfathomable!"

"Indeed, it is true. Daily, I find my strength and control waning. I am helpless to do anything about it, other than pray for time to defy the laws of physics and bring November the twenty-eighth sooner than normal. It is entirely possible I may lose my mind for wanting you if the next ten days creep by."

"Oh, the tragedy! A fine mind such as yours, sir, must be protected at all cost. Then I shall increase my prayers. Perhaps with the joint effort, along with Jane and Charles who are likely appealing to the heavens as well, God's heartstrings will be tugged to perform a small miracle."

He was still fixated on her ear, which was wreaking havoc with her insides. It didn't help that his eyes had assumed a dreamy glassiness and were darkening with desire.

Goodness gracious but we are a pathetic pair of romantics.

Attempting a jest, her voice came out as a susurrant mumble. "If you want to know the truth, William, I shall confess my severe weakness, with the warning that it may result in uncontrollable laughter or possibly another round of improper kisses."

Darcy agreed to take his chances, so Lizzy recounted her morning of staring out the window, eyes drawn as if magnetized to the gap in the trees. He did chuckle and bestowed a kiss. Attempting to keep the kiss light and under control failed spectacularly, Darcy once again calling upon some internal reservoir of fortitude that Lizzy appeared to lack.

"We are quite the pair of hopeless romantics, are we not?"

His gruffly spoken, rhetorical question, echoing her thought just seconds before, brought on a case of giggles. Tension momentarily eased, Darcy roughly cleared his throat and continued in a regulated tone, "I did have another purpose in stopping by, not that kissing your lips isn't a justifiable reason. This trip to Town was an abrupt decision, and I worried I had not explained the necessity as fully as I ought to have done."

"You are an important man, my love. I may not yet comprehend the intricacies of your myriad business affairs, and probably never will, but I know it consumes large portions of your time and is necessary. You need never fear I shall be demanding or jealous in this."

A row of small creases marred his perfect brow, and he squeezed her hands. "I see I was wise to take the time to talk to you, Elizabeth, as there are misconceptions in your kindly meant speech. For one, I have no intention, ever, of placing my business affairs over you, and the family I pray we shall one day have. I am grateful for your willingness to be undemanding. However, if I ever slip into a pattern of ignoring my duties as a husband and father, I insist you bring it to my awareness. Those roles will always be of principal importance to me."

Her answer was a firm nod and a smile. Pleased with that, Darcy went on. "Secondly, the fact is, my various business concerns, both in London and at Pemberley, consume my time because I have *wanted* them to. I derive tremendous pleasure from engaging in financial ventures and estate management. I doubt this desire and satisfaction will change, to be honest, only the quantity of time I spend doing it. To be frank, until I met you, I had little else to enjoy in life. Work is a far better alternative to boredom and loneliness than what most men of my station do with their time, trust me."

The fleeting expression of distaste spoke volumes about his meaning. Lizzy chose to let that topic alone, but she did silently thank God for bringing her a man like Mr. Darcy rather than one of those others he alluded to!

"Once we are married, I will have other activities to bring me pleasure." The salacious grin now on his face, while raising a blush to her cheeks, was preferable to the grimly pressed lips of a moment ago. "And that brings me to the reason I am making all these annoying journeys. I want our beginning months as husband and wife to be as carefree as possible, Elizabeth. Not that I have tended to travel to London often in the winter, but I am looking even beyond that. With Mr. Daniels' assistance, I am arranging my various affairs so he will not have to bother me unduly.

Unfortunately, just about everything in this era of complicated legalities requires piles of documents to be drafted, signed, notarized, distributed, registered, and on and on. My solicitor and his team are working overtime."

"And being paid well, I presume."

"Oh yes." He laughed, leaning back into the sofa for the first time. Relief and happiness shone in his countenance. He dropped his hand to her knee and caressed it lazily. "Every penny is being earned and willingly paid so I can be alone with you and unfettered from all pressing matters. To state it another way, my love, as terrible as it is to separate during this special period of betrothal, the sacrifice will benefit us later."

"I cannot argue on any point. And perhaps it will ease your terrible feelings about our separation if I remind that you shall fortuitously miss out on the grand ball the Lucases are holding next Saturday."

"I realized this morning and did send a note of explanation to Sir William. I promised to try to complete my business in time to drive back, although it is unlikely." Pausing for a moment, the eyes resting on her face penetrating, he then asked, "You will attend the ball, then?"

She was startled at the question and the odd discord in his voice. "I planned to, with my family and you and Mr. Bingley. Indeed, I was only teasing. I know you like Sir William. We will miss your presence tremendously, of course. Worst of all, I shall be losing my favorite dancing partner. You never miss a step or trample upon my toes. Imagine how mangled I may be when you next see me!"

"So, you shall dance. I see."

Her efforts to jest had clearly failed. Holding in her giggles, she smiled serenely. "Only with decrepit old gentlemen, like my father, if I can drag him onto the floor. And Mr. Bingley, if I can tear him away from Jane for one dance." She held up her left hand, wiggling her fingers so that the sunlight sparkled off her engagement ring. "I am an engaged woman. No unattached male dances with a lady he cannot flirt with."

Her attempt to placate with truth spoken humorously was ineffective. Darcy narrowed his eyes farther, and the muscles in his jaw visibly tightened. Still more amused than concerned, she softened her tone. "You have been to enough Meryton assemblies by now to surely know that none of the men can compete with you. Not a one stirred my interest before meeting you, so how could they now? Rest easy, my love, as you have no cause for jealousy."

"I believe we establish several weeks ago that I am a possessive man, Elizabeth. Jealousy is a natural reaction and I shan't apologize. Nor do I see it as a weakness, but as a trait any sane man should have when he loves passionately. Additionally, when the woman he loves is beautiful, witty, physically desirable, and near perfection, a sensible man will anticipate jealousy arising frequently."

She vividly remembered their heated argument in the garden after he observed her playful antics with Matty Beller. That incident recalled her raging jealousy over Caroline Bingley, a woman Lizzy had done her best for the time being to pretend didn't exist.

Closing her eyes at the uncomfortable memories, she rested her head on his shoulder and curled against his body. Momentarily mystified by the unexpected action, Darcy stiffened slightly but quickly recovered and wrapped his arms around her.

"Forgive me," she whispered. "I know better than to tease about that. You have nothing to fear, my love. You are the only man I want, now and forever. However, if it distresses you to think of it, I shall not attend the ball. I would miss you too much to enjoy it anyway."

After a brief silence, he relaxed fully and kissed the top of her head. "It distresses me that I shall miss an opportunity to be at your side, proudly escorting the most beautiful woman in Hertfordshire. My peevishness is from that more than actual jealousy. I want you to go and enjoy yourself, Elizabeth. Just not *too much*, how about that?"

Answering with a hushed chuckle, she snaked her arms around

his waist and nestled deeper into his warm embrace. The feelings of peace and harmony drifted over and through her. Desire, never far away when in the same room with William, simmered under her skin. For the moment, she was content to bask in the love between them. In contented quiet they held each other, the marvelous lulling interlude abruptly shattered when the mantel clock loudly struck the eleven o'clock hour. Darcy jolted into a half rise, which might have toppled Lizzy onto the floor if she hadn't jumped out of his arms and briskly scooted to the other end of the sofa.

"Good God! For a moment I thought sure it was your father barging in with a primed musket!"

Giggling a tad shakily from being startled as much as his exclamation, Lizzy assured, "You are safe. Papa is off on some sort of estate business, or so that was the claim for escaping the house today."

This belated news seemed to cheer Darcy considerably. "Now you tell me! Alas, another missed opportunity for inappropriate behavior as I must be on my way."

Pausing, his eyes drifted from her mouth down to the tops of her breasts, which were, she just then realized, exposed to barely an inch above her nipples, thanks to her loose morning dress slipping lower while slumped against his body. Moreover, the recent fright had caused her to breathe hard. With each deep inhale the pale mounds rose, an effect not likely to stop anytime soon with his darkening gaze staring directly at them.

"Of course, arriving at my destination later than planned is not an unpardonable transgression."

Those huskily whispered words trailed off when he closed the gap between their bodies. At the bumping contact with her knees, he clasped onto her legs and, almost absently, draped them over his. The movement was smooth and slow, yet it shifted her balance so that she ended in a moderate recline, the tall, padded sofa arm behind her back. Whether this was his plan or not, her determined lover leaned closer without the tiniest hesitation.

Lifting his right hand, he touched his fingertips lightly to the nape of her neck. Delicately, he glided across the slim contour of her collarbone until meeting the edge of her garments, which already teetered precariously on the extreme curve of her shoulder.

Darcy flicked his eyes up for a split second, perhaps asking for permission or showing her that, while inflamed with desire, he was in control. Whichever the impetus for diverting his attention from the rapt focus upon her breast, Lizzy had no time to respond before he had returned to his provocative scrutiny. In truth, if given several minutes, she would not have been able to formulate a coherent thought. Undoubtedly, her glassy eyes and parted lips were all the reply he needed anyway. Undeterred by the fabric layers, he nudged them past her shoulder and traced a slow path along the ribbon-edged bodice downward.

The wood sofa corner digging into her back and the air cooly wafting over her bared shoulder registered hazily upon Lizzy's mind. There were far too many pleasant sensations rushing through her body to bother over such trifles. For instance, she was acutely aware that the fabric covering her left breast now perching dangerously close to her pebble-hard nipple. She was even more aware of William's fingertips steadily approaching the sensitive, virginal flesh.

Torn between closing her eyes and enjoying the unique thrills of pleasure, she kept them half-open to enhance the bliss with the visual. The sight of his strong hand, tanned golden from the sun, brushing over the creamy skin of her chest was bizarrely erotic. His long, elegantly shaped fingers stroked firmly, the mildly calloused pads intensifying the emotions. Fire flooding her veins, Lizzy was amazed that her skin wasn't red as a ripe cherry. She focused all her energy on not squirming in desire, hands pressed harshly into the sofa seat for support.

What will he do next? The possible options flashing through her dazzled brain unprepared her for the reality.

Reaching the swell of her left breast, he hesitated for a moment, warring, she suspected, with the urge to push the fabric aside. The merest prod of his thumb would free the rosy tip aching for his touch. Instead, he drifted up and over, until poised at the shadowy crevice separating her bosom. Dipping the end of his index finger halfway into the narrow gap, he then splayed his hand fully onto the soft pillow. Simultaneously, he dropped his head and pressed his mouth to her bared, as-yet-untouched right breast.

Lizzy gasped. Succumbing to the escalating euphoria, eyes closed and head weakly flopped onto the sofa back. Her hands, which had at some point knotted into fists and dug into the cushion, uncurled and jerked upward to clutch his upper arms.

Darcy did not move. No increase in the pressure of his mouth. No parting of the moist lips on her chest. No probing or squeezing with his right hand. He simply maintained the contact for what seemed like hours but was only a minute or two. Finally, after the faintest nuzzle of his face against her breast, he pulled away, shaky hands readjusting her bodice in the process. Once satisfied she was reclothed to proper modesty levels, he sat up straight and met her eyes.

The expression he wore would forever be indelibly painted upon her mind, yet she would never be able to adequately put the look into words. *Rapturous joy* and *transcendent love* were as close as she could describe, although that wasn't nearly accurate.

"I believe that shall tide me over for the week ahead and give me something sweet to dream about. I shall pray the same for you, my darling. So very soon we shall be able to enjoy each other to the fullest, without any reservations."

Smiling, he clasped her hands and stood, bringing her with him. Placing their hands upon his chest, he bent for a chaste kiss on her lips. "I will be counting the days until I am again in your arms,

Elizabeth," he whispered against her mouth. Withdrawing, he peered earnestly into her eyes. "I am more bewitched by you than I was when I proposed. I love you, Elizabeth, with all my body, heart, and soul."

"I love you, William——"

Her declaration was cut short by an abrupt, bone-crunching hug. "I will miss you terribly. Stay safe, my heart."

Releasing her as abruptly as he'd embraced her, Darcy pivoted and lurched toward the door, tossing, "I will be back on Saturday," over his shoulder. In a flash, he was gone.

～

*E*ventually, Lizzy regained her breath and composure. Able to face the day in better spirits than initially anticipated, she was pleased Jane had followed through on Mary's suggestion to visit with the Lucases. Before they finished lunch, a return message from Lucas Lodge assured them they were welcome, and a wonderful afternoon respite was enjoyed by all—excepting Mrs. Bennet.

Pleading lethargy, overwrought nerves, and symptoms of an oncoming cold, she decided to stay at Longbourn. When they returned late in the afternoon, she was lying on the couch with a flushed face and fanning herself vigorously. However, no amount of peakedness or upset nerves prevented her insisting they repeat the conversations word for word.

"Jane dear, was Lady Lucas able to solve the problem with Mrs. Goulding's lady's maid?"

"I believe we shall have a positive outcome, Mama. Lady Lucas is amazingly skilled at such matters, I daresay. She spoke with Mrs. Goulding over tea twice this past week. By the end, Mrs. Goulding was praising her maid and weeping at the very idea of losing her but insisting she be given as a 'gift' for the new lady of Netherfield!" Jane laughed while shaking her head. "I know not how she accomplished it, but I am to meet with the woman, a Miss Peyton, on Wednesday. I think I will ask Mrs. Nicholls to join me. She is new as Netherfield's housekeeper but has years of experience and, Mr. Bingley informed me the other day, served as a lady's maid herself. Her insights will prove valuable. Better than mine, of that, there is no question."

Mary paused in her piano practice, a puzzled frown creasing her brow. "I never fathomed selecting a servant who laces up stays and fixes hair would be such an ordeal."

"I thought the same, Mary. Much ado about nothing, if you ask me."

Jane gently admonished, "You can say that, Kitty dear, because you leave your hair loose most of the time and, sweet Mary, you only dress your beautiful, black hair into a severe knot. Perhaps once Lizzy and I are gone, Betsy will be able to focus her skills on you two."

Kitty had immediately lifted her hands to fluff the thick, tawny curls falling in a wave down her back and swayed her head side to side so that the tresses bounced prettily. "I maintain it is a travesty to conceal and restrain these lush locks, which God gave me, may I remind. Besides, all the pulling and tugging, and those pins stuck into my scalp give me a headache."

Mary's expression transformed from baffled to prudish disapproval at Kitty's words and antics, and then to borderline panic —probably from the vision of an ostentatious coiffure à la Betsy.

Fearing Kitty would next launch into another anti-corset tirade, they let the topic alone, opting instead to relive the hours at Lucas Lodge minute by minute while answering Mrs. Bennet's questions.

What did they serve as refreshments? How were preparations for the autumn ball coming along? Did Lady Lucas have any town gossip to report? Not that Mrs. Bennet asked this directly, preferring the code phrase "news from the village of vital importance."

Did Maria Lucas have any suitors calling? This was asked because *nothing* would be worse than for Miss Lucas to become engaged to a gentleman of greater worth or prestige than Mr.

Bingley or Mr. Darcy! As unlikely as the possibility of this was for Maria Lucas especially, or anyone in the area for that matter, Mrs. Bennet conveyed her anxiety over such a horrific development at least twice a week. Once relieved on that count, it was essential to verify that Lady Lucas had asked about the wedding plans, which the girls assured she had, at length. Whether this was entirely accurate is debatable, but Mrs. Bennet was content.

"How was your visit with Charlotte, Lizzy?"

"Wonderful. We truly enjoyed our company, almost as if the past year had never happened. Of course, it helped not having Mr. Collins lurking in the background in hopes of overhearing something to report to Lady Catherine."

"Really, Lizzy, do you think he does that?"

"I am sure of it, Mama. When I visited with Charlotte the last time, after we returned from London, I told her about the necklace Mr. Darcy gave me for the wedding. Why you should have seen how his eyes bugged! I thought he was far enough away not to hear our conversation, but he must have hearing like a dog."

"Makes sense," Kitty interrupted. "He is the old harpy's pet dog, after all."

"Kitty! For shame!" Mrs. Bennet exclaimed, waving her fan furiously. Kitty shrugged, unashamed.

"Well, be that as it may," Lizzy resumed after winking at her younger sister, "Mr. Collins jumped out of his chair and scurried from the room. Charlotte whispered, and this is verbatim, 'He has gone to write that down before he forgets. Lady Catherine will be furious!' We shared a good laugh, I confess without a bit of remorse."

"Poor Charlotte," Jane said sorrowfully.

Mrs. Bennet's fan snapped closed. "Why 'poor Charlotte'? She has a house of her own and security. We all thought she was doomed to be an old maid! To be saved from that fate is a cause for rejoicing, not pity. My word!"

Surprising everyone, Lizzy nodded her head. "While I do not

deem remaining unmarried a doomed fate, I have discovered my heart softening toward Charlotte's choice. I know"—she smiled at her sisters' collective amazement—"my change of tune is a shock. Mr. Collins is ridiculous and a nauseating toady, and I still shudder when recalling he offered marriage to me." She sent a glare toward her mother. "Nevertheless, he does care for Charlotte, never mistreats her, as far as I can tell, and has provided her a stable life with a good home. She is more suited to being a rector's wife than I would have suspected, and for certain far better than me. Charlotte seems content, I think, and perhaps that is what matters most."

Having ignored Lizzy's glare, Mrs. Bennet gushed, "So true, Lizzy! Charlotte made an excellent decision. I daresay, your refusal produced an outcome in everyone's best interest."

"You judge Mr. Collins too harshly, Lizzy," Mary remarked blandly. "He is a gentleman and has devoted his life to serving God. That is a noble calling with heavy burdens and, as such, is worthy of respect."

Lizzy wasn't sure how to respond. Mary had a point, although her innocent view of the goodness of people, even those in the church, was flawed. Still, this was Mr. Collins she was talking about. Lizzy may have been willing to agree that Charlotte hadn't made a terrible decision in becoming his wife, but going so far as to use words like *noble*, *gentleman*, and *respect* in conjunction with Mr. Collins left a bad taste in her mouth. Her mother jumped in, saving her from formulating a pleasant reply.

"Right, Mary! A girl can do far worse, believe me. A man like Mr. Collins is bendable, easy to please, and undemanding. Charlotte can manage a husband like Mr. Collins as she is much like you Lizzy."

"What do you mean, Mama?"

"Only that she has a strong will. She is not as stubbornly pigheaded as you, few are, I daresay. You tried my nerves no end since the day you were born. At times, I do pity Mr. Darcy, although he is nothing like Mr. Collins. In Charlotte's case, with a tenderhearted, malleable man like Mr. Collins, I doubt he pressures her unduly, if you take my meaning."

Her mother's disjointed ramble made little sense, except for the last statement. Oh yes, Lizzy took her meaning. A swift exchange with Jane proved her sister did as well.

She is wondering, as I am, how we walked blindly into what promises to be another talk imparting wisdom about the marriage bed and what we can say or do to avert the horrifying inevitable.

Evidently, her younger sisters were of the same mind. Mary pounded loudly on the pianoforte, playing a jaunty tune Lizzy wouldn't have thought was in her musical repertoire. Kitty jumped to her feet and insisted in a boisterous voice that everyone observe the latest tricks she had taught her fast-growing puppy. Jane, bless her heart, blurted into a descant about the weather.

Lizzy groped for the one subject sure to overshadow all others. "Lady Lucas did say that the Bennet wedding will be the most spectacular event to happen in Hertfordshire in decades." Lady Lucas had said no such thing, but Lizzy was desperate! Tragically, the bald-faced lie failed, as did all the rest.

"One never knows how a husband will be, of course. Hopefully Lady Lucas taught her daughters well, as I have attempted to do with you four. Alas, I missed my chance with sweet, innocent Lydia. Who knows what she has suffered?" Her sigh was a half sob. "Whether Charlotte needs to be firm with Mr. Collins is none of my business. I only bring it up as an example for the two of you."

Since diversion had not worked, Lizzy opted for the tactic of ignoring her mother. After all, her sermonizing never lasted too long. There were a limited number of euphemisms for sexual intercourse in her vocabulary, and the agitation the subject roused usually reached an unsustainable level in fifteen minutes maximum. Picking up her book and feigning deep absorption, she peripherally saw Jane doing the same with her needlepoint.

Either unaware no one was listening or indifferent, Mrs. Bennet rambled on, fan briskly flapping and eyes on the ceiling. "A woman's monthly courses are a legitimate impediment to intimate relations. The very idea of doing… Well, it is appalling! Men never pay attention to a women's schedule, nor is such a personal topic ever to be discussed. Remember that, girls. Always be vague, as is proper. A wife should never lie outright. Perish the thought! A decent, respectful gentleman would never dream of asking directly, and you are not to blame for their assumptions."

Glancing to Jane, they shared a roll of their eyes and swift smirk before resuming their feigned intent fascination with the items in their laps.

"Perhaps my suffering with headaches and nerves has been a blessing in disguise. Not that I wish such a debilitating ailment upon either of you, my dears. Just remember that when ill, a gentleman will understand a wife is incapable of activity that may well increase her pain and distress. Truthfully, what proper lady would not suffer from a headache at the very idea of a man's advances? Performing one's wifely duties is an expectation and honorable. The blessing of children, only created through the act, as confounding as that is— why would God do such a thing? I cannot comprehend it… Hmm… where was I? Oh, yes, the blessing of children is a reward for your perseverance and faithfulness to your vows. And there is some comfort in the warmth to be found, the companionship…"

Lizzy lost track of the discourse. Mary had given up on the lively tune and finally on entertaining with the pianoforte altogether. Somewhere in the middle of it all, probably around the mention of "wifely duties" or perhaps earlier, when menstruation and "intimate relations" were said in the same sentence, she and Kitty had slunk away. Just as Lizzy was debating whether it was time for her to do the same, Mrs. Bennet's tone altered into the lilt of a question.

"You did say, Jane, that Netherfield has a well-appointed bedchamber separate from Mr. Bingley?"

Jane automatically nodded and, out of habit, opened her

mouth to reply, but her mother had presumed the answer and wasn't even looking at her eldest daughter. Oddly, she was staring at Lizzy.

"Be sure the door has a sturdy locking mechanism, not that you, Jane, should have a need for it."

Lizzy groaned, the sound drowned out by her mother's increasingly shrill voice. *Thank goodness Aunt Gardiner talked with us,* she thought, eyeing the open doorway longingly, *or I'd be searching for the deepest, darkest cave in England to avoid getting married.*

"The important point to remember, girls, is to be firm with your husbands. Naturally, you must submit when necessary, as is proper. However, there are ways to avoid this honorably, as I have revealed to you both. Jane, you should have no problem in this regard, as Mr. Bingley is so amiable and gentlemanly. Lock or no, he would never force himself upon you, so you can rest easy, my dear. It is you, my Lizzy, whom I fear for."

Swiveling her eyes back to her mother's face, Lizzy frowned. "Whatever do you mean, Mama?"

"Oh, Lizzy!" Mrs. Bennet sat up, eyes teary and face seamed with deep concern. "Mr. Darcy is so proud and arrogant! I know he has tempered, according to you, but how long will that last? He is a gentleman to be sure, but he is also a man of substance who is accustomed to dominating and having his orders abided by without question. He is a man used to being in control. You may well learn, I dread, that his demands upon your person will be tremendous. Judging by how he looks at you, well, it is assured."

Frankly, she had no worries over William's "demands upon her person" since she fully intended to be making *her* demands upon *his* person as often as feasible. Nevertheless, in the way her mother couched the idea, Mr. Darcy sounded like a monster. How could she speak of him so negatively?

Lizzy could not immediately think of the words to defend him, and her mother provided no time to collect her scattered thoughts.

Apparently mistaking Lizzy's stunned expression as panic, Mrs. Bennet leaned over and patted her suddenly ice-cold hands.

"There, there, Lizzy. Do not fret. You are a strong woman. If anyone can handle a man like Mr. Darcy, it is you. Besides, I am confident the pressure will subside once you have provided him with an heir. That is what is most important to men of his station. Pray, my dear, that you are not like me and that you birth a boy first. After that, things shall go better. Men with social requirements, such as Mr. Darcy, do not wish their wives to be indisposed by frequent confinement. He will want you to stay pretty and svelte, to be the elegant lady at his side. These great men always have mistresses to take care of their baser needs, leaving the wife free to fulfill her household and social duties. Quite probably Mr. Darcy has already established an arrangement of this nature. I have suspected as much, what with his frequent and extended stays in London."

"Mama!"

Jane's shout silenced the awful words spewing from their mother's mouth. Jane looked no less flabbergasted than Lizzy felt, but at least *she* had found her voice—Lizzy was absolutely speechless. She sat on the sofa completely frozen. Her head spun and a black curtain was blanketing her sight.

I am going to faint.

Oddly, the prospect was appealing. Oblivion was better than the pain slicing through her body. She was surprised not to see a pool of blood by her feet. Stars began to flicker before her eyes as her mind screamed, *Breathe! You need air!*

Jerking to her feet, she swayed dangerously and stumbled from the room. Faintly, she heard Jane speaking in an uncharacteristically harsh tone, but she was too distraught to care. Instead of listening, she made her way outside, the need for fresh air and solitude determining her steps. She wound up at the garden bench she so often sat upon with William's arms embracing her and his lips pressed to hers. But whatever comfort and reassurance she unconsciously sought was not to be found.

William loved her, of this she held not a shred of doubt. Yet was there any truth to her mother's claims? Sifting through them one by one, a laborious process with a clouded brain, Lizzy discarded most as outrageous-or she tried. In truth, her attempts at moving past the reference to mistresses, in the plural, were futile.

"Lizzy, there you are! I should have known you would come here. You must not listen to a word Mama said. You know as well as I how ridiculous she is on this subject."

Jane's sweet voice and tender embrace were immediately soothing. Laying her head onto Jane's shoulder, Lizzy attempted to relax.

"I know Mr. Darcy is not the man Mama described just now. He is wonderful and kind and loving. How could she say such things, Jane?" Springing to her feet, Lizzy paced over the cobblestones. "Oh, I can see past most of it, truly I can. But…do you ever wonder, Jane, about Mr. Bingley? About his…past?"

"With women, you mean?" Jane's whisper finished what Lizzy could not say aloud. "No, not really," Jane answered. "I suppose he must have…*experience*, I believe is the polite way to put it. I do not want to know of it. Whatever past he has is irrelevant now. I shall be Charles's wife, and I trust in his love and promised faithfulness. The same is true of Mr. Darcy. Trust your heart, Lizzy."

～

*E*lizabeth Bennet, soon-to-be wife of an amazing man she loved with every ounce of her being, had a terrible week.

On that first night of her separation from Mr. Darcy—he in London and she in Hertfordshire—the relatively minor geological distance dampened her spirits. Of far greater weight were the lingering words from her mother and the conjured images and fears they aroused.

Placated to a minimal degree by Jane's calming presence and wise words, she faked her way through dinner and for one hour in the parlor afterward. Mrs. Bennet appeared to have forgotten all about the exchange, Lizzy unsure whether to be relieved or furious. On the whole, the strain was too intense, so she retired early.

Curling into a ball under the heavy blankets and down-filled counterpane, she welcomed the peace of her dreams. In and of itself, this was a typical nighttime wish, as her dreams for weeks had predominately included William. After Mrs. Gardiner's informative lecture that ranged from the specifics of male anatomy to biology to sexuality, her dreams had evolved. Upon occasion, they were the carefree, chaste, sweetly romantic interactions from before. With increasing frequency, her dreams were vivid, intense, passionate interludes which caused her to wake abruptly, gulping for air, with her body flushed and aching from unfulfilled desire.

Despite being a bit frustrating to jolt awake in the middle of the night in a state of intense concupiscence, Lizzy relished those dreams. Tonight, thanks to her adoring mother—sarcasm intended— her inner turmoil, and the early hour did not bode well for a restful slumber. She fully expected sleep to evade her, and to then toss and turn fitfully. In the end, that might have been preferable.

She did not stir when Jane came to bed and slept dreamlessly for a time. That night's slumbering vision, when it came, began similarly to most of her unconscious fantasies involving William.

The setting was a bedchamber unfamiliar to her, although when the only visible feature is an enormous bed, identification is difficult. On most nights, as well as this one, the assumption that it was the master's bedroom at Pemberley gained veracity by the appearance of William. He either entered through a doorway vaguely outlined in a blank wall or materialized as if from the air, as he did in this dream.

However he arrived, his handsome face was relaxed and happy, and he gazed at her with adoration. The passionate countenance seen in waking life on those handful of occasions when emotions were let loose, was on full display in all of her dreams. Every feature was crisp, from the tousled, brown hair to his clear, blue eyes, and from the tantalizing cleft in his chin to the provocative patch of chest hair peeking from his open shirt collar.

Alas, no matter how hard she prayed as she drifted off to sleep, he always wore trousers and a shirt, that being the most undressed state she had ever seen him in. Apparently, her subconscious still could not fabricate a nude William, despite her aunt's descriptions of the male physique. Some details were destined to remain mysterious for a while longer.

Dream Lizzy always wore a loose, lightweight chemise, one of the frilly, new purchases from her recent shopping expedition. Judging by the avid scan of her body from head to toe, dream William was wildly enticed by her attire. He would rush to her, eager to touch her flesh. Enfolding her in his strong arms and crushing her against his firm chest, he would capture her mouth in a penetrating kiss.

On most nights, at this point, the dream varied. He might peel the gown off her shoulders as they stood near the bed, his caresses and kisses moving over her inflamed skin to places as yet untouched by him in life. Three or four times, they were suddenly on the bed, limbs entwined passionately. Once she vaguely recalled them falling to the carpeted floor, and a few times, a huge sofa spontaneously popped into the scene.

In every dream scenario, Lizzy's heart soared, and her ardor rose to unimaginable heights. This building of sensation—blissful, rapturous, consuming sensation— inevitably caused her to wake, her body aroused and on the brink of a craved for, mysterious physical release.

On this night, passionate arousal was not what woke her with heart pounding and body throbbing.

All had begun the same, William kissing and caressing in his gentle, loving manner. Dream Lizzy waited for the sweet spark of heat, for the tingles and shivers to erupt where his fingers danced on her skin, and for the rush of warm moisture in her womanly core. She waited for the anticipated ecstatic response...and felt nothing. Or rather, she felt an unwanted, contrastive response. Her skin grew ice-cold, her belly clamped into knots, and her lungs were desperate for air. Unnamed fear swelled inside her chest, expanding and ripening into full-blown panic.

I cannot do this. I will disappoint him. I cannot please a man like him. I have no idea what to do.

Unsure whether she shouted it in the dream or transmitted her thoughts by struggling to escape his embrace, dream William received the message. He did not care—at least, not initially. His handsome face—moments before awash with love and tenderness—altered into the proud, arrogant mien she'd first glimpsed at the Meryton Assembly. Lips pressed into an angry line and eyes hard as ebony, , he held her so tight it was painful about her body, and then he roughly propelled her toward the bed.

In a state of hysteria, her frenzied thrashing and screams to stop escalated. Abruptly releasing his hold, he stared down at her with absolute disgust. William, both the dream version and the man she loved in waking life, was gone. An extreme, mutated version of Mr. Darcy had taken his place. This Mr. Darcy was far worse than she had ever imagined, even at the height of her dislike for him. Anger, pure hatred, disdain—all of these and other awful sentiments shone from his stony eyes.

He did not speak aloud, but she heard him anyway. "You are a child. How could you please me? I've been with skilled women all over the world. Who are you to compare?"

As the final nail in the coffin, he turned away...into the arms of another woman—a gorgeous woman with massive breasts, who smirked at dream Lizzy as she slid her arms around his shoulders and melted into his kiss.

Lizzy launched upright in bed, the scream caught in her bone-dry throat.

Any hope that the cloudless cobalt sky and shining sun that Tuesday morning would lift her spirits and warm her heart was dashed thanks to the London newspaper read over the breakfast table. Handed the social news sections while Mr. Bennet read of world events and politics, Lizzy scanned the gossip column by habit. It was a mistake. The top news bits were four reports of the latest whispered mistresses and *affaires de coeur* amongst the *bon ton*.

Hastily flipping to the literary section, the headline story was of Lord Byron's newest publication. Surely an article about a book of poems, the primary work a fable about a monk, was a safe read, right? Apparently, it was not her destiny that morning to avoid reminders of illicit dalliances. The writer of the piece barely mentioned *The Prisoner of Chillon, and Other Poems.* Instead, the focus was on Byron's affair with Claire Clairmont, formerly linked with Mary and Percy Bysshe Shelley in an infamous, scandalous ménage à trios and who was now rumored to be pregnant with Byron's child.

Tossing the paper onto the table with a grunt of disgust, she further startled her half-asleep family by jolting out of her chair and stomping out of the room, leaving her plate untouched.

From there, the week proceeded from bad to worse.

Every night, without fail, the horrible nightmare came. Over and over and over, his beloved face would twist in anger and disappointment, stabbing her soul. Always, some woman, the face changing and often hazy, would clutch him, kissing and touching as the entwined duo faded into the shadows. Dream Lizzy would be left standing alone, sobbing and wretched. Unable to bear the pain, Lizzy would wake in a panic, her heart pounding and lungs burning.

Jane had forever been a solid sleeper, but how she slept through Lizzy's thrashing was a mystery. Lizzy was glad of it though, as she absolutely did not want to talk about the nightmares or her chaotic emotions.

Nevertheless, despite Jane's unawareness of Lizzy's traumatic nightly visions, Jane knew her sister well enough to pierce through the feigned normalcy Lizzy tried to project in front of her family. No one was fooled, although to everyone besides Jane, Lizzy's dolor was merely the result of missing Mr. Darcy.

Mr. Bennet, who was hopeless in dealing with female moods, retreated to his library. Whether due to conscious regard for Lizzy's malaise or regret over her hideous speech, Mrs. Bennet never again broached the subject of future husbands and marital counsel. This development was a huge relief to all four of the Bennet daughters!

Mary was flummoxed by Lizzy's depression over a man being absent for a few days, the concept utterly inconceivable to her. After a handful of piously intoned platitudes gained nothing but stinging retorts from Lizzy, Mary gave up on her brand of comfort. Kitty tried to cheer her sister but was far too self-centered and flighty to fret over Lizzy's emotional state for long. After all, if a cute puppy or a parlor game didn't do the trick, what else was there?

Honestly, Lizzy was glad when they finally left her alone. She had always preferred solitude when troubled, ideally out of doors where the clean air and open vistas calmed her nerves and renewed her senses. Alas, the weather insisted on being unpredictable and volatile, another reason why that week was terrible.

Decreased temperatures, spates of wind, and intermittent drizzling rains forced Lizzy to remain indoors. Normally impervious to inclement weather, with her wedding a week away, even hale and hearty Lizzy Bennet was not going to risk an autumn fever. Thus, she had scant to do but stare at the gloominess outside, which matched how she felt inside.

I miss you, William. I miss you so much my entire body hurts. Please hurry back to me.

His letters helped tremendously. In that week alone, Lizzy received nine envelopes addressed to her! The red wax stamped with his seal indicative of passionate love, so he wrote. The double-sided pages contained line after line of romantic sentiment, expressions of his grief in being parted from her, his longing to hold and kiss her, and his impatience to be her husband. After his loving greeting, each letter began, "In X days, you shall be Mrs. Fitzwilliam Darcy."

Despite this concrete evidence of his devotion, Lizzy's subconscious stubbornly refused to relinquish her fears and insecurities. It was not until Friday, a short break in the nasty weather providing a window of opportunity for a vigorous walk, that she gained some clarity and improved her outlook.

"Assess what you know to be true," she said aloud to herself while trudging through a deserted field of yellowed, knee-high grasses. "William loves you. He is an honorable man, who is devoted to his family—a gentleman in the purest meaning of the word. He is kind and...he loves you."

Always, inevitably, she came back to that incontrovertible fact. He loved her. He had proven his love in a thousand ways for close to a year. There was no possibility of her doubting his love. With his love and because of his love, he desired her physically. No question of that either!

Where she stumbled in her confidence was concerning her ability to please him in the physical realm, as probably all virginal brides had since Eve. What caused deeper anxiety were the subtle doubts of her competence and worthiness to be Mrs. Darcy of Pemberley that had crept inside her brain. There had been conversations and incidences, particularly while in London, when the reality of his worldliness, education, refinement, and superior station forcibly hit her.

William had divulged fragments of his business affairs, life at Pemberley, and noble family, but for every piece of the Fitzwilliam Darcy puzzle she snapped into place, there were a hundred more lying in a jumble. His stated reasons for secrecy--the pain of lost loved ones weighing upon his heart and the preference to share once at Pemberley--made perfect sense. Lizzy had never questioned his motives or was suspicious. Until now, thanks to her mother instilling distrust and weakening her faith!

Ignoring the damp, Lizzy plopped down on a sun-warmed rock and stared up at the sky. As much as she wanted to curse her mother and place the blame upon her shoulders, Lizzy knew her mother's words held no power unless the thoughts had already been buried deep within her mind.

Was he the type of man who entertained women of ill repute? It was so outside his character that she could not fathom it! Then again, look at Lord Byron. A man who wrote the most beautiful love poems was a notorious rogue if even half the rumors were true, and he was only one famous example.

What her mother had said about men of Society and mistresses was true. If one listened close enough, murmurs of the same were rampant right in sleepy, boring Meryton and the surrounding villages. She could name three widowed women off the top of her head who were reputedly "available" for men in need. Polite ladies pretended not to hear such tales—and also pretended not to gossip about it—yet somehow whispers spread.

Local shenanigans had nothing to do with Mr. Darcy, of course. They only served to remind Lizzy of the wickedness of the world, the decaying morals—the human condition, if you will, that far too often justified less-than-perfect behavior.

William had said, numerous times, how he abhorred the attitudes and activities of Society, and she believed him. However, by all accounts, it was wholly acceptable for males to follow different rules when it came to their physical urges. Her William was a healthy, robust, virile man possessing an intensely passionate nature, as she knew oh so well.

"No, I don't want to know the details of that portion of his past. Not ever," she said to the sky. "I only hope Mama is mistaken and that his affairs are past and will remain so."

It came down to her fears and uncertainty—right or wrong, valid or nonsense—and their promise to be honest with each other. She wasn't sure how to broach the subject or what she would say, but she trusted her beloved William to comfort and reassure. No matter how difficult the conversation or painful the answers, the burden pressing upon her shoulders eased once she decided to talk openly with him.

So why did she continue to have that hideous nightmare?

11

SIGNIFICANT INTROSPECTION

*D*arcy's week away from Hertfordshire was fantastic—at least in comparison to the week suffered through by his beloved Elizabeth.

With spirits fortified by his spontaneous visit to Longbourn, the initial leg of his journey was, indeed, close to fantastic. Unbeknownst to his beautiful and so very sensuous fiancée, London was not his immediate destination. Rather, upon reaching the busy north-south thoroughfare, the driver turned north. Just under five hours later, the coach pulled into the wide, circular drive fronting the two-story brick entrance of the White Stag Inn.

In contemplating where to spend their wedding night, Darcy had immediately crossed off staying at Netherfield or Darcy House in London. He had learned to tolerate Elizabeth's family, and had even grown quite fond of Mr. Bennet and, to a lesser degree, the vivacious Kitty. Nevertheless, he needed to be alone with Elizabeth, far away from Bennets and Bingleys, and this meant traveling some distance after the wedding reception.

Going south to London—while closer and therefore shortening

the time between the vows and finally, blissfully, making her his wife physically—would put them farther away from Pemberley. His greatest wish was to be with Elizabeth in the place he loved most in all the world. Therefore, they had to travel north.

Located past Bedford, the White Stag Inn was one of four coaching inns Darcy patronized on his many jaunts between Pemberley and Darcy House. Depending upon road conditions, weather, the fatigue of the horses, and other various concerns, which inn he chose for the two-day journey differed, but the White Stag was his favorite. The distance from Longbourn was farther than he preferred for a wedding-day journey, but it would decrease the final leg to Pemberley, which would still require nearly all of one day to reach.

The inn nestled in a shallow, verdant valley with a pristine river and modest-sized lake. The small village was nothing to brag about, but it was well kept and boasted enough shops to entertain, if they wished. All in all, the locale was perfect for a romantic honeymoon, and the owners of the inn, Mr. and Mrs. Hamilton, were delightful people whom he trusted to make their stay special.

He had corresponded with the Hamiltons shortly after his engagement, and he trusted them to provide all he had requested, and probably more. Visiting in person was not truly necessary, but he would rest easier after speaking with the Hamiltons. Call it evidence of his need to be in control, but Darcy was not taking any chances on their initial days, and nights, as Mr. and Mrs. Darcy being less than perfection.

Additionally, he had only boarded in the smaller rooms for single men and eaten hasty meals in the pub. Peripherally, he was aware that the White Stag's accommodations included private dining and luxury suites, hence his choice to stay there with Elizabeth, but he had never viewed them or studied the inn with a wife in mind. One night was all he needed to be satisfied on all counts. The following morning, he departed the White Stag Inn for London.

Bypassing the side road to Longbourn was an unhappy reminder of the long, lonely week stretching ahead. Adding to his gloominess was his empty townhouse.

Lord and Lady Matlock had rescued a restless, bored Georgiana, and the trio was visiting friends in nearby Essex. Darcy was thankful his sister wasn't sitting about the house with only Mrs. Annesley for company while waiting impatiently for the wedding. The Matlocks' last-minute invitation was great for his sister, even if it meant a too-quiet house for him.

That left his cousin Richard as the only person he cared to socialize with. Unfortunately, aside from one dinner, the colonel was snowed under with work. "I asked for your wedding off, and apparently the generals had a confab to devise ways to make me pay," he exasperatedly related to Darcy on their lone evening of bachelor debauchery—Richard's phrase. Undoubtedly a massive exaggeration, but regardless, Colonel Fitzwilliam was unavailable.

There was nothing to do but read, or attempt to read, and write Elizabeth letters of increasing romanticism. "You are pathetic," he frequently muttered, and kept on writing.

Elizabeth wrote to him as well, but only twice. The small number of letters did not bother him unduly, as she had friends and family to occupy her time. The sensations of unease he experienced were triggered by an indefinable, underlying tone to the sentences and paragraphs.

Did he imagine a lack of cheeriness? Was her use of endearments and romantic phrases minimal merely upon comparison with his flowery prose? Were the two, one-page letters an indication of trouble between them, or merely that she was busy? While he did not want her to pine for him, it was a blow to his ego to imagine her blithely carrying on with life to the point of having no time to write him.

It is only a week, for goodness sake, he told himself, but that fact not soothe his mind.

He gained scant clarification re-reading the other letters she had written to him. There were only three, for one thing—not a significant quantity to claim knowledge of her letter-writing style. Furthermore, two of them had been written during his first trip to London, when they had been engaged barely over a week. The difference between those two and the one received when he stayed in Town after the shopping expedition were considerable, as one would expect. By then, they were far more relaxed and familiar with each other. Elizabeth's playfulness and love had shone through in the third letter, which, he noted, was three pages, front and back.

With insufficient evidence and unable to resolve the matter anyway—if there even *was* a "matter" to resolve—his only choice was to hurry through his business and get back to Hertfordshire.

The bulk of his week entailed extended hours in one of the luxury conference rooms inside the elegant building housing the law offices of Daniels & Sons. The original Mr. Daniels of the business's name had established his practice three generations past with a hope of sons in the plural—a hope as he only had one child at the time, a boy not yet two years of age. Darcy's grandfather, James Darcy I, had been one of young Mr. Daniels's first clients, the two men having met as youths in boarding school. A second Daniels son did come along, and amazingly, both chose law as their profession. Over time, more clients and more Daniels were added to the firm until the present day, with over a dozen doors bearing a *Daniels* nameplate.

Mr. Andrew Daniels, the grandson of the founder and current leader at the firm, had two sons working alongside him—Joshua and Jeremiah—a third in law school, and two or three others yet at home (Darcy had lost count). This boded well for the future success of the firm, as well as a continuing, solid relationship with the Darcys of Pemberley.

What this historical tidbit meant was that the solicitors at Daniels & Sons were intimately involved with all of Mr. Darcy's business and personal legal affairs. It was Mr. Andrew Daniels himself who oversaw the bulk of Darcy's business, although Mr. Joshua Daniels, the eldest son, had assumed a portion of the duties and was present at most of the meetings. Darcy trusted them both explicitly. Nevertheless, he made it a rule never to sign anything without reading it thoroughly and having every question answered to his satisfaction. Obviously, this took time, thus contract reading being the main time consumer of his days in London.

In between, when desperate for physical exertions, he twice visited Angelo's Fencing Academy. He also squeezed in more shopping. Now that he had bravely ventured into the realm of purchasing feminine items, and triumphed beyond his initial expectations, it was akin to a fever racing through his veins. The plethora of fabulous objects available to gift to his adorable Elizabeth begged to be bought.

By the end of the week, another shipment of boxes containing various trinkets with personal notes attached was on its way to Pemberley. By express courier, he sent the comprehensive pages of instructions for Mrs. Reynolds and Mr. Taylor, this to be his last correspondence with the Pemberley staff before the wedding.

His shopping wasn't exclusively for Elizabeth, however. Mr. Meyer had completed Darcy's wedding suit, delivering it to Darcy House while Darcy was in Hertfordshire. The suit was secure in a garment bag and hanging in his dressing room, so his first order of business was trying it on.

While assisting, his valet, Samuel Oliver, calmly informed him of his plan to freshen Mr. Darcy's supply of cologne, as well as acquire new shaving equipment, toiletries, and various necessary accessories, such as stockings and handkerchiefs, while in Town. Rather shocked it hadn't occurred to him sooner, Darcy figured it was wise to do a bit of resupplying for himself. A new banyan and slippers, nightshirts he frankly hoped not to wear, a brand-new, fashionable top hat for the wedding, two pairs of shoes and new Wellingtons, and random articles of clothing for no reason other than they appealed to him.

Honestly, aside from the robe and slippers, he needed nothing. Tramping through stores was a way to kill time before returning to the empty townhouse.

By late on Thursday, after a final meeting with Mr. Kennedy, the tradesman at the Royal Exchange who had arranged all the redecorating needs for the private suite of the Master and Mistress of Pemberley, Darcy was beginning to think he could wrap up his business early on Saturday. If so, then he would make it back to Hertfordshire in time to join Elizabeth for the ball at Lucas Lodge. A hastily dispatched missive to Elizabeth ensured of his return on Sunday, at the very latest—maybe on Saturday.

He should have known better than to make such a promise. As the Scots poet Robert Burns wisely wrote, "The best-laid schemes o' mice an' men…[often go awry]."

～

The first delay was a riot at the London docks late Friday night. As riots can go, it wasn't too extreme. The ruffians torched the cargo of one ship, and in the ensuing violence, three men died with several wounded before the enforcers paid by a coalition of ship owners managed to get it under control. The ships Darcy partially owned were not directly involved, but near enough to the riot that a handful of dockworkers employed by the partnership became accidentally drawn into the fray. Thankfully, none of them were amongst the dead or wounded, but as Darcy happened to be the only owner currently in London, he felt it was his duty to check into the matter.

That task ate up the whole morning and into the noon hour, making him tardy for his final appointment with Mr. Daniels. Rushing up the stairs, Darcy barged through the door to the meeting room only to discover it empty. Momentarily baffled, Mr. Daniels soon appeared and informed Darcy that the gentleman they were scheduled to meet had also been waylaid. A series of rather comedic errors involving a horse throwing a shoe, a sick child, a dog bite, and something about the document transcriber's hand getting smashed by a commode lid. Darcy had a difficult time finding the humor in being hindered yet again, although the commode lid imagery did make him smile.

The result being, there was no way to wrap up his day and reasonably travel to Hertfordshire in time to prepare for the Lucases autumn ball. An assembly which, frankly, if not for the joy of dancing with Elizabeth, he had little interest in attending—no offense to Sir William, whom he respected and rather liked. Balls simply weren't on the top of his list of entertainments.

Settling in for another boring night of missing Elizabeth, he prayed for sweet dreams to tide him over until the morrow. With orders to have his horse ready and waiting by the front door at nine o'clock sharp, he retired for the night, confident that with his swift stallion, he would be holding Elizabeth in his arms by noon at the very latest. Alas, he was overconfident again as it turned out.

"It is your choice, of course, Mr. Darcy. However, with those ominous clouds, I do strongly encourage you to take the carriage, if you must leave at all." Darcy stood at the window, glaring at the black-cloud-covered sky and pretended to ignore Mrs. Smyth's advice.

Damn it all to hell.

The housekeeper was correct, and he knew it. She hadn't needed to say it, in fact, as he had recognized instantly upon rising that venturing out on horseback was perilous. Parsifal was as surefooted as a horse could be, but slick roads and pouring rain, not to mention the inevitable lightning and wind, were unsafe even for him. Additionally, while Darcy was strong as an ox and not susceptible to illness, with his wedding four days away, he wasn't so foolish as to risk a cold or injury.

"Have the coach prepared," he commanded, a bit ashamed at the rude tone, but he wanted to be clear there would be no further arguing over the decision. He *was* leaving that morning and *would be* in Hertfordshire that night if he had to crawl through the mud to get there!

Two hours later, the coach had barely passed the outskirts of London. If it had been a clear day, as it most definitely was not, the outline of the city buildings would still have been visible on the horizon.

"Sir?" Mr. Anders's yell from his driver's perch was a mumble to Darcy inside the carriage. Ears ringing from the sizzling cracks of lightning and simultaneous booms of thunder shaking the coach, he had to guess at half of the coachman's words. It wasn't too difficult to figure out the message.

"We must stop and wait for this to pass or we will be crawling through the mud!"

Thankfully, neither the horses nor the wheels became mired in the thickening sludge as they slogged along for another thirty minutes until reaching the next coaching inn and pub. The rustic establishment was not the type of place Darcy typically chose as a resting point, but it was sturdily built, and the tables and floor were moderately clean, as were the serving wenches and barkeep. That was encouraging.

The foursome made up by Mr. Darcy; his valet; the coachman, Mr. Anders; and the under coachman, Mr. Gowan was not the only traveling party seeking refuge from the downpour, although there were not as many as one would think. Presumably, most people were sensible and had not been stupid enough to attempt traveling in the first place. Therefore, the rooms were crowded, but not to full capacity, so they found a table to themselves near a back window and not too far from one of the four fireplaces. Surprisingly, the food was decent and the ale passable. As the storm showed no immediate signs of diminishing its fury, they settled in for a long wait.

Darcy chafed at the setback and, in his annoyance, drank the first two mugs of ale faster than he should have. It seemed to be a common mistake, judging by the quickly mellowing throng. After a while, the many stranded travelers and those locals who had nothing better to do during the deluge than share a pint or two with friends grew increasingly animated. Laughter was rampant, and probably due to the effects of alcohol as much as the compulsion to drown out the relentless pounding of the storm, one man pulled out a battered guitar and another man a fiddle. In short order, a spontaneously formed minstrel group was performing to rousing cheers and singing.

There was no chance of the eclectic troupe of musicians being hired to dazzle at Vauxhall Gardens, but they served a purpose. After the third ale, or maybe it was the fourth, Darcy wasn't nearly as distressed over being stuck far from his destination. Nevertheless, as soon as the lightning stopped and the rain slowed to a steady drizzle, he was ready to attempt the journey.

Mr. Anders, ever the consummate professional, had nursed one mug of ale, as had Mr. Gowan, so the drivers were in complete control of their faculties. Mr. Oliver had also kept his composure, Darcy suspecting he only pretended to drink his ale, so between the three servants, Mr. Darcy's dignity was maintained as they exited the pub—or rather, at least he didn't fall face-first into the mud and he required only moderate assistance climbing into the carriage.

On the road again, the coach inched determinedly onward, thanks to Mr. Anders's excellent skill and the rested animals. Twice, they ground to a halt, one wheel sinking into the muck, requiring the efforts of all four men to free it from the trap. Two other times, the impediment was debris from downed trees obstructing the road, again necessitating concerted effort and brawn to remove the blockages. Between the slow pace and frequent stops, the carriage pulled into the Netherfield driveway well past dark—not that it was discernibly darker than it had been all day.

Exhausted, filthy, starving, and fuzzy headed from the ale, Darcy didn't give serious thought to visiting Elizabeth. In truth, it took his last ounces of strength to climb the stairs, bathe, choke down enough cold food to take the edge off his hunger pangs, and fall into the bed. He slept so deeply that if he did dream of his beloved, he had no memory of it.

h! To rise in the morning after a blissfully restorative sleep and have your waking thought be, I shall be embracing and kissing my sweet Elizabeth in just a few hours.

Darcy shot out of bed and dashed to the window. Yanking the drapes aside, the blast of brilliant sunlight blinded him, but he still released a whoop of joy. Ringing for the maid and ordering coffee, he was at his desk dipping his quill into the inkwell before the tray of piping hot beverage arrived.

My Dearest, Precious Elizabeth,

Please accept my humble apologies for greeting you, my beloved, in this impersonal manner. Rest assured that as soon as humanly possible, I shall greet you with my arms tightly about your warm body and my lips resting upon your sweet lips, as they were created to do. My most fervent prayer is to allay any fears you may have regarding my well-being. I am safe at Netherfield, having arrived long after dark. Bingley was nearly required to physically restrain me from rushing back out the door and into your arms. Reason prevailed, but only when Bingley pointed out that, as you might have been long abed, rushing into your arms would raise a few eyebrows! Frankly, his words fleetingly had the opposite effect, as the vision of you abed was more than slightly appealing.

290

Nonetheless, as you have now surmised, I remained at Netherfield.

I impatiently await your presence to assuage my aching heart. I wished to ride to Longbourn at first light, but, again, Bingley's rationale prevailed. As it is, this missive is undoubtedly disturbing your breakfast, but I can wait no longer! The carriage is for you, dearest, and Jane as well, naturally. If your desire to see me is even half as profound as my need to see you, then you are already racing to the door! Hurry, my love.

Yours forever, Fitzwilliam Darcy

She would laugh aloud at his exaggerations, he knew, not that a good portion of his note wasn't precise. He had yet to speak with Bingley that morning—a glance at the clock showed the minute hand almost to half six—but could rightly guess the younger man would balk at descending upon Longbourn or sending the carriage at this impolite hour. Darcy suspected Elizabeth would not protest if he showed up on her doorstep no matter the time. Her father and mother, on the other hand, would be slightly put out.

The real deciding factor in waiting until a reasonable hour was the sorry state of his person when he took a long look in the mirror. The effects of drink and a strenuous journey had disappeared with hours of heavy sleep. The effects of accumulated layers of mud washed off negligently as they were last night were another story. His reflection was downright ghastly. A soaking bath was the first order of business, followed by a shave and trimming his unruly hair. He didn't want to frighten his betrothed into a heart seizure days away from their wedding.

Not quite four hours later, an outrageous length of time as far as Darcy was concerned, he planted himself in front of the window facing the gravel driveway. He honestly was not aware of the coiled energy causing him to pace until Bingley laughingly admonished, "Darcy! For pity's sake, man, please sit down. You are wearing a hole in my carpet."

Sure, it was easy for Charles to sit calmly in his chair. He had been in the company of his betrothed every day all week.

"What could possibly be taking her…them, so long?"

"Be patient, Darcy. It is quite early, and the carriage left not an hour ago. Women need time to prepare, trust me. You might as well start getting used to delays. My sisters are always late."

The last thing Darcy wanted to hear was even the remotest reference to Caroline Bingley. A sharp retort on his lips, his attention was diverted by a flash of black beyond the trees. *Yes.* Aware on some level that his beaming grin and bouncing leap in the direction of the door made him appear foolish, he simply didn't care, not even when Bingley's laughter nipped at his heels. Luckily, the butler had noted the arriving carriage and had the front door open, although he was forced to skip to the side or be bowled over. Darcy was down the steps and had flung the carriage door wide before the vehicle came to a complete stop. Revealing her anxiousness, Elizabeth had already half risen from the bench, her smile as giddy as his and her eyes were dancing.

Propriety be damned, he reached in, encircled her slim waist with his broad hands, and lifted her out of the carriage. When her toes were touching the ground, he let go only long enough to grab her into his arms, twirling about as they laughed. Truthfully, why he held himself back from kissing her passionately on the spot was moronic— some residue of what constitutes gentlemanly behavior pounded into his brain since he was able to toddle.

Instead, he cupped her face and leaned close, whispering, "I love you, Elizabeth."

"Why, Mr. Darcy, I get the impression you missed me just a little."

"More than I have the words to express, my sweet. Nor would I want to try. From this moment onward, only happy words of love, if we must use words at all over other, preferable methods of expressing our joy." As he hoped, his suggestion brought a tint of pink to her cheeks, and she ducked her head. Clasping his arm, she nudged them toward the door.

"We feared your breakfast might have been interrupted," Darcy explained loud enough for Charles and Jane to hear as they climbed the steps and entered the foyer. "I confess the early summons was entirely my idea. Bingley sternly exerted his good manners and sense of decency. He is not to blame for my blatantly ignoring him and badgering of the staff to do the same."

Laughing, Jane lightly touched her future brother's forearm. "Do not concern yourself, Mr. Darcy. Neither Lizzy nor I felt put upon. In fact, not a word of protest was given, nor did my sister waste seconds to frame a witty retort to Papa's tease."

"Indeed, that says it all then," Bingley proclaimed, smiling at Elizabeth. "Just in case we caught our ladies with their hunger unsatisfied, we have a light repast prepared in the breakfast room. Come!"

"I could not eat a bite earlier, so I am starving," Darcy murmured after sneaking a kiss to Elizabeth's cheek. "Even so, what I truly hunger for are your lips. Perhaps a brief detour into yonder closet, Miss Elizabeth?"

"You, sir, are incorrigible!"

"Guilty as charged. Was that a yes, then?" It was a spontaneous joke, but he still felt faintly disappointed when she chuckled and shook her head.

The quartet, clustered at one end of the table, relaxed into the joyous reunion. Darcy truly was famished, eating heartily while chattily reporting the highlights of his week in between bites. Elizabeth nibbled and sipped absently, seemingly content to allow him to do all the talking. Gradually, the vague sense of disquiet stirred while reading her two letters, which he had all but forgotten, rekindled. As with her writing, he could not pin down the cause of his nebulous feelings but could also not shake them.

For instance, she held his hand a bit too tightly and was adverse to letting go, even when he needed it to cut his meat. Her eyes did not leave his face except for when he peered directly at her for longer than five seconds, her gaze always sliding away before he could decipher the odd shimmer within. A smile curved her plump lips but it never wavered, as if it were painted onto her face or molded from plaster.

Strangest of all, she said very little aside from a handful of perfunctory comments and superficial questions. Of note was when candidly recounting the evening of "bachelor debauchery" with Richard. He suspected she was not listening to a word he said since she had yet to laugh or insert a single sportive wisecrack, a suspicion verified when, in the middle of a sentence, she leaned into his side and interrupted.

"William," she whispered softly into his ear, "I am elated to have you back. I missed you terribly and was devastated not to see you yesterday. Nevertheless, I must scold you for venturing into the storm. You could have been injured or—" She gulped. "What would I do at the altar with no groom to wed me?"

He apologized profusely and sincerely. Each of them tried to make a joke out of the painful separation and of what could have been a tragedy. He told her of the journey, focusing on the pleasanter portions at the pub and glossing over the violence of the storm and the resulting road hazards. She seemed placated but not exactly cheered either. Simply put, she wasn't the Elizabeth he knew so very well, and he had to find out why once and for all.

As the meal drew to the end, Bingley and Jane suggested a walk in the garden. Although the paths were likely to be wet, the sun was shining for the first time in days. Frankly, the prospect of an invigorating walk was highly appealing. A sidelong inspection of Elizabeth's face changed his mind.

Rising from the table, Darcy stayed Elizabeth with a light press of his palm upon the small of her back. She glanced upward with a questioning lift of her brow, but Darcy directed his attention to Bingley. "A walk does sound lovely, Charles, now that the weather has decided to behave. If you do not mind, we shall join you in a bit. I have a gift for Elizabeth in the library which I can no longer wait to give."

Bingley was understandably puzzled since he had not seen Darcy go anywhere near the library all morning, but he rapidly recovered, smoothing his features and leading Jane away.

"Another gift, sir? At this rate, I will be doing nothing but shopping for the first week of our marriage just to catch up," Elizabeth said as they crossed the library threshold. Her attempt to tease was strained, as all of them had been that morning.

Leaving the door partially ajar, Darcy guided her to a far corner within eyesight of the entrance but well away from any curious listening ears. Rather than speaking, he enfolded her in his arms and bent to deliver the ardent kiss his soul had craved for over a week. Truthfully, it was a chaste kiss compared to the one he hungered to engage in, but he knew letting loose his need for her, even in a tempered fashion, would consume him.

It was extremely difficult to remove his lips from the warm, satiny skin of her neck, and harder still to release her from his embrace. Her passion-glazed eyes were nearly his undoing, but then he gleaned a hint of questioning deep within their chocolate depths. Talking to her was, at this juncture, more important.

Steering her to the sofa, they sat with knees touching and hands entwined. "Forgive me, Elizabeth, but the gift was a small deception. It is time for you to tell me what has been troubling you."

Her eyes widened and then swiftly darted to the side. "What do you mean?"

"My darling, do not play coy with me. We know each other well, do we not? I have felt that something was amiss all week. Your letters

SHARON LATHAN

were not as merry as I thought they should have been, but I was willing to believe it my overwrought imagination. Now that we are together, I know that was not the case. You are not your usual lively self, Elizabeth. The fact that you missed a dozen chances to tease me is evidence enough. I can sense your distress." Lifting one hand, he brushed his knuckles over her cheek, then gently used two fingers to turn her face toward him. "Please enlighten me. Allow me to comfort you, beloved."

She did not glance away but was obviously struggling. He waited, willing his muscles to relax and face to remain neutral even though his stomach churned. Finally, she inhaled and spoke, the words halting and her tone heavy.

"You are correct, William. I am troubled. I need to speak of…a delicate, uncomfortable matter. Please, will you promise not interrupt? I do not want to talk of this. It will be difficult for me, and I will lose my nerve or train of thought if you interject."

Elizabeth wasn't a woman who exaggerated or dramatized a mundane problem. Her statement and the weighty emphasis revealed this wasn't some minor wedding dilemma or premarriage jitters as he had presumed. He was seriously alarmed for the first time, making it nigh impossible to promise restraint. He had to trust her, however, so he bobbed his head once and said, "I promise."

After another deep sigh, and with eyes focused on their clasped hands, she began. "Some of it is nonsense, I admit—me, just being a silly girl, a maiden with what I suppose are the normal fears faced on one's wedding night. The unknown and the possibility of pain, which no one looks forward to." She released a soft chuckle and briefly met his eyes.

He smiled, but she had already resumed her scrutiny of their hands. "Additionally, for me, there is the worry of displeasing you, of not bringing you the pleas—joy you are expecting when we are… together for the first time, and perhaps first several times."

Darcy instinctively opened his mouth to refute such baseless worries but remembered his promise and clamped his lips tight.

Not bring me pleasure? Ah, my sweet Elizabeth, if you knew the depth of pleasure you give me by a mere kiss or touch of your hand, there would be no way you could question the rapture I shall experience when being inside of you.

"My aunt Gardiner, you may be surprised to learn, spoke to Jane and me at length, and in explicit detail. Suffice it to say, we were educated to a degree not expected for most young, unmarried ladies."

Her cheeks were flushed a delightful shade of pink, and he knew she would look at him while such intimate "explicit details" swirled in her head. He wanted to laugh—envisioning Mrs. Gardiner having a frank talk about sexual relations with her two virginal nieces was highly amusing! He sent a prayer heavenward for women of common sense like Mrs. Gardiner, and felt the tension in his muscles ebbing away. He could relate to Elizabeth's anxieties better than she realized.

"For the most part, none of these concerns greatly bothered me. I trust us, our love, and while it may take me a while to…be the wife you deserve in the…bedroom, I haven't doubted our future. Or at least I didn't think I did."

A pause, another huge inhale and exhale. "I began having nightmares the night you left for London. And I know why, and this is the most difficult part for me to share."

She released his hands and stood, walking a few feet away and turning toward the wall. Averted eyes shining with unshed tears, fingers kneading the edges of the fichu draped over her shoulders, and chest rising jerkily with each labored pant, she proceeded to report Mrs. Bennet's marriage "advice" and her expressed fears for Elizabeth's safety as his wife.

Darcy's dismay turned to vexation, then to anger before accelerating into rage. He was so stunned that for a time he could not have spoken if begged to say something. The emotions coursing through his body were too numerous to decipher. Primarily, he was furious that Elizabeth had been forced to endure this torturous pain, while also mortified and profoundly offended that Mrs. Bennet would besmirch his character.

Topping it all and sending him over the edge into blind, murderous wrath, was Mrs. Bennet's assurance of his future unfaithfulness and claim that he already kept a mistress, this one reason why he had gone to London.

"No!" he roared, shooting to his feet. "I will not hear another word! This is unconscionable! How could your mother say such things? Elizabeth, you must surely know this is entirely untrue. It's absolutely false."

She had violently started, swirling about and then taking a half-dozen steps backward when he jumped up. Her eyes were round as saucers, and mouth agape—and there was something in her eyes.

Frozen, incapable of inhaling deeply, he could only gasp faintly, "My God, you do!" Unable to bear it, he turned away and clutched onto a nearby bookcase for support.

This must be a nightmare. Wake up, Darcy! After all we have been through, surely our love will not die now, over this. It cannot be happening.

The silence stretched, seemingly for hours, although he knew it could not have been long or the pain would have killed him. A tentative touch on his arm brought him back to reality.

"William, please listen to me. I know you are not the man my mother spoke of. I never, not for a second, entertained the notion. I know you love only me, and would never hurt me. Our relationship is special, our love superior to that of my parents. In this I am absolutely confident."

Her tender, truthful voice soothed him. The pain and rigidity eased. But he sensed a caveat coming, and was not strong enough to handle whatever doubts might be visible on her face.

"William, you must try to appreciate that there is much I do not understand about your world, or your past for that matter. I know you are not a rake, but I do read the Society pages, the scandals and gossip. You have spoken of it yourself. It is…confusing." Her voice

broke, catching in a sob. "I don't want to know about your…
experiences, so I am not asking for that. Perhaps I am an utter fool
but I need your reassurances. You must help me to understand,
please?"

*My experiences? All of this hinges upon my past experiences? Will hearing
the truth ease your mind and reassure? Or will it cause you to question my
maturity, manhood, and competence from a different angle?*

Sighing, he turned around. Tears streaked her face, and Darcy
wiped them gently away. "Forgive my outburst of anger. I should not
lose my temper so."

He kissed her lips, a feathery touch, then drew her to his chest.
Holding her in silence, he desperately tried to sort his thoughts. How
in God's name could he explain himself to her clearly?

"You are correct in that I must make you understand if I can. It
will not be easy for me, I warn you. This is an awkward topic and
involves delving into areas that remain painful for me. It will be my
turn to beg your indulgence and patience in listening to me with an
open heart. Can you do this?"

Lifting onto her toes, she kissed with the same featherlight
pressure. "Of course I can, my love."

Sitting again on the sofa, Darcy leaned forward with his elbows
on his knees. Where to begin?

"My earliest memories of my parents are of love—love for me,
and, later, for Georgiana. Love for family and friends. Love for
Pemberley and the people who depend upon the estate for their
livelihood. But above all of this, it was the love my mother and father
had for each other. A child takes such emotions for granted, of
course. I did not recognize the special emotion as the rare gift it was.
All I knew was that my parents were happiest when together, and
somehow sadder or less animated when apart. It was obvious how
their faces shone brighter when they saw each other and how they
were forever touching each other—nothing wildly inappropriate, of
course, but different than other couples. I started to notice how doors

normally open in the daytime would be inexplicably locked, and that my parents would disappear at odd times only to return an hour or two later with a particular glow upon their faces."

He chuckled lowly. "Naturally, I had no idea what this meant until quite a bit older. Once, when I was perhaps nine or ten, I entered the parlor and caught my mother sitting on my father's lap. They were kissing, not unusual in and of itself, but in a manner I had never seen at that point in my life. I left abruptly and went directly to Mrs. Reynolds. I was not upset, just curious. I shall never forget how she laughed, playfully pinched my cheek, and said, 'It is perfectly natural, so never you mind. Someday you shall understand. But, in the future, Master Fitzwilliam, you would be wise to knock before entering a room.' Thereafter, I always did."

Darcy paused to collect his thoughts. Those were the happy memories easy to relate. Swallowing, he closed his eyes. "You know that Georgiana was born when I was almost twelve. What you do not know is that my mother was very ill all through her pregnancy. Georgiana's birth was difficult as well, so I gleaned, and my mother almost died. In fact, she remained on the edge of death for weeks. My father was beside himself and in no shape to console me. Worse, I had come to rely on his temperate nature and implacable steadfastness. James Darcy was the type of man who could handle any crisis with wisdom, humor, and patience. These are not traits borne from a child's hero worship of his father, Elizabeth. It was his reputation, the known facts. He could not handle my mother's illness. Not at all. He rarely slept or left her side, and in his face was a fear I had never seen before. He was terrified of losing my mother."

The pressure of Elizabeth's hand over his clenched fist startled him, unaware in his preoccupation with past pain that she had scooted closer. Smiling wanly, he went on.

"She did recover, although never fully. She was fragile, weaker, and easily exhausted. Life returned to normal more or less. The death of my grandfather happened that next year, a horrific blow for all of us, although that tragedy does not directly impact this topic. Nevertheless, it added to the stress on my mother. Father hovered over her constantly, his focus so intent that he ignored me and Georgiana, to a degree. I mean no accusation, as I understood it then and do so even more now, having fallen in love with you. Still, it was a puzzle to me. I was, you see, a precocious youth, always demanding knowledge, often about subjects beyond my comprehension. My father and grandfather encouraged my thirst for education. My mother and Mrs. Reynolds, conversely, were forever endeavoring to make me less serious and to laugh more—a vain effort, for the most part."

He chuckled at the remembrance and looked at Elizabeth for the first time since launching into his narrative. "Remember at Netherfield, when you teased me about being proud and that you 'dearly loved to laugh'? It was as if my mother were in the room putting those words on your lips. You are so like her, Elizabeth. Wittier, perhaps a bit more caustic, but like you, she was amused by the smallest things. Even when ill, that did not change."

She smiled at him, her eyes warm and filled with love. It gave him hope that this conversation would not be the trial he feared or have a negative outcome. Leaning, he kissed her again, needing the strength found even in a glancing touch of her lips.

"I digress," he noted, clearing his throat. "The point was my curiosity. You see, as I observed the interactions between those married people in our family and social circles, I began to comprehend the differences. It isn't the only subject I was inquisitive about, to be sure, as Mrs. Reynolds will delight in telling you." He smiled wryly, then shrugged. "I began to understand that people married for many reasons—for security, to advance a position in society, pure lust, or to further a family line and inheritances. Despite aspects of validity to these reasons, none of them, if the sole reason, brings true happiness. My parents possessed true happiness. They were blessed, and it was because they loved each other. I was too young to fully grasp all of it, yet even then, I vowed to have a marriage like my parents."

Sitting back into the sofa, he leaned his head against the wall and again closed his eyes. Clasping Elizabeth's hand tightly, he allowed the grief to creep into his voice.

"I was seventeen when my mother died. Immediately after the funeral, my father retreated to his bedchamber. He did not emerge for a month, and when he did, he was a changed man. Gone was the light from his eyes, and the quick smile never reappeared. He had aged, his face deeply lined and hair shot through with gray. He sank deeper and deeper into an abyss. I know, without a doubt, that he would have died before that year was over if not for my Uncle George. A year after my mother's death, my uncle arrived from India. I have no idea what he said or did, but somehow, he reached through the…well, the insanity of grief is the only apt description. Father never fully recovered and was never the same, but Uncle George brought him back to us for a while longer. I shall forever be grateful to him for that."

He had to stop talking or would succumb to the tears. Reliving the trials of those years was extraordinarily painful, yet it was the only way to explain his thinking, his choices in life, and why she could trust him to be faithful to her until his dying breath.

A full five minutes had passed before he was capable of resuming the tale. "A sensible man would probably regard my father's profound grief as a justification for avoiding all-consuming love. If so, then I am not a sensible man. Watching my father, even in his misery, heightened my resolve to have the same love."

He rose to his feet and walked to the window, but lost to memories, he saw nothing outside. "That next year I left for Cambridge. I had planned to go sooner, but mother's death had put that on hold. It was the relief I needed in most respects. I had never gone to boarding school, due to my mother's poor health, so university was a completely unique world for me. Exciting, yes, but also intimidating. I relished the education, of course. Learning is like breathing to me. It was in the social arenas where I failed. Spectacularly. I doubt you are astounded to hear me confess this."

He looked at her then, smiling when she laughed and shook her head.

"Oh, my love, if you think I am bad now, imagine how I was ten years ago. I was incredibly naïve as having been quite sheltered. Pemberley is isolated, Lambton small, and between my parents preferring Derbyshire and mother's ill health, journeys into London were rare. My previous exposure to large crowds and society was minimal, and then suddenly I was thrust into it. I have never made friends easily, and I enjoyed few of the entertainments the university men partook of. Gambling, drinking, carousing...none of it interested me. More to the point, I abhorred it. Men like Wickham, for example, consider those as the primary purpose for attending university. I was there for the education, a shocking thing to many, and spent my leisure in quieter pursuits. As now, I took pleasure in billiards, chess, fencing, and riding, of course. My friends were those gentlemen who were of like mind. Richard was my main companion, but others too, all of whom are still dear friends you will meet in due course."

Pausing again, he returned his sightless gaze to the window and rubbed the back of his neck. *Dear God, help me to explain this properly without sounding the fool.*

"As for women...it would be a lie, Elizabeth, for me to claim I made a conscious vow of chastity. I felt no calling to be a man of the cloth or anything of the sort. I was a man in my prime, as the saying goes, with urges I very much longed to gratify. Honestly, I fully intended to do so somehow, somewhere, with someone. There were opportunities, many of them, but I refused to selfishly slake my appetites in a demeaning manner. My father taught me values and morals, and the example of my parents' relationship and the only vow which I had made were never far from my thoughts."

"I had some vague notion of an acceptable situation outside of marriage, but what that was I cannot say. It certainly wasn't what I saw from men like Wickham. They bragged of their sexual conquests, were lewd and crass—not my concept of how a gentleman behaved. There was never any affection or kind regard for the women they used, and the justification of the women being of a low station or...paid for made no sense to me. Were these men not as immoral and low if they partook in the activity? It disgusted me."

"Despite all of this, I was extremely happy at Cambridge. I loved those years and was sad to see them end. By the time I left, I had mastered the forbearance and temperance that are innate in my character. It was not easy, Elizabeth, I cannot pretend it was, but I had remained virtuous."

Beginning to believe this story would never end, Darcy started pacing. There was yet more personal tragedy and grief to relate.

"Not two months after my return to Pemberley, my father unexpectedly collapsed. It was his heart, according to the physician, and a week later he died. There I was, twenty-two years old, with a devastated eleven-year-old sister and an enormous estate squarely upon my shoulders to manage. There are not words in the King's English to describe how overwhelmed life became. Thank God for Mrs. Reynolds. She assumed charge over the household staff and upkeep, and Georgiana too. Mr. Wickham, my father's steward, was a remarkable man. Without those two, along with Mr. Taylor and the rest of the staff and tenants, Pemberley would have fallen into a waste. I was an apt pupil, fortunately. Even after Mr. Wickham's tragic death about six months later, I had learned enough to keep my head above water barely. Lord Matlock assisted me tremendously and found my current steward, Mr. Keith. It took a very long while, over two years, before I felt as if my feet were on solid ground and I could breathe again. I suppose the only positive to those horrific years was that minor concerns like sex were completely buried."

He laughed shortly and stopped pacing. He sensed Elizabeth's eyes on him as he had talked, but her thoughts were a mystery. While he appreciated her keeping the promise not to interrupt, it was unnerving to have a one-sided conversation. Unsure what he would find, he pivoted about.

Elizabeth sat on the edge of the sofa, hands folded in her lap, chin lifted and bright eyes gazing steadily. With relief, he saw love and sympathy in her face, but before it weakened his resolve to finish, he inhaled and plunged on.

"It was about this time when subtle and not so subtle hints to enter Society came to my attention. New demands I had no desire to be a part of were placed upon my shoulders. It is my responsibility to interact with the *ton*, but God how I hate it! I'm not sure if you appreciate how much of an agony it is for me, Elizabeth—or was, I should say. I am still uncomfortable, introverted, and not well-skilled in conversing with people, but believe it or not, I am a charmer compared to how I was just five years ago."

She laughed at that, as he'd hoped, giving him the courage to wrap it up. Stepping closer, he got to the meat of it.

"I learned to enjoy some of the social life. It can be entertaining, I admit. What I despised was the portion I was expected to focus on —finding a wife. With each passing year, the pressure increased. My problem was not a dearth of candidates, believe me. I was the perfect catch with wealth and position. I could have been married a dozen times over, Elizabeth, or had any of the multiple married women who blatantly offered themselves to me as a diversion from their boredom and empty marriages. I wanted none of them. I wanted what my parents had and despaired of ever finding it. I know it makes no sense, and probably any of the men I know would judge me insane or deficient somehow, but with every deceitful, insincere woman who was thrust into my path, wanting me only for my money, my physical desires faded away.

"I began to believe I would never find what my parents shared, that such a love was not destined to be my fate. I knew I was growing bitter and weary, but I could not stop it. And, yes, I worried that something *was* wrong with me. At times my sexual needs would hit me, excruciatingly so, and I would teeter on the brink of doing something stupid. Not quite so stupid as marrying Caroline Bingley, but you get the idea."

Another spate of laughter, Elizabeth joining in even with her eyes swimming in tears.

"Mainly, surprising even me, to be honest, I hardened my resolve. I told myself that if I could not find a woman to love, who loved me for me, then I would not marry. Future heirs and Pemberley be damned. I am a profoundly stubborn man, my love if you have not realized that already. Once I set a course, I am loyal to it."

He paused again, this time for effect. Setting his face into a somber expression, he stared gravely into her eyes.

"What all of this meant to me, Elizabeth, is the unwavering conviction that if I were so fortunate as to find that elusive woman, I would be devoted, faithful, and enduringly thankful until my last breath, and hopefully on into eternity."

Crossing the remaining space between them, he knelt before her and enfolded her hands in his. "What this also means, in case you haven't put it together, is that I am as chaste as you. Dearest, precious Elizabeth—I saved myself for you, long before I knew who you were or even if you existed. As trite as that sounds, it is the truth. My principles, my pride, if you wish, would not allow me to be with a woman unless I loved her and was married to her. Strange as that is, there you have it. Call me a hopeless romantic."

Reaching up to cup her wet cheeks, he whispered, "Now I can see that my decision to wait for you, to trust that you existed, was a worthy one. I have no doubts we shall be marvelous together, in every way, and especially in our lovemaking, even from the very start. How could it not be perfect, beautiful, rapturous? Furthermore, when I stand before God and vow to love and cherish you forever, to be faithful only to you, I will mean it with all my soul. I will never, ever want anyone but you, Elizabeth. This you must believe."

"I do!" She flung her arms around his shoulders, half falling into his body. If he hadn't firmly balanced on his knees, they would have tumbled to the carpet. Upon later reflection, he wished they had, but at the moment, it was bliss to feel her happiness.

"Thank you, William, for sharing your life with me. I know it was painful, and I am sorry for being so silly."

"Do not apologize, love. Promise me you will never apologize for talking to me about any subject. It is my mistake for being so guarded." He squeezed her tighter, then withdrew just enough to meet her eyes. "Elizabeth, you must also trust that I would never force myself upon you in any way. Your wishes, requirements, desires…everything and anything to make you happy are of paramount importance to me. I cannot fathom our relationship ever disintegrating so that we do not desire each other, physically or otherwise. But whatever may happen, I will respect you and never cause you harm—"

It was her turn to interrupt, doing so with a kiss. Further vocalizations were mostly monosyllables, the only string of words being multiple "I love you" declarations.

12

SUPREME TEMPTATION

Two more days. Elizabeth will be my wife in two more days.

Darcy stared at the calendar atop his desk, a smile spreading simply by seeing the ink circle marking November the twenty-eighth. Each morning for nearly two months he had crossed off the previous date yet had often felt as if the wedding day grew no closer. Now, finally, the day his heart and soul would be complete was almost here.

Hopefully, these final forty-eight hours will not crawl so slowly it feels as if the clock is turning backwards.

Standing, Darcy stretched and yawned. As he did every morning immediately upon rising from his bed, the drapes had been drawn open, so he could survey the weather. Not a cloud was visible in the whole expanse of the vibrant-azure sky. If one did not know it was late November, the brilliant sunlight would have deceived. Evidence of winter was there on closer inspection, of course, as was the aftermath of the heavy rains in the dozens of muddy puddles and temporary ponds.

The horrendous storm which caused him troubles had left a wake of disasters over a substantial portion of Hertfordshire, northern London, and the southern tip of Buckinghamshire. The newspapers yesterday and that morning reported flooding, roads washed out, lightning strikes with resulting fires, injuries, and, tragically, deaths. He should never have let his selfishness overrule common sense. He had risked his own safety—a foolishness Elizabeth had reminded him of several times yesterday—but far worse was the peril he had forced upon his servants. It was sobering, and he would not forget the lesson learned.

However, Darcy was not the type of man to flagellate himself. These were the last two days of their betrothal season, and while he would gladly welcome the miracle of the hours zipping by, since that was improbable, he planned to make the best of it. What that would entail, he had no idea. Then he remembered that today, or certainly by tomorrow, wedding guests would descend upon Longbourn and Netherfield. Boredom was unlikely.

Sure enough, before noon both households were welcoming visitors: the Gardiners arrived at Longbourn, and the Matlocks, with Georgiana and Colonel Fitzwilliam, descended upon Netherfield. The women at Longbourn were consumed with creating the flower bouquets, the endeavor likely to take the entire day, so Darcy had been warned. Resigned to this reality, the Longbourn servant delivering a missive from Miss Elizabeth shortly after two o'clock was unexpected. Grinning, he instructed Georgiana to hastily grab her coat and bonnet for a trip into Meryton. Thrilled, she did so without question, Richard coming along as well, and a half hour later the four of them were strolling along the wooden walkways of the modest village with Elizabeth as a guide.

"A ribbon crisis? That is what you fabricated to get out of the house?"

"Whatever do you mean, Mr. Darcy?" Lizzy declared, brows high and eyes wide and innocent. She even patted her heart and added a gasp of shock. "Are you suggesting I misplaced an entire box of ribbons *on purpose?*"

"No! No, of course not. How silly of me! Forget I said a word." Darcy pressed her hand firmly against his arm, sighing sorrowfully. "I only pray the draper has more in stock. We cannot proceed with the wedding without the full complement of ribbons."

"Oh, I am sure he does! Besides, these missing things usually do turn up. In fact, I suspect someone at Longbourn has stumbled across them by now. Probably my aunt Gardiner. She is cannily akin to a bloodhound in locating misplaced objects."

Laughing, they enjoyed the short respite as thoroughly as they could under the time constraints imposed by last-minute wedding preparations. Georgiana was charmed by the village, although her enthusiasm was mainly in being with Elizabeth. The short trip ended with an even briefer pause at Longbourn to introduce Colonel Fitzwilliam and Miss Darcy to the Bennets. That meeting went predictably.

By the time Darcy, Richard, and Georgiana returned to Netherfield, the Hursts and Caroline Bingley had arrived.

"Terrific," Darcy muttered grumpily upon espying the familiar coach in the drive. It was a sentiment of which neither Colonel Fitzwilliam nor Miss Darcy could disagree.

As per the agenda for the final days and evenings, the brides and grooms would honor tradition by not seeing each other after sundown on the eve of the wedding, meaning they would dine apart. For tonight, however, Mr. Bingley had offered to host at Netherfield. It was the sensible choice, presuming the likelihood of some of their families arriving that day. As it turned out, *everyone* arrived that day. It was, for all intents, a prewedding reception.

When the dust finally cleared, and the last visitor had departed with the rest retired to their guest quarters, the grooms and Richard Fitzwilliam met in Bingley's private sitting room.

"Well, that went swimmingly, I'd say." Richard handed a brandy to Darcy, who grunted, then took a large swallow.

"As swimmingly as in a river of piranhas."

"Oh, it wasn't that bad—maybe sharks, or stinging eels, but not piranha level."

Bingley smiled at Richard's humor but looked a bit dyspeptic and also gulped at his brandy. "We may as well accept it, Darcy. After all, we will be family in two days so these gatherings, while hopefully rare, will happen from time to time."

Now it was Darcy's turn to look ill.

"Does Mr. Hurst ever smile?" Richard blurted in a tone of sincere curiosity.

"Sometimes, I think." Bingley frowned, then shrugged. "Can't recall to be honest."

"Huh. Well, here is to family." Richard lifted his glass. "Got to love them, for better or worse, sickness and in health, richer or poorer... Wait, that is for spouses. What are the rules for family again?"

"That is the real tragedy. One has no choice in the matter and is stuck with them," Darcy grumbled.

"Yes, well, cheer up, Cousin. You have me! That is a stupendous blessing from the Almighty. And soon you shall have Bingley here. We make up for a dozen Mr. Hursts or Mrs. Bennets."

"I suppose I will have to give you that," Darcy admitted grudgingly, and then he laughed.

Richard joined in, but Bingley was quiet, eyes faintly troubled and a frown creasing his brows.

"What is it, Charles?"

"Was Caroline..." Bingley paused. "That is, did she do or say anything I am unaware of?"

Richard shook his head, but it was Darcy who spoke. "Surprisingly, no. In fact, I don't think she said much at all. She sat with Mrs. Hurst the whole night. I know she never approached

Elizabeth, at least when we were all together. I was watching. I think the time away did her good, truly I do. But really, what does it matter for the present? We should put all this aside and focus on what is important. The reason we are gathered here in the first place."

"Here! Here!" Richard raised his glass, but only halfway. Staring at Darcy with a comically confused expression, he asked, "And why was that again?"

Darcy shook his head, helpless but to laugh. Casting aside the serious, negative topics, the trio of friends chatted and drank for a while longer.

"I almost forgot," Richard slurred sometime later. "Georgie asked me what I thought about braving the dirt trails meandering prettily through the nearby meadows for an extended walk in the crisp air and sunshine. Or some such poetic blither. This would be for tomorrow, that is. Or is it now today? What time is it anyway?"

"Time for us to pour you into bed, Colonel. And pour ourselves, for that matter," Bingley noted, a bit slurry as well. "As for the walk idea, it sounds like a feasibility. What say you, Mr. Weather Predictor? Will the pleasant weather last?"

"I am not as sensitive to the climates here as I am in Derbyshire, but I think it will. I am basing that on the *Farmer's Almanac*, to be honest. At any rate, getting out into nature for more than a short jaunt would be wonderful. I hate being cooped up."

"Says the man who will soon be married and staying cooped up for days on end." Richard wiggled his brows and leered.

"Yes, but I will at least be exercising."

Loud guffaws came after that suggestive jest, and from there the inebriated conversation went into bawdy realms best left unrepeated. It was probably a blessing that none of them remembered most of what was said from that point onward.

❧

*T*he following morning, one day before the long-awaited wedding, the three gentlemen luckily remembered the discussion of a walk.

Or rather, they remembered when Georgiana loudly and painfully screamed at them about it. Several pots of coffee and solid food in their stomachs later, her voice wasn't as shrill—strange how that happens—and the prospect of so much bright sunshine piercing into their aching skulls wasn't quite as nausea inducing.

Despite lacking a high degree of eagerness initially, the recovering grooms were willing to do anything if it meant being with their ladies. Ever adventurous, Colonel Fitzwilliam would not have been left behind barring someone tying him up with chains, and even that may have failed. Lord Matlock was content to quietly pass the day with Mr. Bennet in the Netherfield library, and Lady Matlock pleaded needing rest for a minor headache. Darcy noted her slight hesitation, suspecting the excuse was a polite way to allow the younger set to have their fun.

As far as they knew, no one asked Mr. Hurst, wherever he was. That left Louisa Hurst, who surprised everyone by chiming in enthusiastically, and Caroline Bingley, who then had little option but to come along.

Naturally, Kitty was up for the challenge, but even if she had a broken leg, she would have hobbled along in order to flirt with the dashing Colonel Fitzwilliam. Mary gave no thought to flirting, but she did enjoy nature, so it wasn't too difficult to entice her away from her books. Furthermore, although it had been less than twenty-four hours since meeting Miss Darcy, the younger Bennet sisters and the shy Georgiana were getting along nicely.

There were dozens of footpaths, of course, but one trail was the shortest, most direct route between Longbourn and Netherfield. More out of habit than any other reason, the walkers set their feet upon this frequently trod course, Charles and Jane in the lead purely by chance. With no destination in mind or time limit as part of the plan, the group of ten strolled at a casual pace, with conversation gay and laughter flowing.

The trail, like all unmaintained, naturally formed tracks, was not level or uniform in width. Some segments were wide enough for four adults to walk shoulder to shoulder, but on average two bodies side by side was the comfortable pattern to avoid a pitfall unseen underneath the tall grass. Due to this reality, the varied paces set by the walkers, the conversation topics, and unconscious choices primarily on the part of the engaged couples, the space between smaller clusters of people began to lengthen.

"I see my cousin has bypassed Bingley and Jane to assume the lead. Not sure when that happened," Darcy noted in a tone of surprise. With his focus captured by Elizabeth's beautiful face, Darcy was amazed he hadn't stumbled into a mud puddle or sink hole in his inattentiveness.

"It must be the military-command attitude taking over. He is used to being a leader."

"Ha! That would be his claim, with a wink and a grin, but I know him too well. It is to be in the center of his female cheering squad, as they hang on his every word."

"You are right!" Lizzy laughed aloud. "Even Mary is smiling and blushing. Goodness, but I never thought I would see the day! The Colonel better watch himself or Mama will never let him leave."

"She would not be the first mother to attempt it, I am sure. Fortunately, Richard can charm anyone, so he is safe. What I wonder is how my dear sister will take the competition. She has been Richard's 'little mouse' all her life and grown accustomed to the devotion." He chuckled, a sly glint in his eyes.

"You are a little devil at times, Mr. Darcy. I am shocked to the core."

He turned to her and winked, clearly unrepentant. "By the way,

Georgiana wanted me to reiterate how thoroughly she enjoyed the outing to Meryton yesterday afternoon."

"As if she did not express her delight and appreciation profusely enough already. I kept looking around to make sure we had not been magically transported to Venice or Paris. I am quite certain that never has a living soul been so utterly delighted by the charms of Meryton. If I had not seen Lambton myself, I might presume it no more than a crude village with mud huts and pigs wandering freely in the streets based on Georgiana's response to our humble town."

"She can be overly dramatic at times. I have no idea where that trait came from," he said in a bland tone and with a perfectly straight face.

After regaining control of her hilarity, Lizzy confided, "I must say, William, that while I am abundantly thankful for Lord and Lady Matlock's willingness to entertain Georgiana so we can have time alone at Pemberley, I tremendously look forward to having her home with us. She is an absolute dear, and, well, Christmas would not be the same without a sister."

Darcy covered her hand with his and tugged her closer to his side, but said nothing. He knew how difficult the changes would be for her, but of course, that was how life was. She was practical, he also knew, and not for a second regretful of the decision to marry him, even though it meant taking her a long way away. All he could do—*what he would do*—was make her happy. So deliriously happy that the moments of sadness and homesickness would be brief and rapidly assuaged.

"So, seriously, where does this propensity for drama come from? One of your parents? You have spoken of their humor. Or better yet, is it a familial connection with a famed stage actor? One of those eccentric Darcys you speak of? How exciting and potentially scandalous that would be!"

Darcy met her impish expression with a teasing grin. "I deem it best to wait until after our wedding before revealing the skeletons hidden in our closets, my dear. Allow me another day of being perfection in your sight."

Lizzy rolled her eyes, harrumphing and jabbing her elbow into his side. "Arrogant man! Must I again chronicle your numerous faults?"

"There is no need. I now have them memorized." He leaned to kiss her cheek. "In truth, neither of my parents was particularly gifted in dramatics. They possessed excellent humor and loved to laugh and jest as you do. Minimal acting skills, however. Of the relatives I know, the tendency runs deepest with my uncle George, particularly, and also my great-aunt Beryl. I long for the day when you can meet them both."

"You have spoken of your uncle, the famed traveling physician. I do not recall an Aunt Beryl. Was the 'great' an adjective or part of the relationship?"

"Both to be honest. Ah, I do not know where to begin with my Aunt Beryl. She is my grandfather's much younger sister, and if it is an exciting scandal you want, then the thrice-married Marchioness of Warrow is as close as the Darcys come—in living relations, that is. Goodness only knows what skeletons exist that I am unaware of. Very soon we shall be at Pemberley, together as a family. I shall happily let you loose in the archival library to read any of the journals you want. As led, you can acquaint yourself with my ancestry and feel the strength of our relations."

"Our relations," she repeated in a whisper, pausing on the trail to stare into his tender eyes. An affectionate, slow smile spread. "I like the sound of that."

Darcy matched her wide smile with one equally as brilliant and filled with love. A generous allotment of raw passion infused his eyes as well, sending pleasant shivers racing up Lizzy's spine. The wild flutters attacking her insides were exhilarating.

Breaking away from the mesmerizing pull of his gaze, her intention to gauge if she could safely steal a kiss, Lizzy's eyes darted up and down the trail. As she had hoped, the colonel and his female retinue were smudges in the distance. Bingley and Jane had paused under a tree off to the left on a secondary trail, Lizzy and Darcy obviously having passed them without ever realizing it. Mrs. Hurst and Miss Bingley, as the slowest walkers, had fallen far behind.

Marvelous. Then, noting the surrounding landscape and recognizing where they were, a stupendously brilliant idea flashed through her brain.

Lizzy jerked her head to indicate the narrow trail veering off to the right. "This is the trail that leads to Willow Bench."

"Is it? I've never come from this direction. It is a reasonable distance from Longbourn, so I can see why it was a frequent destination for you."

Lizzy nodded, smiling at her fiancé archly. "Shall we?"

Darcy grinned and stepped onto the track. "I cannot think of a reason not to."

~

"Where are they going?" Caroline Bingley asked shrilly. "Should we follow? It is quite unseemly for them to be unchaperoned!"

"They will be married tomorrow, Caroline." Louisa's sigh was long-suffering, and she rolled her eyes. "If they haven't managed a few unchaperoned interludes by now, I would be amazed."

Caroline sniffed. "I am quite sure you are right. With a woman like her, inappropriate behavior is to be expected."

"Oh, Sister. You are so amusing in your ridiculousness. I have delighted in the spectacle, truly I have. Now, however, it is past time for you to cease your obsession."

"Obsession? Over Mr. Darcy? Absurd! I care not one whit for the man!"

"Indeed," Louisa drawled. "How could I *possibly* believe otherwise?"

Caroline stopped walking, an expression of complete exasperation on her face as she stared at her older sister. "Louisa, how many times must I remind you that it is our brother who will suffer from this disgrace?"

"And, Caroline," Louisa snapped the name, "how many times must I then ridicule you for such stupidity? If Charles should suffer in his marriage, it is his choice nevertheless and not our place to interfere. But, as I have kindly said a million times now, hoping you would come to understand the truth yourself, there is no disgrace to be had. Jane Bennet is a lovely lady, and they will have a marriage as fine as one can find in this world."

Even though the harsher spoken admonition did not appear to have had the slightest effect on Caroline, whose face was stiff and cold, Louisa softened her tone and touched her sister lightly on the arm. "You, on the other hand, will never have a marriage at all, fine or disgraceful, if you keep to the course you are on. That is my advice to take or leave. For the present, we shall continue walking. For the remaining time we are here"—Louisa hardened her tone—"you, dear Sister, will smile and be graciousness itself. Do you understand?"

Caroline lifted her chin, her cool eyes narrowing. "If I do not?"

"Then the next time Charles sends you out of his sight, Mr. Hurst and I shall be unavailable and will suggest Aunt Agatha on the Isle of Arran. Perhaps Scotland will be far enough away to free you from the distress of witnessing our brother and Mr. Darcy *suffering* in their marriages."

Caroline blanched whiter than a ghost.

Evidently, there was a possible fate worse than losing Mr. Darcy.

*O*blivious to the sisterly chitchat occurring on the trail behind them, Darcy and Lizzy continued to laugh and leisurely stroll. Willow Bench held special memories for them, although they had only met there twice. Each of those times had been accidental, and the encounters as different as night and day.

On a hill off to the left of the trail, the copse of six old willow trees with leafless branches swaying in the gentle breeze appeared rather sad and lonely. Still, even with the lack of sheltering foliage, they were isolated and beyond eyesight. The location was perfect for two people wildly in love, but also dangerous, which is why Darcy already knew the answer to the question he asked.

"In all our walks, why have we not taken the time to visit your childhood sanctuary?"

"Because you, Mr. Darcy, are a proper gentleman who would never, not even if told the very fate of the world depended on it, do something as outrageously indecent as to be alone with his fiancée! The very idea is shocking and unfathomable."

"Ah, yes. That is so. I am a rock in that regard." He paused, sighing heavily. "Still, it is a shame to waste a lovely day, and I have noticed that you are appearing a bit weak, Miss Elizabeth. I would hate to overtax your fragility, but then again, I am vastly concerned for your health, so perhaps a sprint would do you good. Get the blood pumping and all that. What say you?"

Her answer was a single laugh, the ringing tones of gaiety floating over her shoulder as she took off running. Darcy watched for several seconds before taking up the chase. Naturally, his long-legged gait could readily overtake her, even with the delay and her impressive speed. Watching her dash with skirts held high enough for him to glimpse flashes of toned, stocking-clad calves was preferable by incalculable measure to winning a race.

Reaching the trees first, she spun around, shouting in triumph. The shout soon morphed into a squeal when he grabbed her around the waist, lifting her high off her feet and crushing against his chest before twirling in a series of circles.

Between laughter and squeals, she begged, "Stop! I'm growing dizzy!"

He stopped the rapid whirling, but the dizziness increased when he impetuously captured her mouth in a passionate kiss. They clung to each other, swaying and with stars spinning inside their heads, and kept on kissing. Within seconds they were fused along every plane, Darcy setting her onto her feet only so he could roam his hands freely over her body.

Wildly out of control, neither knew who broke the contact or why, but they pulled apart and mindlessly retreated to opposite sides of the copse. Collapsing backward into solid willow trees, they stared at each other with passion-drugged eyes for a full five minutes. Each of them gasped for air, the breathlessness having nothing to do with the sprint or the twirling.

Darcy leaned against the trunk, hands rigid with palms flattened harshly into his thighs as he frantically grasped onto the remaining threads of control. If he did not regain his equilibrium soon and force a specific organ to behave, Elizabeth would become his wife in one sense of the word in the next ten minutes. Of all the occasions where his restraint had teetered, this was a hundred times worse.

God help me, he silently begged, *and please don't move or say a word, Elizabeth, or I will be lost.*

"I love kissing you!"

Darcy groaned at her blurted comment, closing his eyes in a last-ditch attempt to remain a gentleman. Looking at her passion-glazed eyes, which were, he had noted, drifting downward to the unmistakable evidence of his arousal, was too much to bear.

"I suppose that fact you have figured out by now," she said, her voice shaky and weak.

He opened his eyes but said nothing immediately. The war raged internally, and the way she was gazing at him was fueling the fire.

"Yes," he finally choked out, through his dry throat, "I have received the message loud and clear. I love kissing you, Elizabeth. Most ardently, and fervently want to do so very much more than kiss you!" He inhaled, clenching his jaw and digging his back into the rough bark. "That is why it is best you stay over there, and I remain here for a while, if not permanently."

At this, she flushed, unconsciously biting the plump lower lip he hungered to kiss, and after another contemplative survey of the bulging member below his waist—which continued to stubbornly resist his monumental efforts to control—she averted her eyes.

Dear God in Heaven, her sweet innocence is as provocative as her womanly passions. How can any man be expected to withstand such a lethal combination?

Darcy felt his muscles tightening, and he involuntarily shifted his weight to take that one step forward which would end irrevocably in making her his. Emitting a growling groan of frustration, he tore his eyes away from the hypnotic allure of her body, following the direction of her gaze.

She was staring toward the meadow he had been racing across on the two previous occasions he happened upon her at this copse of trees. Ten or so feet away was the tall wooden fence he and Parsifal had jumped over, Elizabeth's anger and worry over that maneuver a comical, touching recollection. She had climbed up the rungs of this fence on both of those unexpected encounters, but her reactions to his two invasions had been altogether dissimilar. At the second meeting shortly after their engagement, he saw her desire for him plainly revealed for the first time in the brazen way she had looked at his body—not the wisest remembrance to dwell upon right now!

Darcy could recall each of those incidents with sharp clarity, the first as distinct as the second because, as he later admitted, he had been crazy in love with Elizabeth Bennet almost from the second he laid eyes on her. Perhaps the intensity of his emotions, denied as they were for months, was partial blame why coming here stirred his lust to a ferocious level.

"What were you thinking when you encountered me here that day? Not a few weeks ago, but last year, after my stay at Netherfield when Jane was ill. You had such a strange expression."

In a mesmerized monotone, he replied automatically, "I thought my dreams had returned to torment me."

"What do you mean?"

I mean, I had dreamt of making love to you, a passionate, erotic vision of our naked bodies entwined and writhing, sweaty and flushed, experiencing a pleasure greater than anything comparable. I mean, I wanted you physically, with such powerful intensity that not leaping off my horse to make love to you right here on the soft earth was the harshest battle I had ever fought. I mean, I was madly, inexorably, and with all my soul in love with you, but had no clue how to deal with it.

"Nothing," he said instead. "At least, nothing we should talk about now, trust me."

They stared at each other in silence for quite some time.

"I know what you are thinking, my love, as I am thinking it too." He spoke softly, seriously, and held her eyes. "What is one day? We love and want each other. We will be married tomorrow, so why not take advantage of our solitude in this special place to consummate our love?"

Pausing, he breathed deeply to still the pounding of his heart. "I want to make love to you, more than I can ever put into words, Elizabeth. I know you want me as intensely. And I shall be honest, at this point proper behavior, being a gentleman, rules, even holy vows be damned, I would consummate our relationship and make you mine."

He slowly shook his head. "The only reason I will not allow it to happen is because we, both of us, deserve better. We have waited a long time to love each other, to become one. Our first time together will be in a comfortable bed in a warm room where solitude is assured, not on the dirt in an essentially public place. It will be special, a precious time of discovery, intimate and beautiful. It will be perfect, I promise you that."

Again, silence fell as they gazed at each other from opposite sides of the small copse of willow trees.

Then finally, Darcy smiled and laughed lowly. "I meant every word, believe me. Nevertheless, I am, in the end, a fallible human who is passionately in love, so let us not tempt ourselves any further."

He pushed away from the tree and extended his hand. After another two minutes, Elizabeth bravely disconnected from the solidity of her tree, which had lent its unbendable strength during her vulnerability. Taking his hand, they left the copse of willows and descended the hill toward the pathway.

Once back onto the trail, Darcy stopped and looked back at the cluster of trees. "I have a feeling neither of us has seen the last of Willow Bench."

Then he smiled down at Elizabeth, who laughed and shook her head. "I have a feeling you are correct."

13

MATRIMONY FINALIZATION

November 28, 1816

*I*n the course of a person's life, there are certain days wherein the collection of hours and minutes indelibly carve into memory—colorful, graphic, defined images painted upon the mind as permanently as if on canvas. Time cannot erase these pivotal events, steeped as they are in profound, rapturous emotion.

Fitzwilliam Darcy and Elizabeth Bennet were blessed to have several such special days already residing within their hearts. Inhabiting the prime location was the pristine memory of the day they declared their love for one another, culminating with Elizabeth accepting William's proposal of marriage.

Upon the dawn of November the twenty-eighth, Elizabeth and Darcy woke from peaceful slumber just as the sun peeked above the horizon. Separated by three miles of a misty moor yet shrouded in shadows, their dreamy musings were identical. Their blissful smiles spreading, they stretched in their individual beds, warm and comfortable, and thought, *Tomorrow I will wake entwined with my love.*

Today was the day Fitzwilliam Darcy and Elizabeth Bennet would be bound before God in Holy Matrimony.

Incontestably, it was the most important day of their lives, a day to greet with receptive hearts and lucid minds—a day to record and savor.

Netherfield Park ~ The Grooms

The two grooms chose to stay sequestered in their private suites until it was time to leave for the church. The decision not to join their guests for the light morning repast was mutual, although for differing reasons.

Charles Bingley was a bundle of nerves. He was not nervous about being married—not at all! The insufferable two months waiting to marry his angel Jane had tried his patience and tested his restraint exactly as it had Darcy's. Weeks ago, he had given up counting the number of times he cursed himself a fool for agreeing to Mr. Bennet's late-November date. That no longer mattered praise be to heaven.

What was important today, and what frayed his nerves, was the pomp and circumstance surrounding the wedding ceremony.

Charles had never handled himself well in social situations where he was the center of attention. In this, he was remarkably similar to Darcy, although the two men reacted to such stressful situations entirely different.

Darcy retreated, as it were, his face and body stiffening, lips clamping shut, hooded eyes hardening, and nose lifting into the air. He unintentionally assumed the pose of an aloof, arrogant, disdainful person, which he was not.

Charles, conversely, became jittery, his smile too big and rather dotty, and his laughter more of a titter. Stringing a sentence together that wasn't an idiotic jumble grew nigh on impossible. It was extremely embarrassing. Despite the misinterpretations Darcy dealt with as a byproduct of his bashful awkwardness, Charles would have taken it any day over transforming into a buffoon.

Therefore, Charles Bingley, Netherfield groom number one, needed peace and calm. All in all, it was best for him to speak to no one until it was time to gaze into his adored Jane's lovely blue eyes and recite his vows.

Netherfield groom number two, Fitzwilliam Darcy, was not the slightest bit nervous about anything. True, he was not fond of being stared at or put on display, but today did not fall into that category as far as he was concerned. The fact that there would be an audience as he stood with Elizabeth to exchange vows was a desirable, welcomed aspect of the day's solemn ceremony.

Each of the carefully chosen attendees were witnesses to the sacred pledges the four of them would freely give and which would be sanctioned by the ordained servant of Christ in the presence of God. In his opinion, this aspect of the matrimonial ritual would not have been written into the Book of Common Prayer if it were not a vital necessity.

Indeed, for Darcy, the sacramental obligations and spiritual importance overrode everything else. Because of this, for the first time since his engagement, and in truth for months before that, he had not awoken to visions of Elizabeth lying naked beside him. The physical desire for her simmered deep within his body, and there was no possibility of his passion for her disappearing entirely, even when standing in front of the altar.

However, for a few hours at least, his heart was fixed upon the hallowed vows he would soon recite. For this reason, the morning hours of solitude were essential for his inner peace and communion with God.

In other respects, today wasn't vastly different than any other day. Due to the feast scheduled immediately after the wedding, he was content with coffee, toast, and a small plate of fruit. Not a typical breakfast by a long shot, but hardly an earth-shattering deviation. Bathing, shaving, dressing—all standard daily activities. Not even having a new suit to put on was all that unusual.

The only serious break from the norm came from his valet, Samuel Oliver.

All through the morning, as was standard with the strictly professional and tight-lipped manservant, the only words the duo exchanged pertained to the clothing and toilette procedures. Mr. Darcy could have been dressing for a shooting or fishing trip, and Mr. Oliver would have performed his assigned tasks precisely the same.

Then, as Darcy was adjusting the cravat pin gifted to him by his sister on his birthday, Samuel casually reached into a drawer and withdrew a small leather box.

Tone as stolid as always, he said, "Mr. Darcy, if I may be so bold as to touch upon a personal subject, I have a gift, a small token of my regard and appreciation. Primarily, of course, the gift is to honor this most auspicious day. I pray for your future happiness with Mrs. Darcy, as Miss Bennet soon shall be, and that your blessings will continue to multiply." Setting the box on his master's palm, the valet popped the lid open. "Familiar as I am with your wedding ensemble and the cravat pin from Miss Darcy, these cufflinks will match superbly. Congratulations, sir," he finished, as matter-of-factly as he had begun.

Darcy was absolutely stunned. He could not recall Samuel ever speaking for that long about anything. Furthermore, aside from a handful of oblique references that always involved his garments or grooming, in the past two months he had said nothing about the upcoming wedding, and now a gift?

Surely such astounding developments are a promising sign.

Darcy did not say this, of course, or hint of his astonishment. Instead, he thanked his valet, gracious but stoic. Overt emotion was clearly not wanted, by either of them. After a single nod, Samuel secured the sapphire-and-diamond cufflinks in place and that was it.

Naturally, Samuel was correct. The cufflinks matching superbly.

Longbourn Manor ~ The Brides

*T*he two brides at Longbourn could not have passed the morning hours in quiet solitude had they begged to do so. Living amongst a family consisting of six females didn't allow for much alone time or gradual waking to a peacefully silent house on any given day. As the brides had known from the start, the wedding day of two Bennet daughters—or, as Mrs. Bennet was fond of exclaiming, "The pinnacle event of the year!"—was destined to be early and chaotic.

It was Kitty who burst through the door when the sun was still partially below the horizon. "Wake up, sleepy-heads! Time for the fun to begin!" She yelled, flinging open the window curtains.

Plopping down between their blanket-draped forms, Kitty added a series of bounces for good measure. Lizzy and Jane burrowed deeper, gripping tight to the covers over their heads. Undeterred, Kitty attacked with well-aimed tickles.

"Mama says you must eat or you will faint at the altar. Can you imagine the horror? Everyone would be talking about the spectacle of a Bennet bride prostate on the floor, and not about the fancy celebration and rich husbands. Come, come! You can sleep later. Oh!" She giggled gaily, "I forgot. You won't be getting much sleep for days and days and days! Oh la la!"

Bounding off the bed exuberantly, Kitty skipped out the door, laughter floating on the air.

"Is she gone?"

"I think so."

"What do you think, Lizzy? Are you worried about losing sleep?"

"I slept very well last night and am pretty sure I can survive a few days without a full night's slumber."

Blanket yet over their heads, the sisters dissolved into silly giggles.

"Did you really sleep well?" Jane asked, stifling her snickers.

"Like a cat after slurping a big bowl of warmed milk. You?"

"I did, surprisingly."

"Were you expecting wedding jitters? You?"

"Not jitters, no. Just normal anxiousness. I did dream that we were walking down the aisle, our gowns perfect, but we had both forgotten to put up our hair."

"Oh, my!" Lizzy laughed, adding dramatically between gasping breaths, "Was our hair mussed and tangled, like mine is most of the time anyway?"

"No, believe it or not. Just hanging down, but, can you imagine?"

"The horror!" Lizzy exclaimed, imitating Kitty. "Did our grooms think we were the most ravishing creatures to walk the earth? Were they *pleased?*"

Jane blushed at Lizzy's insinuating drawl but laughed as she replied saucily, "I am certain they were, but, sadly, the dream did not show that part."

"Has Charles ever seen you with your hair down?"

Pausing for a moment of reflection, Jane shook her head. "I do not believe he has. It had not occurred to me, to be honest."

"Well, he is in for a treat. You have fabulous hair," Lizzy asserted confidently. Tossing the blankets aside, she sat up in bed and gazed at her bed-tousled, gorgeous sister. Smiling, she patted Jane on the cheek. "Indeed, he will be delightfully overwhelmed, sweet sister. Kitty is correct—you will be missing lots of sleep."

Returning the smile, her cheeks still prettily pink, Jane tugged on Lizzy's dangling braid. "I shan't be the only one. And as you said, we can survive."

Another laugh, a soft one, then Lizzy sighed. "Dear Jane, I shall miss you so!"

"I shall miss you too. Our lives will be different. Better, hopefully, and certainly not worse, but assuredly different. It will take some adjusting."

"Christmas will be difficult. I can't imagine it, to be honest. Pemberley is so beautiful, but I suspect it won't feel like home. I wish we could be here instead."

"You might be surprised how quickly Pemberley will become your home, Lizzy. But even if not, it would be foolish to journey back so soon. Mr. Darcy was wise to refuse."

"I never asked him. Oh, you were right, Jane," Lizzy admitted at Jane's raised brows. "It was ridiculous for me to even think of it. There are a dozen sensible reasons to stay at Pemberley. But I know William. If I asked to come home for Christmas, he would agree. That is how wonderful he is, and it would have been selfish of me. Besides, Georgiana will be there, and possibly Lord and Lady Matlock. I don't know what their winter plans are but assume they will reside in the country as most people do. They must live nearby. Or rather, Matlock Bath is near Pemberley. I have no clue where the Matlock estate is, to be honest, or even what it is named."

Falling back onto the pillow, she stared up at the ceiling as she laughed. "I have much to learn! William did say he has friends in the region. He mentioned the Vernors and the Sitwells, whom I gathered were within a reasonable distance, and he spoke of another gentleman from university who lives in Staffordshire. Or was it Leicestershire?" She frowned, then gave up and shook her head. "Anyway, surely there will be some holiday entertainments to be had. Besides, even with people I do not know, I shall be luckier than you in one regard." She turned her head and grinned.

Jane narrowed her eyes, knowing that look. "How so?"

"You get to have Caroline Bingley!"

"Oh, you!" Jane pummeled her with the pillow. A brief spat of childish play ensued but was interrupted by Mrs. Bennet hollering for them to come eat.

With the help of two sisters, their mother, and every maid in the house, Jane and Lizzy were pampered, primped, powdered, and prettified without lifting a single finger. Betsy was assigned to their hair, the final coiffures elaborate but elegant. By nine thirty, they were declared the most perfect, resplendent brides ever to be wed in all of Hertfordshire. Obviously it was a prejudiced assertion, but Jane and Lizzy were also awed by the visions of magnificence reflected in the tall mirrors.

With so much fuss and fun, neither bride had a spare second for nerves to set in. Only when settled into the carriage, with their father sitting across, did they have a chance to breathe.

For the short drive to All Souls Trinity Church, the ancient house of worship constructed of grey-stone and located on the far side of Meryton, they relished the quiet. It was a welcomed twenty minutes of calm reflection to prepare their hearts for the momentous ceremony.

Mr. Bennet smiled softly, his tender, slightly sad eyes moving back and forth between his two eldest daughters. Lizzy tried to think of a jest to ease the tense emotions she knew they were each feeling. But the wrong word and the tears tenuously held in check would spill, so she said nothing. Then, as the carriage crested the rise and the church's bell tower popped into view, Mr. Bennet broke the silence.

"It is said that tears are expected at weddings, although I believe it is supposed to be the brides who cry with joy. Good thing you have your handkerchiefs handy, but I brought several extras along in case. Just bear in mind that it is not an unending supply, so be careful not to drop the bouquets or accidentally untie a bow, or your mother will have used them up before you two need them."

Ah! The laughter they needed—and precisely as the carriage jolted to a halt. Faces merry and eyes sparkling, they clasped their proud papa's arms, ascended the stone steps spanning the entrance to the church, and stopped before the massive solid oak doors.

All Souls Trinity Church, Meryton
~ The Wedding ~

*I*n a separate room inside of the church, the two grooms waited for the agreed upon signal, yet were still startled when it came. The sharp rap on the door was immediately followed by the appearance of Colonel Fitzwilliam's solemn face squeezing into the gap.

"It. Is. Time," he intoned sonorously. "Thy brides hath cometh and shalt soon enter the holy church. Thy attendance is requested forthwith." Then he grinned and shoved the door wide.

Bingley chuckled, or tried to. To Darcy, it sounded more like a weak wheeze, not that he paid much attention to Bingley or his cousin. Calmly passing by the still-smirking Richard, Darcy walked into the church with Bingley a step behind. Together they crossed the transept until standing to the left of the priest. Reverend Jenney, resplendent in his official robes, stood in the center of the chancel, his hands folded over a well-used Book of Common Prayer. He greeted the grooms with one bob of his head and the tiniest possible lift of his lips before returning his eyes to the closed doors at the far end of the nave.

For weeks, Darcy had passively listened to chatter about the desire to adorn the ancient brick church with flowers, ribbons, and candles. Frankly, he didn't care about the chosen flowers, the ribbon colors, or if there were decorations at all for that matter. His only desire was to marry in the Pemberley Chapel, but even there, he would not have expressed an opinion on the decor.

However, when he detected Mrs. Bennet's dismay over the rigid Reverend Jenney's refusal to permit garnishing the pews with even a single flower and later ascertained that Jane and Elizabeth were saddened by this as well, he decided to intervene. In truth, as a man of deep faith, he tended to agree with the parish priest on maintaining the solemn atmosphere befitting a sacred place of worship. Then again, were not flowers God's gift of beauty and color? What harm was there in a few ribbons and fragrant blooms if he promised to restrain Mrs. Bennet?

Now, as he swept his eyes over the interior, he was thankful for his powers of persuasion. Mrs. Bennet, Darcy had to admit, had far exceeded his expectations, the resulting floral display tasteful and modest by anyone's standards. She had beautifully arranged small clusters of winter blooms with narrow ribbons of white and gold tied around them. Adorning the aisle end of each pew was one bouquet, in the center of which was a single, tall, lit candle. The overall effect was stunning and elegant.

These details he registered swiftly and might not have noticed at all if not for repeatedly reminding himself that this day was special as no other day in his entire life had been or would ever be. He would later regret it if he could not recall these seemingly minor elements. Thus, after first checking the main door and ensuring it was still closed, he scanned the church wall to wall. Peering into the pews, he acknowledged his family, smiling at each one.

Lastly, he swiveled his eyes to the left, where a few paces beyond Charles Bingley stood the two individuals chosen as the official witnesses.

As the only man well known to both Bingley and Darcy, Colonel Richard Fitzwilliam had been the obvious choice as groom's attendant and official witness. Even if Bingley hadn't been well acquainted with the colonel, or had desired another gentleman as his designated attendant, Darcy would have insisted on his cousin for himself. The two men teased each other mercilessly, but they were closer and dearer to each other than any two real brothers could be. Dressed in his full colonel's regalia, medals shining upon his chest, Richard cut a striking figure.

It was no wonder Mrs. Bennet spent as much time staring at him as she did the two men about to wed her daughters. Nor was Darcy surprised to note that Kitty wore an expression that was a cross between flirtatious and pouting. Neither she or her mother had been thrilled at Jane and Lizzy's designated bridal attendant, but no amount of begging changed their minds.

As the next eldest Bennet daughter, Mary was the proper choice. However, Darcy knew that, beyond propriety, they had wanted Mary for her soberness and deep faith. For both, the latter especially, Darcy was pleased with the selection. The Longbourn maids had managed to talk Mary into styling her hair, adding a bit of jewelry, and wearing a dress with some lace and frilly bits, the result making her almost pretty. Kitty would have presented a more attractive picture next to the dignified, uniformed Colonel Fitzwilliam, but with Mary at his side, there was no chance of coquetry causing either to forget their solemn purpose.

The dull clang of the bell high above in the church's tower signaled the ten o'clock hour. Darcy and Bingley swung their eyes immediately to the entrance. Colonel Fitzwilliam's timing proved to be perfect, allotting the grooms exactly enough time to assume their proper positions and canvass the scene without a spare moment to become impatient or engulfed by nerves. At the fifth chime, the double doors slowly swung inward, the brilliant sunlight streaming inside. For the minuscule span between the fifth and sixth chime, the portal was empty. Then, as the sixth stroke rang crisp and clear through the open archway, three figures appeared.

Darcy doubted an earthquake could have torn his gaze away from Elizabeth.

"Keep breathing, Darcy."

"Same to you, my friend."

Before the tenth, and final chime had faded into silence, he realized that Bingley's whispered words had not been an attempt at humor but were words of advice meant for them both. The vision of Elizabeth, his bride, had wrest the air from his lungs. It took him several seconds to recognize that the stars swirling in front of him were not solely the result of the magical moment.

My God in Heaven—she is stunning.

One hand lying daintily atop her proud father's left arm, Elizabeth glided down the aisle, a pure vision of flawless beauty. Her rich, coffee-colored eyes sparkled with the unique blend of vivaciousness, intelligence, and wit that had captivated him the second he'd beheld her at the Meryton Assembly so long ago. Of her many exquisite features, Darcy adored her eyes above all. Today especially, her superlative eyes shone with transcendent love directed solely at him. He could happily stare into her eyes for eternity, and if not for a hushed voice buried inside his head reminding him to savor every detail, Darcy would never have been able to look away.

Somehow, he did and was struck anew with breathless bedazzlement.

Elizabeth wore a gown of creamy-white silk gauze under a transparent overdress of Madras lace woven with tiny, vaguely heart-shaped silk-satin accents. The squared bodice was modestly cut, trimmed with delicate lace and champagne-gold satin ribbons sewn into a beautiful design of narrow horizontal bands and vertical scallops, which curved over her full breasts, down the front to the hemline. The slightly puffed, capped sleeves were embellished with the same satin ribbon and lace trim. Spanning her slim waist was a sash of deepest gold tied into a bow at her back.

Her luxuriant tresses were styled in an elaborate weave of curls and braids with thin gold ribbons entwined and tiny buds of baby's breath and lavender inserted. In her right hand, his mother's engagement ring sparkling in the light, she held a bouquet of honeysuckle, lavender, and, to his utter amazement, clusters of cobalt-blue Jacob's ladder. The splash of blue with the purple was sublime and complemented the sapphire-and-diamond necklace encircling her creamy, slender neck.

From the top of her coiffed hair to the tips of the white satin slippers peeking from underneath the hem of her gown, she was extraordinary. The proper names and descriptors for Elizabeth's wedding ensemble were largely unknown to Darcy, of course. His awed appreciation was for the combined effect, which was devastating to his senses and made it extremely difficult to catalog the specifics. In his urgency to have her close, the time from her entrance until she was standing before him felt like an hour, but there still wasn't enough time to absorb her perfection.

Mr. Bennet stopped at the end of the aisle, and only then did Darcy remember Jane was on his right! The oversight, under different circumstances, would have mortified him, but at present he could not muster the slightest remorse. Darcy doubted Bingley was paying any heed to Elizabeth either. Eyes locked onto his bride, he waited for the proper ceremonial initiation, a task he found exceedingly difficult to do patiently. Judging by the expression on Elizabeth's face, and her involuntary step forward, she also struggled to remember the rituals. Wanting to laugh aloud, he curled his lips into a soft smile instead.

～

"*R*emember, don't signal to open the doors until the exact moment I ordered."

At Mr. Bennet's reminder, the young curate standing on the top of the outside steps in front of the church's door folded his hands in a praying posture and inclined his head.

"What are you up to, Papa?" Jane asked.

"You two want to make a grand entrance, do you not? Trust me," he added, winking. "You two just concentrate on breathing. I can't drag both of you down the aisle."

Waiting for whatever he had up his sleeve, the brides took his advice. As they breathed slowly and deeply, keeping themselves calm, the remaining handful of minutes ticked away. Despite expecting it, at the reverberating gong from the bell high above their heads, they both jolted a foot in the air.

"Another reason to wait a bit longer," Mr. Bennet drily noted, Lizzy and Jane giggling with a slightly hysterical edge. At the fifth chime, he nodded to the curate, who yanked on the rope beside the left door. Before the echo faded, the doors were already swinging inward.

"Not yet," Mr. Bennet murmured when they instinctively shifted their weight forward. "Grand entrance, remember?"

The sixth chime struck and with a lowly commanded, "Now," Mr. Bennet led them over the threshold and into the church. He paused again at the invisible line separating the narthex from the long aisle that divided the nave into equal halves. Whatever additional dramatics her playful papa had planned, Lizzy no longer cared. Her gaze had instantly snapped to the other end of the aisle, and after that she saw nothing except for William.

How handsome he is. And he is mine—all mine.

He wore an impeccably designed and tailored coat of merino wool, and coal-black and form-fitting breeches in the same material secured just below his knees with gold buckles. White stockings encased his muscular legs, of course, and his polished black leather shoes gleamed. As she decreased the distance between them, the extraordinary design embroidered over the entire front of his ivory satin waistcoat came into sharper focus. It was ornate and colorful, as she knew was not his ordinary preference, but utterly stupendous and suitably unique for this singular day.

Georgiana's birthday gift, the diamond-shaped stickpin embedded with diamonds, amber, and deep-blue sapphires was eye-catching in contrast to the stark-white cravat. Not until later would she notice the sapphire cufflinks, remarking then that their ensembles were impressively coordinated.

A majority of the minutiae escaped her initial scrutiny. She might have floated on air or passed by empty pews for all that she was aware of during her passage down the aisle. As stunning as the figure he cut, it was his face that captured all her attention and implanted into her memory in sharp detail.

Hundreds of times she had seen his absolute love for her expressed within his blue eyes and unguarded visage. None of those times prepared her for the raw emotions visible now. Tears were prickling the insides of her eyelids and her heart thudding against her ribs. She sucked in her breath, unaware they had reached the halting point until her father tightened his arm as a subtle reminder. Heeding the clue, she stopped midstep, emitting a feeble laugh, which then reminded her to heed her father's earlier advice.

Concentrate on breathing, Lizzy.

Then William curled his full, kissable lips into a soft smile, and she forgot all about breathing once again.

~

"*D*early beloved," Reverend Jenney boomed, "we are gathered together here in the sight of God, and in the face of this congregation, to join together these men and these women in Holy Matrimony; which is an honorable estate, instituted of God in the time of man's innocency, signifying unto us the mystical union that is between Christ and His Church; which holy estate Christ adorned and beautified with His presence and first miracle that He wrought in Cana of Galilee, and is commended of Saint Paul to be honorable among all men, and therefore is not by any to be taken in hand unadvisedly, lightly, or wantonly, to satisfy men's carnal lusts and appetites like brute beasts that have no understanding; but reverently, discreetly, advisedly, soberly, and in the fear of God; duly considering the causes for which matrimony was ordained."

After a short pause—even priests can be dramatic at times—he continued, "First, marriage was ordained for the procreation of children to be brought up in the fear and nurture of the Lord, and to the praise of His Holy Name. Secondly, marriage was ordained for a remedy against sin and to avoid fornication, that such persons as have not the gift of continency might marry, and keep themselves undefiled members of Christ's body. Thirdly, marriage was ordained for the mutual society, help, and comfort that the one ought to have of the other, both in prosperity and adversity: into which holy estate these two couples present come now to be joined. Therefore, if any man can show any just cause why they may not lawfully be joined together, let him now speak, or else hereafter forever hold his peace."

This time, the pause was longer and not for dramatic effect. The wait of some two minutes, while rarely resulting in anyone speaking out, was a serious obligation. When not a peep was heard from amongst the assembly, Reverend Jenney closed the Book of Common Prayer to train his stern gaze on the brides and grooms. Searching each of their faces one by one, he recited the next series of memorized lines.

"I require and charge each of you, as you will answer at the dreadful day of judgment when the secrets of all hearts shall be disclosed, that if any of you know of any impediment as to why you may not be lawfully joined together in matrimony, you do now confess it. For be ye well assured, that so many as are coupled together otherwise than God's Word doth allow, are not joined together by God, neither is their matrimony lawful."

Thankfully, the priest did not drag out the process. With an abrupt change in demeanor, he smiled, flipped the book open, and turned to Bingley and Jane. As the eldest Bennet and the first to become betrothed, they had all agreed it only proper for them to speak their vows first.

Darcy managed to pull his eyes away from Elizabeth after a brief struggle and was somewhat amazed to discover that observing his friend and very-soon-to-be sister declare their solemn promises was profoundly moving. The mutual expressions of raw devotion were, Darcy knew, a mirror image of the emotions he was feeling.

The display increased the joy in his soul, and he recognized the same had touched Elizabeth when he again beheld her face.

His heart pounded forcefully, and flutters of happiness rushed through his body. At long last, the time had arrived. The sacred words, sweeter than any he had ever heard outside of Elizabeth's "yes" to his proposal, were now to be uttered.

"Fitzwilliam Alexander James Darcy, wilt thou have this woman, Elizabeth Nicole Bennet, to thy wedded wife, to live together after God's ordinance in the holy estate of matrimony? Wilt thou love her, comfort her, honor and keep her, in sickness and in health? And, forsaking all others, keep thee only unto her, so long as you both shall live?"

"I will," he enunciated crisply, eyes fixed on her face. *With all my heart and soul, to beyond my life on earth.*

"Elizabeth Nicole Bennet, wilt thou have this man, Fitzwilliam Alexander James Darcy, to thy wedded husband, to live together after God's ordinance in the holy estate of matrimony? Wilt thou obey him and serve him, love, honor, and keep him, in sickness and in health? And, forsaking all others, keep thee only unto him, so long as you both shall live?"

"I will," she declared as firmly as he. And then she smiled.

Darcy's knees nearly buckled.

Addressing Mr. Bennet, the priest asked, "Who giveth these women to be married to these men?"

"I, Thomas Bennet, father of Jane and Elizabeth Bennet, do giveth these women to be bound in holy matrimony to these men."

On cue, Elizabeth released her father's arm as he turned to his eldest daughter. After bestowing a kiss to Jane's right hand, he then placed it upon Reverend Jenney's right hand and stepped back to Elizabeth's side. At a nod from the priest, Mr. Bingley laid his right hand atop Jane's. The final vows of bonding were repeated, first by Charles and then by Jane, followed by the ring placement ritual.

Once again, though Darcy had anticipated being frustrated

having to wait for Charles and Jane, he was overjoyed. His sincere affection for his longtime friend meant that his delight in Charles finding his true mate was genuine. Love was a gift, as he knew better than most, and he truly could not have been happier for his young friend. Additionally, as with the declaration portion of the ceremony, his heart leaped to unimaginable heights as it was now their turn to take the final vows which would irrevocably bind them forever.

After Elizabeth's petite hand was laid atop the priest's, Darcy eagerly covered it with his palm and curled his long fingers over it, loosely clutching. His penetrating gaze on Elizabeth, he repeated slowly and clearly, "I, Fitzwilliam Alexander James Darcy, take thee, Elizabeth Nicole Bennet, to be my wedded wife, to have and to hold from this day forth, for better, for worse, for richer, for poorer, in sickness, and in health, to love and to cherish, till death us do part, according to God's holy ordinance: and thereto I plight thee my troth."

Glistening tears had formed in Elizabeth's eyes, her rapid blinks stopping all but one, which escaped the corner of her left eye. Darcy yearned to wipe it away, for no reason other than to touch her precious face, but he resisted the urge. Surprisingly, she repeated her vows with only a faint tremor.

"I, Elizabeth Nicole Bennet, take thee, Fitzwilliam Alexander James Darcy, to be my wedded husband, to have and to hold from this day forward, for better, for worse, for richer, for poorer, in sickness, and in health, to love, cherish, and to obey, till death us do part, according to God's holy ordinance: and thereto I plight thee my troth."

Eyes never leaving the beauty of her face, Darcy reached into his waistcoat pocket with his left hand and placed the slim band of gold upon the open Book of Common Prayer held by Reverend Jenney. Covering it with his fingers, the priest closed his eyes for a silent prayer, then handed the ring back to Darcy.

Only then did Darcy release Elizabeth's right hand, immediately clasping her left. Sliding the narrow band embedded with tiny diamonds halfway onto the fourth finger, he poured all his immense love into his eyes and voice.

"With this ring, I thee wed: with my body I thee worship: and with all my worldly goods I thee endow. In the Name of the Father, and of the Son, and of the Holy Ghost. Amen."

Another tear slipped down her cheek and a sob caught in her throat. Darcy squeezed their now-entwined hands, fighting his own emotions. Kneeling beside Charles and Jane before Reverend Jenney at the altar, they bowed their heads and closed their eyes.

"Let us pray. O, Eternal God, Creator and Preserver of all mankind, Giver of all spiritual grace, the Author of everlasting life: Send thy blessing upon these thy servants, these men and these women, whom we bless in thy Name, that, as Isaac and Rebecca lived faithfully together, so these persons may surely perform and keep the vow and covenant betwixt them made, whereof these rings were given and received are a token and pledge, and may ever remain in perfect love and peace together, and live according to thy laws, through Jesus Christ our Lord. Amen."

"You may rise," he said, the couples doing so. Per the ritual, they joined hands once again with the priest—as best they could with so many hands—and kept still as he drew out the final, official proclamation.

"For those whom God hath joined together, let no man put asunder. Forasmuch as Charles Bingley and Jane Bennet, and Fitzwilliam Darcy and Elizabeth Bennet, have consented together in Holy wedlock, and have witnessed the same before God and this company, and thereto have given and pledged their troth each to the other, and have declared the same by giving and receiving of a ring, and by the joining of hands: I pronounce that these two couples be man and wife together. In the name of the Father, and of the Son, and of the Holy Ghost."

"God the Father, God the Son, God the Holy Ghost, bless,

preserve, and keep you all; the Lord mercifully with His favor look upon you all; and so fill you with all spiritual benediction and grace, that ye may so live together in this life, that in the world to come ye may have life everlasting. Amen!"

Elizabeth Bennet is now Elizabeth Darcy, my wife! Praise God!

Darcy had, quite literally, never been happier in his entire life, and the urge to whoop and dance with joy was intense. Glancing at Elizabeth's face, he saw the same measure of joy in the eyes fixed upon him. Before they were forced to stop the intimate exchange and join the priest at the Lord's table for communion, she whispered, "I love you, Husband."

From that moment onward, all other words barely registered. The recited Psalms, sacred hymns, and final prayers pierced deeply into his soul, but only because he had memorized them all years ago. Walking up the aisle with his wife on his arm, Darcy finally felt complete. As much as he longed to take her into his arms, the last task before exiting the church could not be forgotten.

Near the entryway to the church was a wooden lectern. Sitting on top and propped at an angle was a large, open book with an ink pot and quill beside. The necessary information of names, parishes of residence, and date had already been written in the designated blanks by the parish registrar, who stood beside the lectern to ensure each of them signed their names in the proper places. While seemingly a small thing, viewing their names linked together and knowing it was the last time Elizabeth would ever sign her name as *Bennet* was profoundly moving.

Stepping aside so Richard and Mary could sign their names as witnesses on each of the two new register entries, Darcy clasped onto Elizabeth's hand. He leaned a hairbreadth away from her ear and whispered, "Mrs. Darcy, I love you, with all my heart."

Instinctively, she turned to meet his eyes, her smile radiant. "Could you repeat that?"

He knew what she meant but said instead, "I love you." He kissed her—brief and chaste, but firm. Then, pulling away, he repeated what she especially wanted to hear and what he knew he would never tire of saying: "Mrs. Darcy."

A crowd had gathered outside the church, and cheers of congratulations greeted the newly married couples when they stepped beyond the doors. Rice, grains, and assorted seeds were tossed into the air and showered them. Laughter abounded, and Lizzy and Jane were frequently waylaid by friendly embraces and congratulatory pats. The twenty-some feet between the church and the open landau took much time to cover, but eventually, the foursome set off. Wheeling slowly through the main street of Meryton, the church celebrants trailed behind, children cavorting and ladies waving handkerchiefs, until they reached the last building.

Gradually the ruckus faded into silence, the only sounds that of the clomping horses and metal wheels. The carriages carrying the wedding guests were farther behind, so for the present, they were alone.

For the span of a dozen heartbeats they stared at each other. Then, as if on cue, all four burst into laughter.

A HOPEFUL FUTURE BEGINS

~EPILOGUE~

*T*wo hours later, the feasting and celebration had concluded —or at least, it had for the new Mr. and Mrs. Darcy.

They had a journey of several hours ahead of them and mutually agreed it was time to depart. A long round of congratulations, best wishes, hopes for safe travels, and mournful farewell embraces and kisses ensued.

Finally, they climbed into the sturdy coach emblazoned with the Darcy crest. While Elizabeth clutched the windowsill and waved at her family and friends, Darcy gave the signaling knock for Mr. Anders to snap the reins.

At Netherfield Park's driveway exit, the coachman steered the horses onto the main road, and the last glimpse of Elizabeth's waving family disappeared.

She scooted back from the window but continued to contemplate the passing terrain. Every tree and bush was familiar. Not a house was driven by that she could not immediately name those who resided within. The numerous pathways and grassy meadows had been trod upon and explored thousands of times.

Memories. Countless memories.

Sighing, the sound a half sob, she bowed her head and closed her eyes against the stinging tears.

"Let it go, my darling," Darcy soothed, one hand gently rubbing the small of her back. "Tears are natural and nothing to be ashamed of. I know how difficult it is to part from those you love, no matter the circumstances. There is no reason to hide your sadness."

Another minute of silent inspection of the Hertfordshire landscape passed—as if she needed to see with her eyes what was forever planted in her mind—and then she melted into her husband's waiting embrace.

Snuggling into his warm body, she rested her cheek against his upper chest, loosely gripping his lapel, and closed her eyes. The finely worsted fabric of his jacket felt wonderful under her skin, and the smell of his cologne was both soothing and stimulating.

He drew her closer, arms tightening, and kissed her forehead. "I have extra handkerchiefs if you need," he said, half serious and half teasing, "but wool is tough, even against tears."

"You are too good, William. I should only be rejoicing this day, not mourning."

He laughed softly. "Oh, I have no fear that the rejoicing shall soon overcome any sadness, my dear wife. Our hearts are too full to be dampened for long."

Oh, how right he is.

Just in the seconds it took him to finish those sentences, her sorrow had largely disappeared. Contentment, happiness, and tickles of desire were rapidly taking over.

Lizzy opened her eyes, the colorful embroidery of his wedding waistcoat was brought into sharp focus. It was a vivid reminder that with the constant commotion during the wedding reception, closer inspection of his garment had been impossible. In fact, they had frequently been pulled apart, and the bustling activity had not allowed them a minute alone or even to speak to each other much.

Well, we are completely alone now, and, we are married.

While not in the best place for the type of "inspection" she wanted to do, they did need to do something to pass the time. Releasing his lapel, she brushed her fingertips over the extraordinary pattern of flowers and vines hand sewn into the silk.

"This is truly astounding. I thought Jane was skilled at needlework, but this puts her to shame. I am a million times worse than my sister so should do the world a service and never pick up a needle and thread again."

Darcy chuckled, and she felt the vibration under her fingers, sending a stream of tingles up her arm. "Mr. Meyer only hires the best. For that reason alone, I trusted him to create this for me."

"I suspected as much. I knew this wasn't your usual preference, but if I ever have the opportunity, I will thank Mr. Meyer personally for forcing you to submit to his wisdom."

As she spoke, he began lightly caressing her arm. She wore a long-sleeved, heavy brocade pelisse over her wedding dress yet still shivered at his touch and closed her eyes to enjoy the instantaneous rush of desire.

Reopening her eyes several seconds later, Lizzy's gaze fell on his hand.

"Oh! What lovely cufflinks. I did not notice before. Are they new?"

"Yes, they are. Believe it or not, a gift from my manservant." He told her the story in brief.

"He sounds like a good man. And he was correct that these would match. We are remarkably color coordinated as if we planned it."

She had remained curled against his side, her head resting on his chest. She did long to see his face, but the intimacy of being held this way was unfathomably intense. Sliding her fingers along the edge of his waistcoat, she toyed with each button as she descended the flat surface of his chest to his abdomen.

He did not move, but his breathing increased, Elizabeth smiling at the reaction the merest brush of her hand could cause.

How bold dare she be? Boundaries no longer applied, aside from their current location, and even then, who would know if she were to take her exploring to the next level?

For what seemed like a long span, she debated and rightfully guessed he was having the same debate.

Then she remembered what he had said the previous afternoon while under the willow trees. Being together fully for the first time wasn't only about the timing or even the vows, as vital as those were. It was about the experience being special, precious, and utterly perfect. A moving carriage in broad daylight, even with the vows now exchanged, was not that place.

So, she pressed her hand over his naval and leaned back in his arms, just enough to see his face. Indescribable love shone from his eyes, and his expression was by far the most relaxed she had ever seen it.

"I love you, Fitzwilliam Darcy, my husband," she declared in a firm tone but softly and tenderly, joy now bringing about the sting of tears.

He did not immediately reply, instead leisurely caressing her arm and neck, then cupping her cheek with his palm. Inclining his head a few inches, he held her eyes for another minute or two of silent communication, finally whispering, "I love you, Elizabeth Darcy, my wife."

And then he kissed her.

For a long, long time they kissed. Sweetly, deeply, and passionately —a sublime connection of lips, breath, and tongue. When they eventually withdrew, she nestled back into the warmth of his embrace and, within minutes, had fallen soundly asleep.

Darcy held his wife, his cheek upon her soft curls as he gazed out the window. Thoughts drifting, he mused upon the past two months, each moment a treasure, even the handful of which had been stressful in some way. All of them were parts of the whole amazing journey which had brought them to the present.

Thank goodness it is finally over, he thought, releasing a heavy sigh.

And, indeed, the first stage was over. Elizabeth was now his wife, as he had yearned for with an intensity that was ofttimes nearly his undoing.

Yet, in truth, this was merely the beginning. Their journey together would span years, on into decades, God willing. What a glorious vision!

Smiling, he rested his head back against the padded seat edge and closed his eyes. As sleep reached for him, he sent a silent prayer Heavenward.

Thank goodness it has finally begun.

$\sim$

THIS END IS THE BEGINNING

**Continue the journey of a happily ever after life with
Darcy, Elizabeth, their extended family, and a host of
friends both new and familiar,
in The Darcy Saga novels by Sharon Lathan.**

ABOUT SHARON LATHAN

SHARON LATHAN is the best-selling author of The Darcy Saga sequel series to Jane Austen's *Pride & Prejudice*.

Sharon began writing in 2006 and her first novel, *Mr. and Mrs. Fitzwilliam Darcy: Two Shall Become One* was published in 2009. With the publication of this novel, Sharon's series of "happily ever after" for the Darcys totals nine full-length novels and one Christmas themed novella.

Darcy & Elizabeth: A Season of Courtship and *Darcy & Elizabeth: Hope of the Future* complete the "prequel to the sequel" duo recounting the betrothal months before the Darcy Saga began.

Sharon is a native Californian relocated in 2013 to the green hills of Kentucky, where she resides with her husband of thirty-one years. Retired from a thirty-year profession as a registered nurse in Neonatal Intensive Care, Sharon is pursuing her dream as a full-time writer.

Sharon is a member of the Jane Austen Society of North America, JASNA Louisville, the Romance Writers of America (RWA), the Beau Monde chapter of the RWA, and serves as the website manager and on the board of the Louisville Romance Writers chapter of the RWA.

Sharon is the co-creator of Austen Authors, a group blog for authors of Austenesque literary fiction.
Visit at: www.AustenAuthors.com

For more information about Sharon, her novels, and the Regency Era, visit her website/blog at:

www.SharonLathanAuthor.com
sharon.lathan@gmail.com

DARCY & ELIZABETH

~ A SEASON OF COURTSHIP ~

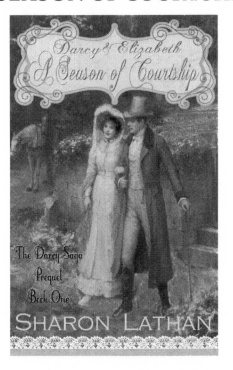

DARCY SAGA PREQUEL DUO BOOK 1

Accepting a marriage proposal is merely the beginning . . .

How did Lady Catherine restore Mr. Darcy's hope to prompt his second proposal? Did Caroline Bingley yield gracefully? Were the Bennets and Meryton citizens approving?

FITZWILLIAM DARCY AND ELIZABETH BENNET ARE BETROTHED!

Readers of The Darcy Saga have shared in the romance, life, and marital escapades of Mr. & Mrs. Darcy. Now the "prequel to the sequel" recounts the weeks in between as two new lovers prepare for happily ever after.

Embark on the journey as Darcy and Elizabeth overcome the rocky past and discover the depth of their love. Delight in budding passion and sweet romance. Enjoy the wedding planning and adventures during the initial weeks of their engagement.

Darcy & Elizabeth: A Season of Courtship

THE DARCY SAGA SEQUEL SERIES

Happily Ever After Comes True . . .

Beginning on their wedding day, Darcy and Elizabeth are deeply in love with one another and excited to begin their marriage.

The Darcy Saga sequel series to Jane Austen's *Pride and Prejudice* is a sweetly romantic, historically accurate tale recounting the daily life of newlyweds Mr. and Mrs. Fitzwilliam Darcy.

Through five novels and one novella, Sharon Lathan presents a vision of happiness in marriage.

Meet new friends and family members. Delve deeper into familiar characters and their futures.
Dwell in the Regency world at Pemberley and London.

Through it all, delight in the unparalleled love story of Mr. and Mrs. Fitzwilliam Darcy.

Mr. and Mrs. Fitzwilliam Darcy: Two Shall Become One

Loving Mr. Darcy: Journeys Beyond Pemberley

My Dearest Mr. Darcy

In The Arms of Mr. Darcy

The Trouble With Mr. Darcy

A Darcy Christmas

"If you enjoy enthusiastic romance passionately written featuring the redoubtable Mr. Darcy and his wife, then "I would by no means suspend any pleasure of yours"!" ~*Austenprose*

MISS DARCY FALLS IN LOVE

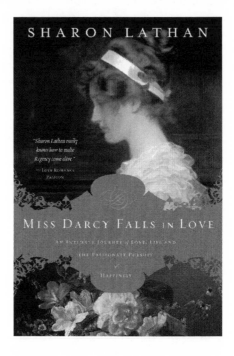

An intimate journey of love, life, and the passionate pursuit of happiness.

Noble young ladies were expected to play an instrument, but societal restrictions would have chafed for Georgiana Darcy, an accomplished musician.

Her tour of Europe draws the reader into the musical life of the day, and a riveting love story of a young woman learning to direct her destiny and understand her own heart.

Miss Darcy Falls in Love

"If you are a Jane Austen fan, if you love historical novels, then Ms. Lathan's wonderfully written, vividly detailed, and sweet romance novel will be one that you don't want to miss out on!" ~***Romancing the Book***

"Sharon Lathan has another home run hit on her hands here. Her name is certainly solidified with what good Jane Austen fan fiction should be. Fast-paced and always full of the romance we all dream about, Miss Darcy Falls in Love is not one you'll want to miss." ~*Austenprose*

"This is a story that fully immerses its readers in the world of the characters, from the rainy streets of Lyon and Paris and the quiet hush of the churches and museums Georgiana visits, to the dazzle and splendor of the society balls that light up the evenings." ~*The Romance Reviews*

THE PASSIONS OF DR. DARCY

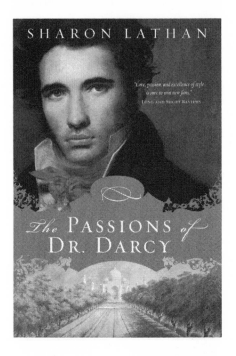

You never know where a life of purpose may lead . . .

While Fitzwilliam Darcy is enjoying an idyllic childhood at Pemberley, his vibrant and beloved uncle, Dr. George Darcy, becomes one of the most renowned young physicians of the day.

Determined to do something more with his life than cater to a spoiled aristocracy, George accepts a post with the British East India Company and travels in search of a life of meaning and purpose.

When George Darcy returns to Pemberley after many years abroad, the drama and heartbreak of his travels offer a fascinating glimpse into a gentleman's journey of self-discovery and romance.

Explore a fascinating and unique aspect of the Regency period, when the British Empire offered the young noblemen of the day promising adventures all over the world.

The Passions of Dr. Darcy

"A splendid tale of one man's determination to be the best in his chosen profession and to find love." ~*New York Journal of Books*

"Lathan obviously spent a lot of time and research to be able to tell of the things happening at this time in history. It is fun, engaging, and full of history. I would strongly recommend this to anyone who enjoys historical fiction. It is an amazing book!" ~*Night Owl Reviews*

"The story is entertaining, especially for those who take pleasure, as I did, in details of 18th-century medicine and learning about the exotic India of this era." ~*Historical Novel Society*

"Lathan is an expert in character development. We travel across every reach of the Indian subcontinent for over 30 years with George, exploring its vibrant and rich history and the intriguing characters that he meets along the way. It was a journey which I was happy to take." ~*Austenprose*

Made in the USA
Coppell, TX
05 September 2020